Praise

"Holy heart palpitations right up to the very last sentence!!!" ~
Wendy, Reviewer

"Loved, loved, loved the entire book and couldn't put it down. Right from the start, it was exciting and unlike any other book I've read." ~
Amanda, Reviewer

"Excellent thriller. You need to put your seat belt on as soon as you start reading this book." ~
David, Reviewer

"With a unique story line, great character development, and non stop action, it's hard to start a new book after this one!" ~
Amazon Customer Review

HEADHUNTER

sands press

HEADHUNTER

PETER PARKIN AND ALISON DARBY

sands press

sands press

A division of 3244601 Canada Inc.
300 Central Avenue West
Brockville, Ontario
K6V 5V2

Toll Free 1-800-563-0911 or 613-345-2687
http://www.sandspress.com

ISBN 978-1-988281-18-6
Copyright © 2017 Peter Parkin
http://www.peterparkin.com
All Rights Reserved

Cover concept Kevin Davidson
Formatting by Renee Hare
Publisher Kristine Barker
Author Agent Sparks Literary Consultants

Publisher's Note
This book is a work of fiction. References to real people, events, establishments, organizations, or locales, are intended only to provide as a sense of authenticity, and are used fictitiously. All other characters, and all incidents and dialogue, are drawn from the authors' imaginations and are not to be construed as real.

No part of this book may be reproduced in whole or in part, stored in a retrieval system or transmitted in any form or by any means, without the prior written permission of the publisher.

For information on bulk purchases of this book or any book published by Sands Press, please call 1-800-563-0911.

1st Printing September 2017

To book an author for your live event, please call: 1-800-563-0911

Sands Press is a literary publisher interested in new and established authors wishing to develop and market their product. For more information please visit our website at www.sandspress.com.

CHAPTER 1

It was one of those days when the silence was deafening. Those days were rare, but there was clearly something in the air today. Perhaps he was being too sensitive this morning; perhaps he was sensing things that didn't exist except inside of his overactive brain. But the commuters on the subway were extra quiet; the breakfast grabbers at his favorite coffee shop seemed subdued – as if they knew a secret that he didn't. He felt left out.

Jeff Kavanaugh walked along King Street West toward his office building at 207 Bay Street. Bay and King intersected and his office was right on the corner. A short walk from the longest street in Toronto, and indeed the longest street in North America: Yonge Street. Jeff loved heading down to Yonge Street at lunchtime – the buzz was overpowering and it always gave his body a surge of adrenaline to finish out the afternoon. By noon he was usually mind-numb. Ready for a nap. His work consisted of mental overdrive – interview after interview, report after report. Enough to suck the life out of anyone, but particularly someone like him whose brain was always working at full speed. It never shut off – sometimes he wished it would.

But there was something in the air. The people brushing past him on King Street had their heads down. Maybe they always had their heads down, Jeff wasn't sure. Had he never noticed before? He always walked erect, head up, looking straight ahead. Confident, perhaps even a bit arrogant. But that was Jeff. Arrogant, intelligent, curious, ambitious. To a fault sometimes. Four hours sleep a night on average, but fresh as a daisy when he awoke. Always ready to take on the day, or anyone who got in his way.

Jeff glanced up at the gleaming towers surrounding him. It was a beautiful July morning – a typical Toronto summer day; hot and humid and it was only 9:00 a.m. This was the one thing that Jeff hated about Toronto. The summer weather was insufferable – fine if you were sitting at home in shorts and a t-shirt, but not so fine if you had to work for a living. And at thirty-five years of age, Jeff still had to work for a living. But he loved working – just not on days like this. He'd rather be up at his cottage on Moon Lake. That was his escape – well, not really an escape. He always took his laptop with him just in case he got the urge to work. And it was rare that he didn't get the urge. But at least he could laze around half-naked while working, and then dive into the lake if he got too hot.

He reached his fingers up to the stiff collar of his white Givenchy shirt and slid them around inside, wiping away the relentless sweat. It didn't make much of a difference – he'd have to do this every few minutes until he reached the air-conditioned refuge of his office at 207 Bay. But wiping away the sweat made him feel better, seemed to stretch the collar making his neck more free to move.

He studied the faces of the other poor souls he passed – flushed and dripping. But all of them with their heads down. What was it about today? Was he imagining this? Was his brain hallucinating, playing tricks on him? It seemed surreal.

Jeff was psychic. That was another aspect of his mind that drove him a bit crazy sometimes. Or as some would refer to it – 'sensitive.' It was powerful, and sometimes he paid attention to it and sometimes he just ignored it. And sometimes it just wasn't there at all. It came without warning and disappeared without apology. It was weird, and it had become progressively stronger as Jeff aged.

He slid his fingers through his thick brown hair. It was moist with sweat, and seemed thinner than it usually did. Probably just the humidity, but he knew that he'd probably be bald by the time he was fifty. He took after his father. In more ways than just thinning hair. He was moderately tall, about six feet high in dress shoes. His eyes were blue, and he had a rugged face; kind of bohemian in a way, but attractive in its own right. His biggest assets were his eyes – penetrating and gentle at the same time. His eyes could disarm any adversary in a boardroom – either by intimidation or kindness. Whichever tactic suited the situation. And he had a swagger that would make anyone take notice. Little did they know that the swagger was caused by a back injury from the days when he played high school football. But even if the swagger wasn't a genuine blue-blooded natural extension of his personality, he knew he had swagger in his brain. So the overall package fit who he was as far as he was concerned. All in all, Jeff felt good about who he was.

He walked into the lobby of his building and squeezed his way into the elevator along with a half dozen others. He pushed the button for the ninth floor, and then glanced around at the other riders. He didn't recognize any of them – he noticed that the elevator was destined for four other floors after his.

Suddenly his body shivered – not a cold kind of shiver, but a scared kind. It started at his ankles and rose quickly to the top of his head. He blinked as his eyes went blurry. The people in front of him were distorted in his vision now. Bobbing heads. He looked up above the elevator door and stared at the floor display. They seemed to be stuck on the sixth floor but he could tell that the elevator was still moving.

The door slid open and he gently pushed his way out, excusing himself politely to the bobbing heads. He took one more glance at the floor display and it still showed 'six.' Yet he recognized his floor and the reception desk. He was clearly on the ninth floor. He made a mental note to remember the number 'six' today. Something of significance would involve that number, he was sure of it. Maybe he'd land a big deal worth six figures? He hoped.

"Good morning, Jeffy. You look devilishly handsome as usual today!" Cathy Ricketts, the receptionist, smiled at him in her usual perky way. She was cute, no doubt. And Jeff had dated her a couple of times. He knew he shouldn't have – not smart to be too close to the people you worked with. But he had found her hard to resist. She was just too cute. Trouble was, he knew she always hoped that another date was just around the corner and he just wasn't interested in her that way. Right now he wasn't interested in anyone that way. He was glad that he hadn't gone to bed with her – that would have made things really complicated. Both times had just been dinner. Innocent stuff.

"Good morning to you, too, Cathy. And you look good, too. You're always the first one I see in the morning here, and the last one I see when I leave. How special is that, eh?"

She couldn't wipe the smile off her face. Jeff found that smile of hers infectious. It made him smile too, to the point where he felt like a goofy kid. But Cathy was a nice way to start the day. He liked her. She was one of the office sweethearts to be sure.

She glanced at her computer screen. "Jeffy, I see you have an appointment coming in at 11:00. Do you want me to send in some coffee?"

"Yeah, that would be great. I know he likes it black, so deliver it that way, okay?"

Cathy looked up at him, and Jeff thought he saw a pleading look in her eyes. "No problem. Will do."

Then he saw something else. A yellowish glow around her head. Almost like a halo. He blinked his eyes a couple of times. The halo seemed to hover around her head with what looked like small tentacles of light streaming upward from the circle. The strange image disappeared before he could blink a third time.

Cathy frowned. "What's wrong, Jeffy? You're looking at me kind of weird."

Jeff clenched his fists hard and instantly regained his composure. "Nothing, Cathy. I think I just need that cup of coffee now rather than later. Send it down to my office, will you?"

She flashed him that infectious smile one more time before he turned and headed down the hall. Jeff kept his fists clenched as he entered his modest office. He didn't know what to make of today – it had started off weird and was continuing weird. Quiet streets, people walking with their heads down, the number six frozen in the elevator, and Cathy wearing a halo. It spooked him. Not the first time these kinds of things had happened to him, which was what spooked him the most. These things usually meant trouble. But this was the first time he had ever seen light around someone's head.

He sat down in his chair, swiveled toward the window that looked out over Bay Street, and opened the newspaper that had been waiting for him on his desk. The number six flashed at him on the front page – almost like a hologram, hovering on top of the day's headline. Jeff shook his head and put the paper down. He gazed out over the street and tried to focus on the day ahead.

Jeff traded in bodies for a living; live bodies, intelligent and breathing bodies. He was a Senior Account Executive with one of the largest executive search firms on the planet, having offices in six countries. His specialty was marketing, having graduated from the prestigious Queen's University in Kingston with a PHD back when he was only a young sprite of twenty-five. His three degrees were in psychology, but he specialized in utilizing psychology as a marketing tactic. The two disciplines were very closely related, much more than most people realized. Psychology was simply utilized to achieve effective marketing.

Jeff had never wanted to be a Psychologist – he only wanted to study it so he would excel at manipulating thinking. Which was what marketing was all about. He was truly a marketing expert and had been supremely successful in placing numerous top marketing executives at some of the most prominent Fortune 500 companies. His acumen was legendary, and he was next in line to become Vice President of his division. He could hardly wait – he was ready for it. Jeff was already pulling down a quarter of a million dollars a year, but he knew that would easily double if he got the VP job. He would also be a solid candidate for a transfer to another country if he advanced to the more visible position of VP. Not that he didn't like Toronto, but he was still young with no ties holding him to Canada. The time to be adventurous would be before he got married and had the obligatory two and a half kids. 'Price, Spencer and Williams Inc.' had a policy of promoting and transferring from within, so he knew his chances were good.

He put his feet up on the credenza and closed his eyes. Just for a few minutes. Just to dream a little. He pictured his chalet-style cottage on Moon Lake – where in fact he'd be heading to this weekend. Jeff was chomping at the bit. He pictured himself sipping a beer on the dock, getting all sweaty, and then just diving into the crystal-clear water. He could practically feel the refreshing water rushing over his body, washing the sweat away replacing it with sheer ecstasy.

He imagined the dock he'd always wanted – a party dock, long and wide at the end, able to easily accommodate a dozen eager partiers. And most of them women – well, at least in his fantasy they would all be women. In reality, most of them would just be his drinking buddies. But he could picture the women in his mind, all in bikinis, all with trim bodies shimmering in the sun that always seemed to shine at Moon Lake. Maybe with the money from his next promotion he'd buy just that kind of dock.

Jeff dozed off into dreamland…

Suddenly he lurched backward. A sound that was foreign. A sharp report. Then another. He swiveled in his chair and faced the open door. He knew he'd fallen asleep but he didn't know how long. He glanced at his watch…almost 11:00.

Now the sound of screams coming from the direction of the reception area. He recognized one of the screams. Cathy!

Jeff flew out of his chair and headed toward the door, blocked for a few seconds by a procession of people screaming and running past his office in the opposite direction of the reception area.

Jeff didn't join them. He ran at full speed the other way, towards the reception desk. There was a knot in his stomach now that got worse with each nervous step. But he kept going. Cathy was in trouble.

He passed several people along the way, some hiding under their desks, others running into closets. He ignored them. He had to keep going. Something was driving him and the feeling of danger was being suppressed by the urgency in his brain.

His feet left the carpeted hallway and his shiny black Pierre Cardin shoes skidded to a halt on the marble tile of the plush reception hall. His eyes came to rest on top of the reception desk where sweet Cathy was laying prone, blood pouring out of the side of her head. She was perfectly still, her eyes wide open and lifeless, gazing at the ceiling. He knew she was gone. Over to one side of the desk was another body – an executive he recognized as Walt Hitchins. Walt was propped up against the wall, almost peaceful in a sitting position. His chest was a mass of red.

Jeff turned his gaze to the other side of the desk. He recognized the monster. The man was standing there with a pistol in each hand, staring dispassionately at Cathy's body. He almost seemed surprised at what he was looking at. Jeff froze as the man turned slowly in his direction.

The monster was Jim Prentice. A man Jeff heard had been fired from the company three days prior. He'd been an Account Executive in the Artificial Intelligence Division. Jeff didn't know the details as to why he'd been fired. It was so commonplace now – who really cared about such things anymore? The strong survived; the weak were left to the trash heap. Jeff was one of the strong ones; Jim had been one of the weak ones. But maybe not so weak after all?

Jeff slowly raised his hands into the air as Jim turned the pistols in his direction. He thought he could see the residue smoke rising from the barrels. But then he saw something else – another halo, but this one was a dark grayish color with streaks of red. It seemed to be pulsating around the perimeter of Jim's head.

Jeff held his breath as Jim cocked the hammers of both pistols, took a step forward, and aimed the barrels directly at Jeff's head.

CHAPTER 2

His face was like one of those Halloween masks – the ones that were simple and looked just like human faces; no deliberately scary features. But those kinds of masks all had the same waxy expressionless stares, which seemed to make them more frightening than the traditional masks of witches and goblins. This was what Jim Prentice's face looked like as he stared down the gun barrels into Jeff's eyes.

Jeff could feel the thumping in his chest, his heart straining at its constraints. His palms were getting clammy and he felt his knees begin to wobble. He'd never stared at death before. Now he had two dead people in front of him, and his own existence seriously in question. For an instant he lamented his decision to run down the hall in this direction. He should have followed the others, especially now knowing there was nothing he could have done for Cathy after all. She was already gone before he got there.

Only a few seconds had passed since Jim had stepped in his direction, but it seemed an eternity. Out of the corner of his eye, Jeff could see that some people were peeking their heads around the sides of their cubicles, watching the standoff. And right now that's what it was. He'd expected Jim to have pulled the triggers by now but for some reason he hadn't. He was staring at Jeff, studying him, his head slightly cocked.

Jeff didn't know Jim very well – those who worked in the AI division on the tenth floor were a pretty secretive bunch. They didn't socialize very much with the employees of the other divisions on the ninth floor. But occasionally the two of them had chatted together, so they weren't strangers. Jeff thought he could maybe use this to his advantage.

Jeff spoke his first words – in a whisper, softly, slowly. "You know me, Jim. I'm Jeff, remember? From this floor, the ninth floor? I didn't see you at the coffee shop this morning. Would you like me to run down there and get you a coffee? I know you like it with cream and two sugars. Would you like that?"

Jim showed no signs of wanting to speak. He cocked his head to the other side and continued examining Jeff, almost as if he were seeing him for the first time. Jeff noticed that the man's eyes hadn't blinked once yet since they had come face to face. Jeff's eyes, in contrast, had probably blinked a hundred times.

"Jim, would you like me to help you? Is there something you need to do today? Anything from your office I can help you take home? I would do that for you – we could then grab some lunch together afterwards, whaddaya think?"

Jeff studied the man's eyes as he spoke to him. They were bloodshot and completely expressionless. Cold, detached. And he couldn't ignore the dark grey and red halo around his head, pulsing, moving – it was hypnotic. Strange. And right on the heels of seeing a yellowish glow around Cathy's head.

Jeff concentrated on keeping his voice soft and steady – making sure that there were no signs of fear. He hoped that Jim couldn't see the drips of sweat that were now falling to the floor from his fingertips. Calm strength was all that could save Jeff now. His only hope.

"Those guns must be heavy in your hands, Jim. Why don't you put them down for a while? You don't need them – you're clearly in charge here today. Everyone knows that. I can put them up in your office for you until you're ready to go home."

Jeff thought he saw a slight movement in Jim's hands. Perhaps he was imagining it, but he could have sworn that the man's hands had fallen slightly. He seized the opening and dropped his voice to a slightly lower octave, and spoke even slower. "I can see your hands getting very heavy now. Those guns weigh as much as two cement bags. You have no choice but to lower your hands. Bring them down to your side, slowly, easy now, slowly, bring them down, down…"

Jim continued to stare at Jeff, transfixed. Then he lowered his hands. That's all he did though – he stood his ground, continuing to stare at Jeff, but the hands dropped to his sides. He was still holding the guns.

Jeff was emboldened. "Now, do me a favor Jim. Release the hammers on the guns. Uncock them. You don't want them going off and hurting your feet."

Jim did as he was told.

"Now, drop the guns gently to the floor, Jim."

Jeff could see the fingers of his right hand begin to loosen. He was encouraged. This crisis may be over in just a matter of seconds now.

Suddenly the sound of a bell. Normally an innocuous noise that was heard several dozen times a day. Today it sounded like a giant church bell. Right behind Jeff the elevator door opened and he could hear the heavy footfall of a man exiting. Jeff's 11:00 appointment had arrived annoyingly on time.

At that moment everything changed. The visitor stopped dead in his tracks – then he was shot dead in his tracks. Jim whipped both guns up into the air and dropped the man with two expert shots to the head. Jeff knew the moment was lost, the trance broken, and now he had to save his own life.

He moved fast, diving sideways towards the side of the desk where the very dead Walt Hitchins was propped up against the wall. Jeff rolled several times as shots now rang out in his direction, tearing into the marble floor and ricocheting off the walls. In desperation, Jeff slid up against Walt, grabbed him by the lapels of his suit and flipped him over on top of himself. Jim continued to fire, several bullets tearing into Walt's thick body. Jeff could feel the cadaver quiver and shudder with each bullet.

Then silence. Jeff peeked around Walt's wide shoulders and saw Jim looking curiously at one of the guns. Then, as if suddenly remembering what to do, he shoved one gun into his belt and slid his left hand into the pocket of his suit jacket and pulled out a handful of bullets. With a flick of his wrist the cylinder of the gun in his right hand flipped open and Jim slowly, methodically, inserted the fresh bullets. Then he raised his head and gazed up the wide spiral staircase that led to the tenth floor. It seemed as if he was done with Jeff now, or perhaps had just forgotten about him since he couldn't really see him anymore – hidden as he was by Walt's bulk.

Jeff watched as the robotic Jim began his deliberate walk up the stairs – no rush, no worry. Just like a machine. He saw him round the spiral curve and disappear from sight.

Jeff shoved Walt to the side and examined himself. He was now covered in blood but he couldn't feel any pain. He pressed and probed and could find no sign of a bullet hole anywhere. He was fine. It was all Walt's blood.

He jumped to his feet and ran over to the staircase. Not knowing why, or what was possessing him, he took the stairs two at a time. He had to try again. More people were going to die today if he didn't. A lot more people. A little voice inside his head was whispering, *"Only you can do this today."*

Jeff ignored his fear and kept going. He reached the top of the stairs to the tenth floor just in time to see Jim raising the gun in his left hand and pointing it at a man cowering in an alcove. In the split second before the gun roared, Jeff noticed the same kind of halo around the man's head that he'd seen hovering around Cathy's. The same yellow glow, the same strange tentacles reaching upward. Then the glow was gone, replaced by blood as the man's head seemed to explode.

Jim whirled around and faced Jeff once again. He raised the gun in his right hand and Jeff's stomach acids rose in his throat. Then he moved his aim slightly to the right, and fired once again. Jeff heard a grunt and a thud, and out of the corner of his eye he could see another suited man collapse to the floor.

Remarkably, Jim turned away from Jeff and walked further down the hallway. He kicked open the door to an office and fired twice. Jeff heard the occupant's scream of terror just before the horrible silence.

Jim spun on his heels, walked across to the other side of the hall and went behind the reception desk. He bent over and dragged a young lady out by her hair. She'd been hiding underneath her desk. She screamed. He slapped her with his free hand.

Jeff stood at the top of the stairs, blocking the way down. Which is exactly where Jim wanted to head right now. With the girl in tow. He wrapped one forearm around her neck with the gun in that hand pointed right at Jeff's head. The other gun hand moved up to her forehead, ramming the barrel against her temple.

She was very pretty. And helplessly sobbing. Jeff knew her as Gaia Templeton – the tenth floor receptionist, gatekeeper of the privacy for the secretive employees of the AI Division. She was a slender girl, probably around thirty years of age. Dark short-cropped hair, jet black eyes. Jeff had talked to her a few times, in the staff cafeteria mainly. It seemed they always took their lunch at the same time. She was nice, and what he liked best about her was her wonderful sense of humor. Always cheery. Well, not today. She was crying today, scared out of her mind. And she had a yellowish halo surrounding her head, with tentacles shooting in the direction of the ceiling. Jeff gulped.

Jim still hadn't said one word. But his intentions were clear – he wanted down the stairs and he wanted to take Gaia with him. He waved the gun at Jeff. The movement of the gun seemed in perfect cadence with the pulsating waves swirling around in Jim's dark halo.

Jeff stood his ground. He whispered to Jim once again, slow and deliberate. "This isn't a good day to die, Jim. Today's Wednesday. Wednesday is a horrible day to die. Let Gaia go and take me instead. Then we'll both die tomorrow–we'll do it together. On Wednesday there is no forgiveness – did you know that? No forgiveness on Wednesdays, just eternal damnation. It is written."

Suddenly an expression on Jim's face. He frowned. And then he blinked. For the first time since this ordeal started, Jim blinked.

Jeff persisted. "Poor Gaia. Look at her face, Jim. She's crying – very upset. And she always liked you too. Did you know that? She's had a crush on you for years. She told me she wished that you were the father of the baby she's carrying."

Jim looked confused now. Jeff was encouraged. 'Confused' was far better than 'robotic.' The man continued his blinking, more rapid now. And the sinister dark halo around his head was beginning to fade. So much so, that Jeff couldn't even make out the flashes of red anymore.

Jeff looked at Gaia's sweet face – she was confused too. Probably wondering where Jeff was going with this pregnancy story. But what made Jeff breathe easier was noticing that her halo too was starting to fade. It was still there but the yellow glow wasn't nearly as noticeable. And the tentacles reaching skyward were completely gone now.

"Put the guns down, Jim. And let Gaia go. She's pregnant and this is very upsetting for her. You don't want her to lose the baby now, do you? A baby she wishes was yours?"

Jim shook his head and removed his arm from around Gaia's throat. Jeff held his palm up signaling to Gaia to stay put and not make any sudden moves. Her halo was completely gone now.

Jeff nodded encouragingly at Jim. His dark halo had disappeared completely now. Jeff whispered again. "Drop the guns, Jim. You know you want to. You're a good man."

Jim let the gun from his left hand slip to the floor.

An older woman sitting on the floor of the hallway suddenly clutched at her chest and cried out, "Help! Please!"

Jim swung the gun in his right hand in the woman's direction. Jeff moved on instinct – diving through the air tackling Jim around the waist, and pushing the full momentum of his shoulders into Jim's hips. They both tumbled to the floor and a harmless gunshot rang out as they fell.

Jeff was on top of the bigger man, and he didn't waste a second. He smashed his fist into the soft inner flesh of the gunhand wrist, causing Jim's fingers to open up. Jeff grabbed the gun and shoved it away, sliding it down the marble tile floor. He raised his other fist and brought it down full force into Jim's face. Again. And again. Then one more time for good measure.

As he gazed at the groaning bloodied face and contemplated whether or not he should hit him one last time, he felt two strong hands grabbing him under the arms and raising him to his feet.

Jeff didn't resist. His fists hurt and his head hurt, and he wished he could just teleport himself to Moon Lake.

CHAPTER 3

No one was allowed to leave. Even though ninety percent of the staff at Price, Spencer and Williams Inc. were near the breaking point, they had to stay. Until the police were finished, which didn't look like it was going to be any time soon.

Jeff was sequestered in the tenth floor boardroom, along with Karen Woodcock, the company's Chief Executive Officer, and Phil Hudson, the Senior Vice President of the Marketing Division – Jeff's division. A paramedic had already attended to Jeff's bleeding fist, and had even offered him a sedative that Jeff politely declined.

Two detectives, faces still pale from the shock of seeing the bloody scenes on both floors, were sitting at the end of the table with their note pads quickly being filled with scribblings.

The detective with the square jaw that Jeff thought resembled the old Dick Tracy caricature was asking most of the questions. He was looking down at his pad, flicking through the pages.

"So, let me see if I got this right. You hid under the body of…Walt Hitchins… down on the ninth, and then followed Prentice up to the tenth. Is that right?"

Jeff winced. "That's right."

"The perp shot Hitchins a few more times while you were under him?"

"Right."

"How could you have been certain that Hitchins was dead?"

Jeff licked his lips nervously. "Well, I didn't have time to check his pulse, but it seemed pretty obvious to me that he was dead."

"Why did you follow Prentice?"

"To try to stop him."

"And you didn't have any kind of weapon on you?"

"No."

The detective grimaced and ran his fingers through his long greasy hair. "Are you accustomed to being a hero, Dr. Kavanaugh?"

Jeff rubbed his forehead. "No, I'm not, Detective."

"So, why this time?"

Jeff sighed in exasperation. "An event like this doesn't exactly happen every day, does it? Does anyone know how they'll behave when it does happen? Geez, I have no idea why I did what I did. Do you? If so, tell me. Please."

The detective ignored Jeff's outburst. "What kind of stuff did you say to this crazy guy?"

"Sir, I'm a psychologist. I know what things to say to calm situations, confuse peoples' thinking, distract them – take their thinking in a different direction. That's what I tried to do with Prentice. And to a certain extent, it worked."

"Well, not entirely, Dr. Kavanaugh. Six people died today at this office."

Jeff felt a lump in his throat. Six people died today. He hadn't counted – had no idea how many had died until the detective just said it. The number six! He'd seen it – in the elevator and hovering over his newspaper! He wasn't going to disclose that to this square-jaw, though. "Yes, but more people could have died. Someone had to do something. Your people hadn't arrived."

The other detective spoke. "Dr. Kavanaugh – you did a very brave thing. We're just trying to provoke some recollections here, so please don't take our questioning the wrong way."

Jeff nodded. "I understand."

The second detective continued. "The hostage negotiators we have on the force use some of the same tactics you're referring to. I know what you're talking about – sometimes they can be very effective."

Jeff nodded again. He was feeling weary all of a sudden – just wanted to go home, or preferably to his cottage. Escape.

"Why did you run towards the reception area in the first place?"

"I heard a scream. Cathy's scream."

"Were you and Cathy close?"

"I liked her, and we'd dated a couple of times."

The detectives wrote some notes down on their pads. The first officer spoke again. "What made you finally tackle Prentice while he was still armed?"

"I had his attention. He'd already let Gaia go, and had dropped one of his guns. But that lady who was having a heart attack started screaming. We lost the moment. Prentice turned his other gun in her direction, so I had to do something."

Both officers were scribbling furiously. "You could have been shot."

"No, I had a strong feeling I was going to be safe – and that no one else was going to get hurt."

"Can you describe that feeling?"

Jeff gulped. He'd said too much. He sure wasn't going to tell these guys that he no longer saw halos over Gaia or Prentice's heads, or that there was no halo over the heart attack lady's head.

"Just a sixth sense, I guess. Can't describe it. Maybe just gut feel?" Jeff knew that detectives related to the words 'gut feel.' He was right – they both smiled and nodded.

The door to the boardroom opened and in walked a uniformed officer. He leaned over 'square-jaw' and whispered something in his ear. The detective nodded and the officer left the room.

'Square-jaw' looked up and then around at each of the people sitting at the table. "The news just got worse. Officers went to Prentice's home and discovered his wife and two children dead – all three were shot in the head." He paused, and Jeff could see tears forming in the tough guy's eyes. "The kids were a boy and girl – only eight and six years old."

There was a collective sigh around the room, and all heads just stared down at the table.

The detectives stood up. "You're all free to go. I think we have all we need from you today. Dr. Kavanaugh was the only one we really needed to talk to anyway. It's good that you other two were here for his moral support. Oh, by the way, we already have a team of therapists here, on both floors. They'll organize the staff and talk to each of them individually after our officers have finished interviewing them. It'll be a long day for them, but we need to talk to them while the details are all fresh in their minds. And it's important that our therapists talk to them right away too. They're going to need the help."

'Square-jaw' stopped short of the doorway, and turned around. He addressed Karen Woodcock. "Ms. Woodcock, why was Jim Prentice fired by your company?"

Jeff noticed Karen fidgeting a bit with her hands. "I hate to admit this, but I don't know. Jim was only an Account Executive in the Artificial Intelligence Division. He didn't report directly to me. I'll have to chat with the Senior Vice President of AI, and report back to you."

"Oh, that's okay. We can talk to that person ourselves. A name, please?"

"Brandon Horcroft. He's away at a conference for a few days, but you can catch him next week."

'Square-jaw' glared at Karen. "With all due respect, this is a pretty serious matter. You contact him and get him back here. We want to talk to him in person tomorrow. Got that?"

Karen just nodded.

Jeff didn't know Karen that well – she was too high up the ladder. He'd only met her at company Christmas parties, and other functions. But he liked her. She was an attractive lady, always dressed conservatively, which she had to for her high position but they were at least the latest fashions. She was a brunette and a tall one, standing at around five feet, seven inches. She had the most mesmorizing eyes, Jeff thought. Jade green. They were the kind of eyes that you couldn't turn away from once you gazed into them. She had class and was good with the staff.

She'd broken the glass ceiling at a fairly young age, and reached the top position despite the no doubt tremendous competition she would have had with the men on the rise. She was a confident lady, but also appeared to be a bit surprised at times that she was where she was. Karen wasn't totally comfortable with it. Probably looking over her shoulder a lot, Jeff thought. She also had the reputation of being an eager delegator – very trusting of her executives and prone to giving them fairly free rein. He'd heard snide comments from time to time, like "we can get away with this – she'll never know," and "she'll approve anything a man puts in front of her." So, Jeff guessed that even though she'd cracked the glass ceiling, she wasn't comfortable in her own skin yet. However, she'd been the CEO now for about a decade, so if she wasn't comfortable by now at forty-five years of age, she probably never would be.

After the officers left, Jeff, Karen and Phil just stood there for a few minutes, pensive in their own thoughts. Phil took the initiative and broke the awkward silence. He walked over to Jeff and put his arm around his shoulders. He squeezed gently. "Jeff, I don't know what to say. We owe you so much. I've never heard of such an act of bravery before. There have been so many workplace slaughters in the last few years around the world, and I've never heard of anyone taking the kind of action you did. I don't think I could have done what you did."

Jeff just nodded, and looked down at the floor.

Karen walked around the table and joined them. She took both of Jeff's hands in hers and held them tightly. "This won't ever be forgotten by us, Jeff. Know that. And brace yourself for lots of attention – from what I know of you, you probably won't enjoy that. But you will get attention – from the company, from the Press, your friends. You'll be a celebrity – and you being a psychologist, you know innately that it won't rest well in your heart. Lives have been lost, you've witnessed a horror first-hand. But do me a favor, and yourself a favor; just go with it. It will be good therapy and will take your mind off the horror of it all."

Jeff looked up and smiled at Karen. And gave her hands a reciprocal squeeze.

Phil opened the door and led the way out of the boardroom. Down the hallway the three of them walked, passing whispering employees along the way. Some were pointing at him, but most of them were simply crying.

They reached the top of the stairway, and had to step around the bloodied bodies of two of Prentice's victims. Before heading down the stairs, Jeff noticed that yellow tape had been stretched across an office doorway – the one that Prentice had kicked in before murdering the screaming occupant inside.

Down the stairs they walked. Jeff found his gait getting slower with each step, knowing what he'd see once he reached the bottom.

Cathy was still there, staring pleadingly at the ceiling. No one had closed her eyelids yet. Walt Hitchins was laying face down, right where Jeff had left him. He looked very dead indeed, with the multiple bullet punctures in his back and a huge pool of blood under his chest.

Karen and Phil escorted Jeff to the elevator. He stepped over his 11:00 appointment lying on his back in front of the elevator door, two perfect red circles in his forehead

They rubbed Jeff's shoulders as he entered the elevator. He turned around and faced them before the door slid shut. He smiled weakly, but was looking past their heads. The only head he could see was Cathy's – but in a different state than the macabre one she was posed in right now across the reception desk.

No – the Cathy he saw was a smiling pretty face looking across at him over a plate of spaghetti.

And he saw a Cathy standing at her front door, leaning seductively in to him as he gently kissed her goodnight.

And a haloed Cathy, whose eyes seemed to have been eerily pleading with him this morning when he had asked her to send down his first cup of coffee.

CHAPTER 4

The horror was everywhere. In each room of his house he saw mirages of bloodied mannequins. Blank eyes staring at nothing; people who used to walk and talk, laugh and frown, were now lifeless. There was no escape. Jeff was hoping that his home would provide a refuge, some modicum of comfort – but the horror was too close to home; home being his heart.

He had taken the streetcar back, along Queen Street East towards his old Edwardian house in an eclectic area of Toronto known as 'The Beaches.' Sitting quietly in his window seat, he couldn't help but hear the conversations throughout the car. They were louder than he would have thought for such a solemn subject. They talked like they knew first-hand what had happened, composing their own embellishments of the story. To them it was just another news item; something horrible that had happened but too far removed from their safe little lives for it to really affect them. Jeff felt some resentment listening to them – but then realized that just yesterday he would have acted exactly the same way as these folks. Nothing like this had ever touched him before.

He paid particular attention to a young couple in the seats in front of him. The girl was talking about a hero, someone who risked his life to take down the shooter and save a receptionist. She described him as a sixty-year old man with arthritic hands, who somehow found the courage and strength to kick the gun out of the killer's hands and hold him captive until the police arrived. And that no less than a dozen people had been shot before the hero finally managed to bring an end to the slaughter. The usual misinformation that immediately followed a big news story.

Part of him wanted to tap her on the shoulder and correct her story – but the more dominant part of him just didn't give a shit. He didn't care if they knew what really happened. Jeff knew what really happened, and he wished he didn't. He felt fairly certain that he would never forget this day for the rest of his life; that somehow it was going to shape him for better or worse. He didn't know which it would be.

As he was getting off the streetcar at his stop he could still hear them talking – including one passenger chatting with the driver, speculating on the cause of the shooting spree. If they only knew that the "hero of the day" was standing right beside them, ready to leave the car. Wouldn't they be excited? A chance to really feel the rush of the moment, experience right from the 'horse's mouth' the same kind of morbid curiosity that caused people to slow down and gawk at serious accidents on the highway. Hoping to see blood, hoping to see a decapitation or perhaps someone kneeling on the ground crying in despair, hoping against hope to see some misery that would make them feel as if their own lives in contrast were blessed. People needed comparisons to be able to accurately count their blessings. Jeff knew this to be true, but always thought it to be a particularly pathetic characteristic of human nature. And he knew that he had been no different. Until now. He knew he was different now. Changed forever in a way that none of those people on the streetcar ever could or ever would understand, unless and until they were confronted with what Jeff had had to face today. Or worse – ever had to do what Jeff had done today.

In his fantasies, Jeff had always wondered what it would feel like to be a hero. Movies always did a good job at creating that fantasy – normal people faced with insurmountable odds who somehow rose to the occasion. The subject of heroism was always romanticized and made people want to be heroes. Made them want to do the right thing and think that if it came to that, courage would be easy to muster. But Jeff hadn't even thought about it – he'd really just acted without thinking at all. Someone he knew was in trouble; Cathy's scream was all it took. His feet had moved seemingly on their own. It would have been so easy to run the other way, but he hadn't. In retrospect, he pondered if that was what being a hero was all about? Not thinking about it? Does courage come from recklessness? Or does it come from feeling protective towards the vulnerable?

After exiting the streetcar at Lee Avenue, Jeff strolled south toward his house, which was only a couple of blocks from Queen Street East, and about one block from the beaches of Lake Ontario. He nodded politely to an old man who was struggling in the mid-day heat, pushing his heavy lawnmower in front of him while his dog ran gleefully alongside snapping at his heels. He encountered his nosy neighbor, Jean, just before walking up his driveway – she yelled over to him, asking something about the shooting. No surprise to Jeff that she knew about it already. He merely nodded to her ignoring her question, then walked up his steps, put the key in the lock and stepped into his private refuge. This is where he thought it would end for a while. But the visions were still with him – in every room of his house. He knew that it was probably because he was all alone and it was deathly still. The stillness reminded him of the silent death that he had walked through to get out of his office building. Death was a quiet thing because around it every living being seemed to become quiet too. It was intimidating, ominous, and a reminder of how life can end so suddenly and without warning. Death made people think, to the point where they pondered their own mortality.

Jeff turned on his iPod and cranked the sound up. Then he scrolled for the heaviest metal music he could find – Led Zeppelin fit the bill today. He needed noise, needed to chase away the silence of death and the visions of lifelessness. At a time like this, he regretted living alone.

He walked back to his front foyer and picked up the mail that had been slipped through the slot in the door. Several items, mainly bills – but one envelope that he knew contained a belated birthday card. He could tell by the feel of it. His thirty-fifth birthday had been a few days ago: June 30th. There were always a few straggler cards and this was for sure one of them. He opened the envelope and scanned the card.

He felt like he'd been kicked in the gut. Cathy Ricketts' distinctive signature was underneath the sweet message that read: "Jeffy, sorry this card is late, but better late than never, eh? You're my favorite person at the office, so I just had to wish you a Happy Birthday! I hope you'll let me buy you dinner to celebrate. Let me know, okay Jeffy?"

She was the only one from the office who had sent him a card, and she was also the only one who had ever called him 'Jeffy.' He had never liked it when she did that, but now he wished he could hear it over and over again for the rest of his life.

The tears came hard and fast. He dropped the card onto the floor and slowly climbed the stairs to his bedroom. He had two bedrooms upstairs – one was his office, and the other was his abode. He chose the abode. Jeff pulled back the sheets and crawled underneath, fully clothed. Then he buried his head in the pillow, feeling the material absorbing his tears. The cool moistness of the cotton felt strangely soothing as he lamented not making the effort to get to know Cathy better. He had felt uncomfortable dating someone he worked with, and now he chastised himself for his stupid rule. But then he might have fallen in love with her, which would have made all of this even worse.

As the tears continued to flow, Jeff couldn't help but think back to how he had felt this morning on the way to work. The eerie feeling as he was walking along King Street, how everyone seemed to look different, walk different. The feeling that everyone knew a secret. A secret he was excluded from.

Then the elevator – the feeling of fear that had come over him, the number 'six' dangling in the air. The pleading look in Cathy's eyes, then the yellowish halo around her head. Then the number 'six' again as he tried to read his morning paper.

Jeff had known something was going to happen – he just didn't know how serious it was going to be. He didn't know what the signs meant. If he had known, he might have been able to prevent this massacre. He started blaming himself, which in his psychologist's mind he knew was a normal post-traumatic reaction.

His mother had been cursed with the same 'gift' that Jeff had. But she hated it, never wanted to talk about it. When Jeff had confided in her she always just brushed him off. She was dead now, as was his dad. He was certain she wouldn't have brushed him off now after what happened today. She would have helped him understand it, he was sure of that. She had been a caring mother, and by avoiding the 'psychic' discussion with him he knew she had only been trying to protect him, keep him feeling as normal as possible. That's why she had always brushed him off, Jeff was sure of it. But this was just too horrible to brush off.

There was, however, one person he could talk to as his mother's surrogate. Her sister, Louise. She loved to talk about the 'gift' and she had it too – in spades. She'd learned to control it over the years, understand it and listen to it. She actually embraced it, but Jeff's mother had always discouraged him from talking to his Aunt Louise about it. And absolutely forbade her to talk about it with him.

But mom was gone now. And Aunt Louise was still here. And she possessed the knowledge that Jeff needed. Knowledge that he wished he'd had before this horrific day had begun. Could he have prevented this day?

He was determined to find out. In case there was a next time.

CHAPTER 5

Mike Slater folded his newspaper carefully as he always did, isolating only the section he was reading. He didn't like to be distracted by the other headlines until he was completely finished with what he was concentrating on.

It was unsettling. Reading about the murderous rampage of his ex-colleague, Jim Prentice. But it wasn't the murderous part that Mike found unsettling – and that concerned him a bit. Instead, it was this nagging feeling in his brain telling him that there was something he was supposed to do, and actually should have done already.

Mike kept reading. Scanning the words, but detached from the story. What penetrated his mind from the front-page story was not the horror of it all, but instead the reminder that he and Jim had been fired from Price, Spencer and Williams Inc. the very same day. Both shown the door by security personnel, each carrying a single box containing their personal possessions. Seeing the looks on the faces of their colleagues – not looks of sympathy, but more of relief that it wasn't them being fired. No one really cared. They only cared about surviving themselves, and couldn't give two hoots about a fallen colleague.

He'd given ten years of his life to that company, and, just like that he was unceremoniously discharged. Thrown away like a bag of trash. He wasn't even sure why he was fired – couldn't remember if they'd given him a reason.

Mike had enjoyed his job. He'd felt more at home there than with his own family, which was odd indeed. Like Jim, he'd been an Account Executive in the Artificial Intelligence division, which meant in the strictest definition that they specialized in placing executives in companies who were tech-driven, companies who needed skilled people to make machines think like skilled people. Mike had a systems engineering degree as well as a degree in psychology. Both those disciplines had given him huge credibility with his clients, as well as the ability to make very clever decisions in deciding who was best for the high-income positions that fell into his lap.

At least he thought he'd made very clever decisions – maybe not so clever? Why else would he have been fired? Mike scratched his head, trying desperately to recall what Brandon Horcroft had said to him. He remembered going into Brandon's office right after Jim Prentice got his bad news – then remembered leaving the building with Jim, accompanied by two burly security guards. That's all he remembered. He couldn't recollect any part of the conversation with Brandon, none of it. Was he still in shock? It had been several days now; surely he would have recovered from the trauma by now?

Mike rose from the kitchen table and poured himself some coffee. Then he paced the room, window to window, but not glancing outside at his beautiful garden even once. He found himself trying to think back – way back, as far as he could. But it was a blur. For some reason his career at PSW was a blur. Was he losing his mind? Is that why he was fired? Early onset dementia? How could he not remember his accomplishments? Had he even had any accomplishments?

He kept pacing – and gradually bits and pieces of scenes came into his head. The movement of his body was helping. Mike was encouraged and he started pacing faster.

He saw a man sitting in the guest chair in his office, fear in his eyes. He saw himself walking around his own desk towards the guest and slapping the man across the face. Then leaning his face down towards his and speaking softly, slowly. He saw the man nodding in obedience, and then rising from his seat. He couldn't make out his face – he was faceless. Mike got the sense that he, Mike, was clearly in charge and the other man was being asked to do something he didn't want to do. He couldn't recall what it was he was demanding of him, but he had the strong feeling that it was something horrible. Was this just a daydream he was having? Or was he reliving an actual moment from his career?

Mike shook his head trying to clear out the cobwebs…and kept pacing.

He saw himself laughing now, and it seemed as if it was a triumphant moment. Two other people were in his office and he saw Brandon Horcroft walking over to him and the two of them high-fiving each other. Then he watched as Brandon withdrew a cheque from the inside pocket of his suit jacket and handed it to him. Mike looked down at the cheque and saw that it was made out to him, in the amount of 100,000 dollars. He heard Brandon say, "That's just the first instalment. When the job's done, you'll get the rest." What job? Mike had a job that had paid him very well. With a regular bi-weekly pay deposited into his bank account. Why was he receiving a cheque directly from the boss?

Then a phrase popped into his head: 'We make people think like machines.' Why was he thinking that? That's not what 'Artificial Intelligence' was – it was the exact opposite. The phrase should have said: 'We make machines think like people.' Mike figured he must just be getting things mixed up. He was so stressed out right now that he wasn't thinking straight. He was hallucinating, distorting things in his head. Sure, that was it – that had to be it.

But why couldn't he remember specifics? In ten years he must have placed a lot of people at a lot of companies, done a lot of interviews, made tons of presentations to tons of companies, and conducted extensive screenings. Why was he drawing a blank?

Mike heard the front door open, and into the kitchen bounded his wife, Jenny, with their purebred golden retriever. She smiled her big smile and gave him an affectionate peck on the cheek. "Any luck in the job hunt today, hon?"

"No, I'm not ready yet."

"Well, you should have come for a hike with Ben and me. It was hot out there, but just beautiful."

Mike ruffled her hair. "Maybe tomorrow Jen."

She wrapped her arms around him tight. "I know you're having a tough time with this, but things will look up. You have everything going for you – it won't take long for you to find another good job. I have faith in you."

"Yeah, you're right. It's just that my mind seems to be blanking out on me – I can't remember very much at all right now. Not even the meeting when they fired me."

"I think that's natural–it's a shock to the system. You'll find it'll get better as each day goes by."

"I sure hope so."

"Well, I'm going to start dinner so you'll have to get out of my kitchen." Jennifer playfully shoved him toward the doorway.

Mike kissed her on the lips. "Okay, okay, I can take a hint! I'll go commiserate somewhere else in the house."

He walked down the hall towards the den...then stopped dead in his tracks.

A phrase popped into his head. And it wasn't just the recollection of a phrase. It was a command phrase...meant for him. One he felt compelled to obey. Mike felt a numbness overtake him as he headed up the stairs. He went straight to the bathroom and stripped off his clothes. He turned on the taps in the bathtub and watched as the water lapped up to the halfway point. Then he turned off the taps, opened up the medicine cabinet and withdrew a single razor blade.

Mike slid into the tub and savored the warmth. He raised his left hand and turned it palm up. Then he calmly slid the razor blade across his wrist and watched impassively as the blood began to pour out over his arm and down into the water. He felt no pain and no trepidation. In fact he felt nothing at all except a mild feeling of satisfaction. For a job well done.

As things began to get fuzzy, the phrase that caused him to make the climb up

the stairs to the bathroom kept playing over and over in his head.
'Thou shalt go forth.'

CHAPTER 6

Brandon Horcroft gazed at his image in the mirror. He had to admit, he was one darn good-looking guy. Modest too, he thought, chuckling to himself. He splashed water on his face and smoothed his longish white hair back just the way he liked it. He had a certain 'look,' and in his view it was important for him to maintain that look at all times. Important for how he felt about himself, but even more importantly for how others felt about him – the intimidation factor, the envy factor, and for just the sheer ability to dominate. Brandon needed to dominate. Crucial in his business – considering who he had to deal with and who his clients were.

He straightened up in front of the mirror to his full six foot, three inch frame and adjusted his red silk tie. It contrasted nicely with his custom-tailored blue linen suit. Brandon was sixty-two years old but looked no older than fifty. He was proud of that, and just loved telling people how old he was – loved seeing the looks of surprise and admiration. Most people were afraid to share their actual age with others – but not Brandon. He enjoyed it.

He turned off the gold-plated tap in his private washroom, and strolled out to the main office area of his suite. Adjoining his suite was also a boardroom where he could hold private meetings as needed, away from prying eyes. His entire suite – the office, boardroom, and washroom – were all super-soundproofed. Not even the yelling that occasionally took place could escape through the walls. And he could fart as loudly and as often as he wanted in his washroom without having the outside world knowing that someone as perfect as him actually had some normal human traits.

Brandon was a psychiatrist – most of the senior staff in the AI division were psychologists but Brandon was the only psychiatrist, thus possessing an actual medical degree. He'd been the Senior Vice President of the Artificial Intelligence division since its inception fifteen years ago. It had been his brainchild, and he treated it as if it was his child. He was protective of it and would continue to be as long as he was alive.

Brandon had been a top candidate for the CEO position ten years ago due to his meteoric success with the AI creation – but he had turned it down. For two reasons: firstly, because he had more power doing what he was doing and secondly, because he couldn't allow anyone else to occupy his position. No one could be allowed to inherit the stewardship of AI. He would destroy it before allowing that to happen.

The tenth floor operation, to the world at large, was a brilliant façade. It generated sixty percent of the revenues of the entire global operation of the company, and it was also the only truly global division. Its fingers reached everywhere and the client base was diverse, to say the least. It included large multi-national companies, universities, military and paramilitary operations, and governments around the world – big and small. The AI division also had secret affiliates, or more appropriately, strategic alliance partners – synergy being the way real business got done these days. Scratch my back and I'll scratch yours.

And with Price, Spencer and Williams Inc. being a privately held company, what the AI division did was beyond public scrutiny. There were two dozen shareholders in the company – most of them being the top executives with a few private investors thrown into the mix. Those private investors were also top clients, and had a vested interest in how well the company did – but most importantly how well the AI division did.

Even though Karen Woodcock, the CEO and also one of the shareholders, had pushed for taking the company public on the TSX and NYSE, Brandon had enough support on the Board of Directors to kill the idea every time the subject was brought up. Most of the board members who supported Brandon were also clients who utilized the services of the AI division, and knew full well that they couldn't risk having the company traded on a public exchange. That would be disastrous for the company – but of more concern than that, a lot of good people would go to prison for the rest of their lives.

Brandon was a bit worried though. For now, he and his division were safe – but if the composition of the board ever changed beyond his control, it might be a different story. To deal with that worry, he received board approval at the last meeting to have a 'shotgun clause' inserted into the company bylaws. This clause basically gave Brandon first right of outright purchase of the entire company if a motion were ever approved to take the company public. Now, Brandon was a wealthy man, but he knew he couldn't afford to buy the company himself – he'd need some help. And he had several board members who would be glad to help him make a hostile offer if it came to that. So, he was feeling pretty good right now; a bit worried but not unduly so.

It had been a week now since the shootings. Brandon had flown back from his conference in Vegas at Karen's request. He normally didn't respond well to orders from her, but for that incident he made an exception. With the cops involved, he wanted to just make the problem go away as quickly as possible. So, okay, an employee went 'postal.' So what? That seemed to happen so often now that the investigations were just a mere formality.

They wanted to know why Jim Prentice had been fired, and Brandon just gave them the usual reason: incompetence. Then they wanted to see his personnel file. He showed them, but there wasn't much in it. The really serious stuff was buried in electronic files that they'd never find. So, he let them see the paper file, which was enough to keep them from looking further.

Brandon couldn't muster up any sadness over the shootings. And he had to admit, he wasn't even sad about not being sad. He had lost three of his people on the tenth floor; they were just mediocre staff and not high-level – so no big loss. He didn't really know the three who died on the ninth floor, and didn't really care either because they weren't from his floor.

What he did care about was what went wrong. What caused Prentice to slaughter his family and six other people? That wasn't supposed to happen. He contrasted that with the suicide of Mike Slater, which he just heard about yesterday. That was textbook. Why did Prentice go so wrong? How had they dropped the ball so badly on that one? Brandon would find out – he'd scheduled a post-mortem meeting tomorrow with some of his top staff, to discuss it and learn from it. And if needed, he'd make some adjustments.

And they would have to do something about this Jeff Kavanaugh guy – his hero status now made him the public face of Price, Spencer and Williams Inc. Brandon could use that to his advantage and, without a doubt, Kavanaugh was also being wasted on the ninth floor. He would have to rectify that – skills like his could be utilized much better on the tenth. They needed some new brilliant blood on the tenth – for the future survival of the Artificial Intelligence project.

Brandon went back into the bathroom and took one last look at his face before heading out for his martini lunch. He knew he was a narcissist. His genius psychiatrist brain had done some serious self-analysis a long time ago. Some of the most successful people in history had been narcissists, Brandon thought proudly. And some of the most dangerous people in history had also been narcissists. Combine that with the sociopath aspect that Brandon possessed, and he knew that he was a force to be reckoned with.

Brandon knew from down in the depths of his cold, dark heart that he was a very dangerous man.

CHAPTER 7

The police somehow managed to keep his name and his face out of the news for an entire week, but Jeff knew not to be lulled into a false sense of security. It was bound to end. And it did.

Jeff awoke to it on a sunny Thursday morning, coffee and briefcase in hand, as he bounded out his front door. He stopped dead in his tracks when he saw the news vans. He knew this was going to happen eventually, but prayed that he might get lucky and escape the onslaught.

Jeff was aggressive and an extrovert to the outside world, but in paradox, he was actually a closet introvert. He didn't relish the spotlight – didn't enjoy nor need attention. He would run in the opposite direction if he saw it coming. This time there was nowhere to run – they were on him in seconds, microphones thrust into his face, yelling out questions. He was stunned – no less than four reporters crowding him on his front steps. Another thing Jeff didn't like was crowds and crowded venues. He needed his space and sometimes became frantic when he didn't have it.

He noticed that his neighbors were all outside enjoying the excitement. The lure of 'celebrity' was intoxicating and they now had a real live one in their midst. Jeff guessed that if the television reporters were here, the newspapers had probably already printed the story as well. He hadn't had a chance to check the morning papers yet, but dreaded what he'd see when he finally got around to it.

He decided that he wasn't going to give these idiots the satisfaction of a story, or even a comment. He angrily pushed his way through the throng, walked down his driveway and started along the sidewalk towards Queen Street. They followed on foot, and he heard the vans start their engines as they began their quest to cruise alongside their reporters. Jeff just kept walking with his head down – unusual for him to walk with his head down, but he wanted to avoid giving them a clear revealing video of his face.

When he reached Queen Street, mercifully, a westbound streetcar had just pulled up at the stop. Jeff leaped onto the stairway and pulled himself up inside, oblivious to the shouts from the reporters behind him. The doors closed and they were off, but the vans kept him in their sights. Jeff glanced back through the window as he weaved his way to an open seat – they were following the streetcar, and they knew where he worked so would probably just park themselves right in front of his building.

He could see all eyes watching him as he took his seat – a rolled up newspaper was on the floor at his feet, and he picked it up and opened it to the front page. There he was – somehow they had gotten a photograph of him; it looked like the one that was used in an announcement when he was promoted a few years ago. And now he knew why everyone on the streetcar was staring at him – they recognized him from the front-page photo.

Jeff read the article – they seemed to have gotten most of the information right, except that they over-dramatized his role, predictably. Drama sold papers. It had been a week since the incident so the facts had gradually, day by day, become less muddled. They used his name in the article, and even managed to post a photo of Gaia Templeton, using her name as well. Jeff imagined that Gaia probably had a fleet of news vans at her house this morning too. He made a mental note to chat with her today, see how she was doing. This would be his first day back at the office since the massacre – the office had been closed for a week, what with crime scene forensics and clean up, let alone the severe trauma of the staff. Jeff had worked from home the past few days, phoning clients, setting up appointments and conducting phone interviews. Now he was back in the rat race and judging by how his morning had started, 'rat race' was an appropriate description.

A young lady across the aisle reached over and tapped his shoulder. She held up her newspaper and pointed at his photo. "This is you, isn't it?"

Jeff just nodded and lowered his head. She swiveled in her seat to face him. "How did it feel? Were you scared?"

He ignored her. Other people chimed in, and turned around in their seats hoping, praying, for words from the hero. Apparently, everyone loves a hero. But Jeff didn't feel like a hero. He felt like a cheap celebrity at this very moment, being celebrated for something horrible. People had died. A charming beautiful lady had died just for being a receptionist. No crime committed – Cathy had just been unlucky enough to be the first person the shooter saw as he got off the elevator. Jim Prentice didn't care who he killed – he was indiscriminate in choosing who would have the honor of losing their lives that day.

The streetcar was abuzz now – people were getting out of their seats and walking to where Jeff was sitting just to get a look at him. Most of them said nothing to him – he felt like a zoo animal. It seemed that because he was a quasi-celebrity now he was fair game – he belonged to everyone for their own gawking enjoyment. They didn't seem to care whether or not he was bothered by it, and they would certainly have been able to tell that he was bothered just by the way he was sitting hunched over, looking down at the floor.

When a man who smelled like he hadn't had a bath in over a week grabbed Jeff's hand and started yanking on it, shaking it, he finally boiled over. Jeff jumped up from his seat and shoved the grungy guy backwards so hard that he bounced against one of the seat frames and collapsed onto the floor. There was a collective gasp from the other riders as Jeff pushed his way to the front of the car, briefcase held out in front of him running interference. He felt a few more hands on him as he made his way, but he was a man on a mission now and he ignored them. He felt the claustrophobic panic that gripped him only rarely, but when it did he had to act on it otherwise he felt like he would simply go mad.

When he reached the front, he leaned down to the driver and said, "Stop the car and open the door."

The driver looked up at him blankly. "Sir, this isn't a designated stop."

Jeff glared at him. "I don't give a shit. I'm designating it as a stop. Let me off now. I'm getting mobbed back there."

"Well, I can't help that, sir."

Jeff reached down and grabbed the lever that he knew would brake the streetcar – he'd seen it used hundreds of times. The car screeched and lurched to the sound of the driver yelling out in horror. Jeff felt a thump, and guessed that a car had rammed into the rear of the streetcar – he didn't care, he had to get out. He then pushed the button on the dashboard that displayed an 'exit' icon and the door folded open. The fresh smell of freedom rushed through his nostrils and he leaped out onto the sidewalk and embraced it. Jeff quickly melded into the walkers on Queen Street to the background noise of the streetcar driver yelling obscenities after him in some foreign language.

*****

"You saved my life and I don't know how to thank you. Tell me how – please."

Jeff was standing at the reception desk on the tenth floor, gazing into the eyes of a still traumatized Gaia Templeton. He leaned his elbows on the counter and answered her in the softest voice he could muster. "It's okay. Knowing you're alive is thanks enough."

She smiled warmly at him. "You were so calm, so cool. And so brave. I still can't believe what you did."

Jeff winced. "I just acted on impulse – I didn't have much of a plan. I just knew that he had to be stopped."

"I have nightmares about it, Jeff. I can still feel his arm around my neck, with one gun up against my head, and the other one pointed at you."

"Have you taken advantage of the counseling that the police offered?"

"No, not yet. I'm not a big believer in that stuff – I'm hoping I can just deal with it on my own."

Jeff pouted. "Not a big believer? That's what I do. I'm insulted, Gaia."

She laughed. "Whoops – big faux pas on my part, eh? Maybe if you counseled me I could become a believer!"

Jeff knew she was flirting with him now. And this time he was determined not to be hung up on his stupid rule about not fraternizing with staff. He was painfully aware for the first time in his young life, that 'life was too short.' "Okay, I'll make you a deal. If you have dinner with me, I'll throw in some free counseling. Whaddaya say?"

Gaia smiled coyly and tilted her head sideways in a way that caused a knot to tighten in Jeff's stomach. She was incredibly cute. "What do I say? I say 'when' and 'where.'"

"Okay, let's say Saturday night, 7:00 p.m., 'Teatro.'"

"Ooh – I love Teatro! I have other plans but they can easily be changed."

Jeff gave her a 'thumbs up' sign. "I like your decisiveness, Gaia. It's a date then."

Gaia chuckled. "Well, since according to you I'm supposed to be a pregnant lady, I do manage to keep my hormones in check, don't I? I can still think straight, despite having to think for two now. By the way, Jeff, what's my due date and am I having a boy or a girl?"

He laughed and gave her one last lingering smile, then turned and headed for the staircase that would lead him back down to his ninth floor office. The dreaded staircase where the final standoff with Jim Prentice had happened. The staircase that the killer intended to leave by with Gaia Templeton in tow.

Suddenly he heard a voice behind him. "Kavanaugh! Wait up a second, will you?"

Jeff turned his head in the direction of the voice, and saw none other than the legendary Brandon Horcroft hurrying towards him. He'd only met him once before in all his years with the company – the man wasn't known as being sociable, and had a reputation for being ruthless and marching to his own drummer. But he was the Senior Vice President of the iconic Artificial Intelligence division, and if he was asking Jeff to 'wait up,' Jeff figured he'd better 'wait up.'

"Hello, sir. How can I help you?"

Brandon reached out and pumped Jeff's hand. "I wanted to shake the hand of the brave man who saved so many lives last week. Our sincere thanks, Jeff."

Jeff just nodded.

"Oh, and I wanted to let you know that I got two calls this morning – one from the police who want to charge you with 'public mischief' for some strange incident on a streetcar this morning. And another call from the insurance company for the Toronto Transit Commission, who want to subrogate back against you for damage that that same streetcar caused to a car that was coming up the rear."

Jeff felt himself blushing. "Sir, let me explain about…"

Brandon waved his hand in the air, dismissing Jeff's explanation. "No need for that – I made both of those problems go away. You don't have to worry."

"Oh…thank you, sir."

"Stop calling me 'sir.' My name's 'Brandon.' From now on, you call me 'Brandon.' Okay?"

"Okay, Brandon." Jeff didn't feel as if that name rolled easily off his tongue, but for this important executive he would do his best to get comfortable with it.

"Jeff, I want to spend some time chatting with you. Is tomorrow, 3:00, convenient for you? My office?"

Jeff thought for a second. "Actually, I have an appointment with an important prospect tomorrow afternoon. Could we make it another day?" As soon as the words left his mouth, he knew it was a mistake.

Brandon frowned and took a step closer to Jeff. "Excuse me?"

"Well, I'm just being honest with you, Brandon. You asked if it was convenient, and it's not."

"Make it convenient, young man. Just make it convenient." At that, he turned on his heel and stomped off back down the hallway.

Jeff's psychologist brain realized in an instant that this little exchange had just given him alarmingly vivid insight into an ego about the size of a jumbo jet. Their meeting should prove interesting; he was curious as to what the agenda was.

And there was no question that his first task when he got back down to the ninth floor was to clear his calendar to make Brandon Horcroft's dictated time "convenient."

CHAPTER 8

"We have two vacancies right now that need to be filled. I'm thinking about you for one of those vacancies. We need some young talent in the AI division, and it's about time we started adding some."

Jeff fidgeted as he listened to the executive. He was thinking that he couldn't recall ever seeing this man in the same suit twice – today he was wearing cream: cream suit, cream shirt, cream tie, and cream shoes. On anyone else but Brandon, the word "gay" would come to mind. But this man was all man, and Jeff could tell that he knew it too. He clearly wore the outfit with pride and probably secretly hoped that someone would have the nerve to make a wisecrack.

"Knock, knock – is anyone home? Earth to Jeff."

Jeff shook himself out of his daydream. "Yes, Brandon. Sorry, I was just thinking about what you said about the vacancies." Jeff lied – he had in fact just drifted off to the man's drone.

"Well, talk to me then. What specifically were you thinking about?"

"Okay, I was thinking about how unsettling it is to be filling one of two vacancies associated with violence."

"Understandable, but remember this, young man. We fired Prentice and Slater before the violence. Prentice went off his rocker and now will probably spend the rest of his miserable life in a mental institution. And Slater took it upon himself to commit suicide."

"Right. But the violent acts were a direct result of being fired."

Brandon wrung his hands together. "Cowboy-up, son. I refuse to be sentimental over a couple of weaklings. What they did afterwards just confirms to me that we did the right thing firing them."

Jeff was taken aback by the cold attitude of the man. He hadn't yet expressed one word of sympathy about the victims of the two employees. Jeff decided to have a little fun and provoke further.

"So, Brandon, how do you feel about the family of Slater? It must have been a shock for his wife to find him in the tub like that – and his two kids; they were just a couple of youngsters. No father now."

"Not my problem. He made a lot of money while he was here, so if he was smart and socked a lot of it away, his family should be well taken care of. If he didn't, well..."

Jeff helped himself to more coffee. They were sitting in the living room of Brandon's palatial office, and the coffee aroma emanating from the silver coffee pot sitting on the table between them was overpowering. He had noticed that everything in this office was first-class all the way, and Brandon went out of his way to make it known that he had a private washroom that Jeff could use if he was "so inclined." He also made a point of advising Jeff to wipe down the gold-plated faucets after using to avoid the "nuisance of lingering water spots." The man was an insufferable egomaniac.

But, could he work for him? The short answer was "yes." Jeff could work for anyone if it suited his career. He didn't have to like them – that wasn't a prerequisite in his mind.

"So, what's your answer?"

Jeff figured this guy was used to getting his way without having to do too much persuasion. Jeff would make him work a little bit harder for him.

"I don't know enough to be able to give you an answer. What does this mysterious Artificial Intelligence division do, anyway? Why is there so much secrecy surrounding it? No one on the ninth seems too sure as to what work actually gets done up here. And generally, the people who work up here don't talk to us down there. So, what would I be agreeing to if I sign on to this?"

Brandon smiled. "Nice to see that you think for yourself. I sensed that about you, which is one of the reasons why I think we need more people like you up here. We're getting 'long in the tooth' and a bit stale."

Jeff smiled back, but knew that this man was patronizing him right now. Men like Brandon didn't like people who 'thought for themselves.' They liked to tell people that they did, but that was only to make others think that their egos were secure. Brandon had an oversized ego, but Jeff knew that it wasn't secure in the slightest sense of the word. If he wanted Jeff to move up to the tenth floor, it was only because it would suit Brandon's plans and make Brandon look good. Jeff wasn't going to make the mistake of kidding himself into thinking that he cared about Jeff's career or for the good of the company. Those things would be secondary to a character like Brandon.

"Okay, so tell me then—what exactly is it that the AI division does?"

Brandon poured himself some more coffee and then leaned forward and lowered the tone of his voice, almost as if he was afraid someone might be listening in. "I created this division fifteen years ago, and due to the specialized nature of what we do, it has to be kept under the radar. We don't want other firms to copy our methods, and we have to respect the confidentiality of our clients as well. If you accept our invitation to join, you will be asked to sign a 'confidentiality agreement,' one that will be enforceable by law and subject to severe financial penalties. So, until you agree to join us I can only give you a 'high level' summary, you understand I'm sure."

Jeff nodded.

"Well then, 'Artificial Intelligence' means, in the simplest terms, the science of developing systems to make machines think like people. So, similar to what you do down there in the Marketing division, we place intelligent people in the right positions with high technology companies, manufacturing firms, government agencies and really any type of firm at all – any firm who requires the need for their computer or machinery systems to take the next step towards intelligent human-like thinking. So, again, like what you do, we match up the right candidates with the right positions with the right companies. No difference there."

"So, why is it so secretive? Why is there this stand-offish attitude between the tenth floor and the ninth floor?"

"Aside from the usual executive search work we do, we also do personal coaching – a huge need these days. Employees occasionally need to be, let's say, "re-engineered." With our staff of psychologists and hypnotherapists, we have the ability to produce the perfect employees to suit the needs of our clients. They come to us screaming for help, and we send them back an employee that is usually pitch perfect. It's cheaper for a client to pay us to change someone than for them to go out and hire someone brand new. If an employee is an introvert, we can make him an extrovert. If someone has phobias such as a fear of public speaking, we can turn that person into a re-born Dale Carnegie. We can do anything because we are solution-driven – and we have the smartest people doing the re-engineering. All modesty aside, we have become famous in certain preferred circles and we have a lock on the market for this sort of thing, and that lock applies around the world."

"So why do you want me?"

"Your bravery in that shooting incident was impressive. And your ability to stay calm in a very dangerous situation caught my attention. Last but not least, your skill at talking a clearly insane man out of finishing what he started left me breathless. And the fact that he could have shot you, but didn't, demonstrated an almost mystical quality you have under pressure. A quality that makes you the 'Teflon man.'"

"Thank you."

"And one more thing – you've been all over the front pages. Even though a workplace shooting is not something any firm would like to have as advertising, in our case you turned a negative into a positive. The 'spin' of having one of our senior people standing down the face of danger is a powerful spin indeed. We need to make you higher profile, use your image to our advantage – and yours. It's the only way we can properly recover from this devastating incident. If I missed this opportunity, I deserve to copy Mike Slater and slit my own wrist."

Jeff was astounded at how irreverent this man was.

"So, you want me for publicity?"

"No, I want you mainly for your talents. But I can't ignore the PR benefits, can I? I wouldn't be a very good businessman if I did."

Jeff admitted that perhaps he was being too sensitive. Brandon talked sense. "No, it's idealistic of me to think that you'd ignore that."

"Good. I'm glad we see eye to eye."

Jeff wouldn't go that far, but best not to admit that to Brandon. "So, what would I be doing upon joining?"

"We'll ease you in slowly, deliberately. At first you'll be involved in the executive placement activities, but we'll swing you in to the personal coaching and re-engineering as soon as possible. That's where the real money is, and where your talents would be best utilized."

"What's in it for me?"

"Your salary will jump immediately from 250,000 dollars to 400,000 dollars – with bonuses on top of that. You'll have a monthly car allowance and a generous expense account. How does that sound?"

Jeff gulped. He just nodded his head, finding it hard to find the words.

"I want an answer."

"Can I have time to think about it?"

"No. And you will need to sign the 'confidentiality agreement' before you leave the room. If you leave my office without accepting the position, it will not be offered to you ever again."

This man played hardball. Jeff decided he would play along with him. He figured – what's the worst that could happen? He could just quit if he didn't like it. "Okay, Brandon – I accept. Give me the form to read over."

Brandon walked over to his desk and brought back a two-page document, already completed with Jeff's name in all the right places. Jeff looked it over – the usual wording, but the difference was that this one didn't expire after a certain time period. The term continued after a resignation, after a retirement, and after a firing – right until death. Till death do us part.

It stated an intent to prosecute to the full extent of the law in addition to a financial penalty of no less than one million dollars. Jeff figured that alone was enough to guarantee silence. He pulled out his pen.

Brandon pushed a button on his phone console and almost immediately a young lady walked into the office through the boardroom door. It occurred to Jeff that she might have been in there listening to every word. She smiled but said nothing. Brandon didn't introduce her. He signed under his typed name, and she signed in the two witness sections – he noticed that the title she wrote in was 'attorney at law,' and it looked like her name was Janice Wilson. She smiled at him one last time, then turned and walked back the way she had come.

Brandon stood. Jeff guessed that the meeting was over. He reached out and shook Jeff's hand and said, "You start next Monday. Report to me here at 9:00 sharp."

"What about the projects I have on the go on the ninth? I'll need time to finish them off or assign them to someone else."

"Well, go ahead and do that then. Tomorrow's Saturday and the next day's Sunday. You have lots of time."

Jeff felt his face start to flush. He knew it wasn't from embarrassment but from instant exasperation. No cottage trip to Moon Lake for him this weekend. "What about my boss, Phil Hudson? Have you talked to him? Or will you talk to him?"

Brandon shrugged. "Your problem, not mine. You talk to him. I own you now – if he has a problem with that, he can come and talk to me."

"He's a Senior Vice President just like you. He might instead choose to talk to Karen Woodcock. Maybe you should fend that off at the pass by talking to him first? Mutual courtesy between colleagues?"

Brandon's face scrunched up into an expression that Jeff hadn't seen yet. His handsome features turned suddenly ugly, and up until this moment Jeff couldn't have imagined how a man who looked like Brandon could even try to look ugly. But he did, and without any effort at all.

"Here are your first few lessons, young man. Take some mental notes: Don't ever attempt to advise me on what to do. And Karen Woodcock is an empty suit; a figurehead, and a shareholder who gives me free rein because she loves her capital gain. Hey, that even rhymes! Phil Hudson is not my colleague – maybe in title, but not even close in stature. I'm the only power that matters around here and it will do you good to remember that."

With that, he guided Jeff by the elbow towards his office door, opened it with his free hand and gently shoved Jeff out into the hallway. Before saying 'goodbye,' he ventured one more statement. "Once you're back down on the ninth floor, go see our VP of Public Relations. There's a morning television show that wants you as a guest. He'll fill you in. You will say yes to this."

Jeff stared back at him, mouth agape, as the office door slammed in his face.

CHAPTER 9

She ordered a Black Russian, and he ordered a glass of red. Jeff watched Gaia closely as she took her first sip of the dark amber liquid. Her lipstick was the color of the drink, and her nostrils flared slightly as she took her first burning swallow.

"God, that scorches." She waved her hand in front of her mouth, fanning the flames. "I think they put too much Tia Maria in this one." She took another sip, and then smiled her cute little smile. "Oh, that's better. Clearly, the secret is to just drink more!"

"I don't know how you can drink those things – too syrupy for me."

Gaia dabbed at her lips with a tissue and whispered, "It's a lady's drink, Jeff. I'd be worried if you ordered one."

"Well, maybe I'll do just that for my second drink, only to show you how secure I am with my manhood."

She winked at him and let it linger while she tilted her head sideways. Jeff felt as if his heart had stopped for just that brief instant. She was adorable when she did that wink and tilt thing. In fact, she was adorable even when she didn't wink and tilt. He had always been attracted to Gaia; whenever they had had lunch together in the staff lunchroom he had wondered what it would be like to date her. But he had that rule – the rule that he regretted now. Now that Cathy was gone. He had missed out on getting to know someone who was probably very special – a moment in time that he could have captured but one that had now eluded him forever. Well, he was determined not to let this moment elude him. He was going to enjoy this dinner at Teatro tonight, enjoy the company of a lovely lady. And if it led to something else, he would allow it to happen. Life was too short for rules.

She was resplendent in a shimmering silver dress, adorned with sequins across the front. It was low cut, but not too low. Just low enough to stimulate Jeff's imagination, but not too low as to taint her classy image. Her skirt came down just below the knees, and her height tonight was raised about three inches by a glittering pair of shoes that matched the hue of her dress exactly. Gaia's hair was short-cropped, which suited her cute pixie face – and her eyes were the blackest Jeff had ever seen. Most people who had jet black eyes had a cold gaze, but not Gaia. Her eyes were warm, expressionful, enquiring. Jeff felt as if he could get lost looking into those eyes.

Jeff ordered a bottle of Chianti to go with the generous plate of antipasti they shared. Gaia ordered another Black Russian. He could tell she was starting to feel the drinks; not drunk, just more talkative as the liquor began to overtake her nerves.

She told him about her life.

Gaia had worked at Price, Spencer and Williams for about seven years – one year longer than Jeff had. She was thirty-two, a little bit older than Jeff had thought, and had joined the company after a two-year stint backpacking through most of Europe. She'd been exhausted after graduating from Western University with a Master's degree in Business Administration and wanted to see part of the world before settling down. Her parents were retired and lived in the resort town of Bobcaygeon, northeast of Toronto. She had two older sisters who lived in the suburbs.

Gaia confessed that she had been engaged once – a love affair that came to a tragic end five years ago when her fiancé died in a plane crash. She hadn't dated too much since then – Matt had been her high school sweetheart, and the imprinted memories of all their years together took a long time leaving her mind at peace.

Jeff couldn't resist the obvious question. "Gaia, you have a Master's degree. Don't take this the wrong way but I'm having a tough time rationalizing your position at Price. You're a receptionist. Aren't you...kinda...underemployed?"

Gaia shifted uncomfortably in her seat. "It would seem so...but that's not really the case at all. Yes, I sit at the front desk, I'm the first person you see when you get off the elevator on the tenth floor, or make the hike up the grand staircase. So it looks like I'm just the receptionist. But my title is actually "Logistics Manager.""

Jeff frowned. "What on earth does a Logistics Manager do?"

"I organize, arrange timing, do a lot of the research for pre-screening of candidates. I also do spreadsheets, PowerPoint presentations, schematics, flowcharts, financial projections."

"Sounds like you should have a private office."

Gaia laughed. "Price is a chauvinistic company – maybe you haven't noticed that?" She laughed again, louder this time. "Even for a woman like me with a fairly important job, they want me out in the open to be seen, for the male clients to see me and even drool over me occasionally."

Jeff could tell that Gaia was getting tipsier with each sip of now her third Black Russian. "You should probably sip that drink a bit slower, Gaia. You're gonna have a whopping headache tomorrow."

She giggled. "You're right, you're right. I guess I've just been a bit nervous – this being our first date and all." Gaia smiled coyly at him. "This is just our first date of many, I hope?"

Jeff rested his elbows on the table, then leaned his head forward and spoke softly to her. "I definitely want to see you again. In fact, I've always wanted to date you but shied away since we worked together. But I don't care about that anymore."

She smiled knowingly. "Yes, I know about Cathy. She told me she'd seen you a couple of times, but that you pulled back."

"Yeah, I felt guilty."

"I have to admit, I was jealous when I knew Cathy had dated you – but then felt better when she told me you put an end to it. Once I knew the reason, I didn't take it so personally that you hadn't asked me out."

Jeff just nodded and lowered his eyes. Gaia reached over and rubbed his shoulder. "It must be hard for you, the memories of what you saw. Cathy…being the…first one…you saw."

"The images won't let go. But having dinner here with you tonight helps a lot, believe me."

"I'm glad."

Jeff decided to change the subject. "So, who do you actually report to?"

"Brandon Horcroft."

"What do you think of Brandon?"

Jeff noticed that she tensed up at that question. "I'd rather not say anything about that right now."

"Okay, who do you do work for, then?"

Gaia relaxed a bit. "The only people who can assign tasks to me are Brandon who's the Senior Vice President, the Vice Presidents, and the twenty account executives…well, correction…only eighteen now with the Prentice thing, and the Slater suicide."

"What about the other 200 employees on the floor?"

"That number's down to 197 now due to the three men killed on the tenth." Gaia sighed, and then continued. "They have their own support staff. For the entire floor I act as the receptionist as well, but my main job is working support duties for the executives."

"Are you satisfied?"

"Well, some things bother me, but they pay me so well I don't know if I could duplicate my salary somewhere else. I just got a raise last week as a matter of fact – I just topped the 100,000 dollar mark."

Jeff whistled under his breath. He found it hard to believe that a support person would command that kind of salary. Then again, he didn't think that at thirty-five years of age he'd be making 400,000 dollars a year either.

"They must really value you."

Gaia winced. "You would think so at that salary, but sometimes I just get the feeling that they want to make it impossible for me to leave. I never get any praise from anyone – sometimes it's a bit discouraging, because I am very good at what I do. But no one seems to care."

Jeff poured some more Chianti into his glass, and took a long sip. "I should tell you – I'm joining the AI division on Monday. As a Senior Account Executive."

Gaia sat back in her chair, shock on her face. "Is that why you asked me out? To find out about the division?"

Jeff felt his stomach churn. "Oh, God, no. I asked you out before I'd even had a chat with Brandon. Remember when we were chatting at your desk on Thursday, and as I was walking away Brandon called out my name?"

She nodded warily.

"Well, that's when he told me that he wanted to meet with me on Friday. I had no idea what it was about."

Gaia crossed her legs, and then drained the rest of her Black Russian. "Okay, I feel better now. Please understand – the AI division is very insular. We're instructed to always be on our guard about anyone who asks too many questions or pries too deeply into what we do."

"What do you folks do?"

"I'm sure Brandon already gave you some kind of an idea."

"He did, but I'd like to hear your take on it."

Gaia whispered. "Jeff, I'm not really comfortable talking too much about it. Maybe when I know you better? And remember, I'm not in the inner circle. I support, only."

Jeff persisted. "Sure, I understand, I really do. But tell me – from your vantage point, what is your biggest observation. You're a smart, educated girl. You have an opinion, I'm sure."

Gaia sighed. "Okay, I'll share some key words with you – and I'm not really in the know. I just support. A lot of what happens happens after I'm finished with what I do."

"Okay, I'm waiting."

"Cloak and dagger, strange meetings, scary clients, lots of cash payments, very close-mouthed to the point of paranoia."

Jeff looked hard into her beautiful black eyes. "Hmm…anything else?"

Gaia leaned her head forward and Jeff saw her eyes skirt briefly from side to side before she spoke again. And she spoke with a strong slur, as the third Black Russian seemed to finally achieve its objective. "People seem to die, Jeff. Clients, employees, contacts – a lot of them just seem to die."

CHAPTER 10

Brandon Horcroft sat at the head of the table, which was where he always sat of course. He even took that seat when Karen Woodcock was in the room. Karen never asserted her right to that seat – she always capitulated to Brandon. Everybody capitulated to Brandon. Which is exactly the way he liked it.

He was hosting a meeting in his private soundproofed boardroom. It was to be only the five of them – he and his four vice presidents. The ones he trusted to execute every little project that he dreamed up. Of course, he let them dream up a few themselves once in a while just to stroke their egos, and, he had to admit, once in a while they had some good ideas. But…only once in a while.

They were indeed good at executing though. Brandon knew that most people didn't have an ounce of strategizing talent in their little brains. Most people weren't creative enough to think outside the box. He wished he were wrong, but he wasn't. And even his narcissistic brain wished there were more people like him. He was never threatened by strong brains – he admired that in people. His own intellect was off the charts, so it was almost impossible for him to be threatened by another smart person.

Sometimes Brandon got weary from doing all the thinking, coming up with all of the ideas and solutions. On one hand, it made him feel powerful knowing everyone looked to his gray cells for their guidance. On the other hand, though, it frustrated him to no end. Once in a while he wanted to just sit back and listen to a good idea.

The things that threatened Brandon were the intangibles – like disloyalty, or disrespect. Challenging him in front of others was another thing that Brandon couldn't tolerate. He knew that smart people will do that, but he wanted those smart people to also respect his superiority – they could be smart all they wanted, but they also had to defer to him. That's what he expected and he knew it was a tall order to expect to find smart people like that – but he would continue to look.

He was hoping and praying that he had found the perfect protégé in Jeff Kavanaugh. If he could just mold him now…

Brandon waited patiently for his entire team to file into the room. Two of them were seated already, scrolling through their iPhones. He ignored them. Instead he concentrated on his fingernails. He studied them one by one, ran his right index finger over the tips of the nails on his left hand, then switched and performed the same procedure on his right hand. That's when he found it – a rough edge on his pinky. Damn! He hated that! The stupid girl was here only yesterday, and he had been so busy he hadn't checked to make sure they were all perfect. He'd have to get her back. Brandon picked up his pen and scribbled a reminder to himself on a pad of paper. 'Manicure – right pinky.'

He looked up–all the king's men were here now. On his right hand sat Cliff Johnstone and Dillon McAffey. To his left were Ray Filberg and Josh Carney. All four looked at him expectantly, anticipating something brilliant. Well, Brandon wasn't sure he had anything brilliant to say today. He just wanted answers.

"Welcome. I'll get right to the point. It's been a couple of months now since the shootings, and I met with all of you shortly after that incident. I wanted to know what went wrong. Since then there has been nothing but silence. Did you think I was just kidding?" Brandon looked around the table, stopping to gaze into the eyes of each of his underlings. His pause was for effect, and he knew it was making them squirm. He couldn't see it, but he could sense it.

"Well? Don't all speak at once."

Dillon McAffey broke the silence. "It may be a general concern rather than a specific one, but since Slater was in my team, I can only address the issue as it applies to him."

Brandon glared at him. "Hello? Don't tell me what you're going to address – just go ahead and address it. Do you honestly need to announce what you're going to say before you say it?"

Dillon shifted uncomfortably in his seat. "Okay, well, in Mike Slater's case, he slit his wrist in the bathtub. It was a few days after he was fired, so he was a little bit late–but he still did it. And he didn't take anyone else with him, which was a good thing. Unlike the Prentice situation."

"You're overlooking the obvious. Why did it take him several days to do it? That's unacceptable."

"I don't know. And you're right, it is unacceptable."

Brandon slammed his fist down on the table. "What do you intend to do about it?"

"I've already begun examining our practices and the integrity of the suggestions. Testing has commenced with some volunteers, to see if certain suggestions take hold when they're supposed to. Our tactics may have to change – or it may simply be a matter of brain overload. Overpowering the suggestions. We may have underestimated the effect that stress might have on someone at the time we want a suggestion to be carried out. A different set of procedures may be needed – perhaps a stress barrier implemented to allow the paramount suggestion to be carried out despite what stress the subject may be feeling."

Brandon nodded. "Okay, now you're talking. It sounds like you're thinking – and at least doing something."

Dillon nodded back.

Brandon turned his attention to Josh Carney. "Your guy was a major fuck up. Prentice was your man, your responsibility. And a slaughter happened, right here in this building. And to his family at home. Brought us unnecessary attention. What the fuck do you have to say about that?"

Josh leaned forward and rested his elbows on the boardroom table. "Okay, Brandon, take it easy. We're dealing with an explosive and unpredictable science here. You may like to think that things will always run perfectly, but be real. Wires get crossed sometimes – people aren't machines."

Brandon laughed. "Aren't you forgetting our secret motto here? 'We make people think like machines' – that's what we do, you moron!"

"Yeah, well, sometimes machines break down. Haven't you ever had a flat tire?"

Brandon got up and started pacing. "I'm not liking your attitude here, Josh. You're treading on thin ice."

"What are you going to do – give me a suggestion?"

"You've already had the suggestion, Josh. You just don't remember it. All I have to do is trigger it, you little prick. So, you better show me some respect. Do you think your staff and clients are the only ones who get suggestions?"

Josh sat back in his chair, and wiped the back of his hand across his forehead. He stared at Brandon, mouth open, not quite believing what he had just heard.

"Yeah, that's right. I cover my bases – always." Brandon swept his hand in the air, gesturing to all four of his vice presidents collectively. "Sorry I had to break it to you like this, but this incident was so severe that I decided to let each of you know how much of your souls I own. You'll continue to get rich working for me, but if you fuck with me, I'll kill you. You should have each clued in by now that getting fired here isn't the same as getting fired somewhere else. And if you speak out of turn and I find out about it, I'll still kill you. You won't see it coming, trust me."

The four vice presidents sat as still as statues, dumbfounded. Brandon laughed. "Ha, you didn't know what you signed up for, did you? It's okay for you to dish it out to others, but God forbid the same thing could be dished out to you. Cowards! Hypocrites! You're all psychologists; you all know the power we hold. None of this should be a surprise to you."

Josh recovered some of his composure and quickly turned the subject back to what they had been talking about before. "I suggest that the four of us meet on this subject and discuss tactics, what went wrong, what we need to change. For some reason Jim Prentice went nuts – the command was skewed, transformed into something else within his brain. I don't know why that happened, but something went wrong.

"I'm hoping it was just an isolated incident, and it may have been. It may have just been due to the makeup of his brain, or he experienced a sudden surge of neuron electricity – maybe similar to why Mike Slater delayed his suicide for several days. Dillon mentioned that it might have been due to the stress of just having been fired – well, Prentice was fired that day too. That seems to be the common denominator here."

Brandon smiled. "Finally, I hear some serious thinking going on here. Good. Do that. Fix it, and report to me what you've done. This will not happen again. If it does…"

Cliff Johnstone spoke for the first time. "Are we done here?"

"Yes, we're done for now."

They all stood, but Ray Filberg had something on his mind. "Brandon, I have a question – a nagging question that I need an answer on."

Brandon frowned. "Go ahead."

"This Kavanaugh guy – he seems to be getting preferential treatment."

"What do you mean?"

"Well, for example, he's a Senior Account Executive but he reports directly to you. Why is that? All the other SAEs report to one of us vice presidents. Why would he come directly in to you?"

"Because he's my protégé. I've chosen him. I want to mold him my way. Jeff Kavanaugh is the future of the AI division. He's charismatic, brilliant, brave as hell, and he looks darn good too. He's our new public face."

Cliff jumped in. "I agree with Ray. It defies protocol and it defies our management structure here. Jeff should be reporting to one of us. This sends the wrong message – undermines us, and is causing a lot of confusion on the floor."

Brandon smiled. "Okay, I hear you, Cliff."

All four vice presidents seemed shocked at Brandon's sudden turnaround. Ray reached out to shake Brandon's hand. "Thanks for listening to us, Brandon. So, you'll fix it?"

Brandon ignored his hand. "Yeah, I'll fix it. Soon, I'm going to promote him to vice president. There! Fixed! Happy now?"

Brandon chuckled to himself, seeing the look of shock on their faces. He loved doing this sort of thing – shocking people. Losers. Be careful what you ask for. He waved his hand at them, dismissing them without a word.

All four turned and shuffled toward the door, silenced by Brandon's arrogant proclamation.

Then Brandon remembered something. "Ray, stick around for a minute, please?"

The other three left and closed the door behind them. Brandon gestured to Ray to resume his seat, the same seat he was in before. Some traditions were important, thought Brandon. Sameness was good sometimes, for both comfort and intimidation reasons.

"Since you raised a specific concern about Jeff Kavanaugh, I'll give this assignment to you. And keep what I'm asking you to do totally confidential. Understand?"

Ray nodded.

"I've noticed that Jeff seems to be spending a lot of time chatting with Gaia Templeton. You know, hanging around her desk, having coffee together, going to lunch. I want to know what's going on between those two. Are they dating? Are they fucking?"

Ray gulped and wrung his hands together. "Brandon, we don't have any rules against office romances per se. There's only an ethical problem if one of them happens to be the boss of the other. But that's not the case with these two."

"Yes, yes, I'm fully familiar with our policies. But when it starts to get blatant and obvious, it's distracting to the other staff. I've had some people mention it to me. And I want Jeff to get off on the right foot here – as I mentioned, he's my protégé."

"Why don't you just ask him yourself?"

Brandon sighed. "Because that would be undignified for someone in my position, don't you think? And I don't want you to do an outright enquiry – I just want you to sniff around a bit."

"You want me to spy on them."

"Call it what you want. Just find out what I need to know without showing your hand or my hand. Understand?"

Ray got up from his chair and headed for the door. He turned around as he put his hand on the doorknob and spoke in a whisper. "I'll do my best."

Brandon closed the door behind him and went into his main office area. He poured himself a scotch neat from the portable bar, then kicked off his shoes and stretched out on his Italian leather couch.

He pondered what he'd just asked Ray to do. Gaia was a mystery to him. She paid him no attention at all, other than as her boss. He wanted more than that, but was too proud to expose himself. He'd never had to approach women before; it was that simple.

Most of the other women in the office threw themselves at him, but not Gaia. He didn't understand it. And now here she was flirting with his new protégé. It pissed him off. Gaia was always the epitome of professionalism around him, never flirted with him, never dressed to attract his attention, never hinted at anything. Brandon wasn't used to this.

It made him want her even more.

CHAPTER 11

It was late September and the leaves on the trees were starting to turn color already. Early this year, Jeff thought. In fact, with every year there were noticeable changes now. The summers came early and left early, winters brought heavier snowfalls, and spring seemed to have just disappeared completely. Spring was now the forgotten season.

The climate changes had forced him to change his own routines. He now opened up his cottage at Moon Lake a month earlier, and closed it down in mid-October rather than November.

Jeff turned north off Highway 401 due east of Toronto, onto Highway 12, which took him through the quaint town of Whitby. He cruised along the main drag, a journey that only took about ten minutes. Then he was out in the country again, admiring the orange and red hues of the maple and oak trees going through their seasonal transformation.

He rolled down the windows and hung his arm out along the side rail. Jeff's hand instinctively hit the 'on' button to his CD player, and he cranked up the sound. Rhianna was singing "Most Beautiful Girl in the World" – he loved Rhianna, and he'd always loved that song. He loved it even more now since he'd started dating Gaia.

The volume of the stereo system was high, but not high enough to drown out the throaty sound of his 454 cubic inch big block engine that was ready and willing to hammer out 370 horsepower on demand. The pride and joy Jeff was driving was a vintage 1970 Chevrolet Corvette Stingray. This was his summer car – during the winter and when he had to haul stuff up to the cottage he drove his Jeep Cherokee. Not as much fun, but a necessary evil.

The Corvette was pure unadulterated fun – it was his dream car, and he loved the style of the model year that he owned. From the years 1968 to 1982, the famous sports car was patterned after the style of the Mako Shark. He loved the smooth lines and the 'looking for trouble' air about it. Jeff had always loved the Corvette ever since he'd been a wee lad, but he totally fell in love with the shark look of his version. The mean machine was a menacing black color and it was also a hardtop – which he felt looked much meaner than the ragtop.

The car got a lot of looks, particularly when Jeff got a little aggressive and let the powerful engine roar off from a dead stop. There wasn't much on the road that could beat his car. And it was indeed a 'babe magnet.' Every date that he had taken out in it had practically drooled – just to be sitting in the iconic sports car.

Every date except Gaia. All she'd said was, "Nice car, but kind of a tight squeeze, don't you think?"

Jeff had just laughed and made a checkmark in his mental notebook – just one more reason why he liked Gaia so much. She clearly wasn't impressed by "boys' toys" or pretension.

They had been dating now for a couple of months, longer than Jeff had dated anyone for quite some time. This alone told him it was getting serious. Gaia was lovely – a captivatingly beautiful girl; in fact she became more beautiful in his eyes the more he got to know her. At first he'd thought she was just pretty, but that word did not even begin to capture the magic that was Gaia. Her smile, her laugh, her love of life and zest for virtually everything – everything except his Corvette Stingray, of course. And she was a wonderful lover, very creative and adventuresome. Jeff had found that a bit intimidating at first, because he wasn't used to it. His love life before Gaia had been pretty normal, pretty traditional. But she had different ideas and he was gradually coming around, opening up a bit more. He still wasn't totally comfortable – but he had to admit it was intoxicating wondering what little things she would dream up next. Sex with Gaia was not only loving, but also fun.

They talked about work quite a bit when they were together, but Gaia still wasn't willing to open up too much about what she knew about the internal workings of the Artificial Intelligence division or its legendary leader, Brandon Horcroft. She seemed somewhat afraid, which really made Jeff curious. Her large salary had probably bought her silence by a man who believed that money could buy anything.

Brandon Horcroft. Jeff had a tough time feeling comfortable around the man. In his entire life so far, he had never met a narcissist in the league that Brandon was in. He had studied narcissists in university, had conducted studies with volunteers, had counseled patients on how to deal with their affliction. But never ever had he met someone who seemed to be as proud of the affliction as Brandon Horcroft.

And Gaia's shocking words to Jeff on their first dinner date: "People seem to die." Those words had left him cold and curious, yet he hadn't explored that statement further with her. He knew she'd had a lot to drink that night and had probably said more than she had wanted to say, so he didn't push it. But he intended to – soon.

Jeff turned off Highway 12, and headed in the direction of the town of Port Perry. A cute little town sitting on the shores of Lake Scugog populated by a large number of retirees who wanted to be on a lake but also within an hour's drive of the big city of Toronto. Perfect for affluent relaxers who wanted the lake life, but also feared being too far away from family, shopping, theatres and hospitals. His aunt was one of those people.

Jeff's Aunt Louise was only fifty-five years old, the younger sister of Jeff's deceased mother. She didn't live on the lake like a lot of other retirees. She had chosen to live on the outskirts of Port Perry, on an acreage – in fact ten acres of beautiful rolling land dotted with groves of spruce, chestnut and maple trees.

Louise had spent thirty years with the Toronto Police Service, retiring at the age of fifty. She had put in thirty years of service, which gave her a full pension. Her rank on retirement was Deputy Chief, and her specialty was homicide. Louise had been personally involved in the investigation of more than 1,000 murders during her career – and when she turned fifty she decided she'd had enough. Retirement beckoned. Then her husband died in an industrial accident in the first year of her retirement – buried alive in an earthmover when twenty tons of an unstable quarry wall came tumbling down.

Louise had been alone for the last four years. But…in reality, Louise was never ever really 'alone' in the pure definition of the word.

Jeff turned into her quarter mile long driveway. He loved this final part of the trip. It was so relaxing – the driveway was like a tunnel; majestic maple trees forming the walls of the tunnel. He drove down the gravel road, red and orange maple leaves drifting lazily onto the hood of his Corvette, twisting and turning in the gentle breeze. The scene suited his aunt.

Louise was waiting for him on the huge front porch of the three-storey Victorian house. The place was huge, and kind of ominous. Spooky, but charming at the same time. Gray stone façade, red cement tile roof, and a well that no longer worked but was maintained as if it did. Flower baskets were hanging from the eaves along the entire length of the covered porch. Adirondack chairs and rocking chairs were scattered along the expanse, adding to the relaxing charm of the estate.

Whenever Jeff came to visit, he just wanted to stay.

He parked his car and walked up the steps to the waiting pitcher of lemonade. She was sitting in one of the rocking chairs and jumped up to greet him when he reached the top of the stairs. She was as youthful and pretty as ever – a carbon copy of his mom, and Jeff got tears in his eyes every time he saw his aunt.

She hugged him without a word, and motioned him over to one of the chairs surrounding the table where the lemonade was beckoning. She poured each of them a glass and then sat down in a padded chair across from him.

"Jeff, you look wonderful."

"So do you, Louise. And so does the house. My God, how do you take care of this big place all by yourself?"

"Well, luckily I can afford maintenance men. And I have a new rider mower, so I cut half the land myself and farm out the rest. And my mower has cup holders and a CD player. So I can have my coffee while I cut the lawn – but to be truthful, more often than not those cup holders are holding cans of beer!"

Jeff laughed as he looked at her. Blonde hair, cut stylishly short, no make-up because she never needed it, tight smooth skin, and a figure that most thirty-somethings would die for. And a smile that was addicting. He loved making jokes with Louise just so he could see her smile. She reminded him so much of his mother, and it was comforting.

"I saw you on that TV show about a month ago, Jeff. I thought you handled yourself very well. And you looked so handsome!"

"Thanks. I'm still not used to this celebrity thing. I wouldn't have done that show if my company hadn't insisted on it. They wanted my presence to put a positive spin on what happened. Kind of an offset to the horror."

"It was indeed a horror. This is the first time I've seen you since that happened – we've talked on the phone a few times and you seemed to be okay, but I wasn't sure. I sensed some internal conflict when we talked. I picked up some vibes of affection and regret for one of the people who was killed."

"Yeah – that was Cathy. We'd dated."

"But you pulled back, didn't you? And that made it all the worse for you when she died, am I right?"

"You're always right, Louise."

"You're not here just to pay me a nephewy visit, are you? You want my help, don't you?"

Jeff nodded. "Mom never let you and I talk about this "thing" we both have, and that she herself had as well. We always respected her wishes on that. But it's about time I started trying to understand it."

"You'll never understand it, Jeff. It's far too weird, and far too unpredictable. But you may be able to learn to listen to it, perhaps control it, and if you're lucky, use it for some good."

Jeff leaned forward in his chair, and took a long sip of his lemonade. "Louise, I saw this thing coming. Everything was strange that morning – people on the street looked different, I saw the number '6' appear a couple of times. And six people were killed at the office that day. And, get this – I saw a bright yellow halo around Cathy's head when I got to work that morning, and then a couple of hours later I saw a grayish halo with pulsating red streaks in it around the killer's head."

Louise just nodded and leaned her chin on her fist. She wasn't going to butt in yet.

Jeff continued. "When I went to the tenth floor and succeeded in talking Prentice into giving up, his halo disappeared. And the girl he was holding hostage, Gaia, she had a yellow halo just like Cathy. But it disappeared as soon as Prentice's halo disappeared. It was damn spooky."

Louise smiled. "You're with Gaia now, aren't you?"

"I don't remember telling you that."

Louise shrugged her shoulders.

Jeff chuckled and continued. "See, this is why I need your help."

"What you saw were auras of death. Auras that were trying to foretell what was about to happen if someone or something did not intervene in time."

"I've never seen auras before. I've seen or felt other things, Louise, but never auras. Why that day?"

"Because...that was the most shocking thing that had ever happened to you, and your sensory perception picked up the energy before it happened. It brought out the sensory skill that you've suppressed for so many years. You've now opened up to it from this event, and I predict that you're now going to experience it again... and again...and again. But only when it's something imminent, sudden, violent. You won't for example, see an aura around my head telling you that I'm going to die in four years' time. That won't happen to you. It will always be something imminent... and violent."

"How do you know this?"

Louise just shrugged again.

"So, what do the colors mean?"

Louise sighed. "There are textbooks that talk about auras. I think they're just trash, designed to take advantage of naïve people. Auras will be different for everyone, depending on the circumstance. The textbooks say that red is the color of strength, passion. A darker red symbolizes quick temper, or someone who's nervous or impulsive. Yellow is said to mean optimism, wisdom. Black is supposed to be the color of protection – or indicative of someone who is hiding something. As far as I'm concerned, it's all just crap."

"Why do you say that?"

"Because, I think it differs with each psychic. And with the moment. Look at me – do you see an aura around my head right now?"

Jeff shook his head.

"And you won't. Because your skill doesn't include this everyday aura vision crap. And the auras you saw have their own color code. The gray with red streaks you saw around Prentice's head, to me, indicated an evil presence that was about to commit an atrocity. And the yellow you saw around Cathy and Gaia's heads didn't indicate goodness per se – it indicated that at that moment in time they were innocent and were about to die. They may not have had any goodness in their lives at all, although I'm sure they did. But at that moment in time they were innocent and were about to die. That's what you saw. And you will always have that same formula from now on – but it will have to be something imminent, sudden and violent. That's how I interpret what you went through, Jeff. Take it or leave it."

"Louise, do you see an aura around my head right now?"

"No, I never see auras. I just understand them."

Jeff drained his glass of lemonade and stood. He went around the table and gave Louise a hug. "You've given me a lot to think about. I have to get going, but I'll be out to see you again real soon. Thanks so much."

Louise hugged him back – then Jeff could feel her body suddenly shudder. She pulled her head back and looked straight into his eyes. Her voice was shaky. "Listen to me. Gaia is in danger–and so might you be; in fact, I'm feeling right this instant that it's more likely you than her. There's a man who's obsessed with her and has been for a long time. It's like a disease with this man. He can't let it go. And he won't show himself, not in an obvious way, because his ego won't allow that. He looks in mirrors, and when he doesn't like what the mirrors show him, he buys new ones."

Jeff knew that his face betrayed his shock. "What…what does this mean? What on earth are you telling me?"

Jeff noticed that Louise's eyes seemed glazed, out of focus. She spoke again – slowly and softly, almost in a whisper. "He's killed before, many times. And he killed Gaia's fiancé. Five years ago."

Jeff felt goosebumps racing up his back and down his arms. His knees suddenly felt wobbly and he gently shook his aunt's shoulders. "Louise, that can't be true. He died in a plane crash. It was an accident. Gaia told me he was a private pilot and his plane crashed into Lake Ontario shortly after takeoff."

Louise's eyeballs rolled upwards and her head began rocking back and forth. Jeff quickly wrapped his arms around her, afraid she was going to faint.

"I can't see this man…can't see his face. But he killed…Matt. Murdered him."

CHAPTER 12

The call came late in the afternoon as he was packing up his briefcase. Annoyed, he answered it even though his instinct told him not to. Not a psychic feeling but more just the feeling that he wanted to go home and didn't want to endure a long-winded phone conversation.

"Hello?"

"Hello, is this Jeff Kavanaugh?"

"Yes, it is. How can I help you?"

"Jeff, my name is Victor Stone. I'm an attorney; I represent Jim Prentice."

Jeff felt an instant knot in his stomach. And images that flashed in front of his eyes; images he'd been trying to forget. Just the mention of the name 'Jim Prentice' brought them all back. Bodies – bleeding bodies, lifeless eyes, blue lips, a once pretty receptionist staring aimlessly at the ceiling.

"Hello? Jeff, are you still there?"

"Y-yes. You just caught me by surprise for a moment."

"Understandable, I guess. Sorry about that. I'll be brief. Can we meet for a coffee? There's something important I need to ask you."

Jeff paused to catch his breath. "Am I being subpoenaed?"

"No, nothing like that at all. But I'd rather explain in person, if that's alright with you."

"Sure. We can do that."

"How about right now? I can meet you in the Starbucks at the corner of Queen and Yonge in about fifteen minutes."

"Okay. I'm just on my way out the door anyway, so that works for me."

"Good. Thanks. And…I know what you look like, from the newspapers and television."

"Right…okay, see you in fifteen."

Jeff hung up the phone and looked out his window at busy Bay Street, cars and pedestrians all rushing to go home. Which was exactly what he should be doing. He admonished himself for agreeing to this coffee meeting, or at least for not asking first what this was all about. He hadn't been following anything to do with the 'incident' since it happened. He'd avoided reading about it, and always turned off the TV whenever coverage began on the News. He didn't know where the trial status stood, or the fate of Jim Prentice – nothing. Which was exactly the way he wanted it.

When he and Gaia went out on dates, they never discussed it between them. They had shared the same horror and neither of them wanted to revisit it. Oh, once in a while when she was hugging him she'd thank him again for his bravery in saving her, but that was pretty much the extent of it. Nothing deeper than that.

And now Prentice's lawyer wanted to meet with him, and it wasn't a subpoena. Jeff figured that eventually he would have had no choice but to face this thing again. There would be a trial, and he would be the prime witness. He knew he'd be called, and had somewhat psyched himself up for that. But until then he didn't want to think about it.

Jeff slipped his jacket on, picked up his briefcase and headed out the door. He passed Gaia's desk along the way and gave her a quick smile. She returned the smile and mouthed the words, "See you tonight." Jeff nodded and headed for the elevators.

*****

"You can't be serious."

Victor Stone grimaced. "Yes, I am. And it's totally up to you. I understand if you don't want to do it."

They were sitting at a corner table in Starbucks. Victor had recognized Jeff the instant he came through the door, and motioned him over to the table. Jeff observed that he was one elegantly dressed lawyer, complete with rings and bracelets. His voice was kind of high-pitched and he seemed a little bit effeminate. But he wore a pleasant smile, and Jeff felt immediately comfortable with him.

He just wasn't comfortable with what he was asking.

"I think I was in shock when you told me what you wanted me to do. I blanked out. So, tell me again, why wasn't there a trial?"

"Well, there was kind of a trial – we call them "mini-trials." It was more like a hearing. At the arraignment, Prentice pled 'guilty' – against my advice. But I made a motion, which both the prosecutor and judge acceded to, to have Prentice examined by a psychiatrist to determine if he was fit to stand trial. So, the whole thing was put on hold until that was done. In fact, two psychiatrists examined him – one chosen by the prosecution and one by me as the defense."

"So, the judge rejected the plea?"

"Yes, he wouldn't accept the 'guilty' plea until the mental state was determined."

Jeff paused to take a sip from his extra bold Starbucks special blend. "This was all resolved pretty quickly, then."

"Yes, it moved surprisingly fast. Both psychiatrists agreed independently that

Prentice was not fit for trial, and presented those opinions to the judge at the next hearing. Right after that, the judge declared Prentice 'UST,' which stands for 'Unfit to Stand Trial.' The prosecution didn't object."

"So, does this mean he gets out soon?"

"No, not at all. The judge has certain latitude in 'UST' cases. He has no authority to release him free to society, not at all. He only has two choices: conditional discharge; or detention in a mental health facility. The judge chose to detain him. Prentice is residing at the 'Lakeside Psychiatric Hospital,' just outside of Belleville."

"For how long?"

"This is where it gets a bit complicated. It could be the rest of his life, or he could be out in two years. The Canadian Criminal Code requires that 'UST' detainees remain there until they are deemed fit to stand trial. Or if the charges are withdrawn – those charges still remain against him, they don't go away. They're really just kind of suspended. So, if he's never deemed fit to stand trial, he stays there forever. But, and this is a big 'but,' – in 'UST' cases, his case must go to a Review Board every two years, at which time the prosecution has to prove each time that the evidence is still prima facie, in other words legitimate and beyond dispute. If they can't prove that, he gets released. If they can prove that and he's still not fit to stand trial, he goes back in for another two years. Then the Review Board process starts again."

Jeff shook his head. "Ridiculous. He slaughtered people. String him up."

Victor Stone lowered his head. "I have to confess, Jeff, that sometimes I have to admit to feeling exactly the same way. But I can never admit that publicly of course."

Jeff raised his cup in a toast. "We can agree in private, then."

Victor clicked his cup against Jeff's, and took a long satisfying sip. "So, what's your reaction to what I've asked you to do?"

Jeff tilted his chair back on its two back legs and rested his head against the wall. "Why on earth does he want to see me?"

Victor scratched the back of his head. "I'm not quite sure. I can tell you this much – Prentice is on suicide watch. He's horrified at what he's done. I mean, killing six people at the office was bad enough, but his family too? The man's a mess. He just wants to die. He can't grasp why he did it, or how he could have done it. Sure, he was upset about being fired, and he remembers that – but beyond that stress point, he doesn't recall too much else. Oh, sure, he has images in his head – he knows he did it. And he remembers you stopping him. But he can't recall what was going through his head when he was committing those atrocities. He said to me that it was almost like he was on 'automatic pilot.'"

"So am I supposed to help with his recovery? Is that what he wants from me?"

"I doubt it – remember, if he's deemed recovered then he no longer fits within the definition of 'UST.' So he'd just stand trial, and then he would willingly plead guilty again. So, this man isn't going anywhere, that's for certain. His life is doomed now, no matter what. He either dies in this hospital for the insane, or he dies in prison. The charges will never drop – they're indisputable. So, for him, the 'UST' two-year rule won't mean very much. And he's allowed to have visitors just as if he was in prison, already convicted of a crime. He can even see people associated with the case, such as you, because for all intents and purposes, his goose is cooked. "

Jeff lowered his chair back down to the floor. "I still don't understand what he wants from me. Just the mere thought of the man and the chaos he caused makes me feel sick to my stomach. I've been trying to forget about all this – and it just keeps pulling me back in again. If it's not TV hosts who want to interview me, it's shock horror fans who want my autograph. It all makes me sick."

"I understand completely. I can't even begin to imagine acting the hero like you did, but I can imagine that the aftermath must be difficult as hell."

Jeff nodded. "It is. I just want to get on with my simple life again – the way it was before all this happened."

"Look, Jeff – maybe all he wants is closure. Maybe he just wants to thank you for stopping him. You may despise him, and I have to admit I did too before the court appointed me to him, but I have to tell you that I feel differently now. If you can block out the images of horror and concentrate on just the man himself, he's a decent sort who is terribly remorseful. He had nothing to gain, and he just wants to die for what he did. It's hard to hate someone like that. And a strange thing for me to say, knowing that he became a monster for a few hours that fateful day."

Jeff stood up and held out his hand. Victor shook it vigorously. "Thanks so much for meeting with me. I promised my client I'd ask you, and I did. So, whatever your answer is, I've done my job."

Jeff turned and started heading for the door. Then he turned back to Victor. "I'm going to think about this, and I'll give you a call. I promise I'll give it serious thought."

Victor smiled. "That's all I can ask. Thank you."

Jeff left the café and walked toward the streetcar stop, casually swinging his patent leather briefcase, trying hard to look and feel nonchalant. But his insides were churning and he was doing his best to resist the urge to vomit. The thought of once again seeing the man who had pointed the barrels of two pistols at his forehead and who had brutally stolen the lives of everyday people, including his own wife and children, left Jeff reeling.

He knew he could simply say 'no.' But along with the stomach cramps, Jeff was getting another feeling – this one was in his head. It was a vague kind of feeling, almost like a voice. And it was telling him to see the man.

Jeff had promised himself that he would listen to these signals the next time they came back. And they were back.

CHAPTER 13

Brandon Horcroft leaned his elbows on the desktop, clasped his hands together, and rested his chin on the resultant double fist. Then he contorted his face into the most threatening look he had in his arsenal. He knew that if he could look in the mirror right now, even he would be scared.

Josh Carney was sitting across from Brandon, shifting uncomfortably in the silence. Brandon just stared at him…and Josh stared back.

"Well, I'm waiting."

"Waiting for what?"

"A reaction from you, some sign of initiative, some semblance of a sense of urgency."

Josh drained his water, and then cleared his throat. "I told you already. The four of us met and have devised some new hypnotherapy techniques. They're in the testing stage right now. We have a few subjects…"

"So?"

Josh leaned back in his chair and crossed his legs, trying desperately to appear confident and nonchalant. "Listen, Brandon. We are your vice presidents. We take responsibility. And we are very good at what we do, as you well know. The techniques we use are powerful, and we're only going to make them stronger with this new stress barrier tactic that we're testing out. It will work…I guarantee it."

Brandon opened his desk drawer and took out two small rubber balls. He held them out in front of him and began squeezing them. A good stress reliever he always found, and it had the double advantage of displaying his strong hands – the incessant squeezing of the balls in front of his adversaries was symbolic of crushing the life out of their scrotums. He noticed that when he did this, his guests always cringed.

Josh looked down at his lap.

"You can keep me posted then, on how that testing goes. But I'm waiting for something else. You haven't shown any initiative whatsoever to an obvious danger. You haven't even acknowledged it yet, let alone reacted to it. I've been testing you."

Josh glanced up at Brandon and frowned, puzzled. "What are you talking about? I anticipate everything in advance. I always take the initiative, you know that, Brandon. That's not a fair statement to make to me."

Brandon rose from his chair and walked around to the other side of the desk, towering over his puzzled executive. He looked down at him and sneered. "Not fair? Poor baby – life just isn't fair for little Joshy. You make several million dollars a year in bonuses alone, and you don't think I'm being fair to you? You sniveling little loser."

Josh jumped to his feet and Brandon noticed that his fists were clenched at his side. "Don't talk to me in that manner! I give everything I have to this job, and I am well worth what you pay me. Christ, the things I've done for you would make my mother roll over in her grave!"

"Well, she's going to have to roll over again, my dear friend. Because there's a job that you've left undone."

"What job?"

Brandon smiled a smile that wasn't really a smile. "You're a little bit slow on the uptake, aren't you? Or…perhaps you just don't want to face the unpleasant truth? Or…maybe you've just turned into a coward?"

"What the fuck are you talking about, Brandon?"

"Jim Prentice was your man, your responsibility. You fired him, but he wasn't really terminated in the true sense of the word, was he? He's still alive. And he's out of our control now."

*****

Jeff watched as the killer was led through the glass doors by two burly security guards. He wondered if they doubled as nurses, trained at giving injections to keep the inmates subdued. Maybe he had the wrong impression of psychiatric hospitals, but he'd heard enough horror stories and had visited enough patients over the years to have an image in his mind. Wrong to generalize of course – some facilities were better and more humane than others. And Lakeside Psychiatric Hospital was apparently one of the best in the province.

During the entire journey to Belleville Jeff had the urge to turn back. Every time he stopped for gas to fill up his fuel-guzzling Corvette, he fought to resist the urge to take Highway 401 west instead of east. But there was a voice inside his head that told him to keep going – that he had to keep going.

Jim Prentice had killed nine people that day including his own family – Jeff found it impossible to believe that he was actually going to pay him a visit. But part of him was also curious – the psychologist part. He knew that in order to glean anything at all from this day he had to think clinically, be devoid of emotion, a fact-seeking mission. And he was trained to do that. He had to call on that training now, more than he would probably ever have to again in his life. It was too horrific otherwise – too surreal to justify sitting and chatting with a monster.

His four-hour drive to Belleville was filled with thoughts. The time just flew by. And the one other item foremost on his mind was what his Aunt Louise had said to him just before he left her. That a man obsessed with Gaia had actually killed her fiancé, Matt, five years ago. Jeff had been thinking hard about that, and he hadn't confided in Gaia yet. He figured it would just be too upsetting for her and…thinking selfishly…he didn't want to dredge up an emotional watershed over someone who was long gone, and someone whom she had obviously cared deeply for. He knew that was the wrong reason not to tell her, but Jeff's feelings for Gaia had become quite strong and he couldn't help himself feeling protective of that new part of his life.

He would tell her in time, he knew that – but he also knew that if he did, he'd have to disclose the fact that his aunt was psychic and that he was also psychic. He really didn't want too many people to know that aspect of him. One of Jeff's deepest fears was that people would treat him differently if they knew, be wary around him, be weird around him. That would be his worst nightmare, particularly if it changed how Gaia felt about him.

But…he had to tell her. He had to be brave enough to expose himself. Louise was clearly overcome with her vision, afraid for him. And indeed, if someone were obsessed about Gaia, enough to have killed her fiancé, then it would be easy to believe that Jeff could be in danger now – and possibly even Gaia. He had a responsibility, similar to how he felt after the massacre. If only he had known enough about the psychic signs he had been getting, and if he'd acted on those beforehand perhaps none of the six in the office would have been killed. He was in the exact same position again. His aunt who was renowned for her accuracy – had given him fair warning. If he chose to ignore that warning, he would be doing so at his peril, and worse, possibly at Gaia's peril.

Gaia had been clear on the circumstances of Matt's death. He had been a private pilot and kept his plane hangared at the Toronto Island airport. On that fateful day five years ago, Matt was flying off to his mother's cottage in the Muskoka region north of Toronto. Right after takeoff he began having problems. His last message to the tower was a 'mayday' and then the little Cessna did a nosedive into Lake Ontario. It smashed into pieces on impact. Matt's body was recovered from the cold depths of the lake – the coroner said he'd died instantly. Sometimes Jeff believed that coroners said those things just to be merciful to the families. Which really wasn't a bad thing at all.

It was declared an accident. There wasn't enough airplane left to do a proper investigation, but the reports concluded that there was some evidence of fuel starvation.

Now that Jeff was privy to his aunt's vision, his mind was going in circles. He knew there were easy methods for a saboteur to achieve fuel starvation. And he knew that Gaia was an enticing enough woman for an unbalanced man to become obsessed over – even dangerously obsessed. She knew a lot of men, and she worked with a lot of men. Was one of them a wing nut?

Now, sitting at a table in the Visitors' Centre at the Lakeside Psychiatric Hospital, Jeff watched a bonafide wing nut coming his way. And he marveled at how normal Prentice looked. He wasn't quite sure what he'd expected, but he had the image in his mind of a man in an orange jumpsuit restrained by a straitjacket.

Au contraire: Jim Prentice was dressed in designer blue jeans, a bright yellow golf shirt, with Sketcher loafers on his feet. His hair was neatly combed, and he was now sporting a beard. He wasn't in handcuffs and his legs weren't in chains. The only apparent restraints were the giants on either side of him, who looked like they could pummel him through a drain in the floor without much effort.

Victor Stone had said that his client was a mess. To Jeff's eyes, he looked like he'd just finished playing eighteen holes. But…Jeff also knew as a psychologist that looks could be very deceiving. Dressing smartly and looking like you didn't belong in a place like this was what the smart ones did. The ones who could still think reasonably clearly. The ones who still had a sense of pride, who possessed some remembrance of who they used to be.

And, hell, trying to make themselves feel good by looking good was just their way of getting through the day. And days in this place must be very dreary indeed.

So, while Jeff was shocked at how good Jim looked, he didn't begrudge him that. Someone without Jeff's education and training would probably feel major resentment though.

The security guards led Jim over to the table where Jeff was sitting and eased him gently into a chair. Which wasn't necessary at all – Jim was not staggering, did not seem to be in a daze, and showed no signs of sedation. He looked…great. He didn't need their help.

But Jeff also knew that this kind of simple gesture of guiding the inmates around was necessary for dominance, for demonstrating control. The inmates, or patients, needed to know the pecking order and the staff was trained in the subtle ways of teaching them that.

One of the guards spoke. "Doctor Kavanaugh, do you wish us to stay here with you?"

Jeff shook his head. "No, that won't be necessary at all. Just remain within shouting distance."

The two guards nodded and walked over to the coffee machine on the other side of the room.

Jim extended his hand out across the table. "Hello, Jeff. Thanks for coming."

Jeff kept his hands on the table. "Forgive me for not shaking your hand, Jim. I just can't."

Prentice nodded and pulled his hand back. "I understand."

Jeff studied his face. His eyes seemed clear, not bloodshot as he might have expected. His face suited the beard – made him look professorial. And his hair was longer than the last time Jeff had seen him. The man looked healthy, calm, respectable.

He didn't look like someone who had slaughtered nine people four months ago. Jeff's quick brain immediately diagnosed Jim as someone who had become disassociated from the mayhem he had caused. A protective barrier had gone up in the man's brain.

"Why am I here, Jim?"

Jim winced and started nervously rubbing his hands together. "First of all, I wanted to thank you for stopping me. I'm not going to bore you with platitudes about how I didn't know what I was doing and all that. We're both psychologists – we understand how these things work and how they can happen. So, I won't insult your intelligence."

Jeff nodded…and waited.

"I've taken lives and I've ruined numerous families, including my own." Jim gulped. "I'm not looking for understanding or forgiveness. I can't be understood for something even I can't understand. Nor can I expect forgiveness for something that I can't be sorry for. Let me clarify – 'being sorry' requires an awareness of having done something wrong. I don't have that awareness – while I have images of what happened and I know from what I've been told that I was the one who did those horrible things, I have no awareness of having done them or why."

Jeff nodded. "I understand what you're saying, but you're saying exactly what you just promised you wouldn't say. You're being clinical which is what your brain has been trained to do. That's why I agreed to come here today – not out of sympathy for you, or a desire to help you get closure. I came here with a clinical mind too – and a scientific sense of curiosity."

Prentice smiled slightly. "I think, then, that we're on the same page."

"Yes, I think we are. But…answer me this. Do you feel anything at all about killing your family, let alone the six people at the office? You seem so…unaffected."

Jim wiped the back of his hand across his suddenly moist forehead. "I try not to think about it. I try not to remember their faces, or the good times. I'm good at blocking things out and I guess that's what I'm doing. And that's all I'm going to say about it, Jeff."

Jeff fiddled with his empty coffee cup while choosing his next words carefully. He was still curious and didn't want Jim's disassociation to cause him to clam up completely. "Fair enough. I understand what's going on in your head – I do. Tell me this, then. What were you feeling that morning? What were the sensations you felt before the...entire thing...unfolded?"

He looked down at his hands, which were clenched tightly together. "That's the second reason I wanted you to come here to see me. I wanted to unburden myself to the one who stopped me. I've puzzled over this for the last few months, and I've had lots of time to think back over all the things I did before this 'thing' happened. And trust me, I just want to die. I don't care about redemption. I may look like I have it all together, but I don't. What I do have is resignation. And if I get the opportunity, Jeff, I'll kill myself. If you handed me a knife right now, I'd plunge it into my heart. There's no point to my life anymore."

Jeff cracked his knuckles. "Jim, if I did have a knife with me, I'd gladly give it to you."

"Well, that's honest. That's the one thing I remember about you, in the few conversations we had back at the office. You were always so honest. I admired that about you, as did everyone else."

"I'm up on your old floor now. I joined the AI division after what happened."

"Jeff, we did massive amounts of hypnotherapy on that floor. Everyone did. In fact, most of the sessions for the highest level clients were performed by Horcroft himself."

"Well, hypnotherapy can be very beneficial in personal coaching. There's nothing too unusual about that."

"Yes, but some that I performed were for pretty unethical reasons, unethical gains. And I know it was the same for everyone else as well. It was very profitable. But the sessions that took place in Horcroft's office – I don't know..."

Jeff leaned forward across the table. "What are you saying?"

Suddenly Prentice developed a twitch in his left eye. Then his head began to bob up and down, resembling a Parkinson's disorder. "Jim, what's wrong? Do you want a doctor?"

Jim managed to shake his head amidst the bobbing. "No, this happens... sometimes. When I remember...mainly."

"Remember what?"

"Anything, really. I get flashbacks, recall...I'm aware of aspects of my job, then

I draw a blank. Jeff, I think I've been hypnotized."

Jeff leaned back in his chair and sighed. "C'mon, Jim. You're reaching."

Jim matched Jeff's move and leaned back in his chair too. The twitching and bobbing had stopped now just as suddenly as it had started.

"You asked me about any sensations I had the morning of the...thing."

"Yes."

"Well, you know of course that I'd been fired several days before. So, there was the trauma of that that certainly affected my thinking, clouded my judgment in the days following. I wasn't thinking straight and I couldn't for the life of me remember any reason I was given as to why I'd been fired. The vice president I reported to, Josh Carney, was the one who gave me the word – but then before I was escorted out of the building I was taken into Horcroft's office. I remember that much, but I don't remember what we talked about. Nothing. A complete blank. But I thought that was strange – being fired by my direct boss, then being taken into the big guy for another talk? What was that all about?"

"Jim, all of this weird stuff may be on your mind, but it doesn't answer my question about sensations. Get back on track."

Jim leaned forward and whispered. "I remember that a phrase was running around in my head, tormenting me...over and over. I don't know why it was there, but it seemed to be powerful as hell."

Jeff grimaced. "You're not going to use the old 'I heard voices' on me, are you?"

Jim continued to whisper. "No, it wasn't a voice. It was like it was something that was a part of me, integral to me. And I can't remember now exactly what it was."

"Any part of it you remember?"

Prentice nodded. "It was something like, 'Go forth.'"

CHAPTER 14

Ray Filberg poured himself another nervous glass of brandy and glanced at his watch. It was 10:00 p.m. and his man should be there right about now. That was assuming the man's head was on straight and his thoughts weren't being jumbled around like they had been lately.

Ray was starting to wonder about all this hypnosis stuff – sure he was a skilled hypnotherapist, hell they all were – but there was so much that could go wrong, so much that they didn't really understand. The human brain inherently possessed the vulnerabilities that allowed it to be manipulated, driven, mind-washed – but it also had the inherent ability to resist at a moment's notice and remember when it shouldn't remember. Remember what it shouldn't remember.

He thought back to that brief meeting with Brandon Horcroft, when he'd asked Ray to spy on Jeff and Gaia. Ray had been shocked at the time, but now in hindsight he wondered why he was shocked at all. The man was a lunatic. Ray shook his head in dismay. *I work for a lunatic. What does that make me?*

Ray had been part of the AI division almost right from the outset. Fourteen stressful years. He knew he should have gotten out when it started getting weird, but he sold his soul. At first he found it stimulating to his psychologist's mind, the extent to which they could push the envelope – and be allowed to do it freely. What scientist wouldn't want the ability to have unhindered freedom to experiment? That's the way he'd rationalized it back then. The human beings he'd manipulated, gradually became less human to him and more just subjects. Objects. Tools. Tools of the trade, no different than computers, cell phones. They were props almost, but very interactive props.

Ray rubbed his weary forehead – a headache was coming on.

He wondered how he had allowed himself to get in this deep. He was a smart man – but the intoxication of unfiltered power and unbelievable levels of income had tainted his thinking. He knew that, and he should have known better. Should have seen it coming. Now he was in so deep he didn't see a way out.

Well, that wasn't quite right. There were ways out, but not any of the choices were good ones. He could go to the police and blow the whistle – but he was too cowardly to incriminate himself.

He could just put a gun to his head, but he was too cowardly to do that too.

He could quit, but that would still be just the equivalent of putting a gun to his head. Brandon owned each and every one of them now, owned their brains, owned their souls. The suggestions, or commands, had already been planted long ago during a session that none of the executives could remember, or would ever remember. Brandon always covered his bases – he was a genius no doubt, but as clear as day he was also a sociopath. And probably even a psychopath, but a rare one, one that most people would never see coming – adorned as he was in pinstripes.

And yet there was one more way out – one that crept into Ray's head once in a while in an especially weak or frantic moment. Brandon could die. He knew in his heart that was the best solution, but once again he was too cowardly to pursue the idea. It wasn't the murder that would be the worst thing for him to grapple with – he'd already engineered several murders so he was insulated now to the guilt. It was just an abstract act for him now. He'd never actually pulled the trigger himself, but had manipulated the events with mind-bending. That made him no less guilty, he knew, but it did allow some detachment.

But if he was going to kill Brandon, he would need help. The genius of the man terrified him, made him the Teflon man in Ray's mind. Brandon's powerful evil charisma made it seem as if he was untouchable, that any attempt to take him out would fail. And if Ray failed he would be a dead man. It was the same feeling that kept normal people from committing crimes – the fear of being caught. He knew that the average human beings wouldn't hesitate to just take what they wanted, or cause harm to those they hated if they thought they could get away with it. What kept them at bay was that fear of capture. Fear of spending a good part of their lives in prison, fear of having people they loved become ashamed of them.

And if Ray failed, he would be paranoid that Brandon would somehow find out that it was him – and Ray would never see the hit coming. He knew that the last thing he would remember before he met his untimely demise would be getting called into Brandon's office for a meeting. That would be it. Brandon would say a pre-planted phrase, and Ray's brain would then go into command action. At that point he would be a walking talking dead man. He'd kill himself within hours or days, and be totally unaware of what he was doing or why.

How did Ray know this? Because this was the way it always happened.

So, he'd need help. He would need his fellow VPs with him on the caper. He thought he could trust them, and sensed that they felt the same sense of despair and hopelessness that he felt. But he wasn't sure. And he had to be sure, otherwise the risk would be too great. What if one of his trusted colleagues betrayed him to buy extra favor with Brandon? And what if each of them were already programmed by Brandon to snitch on anybody who planned anything nefarious against him? It was possible – a thought that Ray found terrifying and isolating. He knew he needed help with this, but was terrified to bring anyone into his confidence. Brandon was genius enough to have covered every possible base.

The lack of options left Ray feeling helpless – and beholden. It was a terrible feeling.

He looked at his watch again: 10:30 now. His man was busy doing what Ray had programmed him to do. After he was finished, the night would be a blank to him. He wouldn't remember what he'd done, why he had done it, and who had commanded him to do it. If all went well. If the suggestion had been buried deep enough to avoid awareness or discovery. Ray wasn't so sure about the science anymore. Mike Slater had taken too long to slit his wrist. Sure, he'd finally done it, but not as soon as he was programmed to do it. He was supposed to have killed himself the very day he'd been fired. Why had it taken several days for the command to move from the subconscious to his conscious brain? Ray knew that if one aspect of the programming failed, then it meant that all aspects had the potential of failing.

And why had Jim Prentice gone nuts? Why had he killed his family and all of those people at the office? He was supposed to just kill himself, in a manner similar to what Mike Slater had done. He knew that Josh Carney was on the carpet with Brandon over that one – Prentice was still alive, and that was unacceptable and somehow Brandon would expect Carney to rectify that. Difficult now with Prentice being locked away in a mental institution.

And his colleague, Dillon McAffey, was on the carpet over the Slater incident – having to account for why it had taken him several days to kill himself. Dillon was worried about it, Ray knew, but at least his guy had finally died. Not so with Carney's man.

But together, the four vice presidents – Ray, Josh, Dillon and Cliff Johnston had pledged to Brandon that they would fix it going forward. Future commands would have a stress barrier built in coincident with the command being planted. Tests so far had proven successful. Ray felt good about that. They couldn't take the chance on having any more messy incidents. Ray wondered how Carney was going to be able to eliminate Prentice though, without it getting messy. Oh, well, he was glad it wasn't his problem. He had enough of his own to worry about. All he cared was that Carney got the job done without drawing attention to the firm. They couldn't afford more attention.

Right now Ray's problem was the Jeff Kavanaugh/Gaia Templeton dalliance.

He glanced at his watch again – 11:00 now. He should have heard back from his man by now. Ray could feel the back of his shirt getting moist with sweat.

While Brandon had clearly assigned the sordid spying task to Ray, there was no way that Ray intended to do the dirty work himself. In fact, he and his colleagues always kept their hands clean. With the skills and power they possessed, they never had to do anything themselves. It was like playing a video game – push the right buttons and stuff just got done. The only side effect was a red and sore thumb with a video game. The only side effect with the mind games was a headache.

And Ray was getting one right now. His man should have phoned him by now with a status report.

*****

Jeff leaned over and kissed her neck as she reached for the remote. He let his tongue slide out and draw an invisible circle on her skin. A soft moan escaped through her half-open lips, and Jeff's tongue sensed a shiver cascading down her neck into her back.

"Did that feel good enough for you to relinquish control of that remote back to me?"

Gaia turned her head and flashed him a sly grin. "You'll have to do a lot better than that, young man. A kiss and a lick just doesn't cut it. And, remember, this is my house. You can't have control of the remote at both your house and mine, you know. It just doesn't work that way."

"But I'm a man. It's kind of written and expected that man controls the remote, and woman controls the kitchen – and the laundry room and all that other domestic stuff."

Jeff ducked as a pillow came flying in his direction. He grabbed one of his own and smacked Gaia gently across the head. She fought back gallantly, sliding her fingers under his shirt and commencing a rapid tickle action in all of the spots where she knew Jeff was vulnerable.

He surrendered, and she responded to his retreat by kissing him full on the lips. Then she sighed. And whispered, "What are you going to do?"

"About what?"

Gaia frowned. "About what you told me about your visit with that…monster."

Jeff grimaced and eased Gaia off his chest and into a sitting position on his lap. "Oh, that. I really don't know what I can do or should do. From his description to me of how he felt, and that phrase that was swirling around in his head, it sounds like he was in some kind of trance – could have been a psychotic episode, and it's possible that he was a closet psychopath already and all it took was getting fired to set him off on his rampage."

Gaia rubbed Jeff's forehead. "Darling, you don't sound convinced."

"No, I guess I'm not."

"What's troubling you?"

Jeff reached his hand up and brushed some hair from Gaia's fringe away from her left eye. "Well, to be honest, it sounded to me like he was under hypnosis at the time it happened."

Gaia frowned. "How could that have happened? He was home when he started his rampage."

"It's not as hard as you think. Hypnosis can have a delayed reaction based on a pre-planted suggestion. It could have been planted in his head days, weeks, months, or years beforehand. It can be done with a simple phrase that if heard again would trigger whatever suggestion was made to him at the time the phrase was first planted."

Gaia shivered. "God, that's scary."

"Yes, it is. And with that part of the phrase he remembered – "Go Forth" – that would be consistent with a hypnotic suggestion phrase. As a hypnotist, you would generally choose a phrase consisting of words a person wouldn't normally hear in the normal course of a day. You wouldn't want your subject acting on the latent command prematurely. I mean, who would say, "Go forth," in normal everyday conversation? So, it's obscure enough to give me the eerie feeling that he might have been hypnotized."

Gaia reached her arms around Jeff's neck and gave him a hug. It felt nice – comforting and warm. As he gazed over her shoulder, he allowed his eyes to wander around the cozy living room of Gaia's bungalow. It was a cute house, located in the Leaside area of Toronto's southeast quadrant. A neighborhood of wartime homes that had undergone a resurgence several decades ago. It was now considered prime inner city, with home prices out of the reach of average income earners. It was a mature area with character and charm, and it suited Gaia's personality, Jeff thought.

Gaia leaned back and whispered in his ear. "If we want to do it here on the couch, I'll need to close the blinds."

Jeff was facing away from the living room window, so he couldn't see the blinds she was referring to. But at the mention of the word "blinds," his vision suddenly became blurry – then it cleared as instantly as it had blurred. A shudder went through his body, and he grabbed Gaia under the arms and thrust her onto the floor in one smooth motion.

She looked up at him in shock and started to protest. Jeff yelled, "Stay down!"

He rolled off the couch and swiveled in the direction of the living room window.

In three giant steps he covered the distance, and then leaped over the recliner that was stretched in front of the window. He yanked on one of the blind vanes, pulling it up so he could see outside.

It was dark, but he'd yanked on exactly the right vane. Staring back at him in wide-eyed shock were two glowing orbs.

CHAPTER 15

Jeff stared right back. He couldn't make out the face of the intruder, only the whites of the eyes shimmering from the light in the living room. Suddenly the orbs moved out of his view, and Jeff could now make out a dark silhouette darting away from the window and across the front lawn.

He spun around and jumped back over the reclining sofa. Gaia was still down on the floor, head slightly raised, tears running down her cheeks. "Jeff, you're scaring me! What is it?"

Jeff went to her and helped her up off the floor. He put his face within inches of hers. "There was someone at the window. I'm going after him. Listen to me – lock the front door after me, and then go lock yourself in the bathroom. Don't come out until you hear me call to you from outside the window. And take your cell phone with you – call the police."

Jeff then turned and ran, yanked open the front door and flew across the porch and onto the dewy lawn. He lost his footing and fell backwards onto his ass. Cursing, he struggled back to his feet and set off running in the direction he saw the figure going.

Jeff was fast, and there weren't many people who could keep up with him when his feet were moving with deliberation. His eyes began focusing in the dark, and since he didn't hear a car engine start, he quickly deduced that the guy had headed across the street and into one of the backyards. Jeff ran in the direction of the house directly opposite because that was the logical choice.

Jeff darted down a driveway, and easily scaled the fence into the neighbor's backyard. He ran to the back of the yard, and scanned from side to side. Then he stopped and listened. A dog was barking and snarling in the backyard behind, and he could hear a man's restrained voice whispering and protesting.

Jeff backed up a few steps and took a good hard run at the high wooden fence, managing to just get his hands onto the top rail. He hoisted himself up and over, landing cleanly on his feet.

He was on the move again now and could feel his heart pounding hard in his chest. He rounded the back of a garage and reached the garden area close to the house. Then he stopped dead in his tracks. A man had his back up against the wall of the house, hands held out in front, trying desperately to keep a menacing German shepherd at bay.

The dog was in a crouch, front legs low to the ground and his head held upward, snarling and growling at the intruder. Jeff could see that the man was about six feet tall, dark hair and wearing a long black trench coat. And clearly scared out of his mind. He could hear him whispering, "It's okay, boy, it's okay." His voice was trembling, and no wonder – the dog was a ferocious looking beast.

Jeff approached quietly – he didn't really have a plan, except that he wanted to grab the guy and drag him back for the police to deal with. But this dog was a complication. He looked up at the house to see if any lights had come on from the racket, but it was all dark. Perhaps the owners were out – he didn't think anyone could sleep through this. The shepherd's snarls alone were louder than most dogs' barks.

Jeff bent over and picked up a rock, figuring he might need it if the dog turned on him. He continued pressing forward as quietly as he could but knew that in just a matter of seconds the dog would react to his presence. Jeff shuddered at the thought.

The intruder suddenly noticed Jeff for the first time, and his face seemed to show some relief. Jeff guessed that even a 'peeping tom' would prefer a beating from his subject to being torn apart by an animal.

Jeff put his forefinger to his lips signaling the man to not talk to him. Jeff now had a plan – he was going to sneak up as close as possible to the dog and try to knock him senseless with the rock. Jeff didn't relish hitting an animal, but his priority right now was to get the intruder – and he knew that if he didn't do something about the dog, one or both of them were going to perish.

Jeff was within a couple of feet of the dog's head now, and the creature still hadn't paid him any attention. The dog was obsessed with the man backed up against the wall, and with every snarl the beast inched his front legs a little bit closer to him. Jeff had no doubt that he would attack the man at any moment. The stranger's hands were still extended in front of him, shaking, and he stole quick glances at Jeff without allowing his eyes to stray from his canine captor for any longer than a millisecond at a time.

Now or never. Jeff dug his feet into the grass and propelled himself forward toward the head of the beast, his hand holding the rock extended back behind his head. But his right foot slipped in the dew as he was pushing off and he fell pitifully short of the massive head, clumsily banging down on the animal's back instead.

The shepherd yelped and turned in Jeff's direction, jaws open, surprise and anger reflecting in his eyes. The rock had shaken loose from Jeff's hand when he'd pounded down on the dog's back, so now he was defenseless. The beast lunged his open jaws at Jeff's face, and he fended him off with his hands. But the dog was relentless – he kept snapping and thrusting, catching Jeff's fingers in his mouth and chomping down hard.

Jeff screamed in pain, and rammed his knee into the animal's groin. He heard a yelp of pain, and the dog rolled slightly sideways. Jeff took advantage of the moment and smacked him hard on the tip of his nose with his fist. Another yelp.

But the dog wasn't giving up – he shook his head from side to side, opened his jowls, and lunged once again at Jeff's face. He could see the fire in the dog's eyes, and he knew the creature was hell bent now on tearing Jeff to pieces.

And out of the corner of Jeff's eye he could see the former object of the animal's anger racing for the garden gate. The gate handle squeaked as he turned it, and the dog twisted his head around in the direction of the sound. Jeff reached his right arm out and scraped it back and forth in the grass, desperately searching for the rock.

The man was out through the gate now, and was running up the driveway.

And Jeff found the rock. He screamed in rage; rage at the animal on top of him, but also an even stronger rage at the thought that the asshole in the trench coat was getting away after all this.

The shepherd turned his open jaws back towards Jeff at the very instant that Jeff brought his right hand down hard. This time he didn't miss. A sickening cracking sound accompanied the rock making contact against skull – the animal squealed and rolled over onto his side. Jeff didn't bother to check if he was still breathing.

He jumped up and ran through the open gate. The intruder was at the end of the driveway now, and starting to run across the street, probably planning to scale another backyard fence.

Jeff found speed in his legs that he hadn't felt since running the hundred-yard dash in high school. The man didn't stand a chance and Jeff was up to him in mere seconds. He felt himself airborne now in a flying tackle, wrapping his arms around the man's waist and slamming him to the ground.

On top of him now, he wrapped both hands over the man's ears and then rammed his forehead into the cement sidewalk. The man went limp.

Jeff carefully eased himself off of the man's back, and slipped his belt out of the waist of his jeans. He roughly yanked the peeper's hands behind his back and tied them tightly with the belt. Then he stood up, tugged roughly on the belt and forced the dazed man into a standing position.

"Walk, don't run. If you try to run I'll ram your head into the ground a second time. Don't test me, buddy."

The man obeyed without saying a word, and Jeff shoved him down the street, around the corner and back onto Gaia's street again. He could see the flashing lights of the police cars – they had arrived fast.

Then he saw Gaia standing on her front porch, talking to two of the officers. She saw Jeff, pointed, and started running toward him. Jeff kept shoving the man forward, and could see that the two police officers were now walking toward him now too.

Then there was the roar of an engine – coming from an unseen vehicle around the corner behind him. He took a quick glance back, just as a purple Dodge Charger came careening around the corner, two laughing teenage boys frolicking in the front seat.

Jeff's prisoner heard the noise too – Jeff reached out for the belt to pull the man off the road and onto the sidewalk. The car was coming up behind them fast and the boys were apparently too busy horsing around to notice that there were police cars ahead. It was swerving from side to side in the street now, and Jeff gave a good hard yank on the belt just as his prisoner leaned himself in the other direction.

Then he was loose from Jeff's grasp and turned straight toward the Charger. He was running now, low to the ground, and clearly had no intentions of getting out of the way of the menacing muscle car.

Jeff watched the man's body collide with the grille of the car and fly over the hood, bounce once on the roof, and tumble lifelessly into the street. His body had appeared to move in slow motion and was almost graceful, balletic, in its movements.

But the grace ended in the street. The mysterious intruder was clearly dead, and Jeff just stood there in shock, not quite believing what he'd just seen.

And he wondered why on earth someone who was caught for merely being a 'peeping tom' would want to kill himself, especially in such violent fashion.

CHAPTER 16

She was a beauty. And he'd wanted her. So badly that he'd kill for her.

Brandon walked through his opulent study, and poured himself a glass of brandy – aged fifty years of course in an oak casket, from the finest distillery in the world. Nothing but the best. This brandy always made him reflect – sometimes farther back than he wanted to.

Her name was Juliet, and he fancied himself as her Romeo. She had soft blonde hair that shimmered like gold in the sunshine. It covered half of her slender back, and swung from side to side as she walked. Sometimes she wore it in a ponytail and it bounced when she ran around the university track. She was a track star, and Brandon cheered for her louder than anyone else had.

But she never heard him.

They were heady days indeed back in New Haven, Connecticut. For a young man from Upper Canada College in Toronto on a football scholarship, Yale was as Ivy League as it could get. Brandon knew he fit right in to a university that had produced no less than five U.S. Presidents and nineteen Supreme Court Justices in its illustrious history. And Brandon got in when he was only seventeen, having finished his high school curriculum at UCC one year earlier than his classmates.

It was 1972 when she grabbed his heart and yanked on it. He was in his fourth year of Sciences, just on the cusp of entering Yale's prestigious medical school. And being that Yale was known primarily as a research university, Brandon felt right at home. He wanted to be a medical doctor, a psychiatrist specifically, and he wanted to experiment. He wanted a blank slate – his brain needed that.

Being well aware of the history of the venerable institution in behavioral sciences, he was excited beyond anything he'd ever experienced before. Even though human engineering at Yale had only enjoyed a fifteen-year history before being discarded on the funding shortfall pile, Brandon knew that the science of improving mankind through medical engineering was still very much a culture at Yale. And the school was full of geniuses – just like him.

He met Juliet through football. Brandon was the quarterback with the Yale Bulldogs, and she was a cheerleader. She actually studied at Yale's sister college, Vassar, the all-female school, but Yale students attended a lot of Vassar's functions, and vice versa. So they all got to know each other. And Juliet and several of her friends were recruited by Yale to be on the cheerleading squad.

She was doing cartwheels on the field just before the Thanksgiving weekend grudge match with hated rival, Harvard, and Brandon forgot all about football. He couldn't take his eyes off her. She took his breath away and he was clearly never the same after that day. It was as if she'd waved a magic wand.

He pursued her with a passion that he'd never felt before. But she was with someone else, her high school sweetheart, and she made it clear to Brandon that he would never have a chance. But Brandon never took 'no' for an answer. He was a star; her boyfriend was a nerd. Brandon had the looks and the smarts and a future that was limitless. He knew she'd eventually see that. But she needed some help.

And Brandon provided that help one moonless night on a deserted street. The boyfriend was crossing the road right at the moment Brandon was accelerating at a breakneck pace in a stolen car. He could still see in his mind the look of shock on the boyfriend's face, as he looked right through the windshield at the moment of impact. He knew that the last image in the kid's mind was Brandon Horcroft, the rival. The kid knew he'd lost the fight for the love of his life, and that Brandon had won. He still smiled when he thought of that delicious moment.

But Juliet was too small-minded to see that the 'hit and run' by an unknown culprit was a blessing in disguise. Brandon waited a respectable three months before asking her out. She still said no. He tried several more times before giving up for good. And vowed that he would never love a woman again. Not that way. He would have them, possess them, make them want him – but never again would he allow himself to be vulnerable. He would take, but never ask, and never ever give.

And when he did finally marry years later, it was her that did the asking. Brandon agreed because her family was rich. He never loved her, even though Hayley was as beautiful a woman as any man could hope to have. Sweet and loving, she adored Brandon to the extent that he knew he deserved. But she wasn't Juliet.

Brandon picked up his glass of brandy and walked up to the second floor of his Forest Hill mansion. The house was far too big for just him, but it was the image he needed. Friends, neighbors, employees and clients needed to see Brandon in all his glory – because that's what they expected, he was sure of that. Someone like him could not possibly live in a normal neighborhood, in a normal house. He needed this house for what it said about him, not for how it made him feel.

He still needed it, and loved it. Even though Hayley had died in it.

Brandon leaned against the doorframe of his large master bathroom, and drained the rest of his brandy. He stared hard at the large Jacuzzi bathtub, then closed his eyes and took himself back ten years.

Hayley's Mom and Dad had just died in a car accident. She had always been extremely close with her parents, and everyone knew she'd fall apart. And she did. With a little help from Brandon. Her parents were her life – she spent more time with them than she did with Brandon. He knew that he'd never get a better opportunity.

Because everyone predicted she would fall apart made what she was about to do…believable.

He'd waited years for this to happen, prepared for it well in advance. Knowing this day would arrive.

That night was still so vivid to him, it seemed like yesterday. Hayley was exhausted. It had been two months since her parents' deaths, and she was still suffering from sleepless nights.

They'd just finished a light dinner of smoked salmon, grapes, crackers and imported cheeses. They were still chatting over their wine, when Hayley finally announced that she was going to take a bath and crawl into bed early. She would try once again to fall into dreamland. But first, the bath.

Brandon bid her goodnight and kissed her on the forehead. Just before she turned away, he leaned down from his tall vantage point and looked straight into her eyes. He said in a slow monotone voice: "Thou shalt go forth."

He remembered the glazed and puzzled look on her face, and her question, "What does that mean?"

He just ruffled her hair and gave her the most affectionate pat on the bum that he could possibly muster – knowing it would be the last.

"It means to have a pleasant sleep, dear."

"Oh, okay." She still had a funny look on her face as she turned around and headed for the staircase.

One hour later, Brandon walked upstairs and headed straight for the master bathroom.

Now, ten years later with brandy in hand, Brandon opened his eyes and gazed at the tub. She was lying in blood red bath water, eyes open and lifeless. Her left wrist bore a gash so deep that her hand was flopping backwards like a broken doll.

Brandon shook his head and blinked a few times – mercifully, the image disappeared.

He smiled at his genius.

CHAPTER 17

Gaia was shaking like a leaf. Jeff had his arm around her, hugging her close, while glancing up at the police officer sitting across from them in the interrogation room. They had been answering questions for an hour already, going over the same things, again…and again.

A uniformed officer came into the room and handed a sheet of paper to the detective. The detective studied it carefully, glancing up a couple of times, and then lowering his eyes to read some more.

Jeff broke the silence. "Officer, can we get out of here? Please? You can see that Gaia needs to get home – she's not doing too well here. I don't think there's anything else we can tell you. The man was just a pathetic 'peeping tom.'"

The detective looked up from his reading. "Yes, yes – Doctor Kavanaugh, you've both been more than cooperative with us. She must be exhausted, I agree."

Jeff stood up and reached down to help Gaia. But the officer raised his hand signaling Jeff to stop. "I just need a few more minutes, though."

Jeff sighed and sat down again.

"I think you'll want to hear this, Doctor Kavanaugh."

Jeff sighed again. "Okay, shoot."

"This man wasn't just a harmless little 'peeping tom.' His name was Herbert Walker. An American, a master aircraft mechanic, and former Army Ranger – Special Forces – now self-employed here in Toronto as a private investigator. Looks like he's been doing that for the last four years. Prior to that, he was a licensed aircraft mechanic at the Toronto Island Airport for six years. And before that, he was with the U.S. Military."

Jeff nodded. "Okay, so he was a highly qualified 'peeping tom.'"

"We found a cell phone in his pocket – with photos of you and Gaia, all taken within the past week. None of those photos ever left his phone – we checked to see if they'd been texted or emailed to anyone, but no luck on that."

"Sounds like good luck to me – I'm glad they weren't emailed to anyone."

"You're missing the point, Doctor. We are curious as to whether he was acting alone, or was being paid by someone to spy on the two of you. Remember, this is what private investigators do – that's why I don't think he was just a simple 'peeping tom.'"

"Who would do that? It doesn't make sense. Neither of us is married or even engaged, so there's no infidelity going on here."

The detective shook his head slowly. "I don't know. That's the puzzle. But, while we don't have any evidence that the photos were given to anyone, we did discover another connection to the place where both of you work."

Jeff sat up straight at this. "What connection?"

"There's a vice president at your firm by the name of Ray Filberg, correct?"

Jeff noticed that Gaia had her eyes open now, and was listening intently.

"Yes, there is. He works on the same floor as Gaia and I. He's a great guy."

The detective winced. "Maybe yes, maybe no – maybe not so great. We traced two phone numbers on Walker's phone to Mr. Filberg. One was his office phone, and the other was his cell phone. And we're searching Walker's office right now – he had a small rented place down on Spadina. We'll look at his computer hard drive, and any hard copy files he had – to see if he had a more formal connection to Filberg, or anyone else who might have hired him to spy on you."

Jeff was silent, not quite believing what he had just heard. Ray Filberg? It didn't make any sense. Then all of a sudden he felt goose bumps running up his back. He didn't know why – there was something just on the edge of his mind that he wasn't capturing, and the shock of the evening and seeing Gaia in the state that she was in was perhaps causing him not to be able to think as clearly or as quickly as he was accustomed to. He would need some quiet.

"Something wrong, Doctor?"

Gaia turned her head and looked curiously at Jeff. She squeezed his hand.

The detective leaned forward across the table. "Doctor Kavanaugh, are you alright?"

Jeff blinked, and shook his head to clear the cobwebs. "Yes…yes. I'm just tired. And confused. Forgive me."

"It's okay, Doctor. You and Ms. Templeton are free to go now. You've had a rough night. And…by the way, I am aware of the rough time both of you had several months ago. Here you are involved with the police again, in another strange matter – luckily not as horrific as the one back in July. Let me just say, before you go, that I admire both of you for your bravery that day – and again tonight. You're obviously very special people."

Jeff and Gaia stood and headed for the door. Jeff turned and looked back at the officer. "Do you think that…Walker guy…deliberately killed himself tonight?"

"We'll never know now, Doctor. But it's possible he just yanked away from you and clumsily lurched towards that car. It's possible it was just an accident."

Jeff scratched his chin. "Possible, I guess – but, as I told you when you were questioning me, it sure looked to me like he had a direct bead on that car."

*****

Ray Filberg was fidgeting – but he kept his hands under the table so that the detective couldn't see his nervous fingers.

"Do you see why I'm asking you these questions, Mr. Filberg? It's one hell of a coincidence that this man, Walker, was spying and taking photos of two people who work at the same firm as you do. And two of your phone numbers were in his cell phone."

Ray was nothing if not good on his feet…or in a chair such as was the case right now. He was a fast thinker, and in this case there was only one story he could make up that might sound plausible.

"That is strange about him spying on Jeff and Gaia. I don't understand that at all. Unless…"

The detective's eyes lit up. "Unless? Unless what?"

"Well…this is a little embarrassing. Do you promise to keep it between you and me?"

"If it has no bearing on the case, you have my promise Mr. Filberg."

"Call me Ray."

The detective leaned back in his chair. "We're both busy men, Mr. Filberg. Tell me what I need to know and you can go."

Ray crossed his legs and brought his hands up from under the table, folding them calmly across his lap. "I hired Walker, yes. But I hired him to put my wife under surveillance. I've been suspecting for quite a while now that she's been…having an…affair. And I did tell him that one of the men I suspected was this Jeff Kavanaugh fellow. I noticed him spending a lot of time talking with my wife at a couple of company management parties we had, and it got me thinking. And she seemed to like him too."

"Okay. Has he been reporting to you yet on any of this, or sent any photos of your wife to you?"

"No, nothing as of yet. I just hired him a couple of weeks ago. I'm thinking now that he might have first been following Kavanaugh since he was my prime suspect, and took photos to prove to me that he's actually with someone else, and not my wife."

The detective nodded. "Okay, this might make some sense." He nodded again. "I think you might have cleared up the mystery for us, Mr. Filberg."

Ray stood. "Good, good. Do you need me anymore today?"

"No, you're free to go. Thanks for your cooperation."

Ray slipped into his trench coat – it was raining hard outside today.

He reached into his wallet and pulled out a photo of his wife, Linda. He showed it to the officer. "Detective, if you find any photos of my wife in Walker's office or on his computer, could you please return them to me? Confidentiality, and all that stuff. I am embarrassed, and it seems now that my suspicions of my wife were unfounded."

The detective shook his head. "You don't have to worry. We've already torn apart his office and found nothing. And his computer also holds nothing of value. And he had no files – at least not in his office or his apartment. He must have kept everything up in his head."

Ray smiled. "Well, if you know anything about these Special Forces guys, their brains are literally metal fortresses, and they are indeed trained to keep everything memorized and in focus. So, not surprising to me at all that he would have very few records."

Ray smiled to himself as he headed out the door. *God, I'm good.*

*****

For the last couple of nights, Gaia had been staying at Jeff's house. Jeff understood—she was clearly unsettled by what happened at her place, and didn't feel safe. Jeff had managed to convince her to get an alarm system installed, and maybe even buy a good watchdog. They both loved dogs so it was kind of a nice thing to do anyway. Jeff suggested she consider buying a Fox Terrier – he had one when he was a little boy. Not only were they great watchdogs with an energetic bark at the slightest sound, but also they were affectionate and one of the prettiest breeds. She agreed to look into both the alarm and the dog.

Tonight Jeff made a nice pasta dinner and they'd relaxed afterwards over a glass of wine…then two glasses. Jeff told her about his latest conversation with the detective. He had told him in confidence that Filberg had hired Walker to spy on his own wife, and that Walker considered Jeff one of the possible candidates who might be having an affair with Filberg's wife. So, that explained the connection between Filberg, Walker, and the spying at Gaia's house. But it didn't explain why Walker ran headlong into the speeding car. Unless, as the detective suggested, it was just a result of Walker lurching away from Jeff's hold.

Gaia seemed to feel a bit better, which made Jeff feel better…almost. There was something gnawing at him, and it wouldn't let go. He needed to clear his head.

After the wine, Jeff walked Gaia upstairs and tucked her in. She was a little tipsy from the wine, so he was confident that she might have her first full night's sleep since the incident at her house. He hoped anyway. Jeff kissed her goodnight and headed back downstairs.

He walked into the kitchen and poured himself one more glass of wine. Then he quietly slipped outside and sat down on one of his padded chairs on the backyard deck. He leaned back and looked up at the stars. Within only a minute or two he saw a shooting star – a large streak of light across the western sky, with a small fireball at the head.

He gasped at the wonder of it. Then he gasped again. At something else.

He bolted upright in his chair, spilling the glass of wine onto his jeans.

Christ, I know what's been bothering me! Right there on the edge of my brain! Walker was a trained aircraft mechanic. He worked at the Toronto Island Airport until four years ago. On the day he crashed into Lake Ontario, Gaia's fiancé, Matt, had flown his plane out of the Toronto Island Airport. That was five years ago, so Walker worked there then. Did he sabotage the plane? Cause fuel starvation? Aunt Louise told me that the man obsessed with Gaia had killed her fiancé. Walker had worked for Ray Filberg. Was Filberg the one obsessed with Gaia, and the one who Aunt Louise had warned would put Gaia and me in danger? Did Filberg hire Walker to kill Matt five years ago?

CHAPTER 18

Brandon Horcroft was in fine form this morning. He woke up with the feeling that the recent disturbing incidents were now behind them. The slaughter at the office had faded from the headlines, the news now shifting to other tragedies and disasters. Prentice was safely entrenched in a mental institution, unlikely to be listened to by anyone. And his vice presidents had come up with the ways and means to ward off stress-related confusion to hypnotic commands.

But still, he had the feeling that they had to kick it up a notch – there were other techniques that he wanted to experiment with, and his instinct told him that perhaps they needed something new in their arsenal.

He strode into the boardroom adjoining his office, and saw that his four vice presidents were already there, chatting together and drinking coffee. They shut up as soon as they saw him. Brandon just loved the effect that he had on these guys.

He sat down at the head of the table, and opened his binder. "Okay, gentlemen, first order of business is the stock market. We've kept a low profile since the...incident...here in July. But, it's time we started trading again. What pigeons do we have on our plates, ripe for the plucking?"

Cliff Johnstone spoke first. "I have one executive I've been grooming. He was sent here for some re-engineering by the company President. My guy's the Senior VP of Marketing—had a problem with being a team player, so I've been using some hypnotic techniques that have had a positive effect. The President is pleased, so he's signed on for a continued coaching contract with us. So...the guy's mine."

Brandon was jotting down notes. "What kind of firm is this?"

Cliff pulled out a brochure from his briefcase, and slid it down the table to Brandon. "This covers what they do. The company is called Oilfield Fasteners Inc. They specialize in heavy duty brackets, drill bits and encasements for the oil patch."

"Why are they based here in Toronto? Should be headquartered in Calgary."

Cliff nodded. "Yes, most of the oil industry support companies have moved out of Toronto long ago. But, this firm's been waiting for an opportunity to merge with an existing and similar company based in Calgary."

"Interesting. Who's the company in Calgary?"

"Western Explorer Ltd."

Brandon was leafing through the company brochure. "I see that Oilfield Fasteners is still a private company. Is Western publicly traded?"

"Yes, it trades on the TSX and the NYSE. Stock is undervalued, and the possible merger with Oilfield hasn't hit anyone's radar. It's been the best-kept secret in the oil patch. The resultant corporation, after merger, will be valued at around four billion."

"How will the purchase be executed?"

"According to my guy – and of course, I know all this only from when I had him under a trance–it will be an all-stock deal. No cash."

"And when will this happen and how certain is it?"

"Three months from now, and it sounds ninety-nine percent certain to go through."

"Okay, let's move on it. Pump twenty million into it, and buy the shares on the NYSE through our little Cayman Islands holding."

Cliff nodded. "Done."

Brandon looked around the table. "I feel this is going to be a very productive day. I'm glad to have some of this horrible stuff behind us and we can get back to what we do best – insider trading! This is the rush, the fun part – hypnosis is just the tool."

All four vice presidents nodded.

Brandon tapped his pen excitedly on the table. "Okay, who's next?"

Dillon McAffey opened his binder. "I've got a hot one for us. Six months ago, I placed a senior executive with Worldwide Autoparts Ltd. As you all know, they're a six billion dollar corporation based in Montreal. And they're publicly traded. Anyway, my guy signed on with me for ongoing training in negotiation skills. I placed him as their new Executive Vice President of Manufacturing, and he talks like a parrot when I have him under. He flies here once a month and spends a week at a time with me for the training. But, get this; the new skills I've given him have already started paying off. He's just about to consummate a contract with Bombardier to provide all of the crucial moving parts for their new executive jet design. Basically, Worldwide is diversifying into aircraft parts due to the slowdowns in the auto industry. Bombardier is projected to produce 200 of these new jets over the next two years, orders already signed around the world. The contract is worth two billion in revenue."

Brandon was scribbling fast on his pad. "Jesus, that's fantastic news. And nothing's been announced to the public or shareholders yet?"

"No, tight as a drum."

"Okay, jump on this one too. Use our company in Luxembourg, and pump around ten million into Worldwide through the TSX. At the same time, sell half our shares in Bombardier – I think we hold those through our Swiss company. Usually, when an outsourcing contract is signed, especially one of this size, the stock is going to tank – but only for the short-term. Then, it'll rebound. So, best we short-sell Bombardier, then buy the shares back after the stock falls at least 10%. Okay?"

Dillon gave the thumbs-up sign, signaling his agreement.

Brandon rubbed his hands together. "Yeah – we're back in the saddle! Not even a little slaughter can keep us down! Okay, Josh, tell me what you've got going."

"Actually, I don't have any hot candidates at the moment, Brandon. I've been busy heading up the re-engineering of our hypnosis techniques." Josh nodded towards his colleagues. "We've all been working on it, but I've been in charge of it. Haven't had time for my usual work for a few weeks."

Brandon just stared at him. The silence stretched out over at least two minutes. He waited until all four of them started fidgeting. Then he spoke. Actually it was more of a sneer. "I hate excuses, Josh."

"It's not an excuse, Brandon. But there's only so much time in the day."

"I don't buy that, Josh. You spend too much time with your family. You can ignore the odd Little League game–that's what mothers are for. Your main responsibility is to me, first and foremost."

Josh just stared at him, speechless.

"Well?"

"Yes, Brandon. You're right."

"Good. At next week's meeting, you better have something for me along the lines of what your two colleagues here have just delivered. Are we clear?"

Josh squirmed in his seat. "Clear as day."

"Good. Glad to hear it. By the way, I haven't had a presentation from you yet on this new stress barrier that you've been working on. I want to hear about it. But, I have to admit, from the Slater and Prentice incidents, I think we may have to face the facts that our rather primitive hypnosis techniques may be meeting some natural human resistance – we could be falling behind the times. There's something new that I want us to look into – well, it's not new at all actually, but it's pretty radical. But we may have to be radical to continue to thrive over the next twenty years or so. It's called Psychotronics, and it is extremely effective for mind control. I don't think we can use it for our insider trading activities but perhaps with some of the military, paramilitary, and counter-espionage contracts we have, it may be ideal."

Ray Filberg spoke up. "I'm familiar with it–that's pretty invasive stuff, Brandon."

"Yes – and your point is…"

"Do we want to take those kinds of risks? I mean, with what we do right now with deep hypnosis and latent commands, it's impossible for it, or us, to be discovered. But with Psychotronics – geez, the risks would be huge."

"No risk, no reward, Ray. You know that."

"Yes, but…"

"No 'buts.' We'll be talking about this some more at a later date."

All four of Brandon's executives looked down at their notes while shifting uncomfortably in their seats. Brandon loved it.

"Okay, Josh. Since you have nothing of a profitable nature to report to us, tell us what progress you've made on the elimination of Jim Prentice."

Josh gulped, and took a sip of his water. "Prentice is still alive. I haven't decided how to handle that yet. Lakeside Psychiatric Hospital is very secure – I don't know how we can get a man in there."

Brandon got up from his chair and began pacing the room. He already knew that Prentice was still alive, so he'd just been baiting Josh.

"Carney, I don't know what to say. You've done nothing about this, and you have no ideas at all. We are exposed, big time, with this guy. Sure, he's locked up and everyone thinks he's crazy – so hopefully no one will listen to him. But there's still a risk."

"I'm sorry, but I don't know what to do about this. I don't know how we can pull off a hit in that facility."

Brandon poured himself a coffee and resumed his pacing. "I think I know how. We have several operatives that we've used before, but there's one particularly creative one that we've all used several times. I suggest we just hand the assignment to him. He'll figure out a way."

Josh frowned. "Who are you thinking of?"

"That Herbert Walker fellow. He's actually Ray's contact. He recruited him about a decade ago, and he hasn't failed us yet. What do you think, Ray?"

Ray avoided eye contact with Brandon. He looked down at his hands, which were now tightly clenched together. "Uh…he's dead, Brandon. He finally failed us. Something happened that I haven't had the chance to tell you about yet."

CHAPTER 19

Ray found himself backed up against the bar in Brandon's office. The man was raging, so loud and continuous that Ray found that it was all becoming a blur of noise; no words, just noise.

Ray held up his hand in the stop sign symbol, and Brandon instantly became silent. But his face wore an enquiring look, head cocked sideways, seemingly waiting for something from Ray that would justify the halting of his verbal outrage.

"Yes, Brandon, I understand you're upset. Herbert Walker died. In fact he did what he was programmed to do. These programs we implement are not logical – they don't give variables to the subject. They don't specify how serious the incident has to be to justify suicide. They lodge in the subconscious and the one I used with Walker merely stipulated that if he was in danger of being discovered, he was to act. This is a sharp contrast to the "Thou shalt go forth" methodology that you use with us executives and our business subjects. Yours is a latent command that is only triggered when you use the phrase at usually a much later date."

Brandon frowned. "Are you finished giving me a hypnotherapy lesson? Are you forgetting that I'm a psychiatrist, a medical doctor? Eh?"

"No, I'm not forgetting that. But for God's sake, don't ream me out when one of our experiments – techniques that you yourself sanction – don't work out the way we want them to. It happened – get over it. At least the man can't talk."

Brandon backed away from Ray, and clasped his hands behind his head. "Well, it sounds like you talked your way out of it nicely with the police. And one thing I do know for sure now is that Jeff Kavanaugh and Gaia Templeton are an item. So, it's not a total loss. We lost a good operative, but I know the story now about those two…and I'll have to think about how to handle that."

"Why don't you just leave it alone?"

"Because I can't, and I'm not going to discuss the whys with you."

"Okay, fair enough."

Brandon walked around his desk and sat down in his chair. Ray was relieved to see that he'd calmed down somewhat. The man's rage seemed to have subsided, but he could tell that he was thinking hard about something – just the look on his face, the furrow on his brow.

"Ray, we do have someone out there who can indeed still talk. And I know for a fact that he is talking. Jim Prentice. I got a call the other day from the lead psychiatrist at Lakeside Psychiatric Hospital in Belleville. He was asking me questions pertaining to Prentice's treatment. Said the man was talking about hypnotherapy – nothing more than that, but the good doctor wanted to know what procedures Jim had undergone. I told him enough bullshit to keep him satisfied for now – we went to medical school together, so he kinda trusts me."

Ray walked over and sat in the guest chair in front of Brandon's desk. "That's not good, but I guess to be expected. He is supposed to be getting treatment there, and his loyalty to the firm is long gone now."

Brandon nodded. "That's what I'm worried about. We have to eliminate him, and soon."

"Have you talked to Josh Carney? Prentice was his man, not mine. Does he have any ideas?"

"Carney never has any ideas. In fact, you will recall that it was my idea to use Herbert Walker – that's why I exploded when you told me he died."

Ray nodded, hoping another explosion wouldn't come until after he'd had a chance to escape from Brandon's office.

"But…I have another idea. I mentioned psychotronics to you guys during our meeting. I want that to be on our agenda for future specific projects. I've studied it quite a bit, and I think it has real merit – for paramilitary projects though, not for insider trading."

"As I said before, Brandon, it's risky stuff."

"Yes it is – but you know me well enough that that doesn't scare me. We have to move ahead in our techniques in order to survive and thrive. And it's evident that some of our tried and true methods are now being circumvented by the human brain. As they say, 'nature finds a way.'"

"But psychotronics involves implants to the brain. So easy to discover."

Brandon frowned. "No, Ray, that's not what it is – not exclusively anyway."

Ray raised his eyebrows in a question.

"Psychotronics is merely the affectation of the human brain with an electronic device. It doesn't have to involve implants at all. In fact, one of the most popular methods used right now, particularly by the Russians, is microwave technology – or specifically ELFs: Extremely Low Frequency waves. The brain converts orders into mechanical precision, without fear, and without memory as to where the orders came from. It's been used by the Russians now for at least two decades."

Ray crossed his legs and sighed. "Brandon, that's the Russians – that's not us."

"True – but we do have contacts there, and some favors that are owed to us. You haven't forgotten, I'm sure, about how we poisoned the Ukraine's President several years ago. How could you forget that? Huh?"

"No, I haven't forgotten that…although I wish I could. The images of how his face transformed into Frankenstein still haunt me. I swear, if we'd just killed him instead of turning him into this grotesque monster, I would have felt better."

"Grow a pair, Ray. It's just business. As you know, in this day and age of the global economy, sanctions are easily and more safely carried out if they're done by parties far away from home. More difficult to trace. The Russians could have easily done what we did, but the traceability factor would have been a lot higher.

"Anyway, I didn't accept payment back then, but got them to promise an IOU to me for whatever I wanted, whenever I wanted it. That time is now. They have ELF operatives who can pull this off for us and put Prentice out of our lives forever. That hospital is not maximum security, there are no armed guards, it may have sophisticated security systems but they will be no match for a team of fearless, robotic, killers."

"You're really going to do this?"

"You bet I am. Consider this our first real-life lab experiment of psychotronics."

*****

Brandon hung up the phone, and found it hard to wipe the smile off his face. It had been easier than he thought it would be. The call to his Russian contact at their embassy in Ottawa had been long but productive. Three days from now – Saturday – would be the day of the hit.

His Russian contact had committed to utilizing two former JTF2 commandos to the operation. JTF2 was the Canadian equivalent of the U.S. Special Forces, and several of them had been declared mentally deranged as a result of the secretive and brutal projects they had been involved in. Two of them had spent time in the Lakeside Psychiatric Hospital after being discharged. Being discarded by their own government, they had gone to the Russians for work. The Russian embassy was more than willing to cooperate. It was hard to get their own commandos into North America, so putting former Special Forces Canadians to work was an easy sell.

The commandos would undergo ELF manipulation at the embassy the day before the assault, would be given their assignments, and Saturday it would happen. They would be as trigger-happy as Brandon wanted them to be – and Brandon definitely wanted them to be trigger-happy. He conveyed that wish to Boris. Boris understood.

The two guys knew their way around the hospital having spent time there, would go in heavily armed, and if caught or killed it would simply be declared by the police that these were two nut-jobs who had an axe to grind against the hospital. Everyone was used to such craziness now, so it wouldn't be a big deal. No one would know that the only real target was Jim Prentice.

The ELF manipulation would make the two men robots – and make the orders clear that Jim Prentice in room 207 was the main target, but that many others also needed to die to cover up the murder. Brandon wanted it to be a slaughter by two mentally deranged men who had a grudge. And the people to be killed would simply be human garbage anyway, so who would really care? Well, okay, some guards, nurses and doctors would die as well – but that was just collateral damage.

Okay, that was done. He'd wait to read about it in the papers. The other problem that was causing him sleepless nights was the Jeff/Gaia issue. He got up and paced his spacious office. Brandon rubbed his forehead and breathed deeply. He had never been able to stifle his feelings for Gaia. She was the reincarnation of his Juliet from his Yale days–the Vassar snob who rejected every move he'd made. Even after he'd killed her boyfriend in that 'hit and run,' she'd still wanted nothing to do with him.

With Gaia, it was like a repeat performance. He'd killed her fiancé in the plane crash five years ago using the expertise of Herbert Walker, but it hadn't made a difference. Invites out for drinks or dinners had been rebuffed every single time. His power and prestige seemed to have no effect on the girl at all. He couldn't understand it. And now she was having a fling with his fair-haired boy, Jeff Kavanaugh. It was driving him crazy. He wanted her badly, and this young hero who was only a fraction as wealthy as Brandon was probably already at third base, if not home plate.

Brandon shuddered at the thought. He knew he shouldn't be feeling this way, feeling this obsessed – but that was just the way he was. There were so many women out there, and he had his pick. Most were shallow enough that wealth and good looks alone would make them fall into bed. But not Gaia. She was different. She was classy. She was choosy. And it felt to Brandon as if he'd failed miserably that he hadn't seduced her into his arms. He knew that when he finally did – either by seduction or some other method – he would feel victory. And he needed to feel that. Soon.

Suddenly the semblance of a plan began to form in Brandon's analytical brain. A brain that was infallible. He smiled. Yes, it could work. This had to be his next step. It could really work.

He sat down at his desk and began jotting down some notes. He paused for a second, realizing for just that second, that it was silly for him to be obsessing over a woman when he had more important things to do. Brandon shook his head and discarded that thought. He had to win this battle and he knew just how to do it. He'd concentrate on more traditional things afterwards.

Right now he had to have her. Had to own her. He knew one of his options was to kill Jeff Kavanaugh, but his intelligent brain threw that thought aside. Jeff was the future of the firm, was the hero of the firm. He had to separate him from Gaia in the best way he knew how. He needed Jeff almost as much as he needed Gaia. Brandon's brain was able to distinguish between the two levels of importance.

He smiled. He was proud that he was able to rationalize things so well. Brandon could win on both counts, with the right maneuvers, executed flawlessly. He wouldn't let his obsession with Gaia interfere with his brilliant instincts as to how valuable Jeff was to the firm.

And Brandon needed to sleep at night. Since the revelations from Ray about what the late Herbert Walker had discovered, he hadn't slept a wink. Gaia's face kept floating in front of his face whenever he closed his eyes. He needed that face in his bed, not in his dreams.

And she would be. Soon.

CHAPTER 20

Jeff was sitting in his car in the underground parking lot of his office tower. He usually took the transit system, but today he'd decided to drive to work. Not because he wanted to treat himself, but because he had a rendezvous tonight. The person he had the rendezvous with didn't know about it though. The meeting would be here in the privacy of the underground garage, where at this late hour of the evening there was virtually no one else around. And the car gave him an excuse to be here – he couldn't loiter; that would be too obvious. So his car was the perfect waiting room.

There were only three other cars in the garage. And Jeff's Corvette was parked close to Ray Filberg's, which is exactly where he wanted it to be.

While he was waiting, he reviewed in his mind the facts that he now knew. Herbert Walker had been killed by the swerving Dodge Charger after spying and taking photos of he and Gaia. And Walker had previously worked as an aircraft mechanic at the Toronto Island Airport at the time that Gaia's fiancé had perished in the plane crash – a crash that was loosely attributed to fuel starvation. His Aunt Louise had told him that someone was fixated on Gaia, and had arranged the killing of her fiancé Matt five years before. And now, once again, Gaia was being targeted – by the same operative who had probably arranged the plane crash. And that operative had a connection to one man at Price, Spencer and Williams Inc. – Ray Filberg.

A faraway metallic door clanged shut, and through the open window of his car Jeff heard the sound of footsteps getting closer by the second. He glanced over his shoulder and could see Ray trudging along, briefcase in hand, looking weary after another long day at the office.

Jeff opened his car door and stepped out, leaning against the fender awaiting Ray's arrival. Jeff had never considered himself a fighter, but he'd had his share of scrapes when he was younger and had always come out on top. And as a former athlete he was in tremendous shape. He knew he could hold his own against almost anyone. He didn't like violence, but he knew it also had a purpose and he wasn't afraid to use it. He also had a temper, a rage that if pushed far enough could erupt in a flash. That flash though had been burning slowly this time, ever since the night Walker had spied on them; he had suppressed it until the right moment. And that moment was now.

He was frustrated that the police bought Filberg's story about hiring the detective to spy on his own wife. And frustrated as well by this psychic stuff – what was the good of knowing something when you couldn't tell anyone? Who at the police would believe him if he told them his Aunt Louise had a psychic vision of someone dangerously obsessed with his girlfriend, and that that same person had arranged for her fiancé to be killed five years ago. Jeff felt impotent, afraid, and alone. He knew something that he couldn't share with anyone because they'd think he was crazy. So, the obsessed person may just get away with it again – and Jeff had deduced from the evidence that the obsessed person was Ray Filberg. And only he could deal with it for Gaia's and his own safety. It was simply pre-emptive self-defense.

"Hey, Jeff. What are you doing hanging around here? Waiting for a pretty girl to show up?" Ray chuckled at his wit.

Jeff pushed himself off the fender without saying a word. He strode over to Ray who was just clicking open the driver's side door to his car. He glanced up at Jeff, a puzzled look on his face. "What's up, buddy?"

Jeff moved fast – grabbed Ray by the necktie, one hand on the bottom wide portion of the tie, and the other on the knot. Then he slid the knot up into Ray's throat until it wouldn't slide any more. Ray choked, and his face turned as red as a McIntosh apple. He feebly banged his hands against Jeff's arms, but all Jeff did was push the knot tighter. The stress that Ray was experiencing caused his throat to contract, allowing more slack for the knot to do its nasty work.

He couldn't talk, but Jeff didn't care. Not at this moment. He wanted him to listen and he knew he had only a few seconds to ask a question before Ray passed out. He was going to use those seconds.

"Okay, Ray. Tell me the real reason you sent Walker to Gaia's house."

Jeff immediately slid the knot slightly down from the man's throat, and waited patiently while he caught his breath. But he kept his hands on the tie.

Ray breathed deeply, and rested his hands on Jeff's outstretched arms. He gasped, coughed and swallowed hard. Then he spoke, slowly. "It's…what I told…the police. I was…having my wife…investigated."

Jeff swiftly slid the knot back up tight against his throat. Ray's face showed panic this time, and his cheeks puffed out like balloons. "Wrong answer. That's bullshit and you know it. I know all about how you hired Walker before – five years ago to be exact – to sabotage Gaia's fiancé's plane. So, why don't you try your answer again?" Jeff slid the knot back down again.

This time Ray brought both hands up to his throat. He made no attempt to fight back, as he probably rightfully knew that his younger and more physically dominant opponent would make mincemeat out of him.

He rubbed his throat, then reached into his mouth and scooped out something gross, flicking it to the ground.

"I don't...know where...you got that information. I've never used...Walker before."

This time Jeff kneed him in the groin and then hit him with an uppercut to the chin, knocking him to the ground. He climbed on top of him and slid the tie knot back up even tighter than the last time. Ray's eyes were bulging out of their sockets now, and his brow was soaked with sweat.

Jeff spoke slowly and clearly. "Did you kill her fiancé? Do you have some twisted obsession for Gaia?" He slid the knot back down again.

Jeff could barely hear the reply. "No...I have no...interest. It's not me."

Rage – Jeff could feel it surging through his veins. He climbed off Ray and started walking back to his car. He had gone as far as he would allow his rage to take him. The man wasn't going to tell him anything, and Jeff wasn't prepared to torture him to find out more. He wasn't made that way. Well, maybe, hopefully, this little episode will scare Ray into forgetting about his wet dreams.

As he was rounding the bumper of Ray's BMW, he heard a noise that caused him to turn his gaze back. Ray was breathing hard and wheezing, with his hand on his chest. Jeff rushed back to his side and slid the tie knot down to his navel. Then he ripped open his shirt, and put his hand on his chest. At that moment, Ray's eyeballs rolled up into his forehead and he exhaled heavily...and with finality. Jeff felt for a pulse–none. He slapped him hard. "Ray, Ray!! Stay with me!"

Jeff panicked. The man was dead! He started performing cycles of CPR on his chest, and with each cycle he pushed harder. He heard a crack as at least one rib broke under his pressure. He ignored it and kept on going. "Ray! Breathe, Ray! Breathe!"

After fifteen minutes, Jeff rested back on his haunches and gave up. The man was clearly dead. He felt like he was going to be sick to his stomach, but he pushed the sensation aside and thought about what he had to do. He had never intended this to happen, but at the same time a tiny thought crept into his mind – he and Gaia would be safe now.

He took some deep breaths and commanded his brain to think fast and logically. First he removed the man's wallet and car keys. Then, realizing that his fingerprints were all over the tie, he removed that from Ray's neck and stuffed it into his pocket. He realized his prints would be on the shirt as well, so he lifted Ray's body up and pulled the shirt down over his limp arms. His last thought was, Could they take prints from skin? I gave him CPR – would my prints show up? He gently rubbed Ray's chest with the shirt, then took a good hard look around the parking garage. No one was around, and there didn't seem to be any security cameras. That didn't mean they weren't there, somewhere, but he didn't see any.

Jeff popped the trunk and hoisted Ray's body up and into the trunk with a sickening thud. Then he tossed the man's briefcase in as well.

Jeff ran to his own car, rolled the shirt and tie up into a ball and threw them into the front seat. Then he pocketed Ray's keys, started up the Corvette, and drove as fast as he could for the exit.

Freedom was what he needed right now – the feeling of the open road, away from the stifling claustrophobia of the underground garage. He'd killed a man tonight – not on purpose of course, but he had indeed killed him. By his own hand.

As he cruised down Queen Street East, he could feel his own heart pounding in his chest. He caught himself looking into the rearview mirror, half expecting to see flashing lights behind him. Every police siren he heard on the drive home was, in Jeff's mind, for him. He was suddenly aware of his bladder – and the more he thought about it, the more he felt like it was just going to explode. Then in an instant it just did, and he could feel the warmth spreading across his crotch and down his pant legs.

He told himself that when Ray was discovered, it would be assumed to be a robbery gone wrong. Heart attack was clearly the cause of death, and the man's wallet was missing.

The sleek Corvette weaved its way home, and Jeff was breathing even harder now. And it suddenly occurred to him that he wasn't breathing hard out of guilt, but out of the fear of being caught. Whatever sadness he'd felt over Ray's death had quickly faded. This surprised him, and he knew he'd have to reconcile this in his mind in the days, weeks, months and years to come. Was it because he'd convinced himself that Ray was a killer? That the man was intent on bringing harm to Gaia? Or harm to him?

Or was killing someone really just that easy?

CHAPTER 21

Jeff took the bus and streetcar into work the next day. He didn't want to go near the parking garage – tried his best to pretend that it hadn't happened. But it had, and he still hadn't reconciled his feelings. He was scared out of his mind about being caught, but logically he rationalized that there was really very little chance of that. He struggled with how he would behave when Ray's death was finally discovered and announced. How would his face look? While shaving, he'd practiced different looks in the mirror: shock, sadness, and surprise. None of them seemed to work, none seemed genuine.

When he got to his office he saw a different girl in Gaia's spot at the tenth floor reception. He nodded politely to her and headed down the corridor to his private office. He noticed that new furniture and a cubicle were being assembled in front of Brandon's office. Puzzled, he shrugged it off and threw his briefcase onto his desk. Then he looked out the window, down at the street that he'd raced away on just last night. He could feel his mouth go dry.

Then there was a knock on his door. He turned around and saw Brandon standing there, resplendent in a black linen suit and bright red tie. Beside him was the new girl who had been sitting in Gaia's spot.

"Good morning, Jeff. I want to introduce you to the new assistant for all you senior folks. This is Carla Matthews."

Jeff nodded, then leaned forward and shook her hand.

"This is Jeff Kavanaugh, Carla. I'm sure you saw his face in the news several months ago. He bravely stared down the killer who took the lives of six of our people."

Carla smiled. "Yes, how could I forget? You were quite the hero, Jeff, and it will be an honor working with you. You're famous – I can hardly wait to tell my family and friends about who I'm now working with."

Jeff nodded politely, then turned his gaze to Brandon. "I'm confused, Brandon. What happened to Gaia?"

"Oh, I've promoted her to the position of my Executive Assistant. It's a big new role for her. She'll be working only for me now. Her cubicle is being built right now, just outside of my office."

"I didn't know. No one told me."

"Well, I'm telling you now. Do you have a problem with that?"

Jeff shuffled his feet. "No, no problem. I'm just shocked at the suddenness of this. No offence to you, Carla. I'm sure you're just wonderful. It's just…a…change I wasn't expecting."

Carla flashed him a flirtier smile this time. "Don't worry, Jeff…can I call you Jeff? I'll take good care of you."

Jeff gave her the once over. She was pretty, no doubt, but in kind of a trashy way as compared to the class of Gaia. He was surprised at how she was dressed. A blouse that displayed more cleavage than was generally seen in office dress, and a skirt that was extremely tight – left nothing to the imagination. And a bit heavy on the makeup. Too much mascara, and bright red lipstick. He shuddered at the thought of working with this person every day, and was surprised that Brandon would hire someone who looked like this for the office. Not exactly the dignified image that Gaia always greeted visitors with.

Brandon shrugged his shoulders. "Well, if all these niceties are over with, let's get back to work. And Jeff, I want to talk to you later about some techniques I want to use with that new banking client of yours."

Jeff looked at him quizzically. *Why was Brandon inserting himself into the process for one of my clients?*

Brandon's eyes glared back at him – they seemed as black as night, and his lips curled up into the most sardonic smile Jeff had ever seen. The man seemed satisfied with himself, and his smile seemed to say, "I've won." Jeff didn't know why he interpreted it that way, but his intuition told him that the man was up to something.

But then he saw something else – something that made his stomach turn. A familiar feeling of dizziness came over him for just a second, then an image flashed in front of his eyes, blocking out Brandon, Carla and everything else in his office. It was like a movie screen, colorful and clear. The image was the front entrance to Lakeside Psychiatric Hospital. Then the still image transitioned to a movie – the front doors opened and Jeff was moving down the hallway, past the reception desk, cafeteria, classrooms and private rooms. Then the movie stopped, and focused back on the length of the hallway. Standing in the hallway were Jim Prentice and several other patients – all adorned in white gowns. But Jim was a giant compared to the others–he was in the middle, with four patients on one side, and four on the other. All men. And all had yellowish halos above their heads. The number nine was flashing in the image.

Then the movie ended – Jeff saw nothing but darkness now, and he could feel himself falling backward against the front of his desk.

Voices now – he could hear them but didn't understand what they were saying. He concentrated, focused, trying desperately to come out of this trance. A trance that scared the shit out of him, and reminded him of a promise he had made to himself after the slaughter at the office.

He could feel his shoulders being shaken now – the darkness gradually shifted to light again, and when his eyes came into focus it was Brandon who had his hands on his shoulders, a look of concern on his face.

"Jeff, Jeff – are you okay? What's happened, man? Do you need the nurse?"

Jeff shook his head slowly, and pulled back from Brandon's grasp. "No…I'm… fine. Just a migraine. I…get them…once in a while."

"Well, son, you'll have to do something about that. Kind of a scary thing to see."

Jeff nodded, staggered around to his chair, and sat down. Relief. He looked down at his hands, the very hands that had killed a man last night. He wondered why they looked so gentle.

CHAPTER 22

Inspector Dan Nicholson of the RCMP stumbled on his way up the stairs to his office on the fourth floor. His Starbucks coffee flew out of his hand, leaving most of the precious liquid sprayed across the stairway wall. He cursed silently.

No time to go back out for another one now. He used his keycard, hearing the familiar click, and opened the door to his floor. Dan never took the elevator – not unless he had to. Just this little bit of exercise, up and down each day, felt good. Sitting at a desk most of the time wasn't good, and he needed to find excuses to move around. Dan wasn't one for structured exercise regimes – too boring. He had to be doing something purposeful when he exercised.

He walked down the hall and nodded to staffers along the way. He had a certain walk about him, one that made everyone sit up and take notice. Long strides, back straight, arms swinging in perfect cadence – almost military in precision. Well, the RCMP did have its roots as a paramilitary organization way back to the 1800s when it was known as the Northwest Mounted Police. And when Dan was a raw recruit training in Regina, boot camp was about as militaristic as it could get. Maybe that's where he got his walk.

Now the Royal Canadian Mounted Police was the national police force for the country, and world-renowned as one of the most prestigious, right up there with Scotland Yard and the FBI.

Famous for the Red Serge Tunic, RCMP officers adorned in those handsome tunics and riding horses were a familiar iconic symbol of Canada. Dan tried to remember the last time he'd worn a red tunic. He thought it was during a parade, but couldn't recall exactly. And that would have been the last time he'd ridden a horse as well – about fifteen years ago.

Dan was proud of the RCMP. He'd joined right out of university after graduating with a degree in Criminology. That degree helped him move up the ladder fast. He had transferred around to different detachments in the early years as a young constable, but then finally settled back in his hometown of Toronto when he joined the Organized Crime division as an investigator.

His segment was known as 'O' Division, and although the division was based in London, Ontario, Dan worked out of the Toronto headquarters on Dufferin Avenue, and worked closely with the Federal headquarters in Ottawa.

Because what Dan did was unique. Organized crime was a particularly difficult assignment, that covered the gambit from the Mafia, to corporate fraud rings, right down to motorcycle gangs. He had to be in the biggest city in Canada to be close to the action, so Toronto was it. And he needed to liaise regularly with the Federal branch in Ottawa because organized crime usually went beyond provincial borders, and a lot of times internationally. So, Dan was kind of a lone wolf.

Dan was an Inspector, one of only 440 such people on the force across the country. And with a total staff count of 20,000 in the RCMP, Dan felt privileged indeed.

But he also felt humble. He was modest to a fault, and that was why most people gravitated to Dan – with their problems, their triumphs, their loves, and their losses. He was just one of those people that everyone loved. He knew it, and that alone humbled him even more.

Everyone also knew that Dan was one of the most committed family men in the Toronto detachment. At forty years of age, he was still in love with his college sweetheart. He and Caroline had been married for fifteen years now, and they were the proud parents of a boy and a girl – the 'millionaire's family,' as Dan liked to joke. It was a joke because he knew he'd never be a millionaire, but as far as he was concerned, having both a boy and a girl made him rich beyond compare.

Dan passed by his secretary's desk. He leaned over. "Good morning, Chrissy. I spilled my coffee."

She faked an admonishing look. "Oh, Dan – not again. If you took the elevator like the rest of us lazy folks, you wouldn't keep doing this!"

He smiled. "I know, I know – someday I'll learn. But, I am a slow learner, you know that."

"Only with coffee and stairways – for everything else you're as sharp as a razor, thank God."

"Thanks. Could you…"

Chrissy cut him off. "I know, I know. Run down to Starbucks and get you the strongest brew of black coffee I can get. Relax for ten minutes – I'll be back with your fix. Don't worry, Dan." She chuckled, picked up her purse, and started walking toward the elevator. She turned around and called back to him. "Watch me, Dan. I'm taking what's called an 'elevator.' All I have to do is push a button, and it comes for me. Isn't that marvelous?"

Dan laughed at her sarcasm. He loved it, loved the way she always teased him. Helped make the day pleasant even when the things he had to deal with weren't the least bit pleasant.

He opened the door to his large corner office, turned on his computer and poured himself a glass of water from the cooler as a stop-gap pending the arrival of his cup of java.

As he did every morning, he swiveled around in his chair and stared at the framed photo of himself, Caroline, Wade and Marilyn sitting in a prominent spot on his walnut credenza. He smiled – to him this was almost like a morning prayer. And since he wasn't religious, this would have to suffice. And this photo was a hell of a lot nicer than a prayer. It's what kept him going, kept him motivated. They were his reason for living and staying alive. In his job, you never knew…

Dan was blonde-haired, blue-eyed, and stood six feet three inches tall. German descent – in the far distance – was responsible for his looks. He didn't speak a word of German and had no desire to. It was the harshest language in the world as far as he was concerned, and he didn't care that it was in his background, he had no desire to learn even one word of German. Spanish, now, that was a different story. He longed to find the time to learn that language, as most of the countries he liked to visit had Spanish as their mother tongue. Most of the time he got by just by hand signals and by flashing his big smile – that's another thing Dan was noted for, his big friendly smile that put everyone at ease. But Spanish, wow, would he love to surprise Caroline one day by saying in Spanish, 'I love you,' with an authentic accent. She'd be so thrilled, and so proud of him. Making Caroline proud of him was one of the biggest motivators to Dan – she just had that kind of effect on him. He loved her dearly, and every woman who knew him also knew that they never had a chance with him because of Caroline. Although many had tried. He just let them down with that big easy smile, and they went away feeling as if they'd been kissed.

Dan looked at his watch – his 10:00 appointment would be here soon. He glanced out the window. Hard to believe it was late November already. Leaves were still in bloom and not a flake of snow had been seen so far. He hoped they'd have some by Christmas – his kids were young and still believed in Santa Clause. Hard to explain a sled and reindeer when there was no snow on the ground.

His meeting at 10:00 was with an executive from Advanced Technologies Ltd., a senior vice president of Marketing who had a story to tell. A weird story. The man's name was Clark Winston, a dynamic up and comer apparently. This assignment had been kicked over to Dan by his superiors in Ottawa. It 'smelled,' they told him. Smelled of something they'd never come across before. It fell to the RCMP instead of local police, because of the fact that it had hints of organized financial crime, and that the firm named in the complaint, Price, Spencer and Williams Inc., had offices around the world. So, if the story panned out, they would need international cooperation.

Chrissy flew into his office with two cups of coffee, black. "I brought two, because your 10:00 is almost due to arrive. And I didn't think it would be fair to have you sitting there with a Starbucks, and him sitting with one of our tacky cups from the machine. Do you agree, boss?"

"Yes, Chrissy. You always think ahead. That's why I may just keep you around for awhile."

She laughed. "You'd be lost without me!"

"In all honesty, yes I would. Show Mr. Winston in as soon as he gets here. And, no interruptions, okay?"

She saluted and left. Dan pulled his service revolver out of his hip holster, and checked to make sure he had six good bullets in the cylinder. Standard procedure before meeting with strangers – you just never knew.

*****

"Did you meet all of the executives at Price during your first meeting?"

Clark Winston sipped his Starbucks. "Yes, they gave me the full tour of the floors, then took me upstairs to the tenth floor, which is what they call the Artificial Intelligence Division. Specialists in executive placements for high-tech companies, and also personal coaching, stress management, etc. I met Karen Woodcock, their President – then she disappeared and I met with a Ray Filberg, Cliff Johnstone, Dillon McAffey and Josh Carney. All four are vice presidents and psychologists. Then they introduced me to the division's head honcho, a Brandon Horcroft. Apparently he's the only medical doctor in the firm – a psychiatrist."

Dan chewed on the end of his pen. "Price, Spencer and Williams is pretty high profile – one of the largest executive placement firms in the world. And...I'm sure you remember back in the summer, that slaughter that happened. One of their senior employees went postal, killed six people in the office and his family of three at home."

"Yes, who could forget? One of their people became somewhat of a hero for stopping the guy."

"Did you meet him?"

"No, and I can't remember his name now, even though the top dog Brandon made great hay bragging about him. Seemed to want me to think of the hero part only and not the slaughter part."

Dan leaned back in his chair. "Okay, carry on."

"Well, Price was the headhunter I went through to land the job at Advanced Technologies. So I already had a relationship with them. After I'd been with the firm for a few months, they told me that I needed help with stress management. And they were probably right – the job is huge and it started getting to me. Anyway, they asked me if I would attend several private sessions at Price that would use coaching and hypnosis techniques to help me. I agreed."

"So, your own company was trying to help you."

"Yes, they were. But I was worried. Stress is a big part of the job, and I really wanted them to think I could handle it. I was determined that even if Price couldn't help me, I would somehow bluff my way into making my bosses at Advanced think I was okay."

Dan blinked several times. "Is it worth it?"

Clark seemed confused by the question. "Well, sure it is. The salary I make is huge."

Dan shrugged. "Okay, continue."

Clark shifted in his chair. "I was assigned to Ray Filberg. He told me how the sessions would go, and that they'd give a progress report at the end to my bosses."

"And you were okay with that? You didn't balk at the confidentiality thing?"

"No, but Inspector, I was really worried. It was clear that hypnosis is a big part of what they do – they made that clear to me. And I've tried hypnosis therapy before, and it's never been successful with me. I can never go under."

"Did you tell them that?"

"For God's sake, no. My survival at Advanced depended on my solving the stress problem, so I played along. I know enough about hypnosis that I figured I could bluff my way through it, pretend that it worked, and just fight the stress thing on my own. I wanted a good report going back to my bosses, and I didn't want them to think that one of the most effective treatments for stress wasn't going to work with me."

Dan poured some water for both himself and Clark. "I understand. Go on."

Clark took a sip and cleared his throat. "The first two sessions went fine, and Ray coached me, did videos of my performance in faux stressful situations, role plays – the whole nine yards. He hypnotized me – or tried to, I should say. I bluffed, faked being under. He seemed to buy it."

"So, things up to that point were going well for you."

Clark stood up and stretched his back, then sat back down again. "Sorry, just a stress relief thing I do."

"That's okay. Are you feeling stress right now?"

"You bet I am. I'm just getting to the good part – the part you're going to want to hear."

Dan leaned forward with his elbows on his desk. "I'm all ears, Clark."

"In the third session, Ray took me to a different room – kind of like a meeting room, but it only had two chairs. One for him, one for me. There was a large movie screen on the wall, with an overhead projector in the ceiling. He used the usual talking stuff, monotone voice, etc. Then he attached an electrode to each side of my forehead, with a power pack sitting in my lap. As he continued to talk, I could feel a gentle current running into my head. Kind of like when you go to physio, and they hook you up. Nothing shocking, just soothing. And continuous. This time I could feel myself actually starting to get really relaxed, almost sleepy. I was thinking that maybe for the first time in my life I would actually fall under hypnosis. Then the movie came on – no sound, just swirling objects. I was told to stare at them, all the while the current was still running into my head."

Dan interrupted Clark. "What kind of images were you seeing?"

"Like those optical illusions, you know? Like a circle that moves in and out and you focus on the middle of the circle and you can't tell after a while if it's even moving. Then three dimensional objects that kept moving and changing shape."

Dan chewed harder on his pen. "So, some advanced techniques, obviously."

"Yes, that's what I figured. But then it seemed to change. Ray pressed a remote and the current to my head increased. I concentrated hard on not letting my discomfort show, but it was uncomfortable. Remember, I wanted him to think I was under. Then the images on the screen started moving faster, more and more confusing – and tiring – to look at."

"Do you think you were hypnotized?"

"No, definitely not – but I was close. Then Ray began to speak. And what he was saying shocked me to my core. I was trembling inside, and hoping to God that he couldn't notice anything on the outside. He began planting commands – asked me to phone him with any corporate changes that could increase the stock price of Advanced Technologies – or decrease the stock price. He wanted information on acquisitions that were being contemplated. I was to call him personally. I kept my head down, chin to my chest."

Dan took another sip of his water. "Jesus. What happened next?"

"As if that wasn't bad enough, the worst was still to come. That Brandon Horcroft guy came into the room, all the lights went off, the screen turned off and Ray removed the electrodes from my head. Then one single bright light was turned on above the opposite chair where Brandon was now sitting. It was pointed right at me – so bright I couldn't see him at all. There must have been silence for at least ten minutes and I could hear Brandon breathing, rhythmically, in and out. The light was very bright and I could actually start to feel the warmth from it. Then he spoke – slowly, deeply, threateningly."

Dan could see that Clark was starting to have some kind of an anxiety attack. His hands were shaking and his forehead was moist. "Do you want to take a break, Clark?"

Clark shook his head and wiped the back of his hand across his forehead. "No, I want to finish. Brandon said four words: 'Thou shalt go forth.' He said that phrase over and over again. I can't even count in my head how many times. Then he said that if I was ever to hear that phrase again, I was to immediately take my own life."

Dan stared at him for a good twenty seconds, mouth agape. Then he reached for his personal recorder and hit the 'stop' button. He looked up at Clark again, and said in a whisper. "I'm going to turn this machine on again and, for clarity, I need you to repeat that last bit to me one more time."

CHAPTER 23

The water splashing over his face felt good – very good. Jeff dried it with a paper towel, popped some drops into his eyes, and made his way out of the executive washroom. He passed by Gaia's new desk, bent over, and whispered a 'congratulations' to her. She looked up at him with a puzzled look, and just shook her head with her lips pursed. Gaia didn't seem overly pleased with her new promotion. She blew him a kiss as he continued on towards his own office.

He closed his door, picked up the phone and dialed a familiar number. She answered on the first ring.

"I was waiting for your call."

"How did you know?"

"We're connected, Jeff, you know that. This time I saw the same images that you did – probably because I've been focusing on you in my thoughts ever since you told me what you saw and felt just before the killings at your office."

"Aunt Louise, this is too weird. Tell me what you saw."

She detailed her vision to him, and it was exactly what Jeff saw when Brandon and Carla were standing in front of him. He got up and started pacing his office.

"I don't know what to say – it's unbelievable that we saw the same thing."

Louise sighed at the other end. "There are some who would say that it's unbelievable that people like us can see anything at all, let alone be in sync in our visions."

"True. And you know, what I saw seemed to be triggered by Brandon – just before it happened his eyes seemed to turn jet black. And Brandon has blue eyes."

"I don't know what to say about that, except that he probably has some connection to the disturbing image you saw. That's what brought it on, and that also means it's probably imminent."

Jeff sat down in his chair and swiveled around to face out the window. "Aunt Louise…have you had any other visions about me?" Jeff was afraid that she might have seen something else. In particular, what happened in the parking garage last night?

"No, no other visions, Jeff. But I have a strong feeling that you've done something that you regret, something that's scaring you."

Jeff paused before answering. "Perhaps so. I need to deal with it on my own."

"I understand."

Jeff hung up the phone and began pacing again. And thinking.

Imminent, she said. What do I do about this? How can I warn the hospital? What can I possibly say? Why would they listen to me?

Jeff checked the memory in his cell phone, and dialed the number to the hospital. As soon as the receptionist answered, he hung up.

I can't do it this way. The phone is the worst possible way to say something weird like this. I have to go there in person.

*****

The first thing Dan Nicholson did after his meeting with Clark Winston, was to put out a 'tag alert' on the firm, Price, Spencer and Williams Inc. This went out over the vast network of interlinked police services, including the RCMP, Toronto Police Service, Ontario Provincial Police, as well as all of the other municipal and provincial police departments across Canada. He then entered a similar alert into the FBI database. The purpose of this 'tag alert' was to exercise his right of supremacy over any criminal issues related to the firm of Price, Spencer and Williams Inc. All other police services had to respect his jurisdiction now, and take no investigative action with respect to that one particular firm. All information had to be relayed directly to Inspector Dan Nicholson of the RCMP. So, if even the most minor incident was reported about Price, it had to be funneled up to Dan.

This was an important step to take. It protected the integrity of the case, made sure only one police service was investigating, and recognized the fact that anything reported about Price could relate in some way to the allegation of insider trading and…basically, murder. If people were being commanded under hypnosis to kill themselves, it was murder. And Dan admitted to himself, it was the strangest case he'd ever come across in his entire career. And would be tough to prove, if it was true.

He then summoned his computer expert, Kent Remington, a corporal in the RCMP, and one of the foremost computer hackers in the world. Dan thanked God that Kent was on their side and not on the dark side. He asked Kent to see what he could do about jumping into Price's Wide Area Network. If Kent could somehow gain access to the WAN, it might open up a world of knowledge about how vast this criminal enterprise was. Or, was it just Ray Filberg and Brandon Horcroft working alone, doing their own little side business?

Then, as his last act of the day, Dan left a message with a Carla Matthews at Price, asking if he could speak to Ray Filberg. She told him that he hadn't come in to work, and wasn't answering his mobile. Dan was using his own mobile, so the phone number didn't tie him to the RCMP. At this point he wanted to stay under the radar. He asked Carla to leave a message with Ray to call him back, saying only that he was a potential coaching client.

Then Dan packed his briefcase and headed home for dinner with his family. On his way out, he smiled his big smile to at least twenty lingering staffers. But on the inside, Dan wasn't smiling. Not even close.

*****

Jeff told Carla he was leaving for the day, and to cancel the rest of his appointments. She protested slightly, saying there was one client already here, waiting in the ninth floor reception. Jeff just said he had an emergency, and everything would have to be re-scheduled.

It was Friday, and leaving early was going to give him a jump on traffic. Jeff took the empty streetcar back to his street, and ran the rest of the way to his house. He packed an overnight bag, jumped into his Corvette and weaved his way out to the 401 East highway grid. In four hours he'd be there. After that, he had no idea what he would do.

*****

Kent phoned Dan at home Friday evening. He had quickly immersed himself into the Price assignment and had bad news to report.

"It's unhackable, Dan."

"I don't even think that's a real word, Kent. At least not for you."

"I know, I know. I can't recall the last time I was stumped. But their WAN is impenetrable. We're going to have to find another way. They have big-time security on their system. It's all tied up in knots."

"Okay. I'll think about it. And you think about it too. We have to find a way in."

"Don't worry. I'll be brainstorming over the weekend."

"Get a life, Kent. Take the weekend off. But, Monday morning we'll talk again, after you've run some searches for ex-employees. I want you to find anything at all related to disturbances, suicides, and murders – tied to anyone who was ever employed by Price, Spencer and Williams. Go back as many years as you can. And… get me the complete data file on that office slaughter that took place there last July. All the marbles. And the hero of the day – I can't recall his name – get me what you can on him. As well as executives Ray Filberg and Brandon Horcroft."

"Will do, boss. Can you tell me what's going on?"

"No, not yet. It's too bizarre to share right now."

*****

It was late Friday evening when Jeff finally pulled into the parking lot at Lakeside Psychiatric Hospital. He glanced around as he was getting out. All looked quiet and serene, belying the insanity of the people who lived inside. This could have been a resort or a country club to the eyes of someone who didn't know any better. He was relieved to see that there were no police cars or ambulances. Maybe his "vision" wasn't so imminent after all. Or maybe it just wasn't going to come true. He hoped.

He strolled through the front entrance and smiled at the girl behind the glass at Reception.

"Can I help you, sir?"

"Yes, you can. My name is Doctor Jeff Kavanaugh. I'd like to see the Administrator, please. A Doctor Olivia Magnusson, if I recall correctly."

"Yes, you have the name right. Do you have an appointment?"

"No, but I was here about a month ago, visiting with one of your...patients. I met Doctor Magnusson at that time."

"Office hours end at 5:00, Doctor. She's left for the day. Can you come back tomorrow?"

"I could, yes. But I would like to see her for just a few minutes tonight. I know she lives here in the complex, so perhaps you could alert her that I'm here? Please tell her it's an urgent matter."

The girl frowned. "Alright. Give me a few moments to get in touch with her, please."

While he was waiting, Jeff glanced down the hallway, the same hallway he'd seen himself walking down in his vision. The hallway where Jim Prentice and eight other patients were standing, all in white gowns.

The hallway was empty now. Presumably, everyone was in their own private rooms, or communal areas.

Suddenly Jeff's vision became blurry. He teetered on his feet as his legs became wobbly. He knew it was happening again, and he leaned against a couch in the waiting area and simply let it happen. And it happened – but this time it was quick. Just an instant. He was looking at a sitting room, or games room – tables and couches were placed in strategic areas, all with perfect viewing opportunities of the big screen television that was attached to a wall. There was no one in the room, but the TV was on. There was a hockey game – he could tell by the uniforms that the Toronto Maple Leafs were playing the New York Rangers. It was the first period, and he watched as a Leafs forward drilled the puck into the back of the Rangers net, making the score 2 to 1 for Toronto.

Jeff shook his head and the image cleared. He poured himself some water from the cooler, just as the young receptionist called out to him.

"Doctor Magnusson remembers you. She'll be pleased to meet with you for a few minutes. Could you wait in the lounge, please? And can I get you a coffee in the meantime?"

"Yes, that would be wonderful, thanks." Jeff thought to himself that a Scotch would go down a lot better right now than coffee.

CHAPTER 24

Jeff was just finishing the last of his coffee, when Doctor Olivia Magnusson came through the door of the lounge. She was dressed in track pants and a sweatshirt, obviously disturbed from what was up until now a relaxing evening. Jeff knew that what he was going to tell her would ruin her evening even more.

He stood up as she came over and they shook hands. She sat down in the leather seat adjacent to his, crossed her legs and leaned her chin on top of her fist.

"So, what's so urgent, Doctor Kavanaugh?"

"Please, call me Jeff."

"Okay, if you'll call me Olivia."

Jeff nodded, and swallowed hard. He had never told anyone about his psychic abilities before, but he'd decided that tonight he had no choice. Let the chips fall where they may, but there's no way she'd listen to him unless he had something to back it up.

"I'm real sorry to have disturbed you tonight, but there's something I needed to talk to you about."

Olivia waved her hand. "Oh, don't worry about disturbing me. I've come to realize that this job is 24/7, made worse by the fact that I actually live here too. I can't escape it."

"Yeah, that must be tough."

"It is, but I'm used to it now. So, is there something about Jim Prentice that you wanted to discuss? He's been a model patient, by the way. I have a tough time imagining him doing what he did."

Jeff scratched his chin. "That's a puzzle to all of us, Olivia. But where the human brain is concerned, I think we both know that some of life's biggest mysteries reside in riddle and may never be solved."

"That's a good word for it – we can try hard to understand the brain, but most of the time the Riddler's work is something we can't overcome. So, what can I do for you at this late hour?" Jeff knew that she was gently telling him to just get on with it.

He felt the palms of his hands getting moist, and he rubbed them subtly against his pants. "Okay, what I'm going to tell you is unsettling. I'll start by going back a few months, to the day when Jim committed his slaughter. You know that I succeeded in stopping him from more murders that day?"

She smiled. "Yes, Jeff – everyone in Canada knows about that, I think. You were very brave and I have to say also that you were a credit to your profession, using your skills of communication to talk him down like you did."

Jeff licked his lips. "Yes, well, there was more to it than that. No one else except my aunt knows what I'm going to tell you. I saw the slaughter coming beforehand – it wasn't entirely clear what I saw when I saw it, but now in hindsight I know the signals had meaning. And I promised myself that if I ever got those signals again, I would react in advance. If I had understood them that day, I could have prevented the killings in the office, I think – not the family members he killed, but at least the ones in the office."

Olivia leaned in towards him and spoke in a whisper. "Are you saying that you're psychic?"

Jeff slowly nodded, apprehensive. "Yes, and so is my aunt. That's why I confided in her afterwards, because I knew she'd understand and help me grasp it better."

"Have you always known this about yourself?" Olivia seemed interested.

"Yes, but I denied it with the help of my mother, and pretty much ignored the signals I've been getting most of my life. When things would come true, I would just shrug them off because most of the time it was just minor stuff. But this slaughter at the office was a hard one to shrug off – it was intense, and accurate. And it turned out to be brutal."

"I understand."

Olivia was starting to sound like a true psychiatrist. Jeff expected that at any moment she'd ask him to lie down on the couch and tell her all about his mother complex.

"And that day, while I was talking him down, I got other signals that told me that what I was doing was working, that the crisis was winding down. So, you call me brave and I appreciate that, but I did have some help."

"I understand."

Jeff wished she'd stop saying that, because he had the feeling that in a few minutes her understanding would evaporate real fast.

"Well, I've had those feelings again, those signals. And they are telling me that something terrible is about to happen here."

"Here? Like in, here at Lakeside Psychiatric?"

Jeff lowered his eyes. "Yes, sorry to have to say. And it feels imminent – how imminent, I can't be sure. But my guess would be tonight or tomorrow."

Olivia sat back in her chair and stared at him silently for a few seconds. "You seem like a rational man. And you're very well educated. You're a psychologist, and I'm a psychiatrist. You and I weren't necessarily taught to appreciate extra sensory perception, but as students of the mind, most of us tend to develop at least a tolerance for it. And an appreciation that it could be real. But, you've thrown me for a loop."

"Yes, I expected that reaction."

"How vivid were these visions, signals?"

"Not vivid in terms of violence – more just symbolic signs that I've come to recognize what they mean. Similar to what I saw that day. Yellow halos over the people who were destined to die, and the number of dead flashing at me in numeric."

"Is it to be a violent act, or an accident instead perhaps?"

Jeff crossed his legs and clasped his hands behind his head. "That's a real good question, and I don't think I have a real good answer for it. I guess I'm assuming it's going to be a violent act, since the symbolism was similar to what I saw before the office incident. And…just a general feeling I have that it will involve violence. As well, one of the symbols showed one of your patients in prominence – in other words, the image of him was larger than the other eight. Which tends to tell me that he's the target and the others are collateral. That's just my interpretation, and I know it's kind of subjective – but I can only go by what I feel from what I saw."

Olivia stood up and started pacing. "Couldn't that also mean that this one person started the accident – let's say it was a fire started in his unit? And the other eight died as a result of that fire?"

Jeff stood as well, and kept her company in her pacing. "Yeah, that could be a possible interpretation. I didn't think of it that way – and maybe my thinking is tainted because the last time I got those kinds of images, there was violence, terrible violence. As I said, it's hard to be objective."

Olivia stopped pacing. "Okay, let's say you're right. What do you imagine? Someone coming in here with guns blazing?"

"Something like that."

Olivia raised her voice a few harsh decibels. "So, should I call the Belleville Police, the OPP, or the RCMP, and have them camp out here for a few days just in case something happens? And how would I explain this to them, to make them want to volunteer their valuable manpower? Officers that could be out doing something else, responding to crimes that have actually happened? In other words, what in the hell do you expect me to do with this information?"

Jeff stopped pacing too. And he raised his voice in response to hers. "Do you understand how difficult this was for me, Olivia? Knowing that you'd probably think

I was a nut? Knowing that anything you did would be acting solely on someone else's daydream? And from someone who you barely know except through the front pages of newspapers?"

"Yes, I do understand – but that's not my problem. Again, what do you expect me to do? Tell me!"

Jeff swung his jacket over his shoulder, and started walking toward the door. Then he turned around and faced her. "I have no right to expect you to do anything. I did my duty; my conscience will be clear. I can't save the world with this curse I have – I'm just stuck with it, that's all."

He turned and pushed open the lounge door.

"Wait a minute! Tell me, who was the one patient who was more prominent than the others? The one you said seemed to be the target?"

Jeff shook his head. "There's no need for you to know that, Olivia."

*****

They sipped their beers slowly, two men who had very little to say to each other. They knew one another, but neither of them were much for small talk. And if they were like that in their younger days, they couldn't remember now. That seemed like a lifetime ago...

The two former JTF2 commandos were sitting in the bar of their Belleville hotel. They had just completed their three-hour drive from Ottawa, and needed to unwind. Both of them were restless, and perhaps the ordeal they had had to endure at the Russian Embassy that morning had contributed to that.

But, they liked their new employer. After being discarded by the Canadian government, they felt like they had some kind of a home again. And soldiers needed that, needed the camaraderie even if they didn't talk that much – just knowing that one guy had another guy's back was comforting. A sense of belonging.

The jobs they were assigned now, though, were pretty mundane. Generally just surveillance of subjects who the Russians wanted to keep their eyes on, infiltration here and there, information sharing. Boring...but it was a paycheck and it made them feel as if some of their specialized skills were still valuable.

This new assignment had some excitement to it though – reminded both of them of some of the stuff they had been commanded to do in Afghanistan. Brutal, but necessary. But so brutal, that they themselves had had to spend a year in Lakeside Psychiatric Hospital, the very place they would be visiting tomorrow. They could do 'brutal,' that wasn't a problem. It's just that the memory of those acts affected both of them after they were sent back home again to the peace and quiet of their own country. So, the hospital stay had been a necessary thing. But, after that, they weren't wanted anymore – except by the Russians.

Being bombarded with ELF microwaves all morning at the embassy was painless – and it was explained to them that their orders would be clear to them, their execution flawless, and the memories of their acts would be blurry if not non-existent. And they would feel no fear, only cold calculation.

But they were warned that their attention to other matters might suffer a bit, so they would have to work extra hard to stay focused until they finished their assignment. Because the ELF treatment caused the assignment itself to be at the forefront of their consciousness. For example, just having these beers tonight was not advisable. They could have too many, or get tangled up with the wrong people – because their judgment would be impaired with respect to other day to day things until the assignment was finished. They had to be extra careful driving as well–their attention could wander.

Jamie and Roger knew all these things – they had been briefed exhaustively. But they were grown men, for God's sake, and they had to have some fun too.

Jamie clinked the glass containing his third beer, with the glass containing Roger's fifth. "What the fuck, eh? Tastes good, doesn't it?"

Roger smiled broadly, and his eyes were swimming with the lovely intoxication. "Yeah, what the fuck. And what the fuck do those Ruskies know, anyway? We'll do their dirty work for them, that's what we do. We don't need their fancy EFU, ELT, or whatever the fuck they call it, to help us be the pros we are. They have no idea what we did overseas. And we always won, survived to be here right now."

Jamie nodded, and then spoke in as low a whisper as a macho guy like him could pull off. "Speaking of getting fucked, see those girls over there at the bar? They look pretty easy, whaddaya say we give em a poke?"

Roger whispered back. "Yeah, I was looking at em too. Dressed like a couple of sluts – they wanna get noticed. Should be easy lays."

"Okay, let's go get em."

Roger put his hand on Jamie's arm. "Not so fast. Let's have a couple more beers first."

"But they could get picked up."

"Who cares – girls like them are a dime a dozen. If they leave, those stools will be quickly occupied by a couple more sluts."

"Yeah, you're right." Jamie raised his glass again. "Let's toast to something, anything, I don't give a rat's ass."

*****

Jeff couldn't get out of bed the next morning. He was staying in a hotel in downtown Belleville, and couldn't think of any good reason to get up. He had been having the same dream over and over again. A man in a trunk, banging away on the lid, screaming in agony hoping against hope that someone would hear him. Jeff would wake up, drink some water, and then fall off to sleep again. The screaming and banging would resume.

He finally gave up and ordered room service. A big breakfast of bacon, eggs, toast and hash browns. He smeared marmalade all over the toast, and then stuck several slabs of bacon on it – just like his dad used to do. Brought back some nice memories of the rare times that his dad actually made breakfast.

After that, he packed his overnight bag and checked out of the hotel. Time to head back to Toronto. Or, maybe not. He was here, he might as well walk around a bit – he hadn't explored downtown Belleville in years. Jeff's best friend from high school, Mike, had grown up in Belleville. The two of them used to drive from Toronto once in a while to visit some of Mike's old haunts. Bars, strip joints – they were young then. Now, at the ripe old age of thirty-five, Jeff wanted to pop into some of the unique shops in the old town center, and perhaps buy Gaia a nice congratulations present.

So that's what he did. And he found the perfect bracelet for her – one that he knew she would wear with the numerous green outfits she had. She loved green. And Jeff loved the way she looked in green.

He stopped for a late lunch, wandered around a bit more, then reluctantly climbed back into his car to start the four-hour journey home. He didn't want to go. He felt he'd failed and still had the sickening feeling that something was going to happen.

He started up the monster engine of his Corvette, pulled out into traffic and began picking his way towards the 401. He glanced at his watch – 6:00. Time had flown by so fast. And now it wouldn't be until at least 10:00 when he finally got home. Well, tomorrow was Sunday – he'd have the day off to relax and get his mind straight. And pray that nothing happened at Lakeside Psychiatric Hospital.

He turned on the radio, and heard a sportscaster discussing tonight's hockey game. It was Hockey Night in Canada, and the featured game was going to be a good one, according to the broadcaster. Jeff turned the volume up – he liked hockey. It cheered him up knowing he could listen to the game on the radio for the entire ride home.

Then he heard something that caused his heart to skip a few beats. The game tonight was between the Toronto Maple Leafs and the New York Rangers. Jeff took some deep breaths, glanced in his rear-view mirror, and squealed the tires as he whipped the car into a quick U-Turn.

*****

It was 6:30 p.m., Saturday night, and Jamie and Roger were on their way. A little hung-over, but not feeling too bad. Probably because they'd both gotten laid the night before. The girls hadn't looked too good first thing in the morning, though. But they'd looked like super-models after ten beers at midnight. Booze had its advantages – it put lipstick on pigs.

Jamie was driving. He turned on the radio and set it to the sports channel. "The Leafs are playing tonight. They're gonna pound the Rangers, I just know it."

Roger laughed. "Yeah, right. I'll put my money on the Rangers."

"Okay, you have a bet. Hundred bucks?"

"Sure, why not?"

They drove in silence for a while. It was late November, and dark already. Perfect for what they had to do.

Jamie broke the silence. "Okay, we'll go in through the roof. Through the ventilation shafts. It's only two stories, so when we go through the ducts we'll be dropping down onto the second floor, which is where we're supposed to be."

Roger jumped in. "Yeah, but first we cut the power. I checked our night-vision goggles and they're working like charms. The intrusion alarms will go off as soon as the power gets cut, but it will take a good twenty minutes for the police to respond way out there."

"We'll be quick. The second floor, and particularly room 207, is what we want. Grenade launchers will make our work fast – no one will be walking around after we work it for five minutes. Then we'll go out the way we came in."

Roger nodded. "Yeah, should be a snap. Those yahoo guards they have won't even have the time to get their guns out of the vault. This will be like taking candy from a baby."

"Yep, and it will be a good payday for a few minutes work."

*****

Jeff sped into the parking lot of the hospital. He knew Olivia wasn't going to be too pleased to see him again, but he had no choice. There had been a detour on his way there due to an oil spill on the road. He looked at his watch – 7:00, and the man on the radio was just starting to call the first period of the hockey game. He didn't have much time.

He went up to the reception desk; to the same girl he'd talked to the night before. "Could I see Doctor Magnusson for a few minutes, please?"

She sighed. "Doctor Kavanaugh – you can't keep disturbing her at these late hours."

Jeff leaned over the counter. "Please, call her. It's important."

The girl sighed again, clearly exasperated with him. Then she picked up the phone.

"Okay, Doctor, she'll be right down." No offer this time of waiting in the comfort of the lounge, or a nice cup of coffee.

Jeff waited, and looked at his watch again: 7:15. He could hear the faint sound of an announcer on the radio. He walked back to the reception desk and the sound got louder. "Is that the Leafs' game you have on?"

The girl smiled. "Yes, it is – but don't tell anyone I'm listening to it. I'm trying to keep the volume as low as possible, but I love hockey and I really love the Leafs!" She was friendlier to him now – now that she was talking hockey.

"What's the score?"

She frowned. "It's one-all. But the Leafs will go ahead."

Jeff frowned too. "Yes, I'm sure they will."

Just then Olivia rounded the corner. She was frowning as well. In a brusque manner, she crooked her index finger motioning Jeff over to a corner of the lobby. "I've heard enough from you, Jeff. I'm not reacting to your vision. Correction – I'm not overreacting to your vision."

Jeff put his hand on her shoulder. "Just hear me out. Today, listening to the radio, I remembered another vision I had – it was last night while I was standing here in the lobby. I saw the Leafs versus Rangers hockey game. The score was one-all, then the Leafs scored and made it two-to-one. In the first period."

Olivia looked at him like he was a crazy man. "So what?"

Jeff swallowed. "The vision ended once the Leafs scored to make it two-to-one. I think that's when it's going to happen. Right at that moment. I just checked with your girl over there–right now the score is tied at one-all."

*****

Jamie was trying to drive, but also trying to listen to the hockey game. The score was tied now and he was getting excited. He knew the Leafs would go ahead any moment now.

Roger was getting anxious – twisting his trigger finger back and forth. Jamie glanced over at him. "Take it easy, Roger. Don't wear that finger out."

Roger laughed. "I'm just getting excited to use it again – been a long time."

"Yeah, I know what you mean. Won't be long now."

Jamie rubbed his eyes. He knew he shouldn't have drunk as much as he had last night. He was paying the price for it now. He looked to his right and could see the hospital now – it was only about 100 yards away as the crow flies, but the road would wind them around a bit until they reached the parking lot. So close he could taste it. But he had to be careful, concentrate. It was so dark already. There was a steep ravine to his right and forest to the left. He clicked on his high beams.

Suddenly Roger yelled, "Look out!"

Jamie saw it too late – the large animal crossed right in front of the big SUV. A damn deer! He swung the wheel to the right but caught the animal with his left front fender. His right wheels were on the gravelly shoulder now, and he swung the wheel again to get the stricken animal off the hood and windshield.

It was slow motion in Jamie's mind, as the SUV lost its edge. It tipped ever so slowly to the right...and then it went over. Over and over, down into the ravine. He couldn't count how many times it flipped, but he did have one count in his mind. There were two loaded grenade launchers in the trunk and he couldn't remember, if in his hung-over state this morning, whether or not he'd double-checked the safeties.

As they rolled to a stop at the bottom of the ravine, he heard the sports announcer yell, "He scores!" Then he heard something else – actually felt it more than heard it. A concussion, a horrible vibration that reverberated through his instantly punctured eardrums, right into his brain.

*****

Jeff glared at Olivia. "Humor me. Tell your guards to get their guns out of the vault. And hit the panic alarm. If I'm wrong, I'm wrong – nothing lost except my self-respect. But you might save some lives if you put this place on alert."

They both turned their heads as the reception girl screamed in delight. "They scored! It's two-to-one! Yay!"

Then they heard the explosion.

CHAPTER 25

"Did you read the headlines this morning?"

Jeff took a long sip of his extra strong brew. "Yes, I did."

A pause at the other end. A pregnant pause. Then she spoke, so softly that Jeff could barely hear her. "I don't know what to say, Jeff. I doubted you, and we came so close to a disaster…"

"Don't worry about it, Olivia. The entire drive home, and all day Sunday, I ran it over and over in my mind. If I were you, I don't know if I would have believed me either."

"Jeff, all I can say is a big 'thank you' for trying to get my attention. I'm just so lucky that there was an accident before the worst thing imaginable happened."

"You're welcome, and don't give it another thought. You're right, we got lucky."

Another pause. "Jeff, I know you sacrificed a lot telling me about yourself… and your secret. I want you to know that your secret is safe with me. And if I can do anything at all for you, and I mean anything at all, please do let me know. I owe you for trying so hard and risking so much to warn me."

Jeff sighed with relief. "That's comforting for me to hear – I don't want that 'thing' to get out about me and I appreciate your discretion. And no, you don't owe me anything."

"You're a good man, Doctor Jeff Kavanaugh."

Jeff hung up and walked down to Gaia's desk – her new desk outside of Brandon's office. That didn't stop him, however, from bending over and giving her a morning kiss. She smiled up at him. A smile that could melt a glacier. "See you tonight?"

Jeff smiled back. "For sure. Your place?"

She nodded, and once again flashed her million-dollar smile.

Jeff went back to his office and closed his door. All was right with the world. Well, not really, but at least he'd be seeing his sweetheart tonight.

He picked up the morning newspaper and read the front page story once again:

Freak Accident Thwarts Probable Terror Attack
The Lakeside Psychiatric Hospital, on the shores of Lake Ontario

approximately twenty kilometers from the City of Belleville, is probably sighing with relief today. A freak car accident seems to have prevented what might have been a horrific terror attack on the hospital.

Details are sketchy at this point, but there was an explosion very close to the hospital Saturday night at approximately 7:30 p.m. – an explosion that was heard from as far away as Kingston.

One of the occupants of the vehicle was found deceased on the slopes of the ravine that surrounds the hospital. Apparently he was thrown from the car as it rolled down the ravine after colliding with a deer. He has been identified as one Roger Tuttle, a former Special Forces officer with the Canadian military.

There was one other occupant of the vehicle, also deceased, but identification is pending DNA analysis. All we have been told is that he is male, but identification papers were destroyed in the resultant fire.

Investigators at the scene have disclosed that automatic weapons were found at the scene along with several hundred rounds of ammunition. In addition, the remnants of two grenade launchers were discovered. One of those launchers had been discharged in the accident, and it is suspected that the grenade blew into the vehicle's gas tank, causing the massive explosion.

Our investigations have determined that former soldier, Tuttle, was a patient for one year at the Lakeside Psychiatric Hospital back in 2010. The hospital will not disclose what he was being treated for due to confidentiality reasons. They did volunteer however that he had served in Afghanistan.

An unidentified source at the Ontario Provincial Police confided to this reporter that the initial conclusion of investigators was that the collision with the deer most likely prevented an attack on the hospital. It was apparent that the vehicle was heading in that direction, and in fact was only two minutes away when the accident happened. The amount of firepower contained in the vehicle caused the police to arrive at no other conclusion than that the hospital was in grave danger. The motive is not clear at this point.

More details to follow on this developing story.

Jeff put the paper down and took another sip of his coffee. It was small comfort to him that he'd been right. If it wasn't for that deer being in the right place at the right time, there's no way the hospital guards could have fended off these guys. The firepower would have been far too much. And if they were indeed military, they had the skill to pull off a slaughter.

And while Olivia's apology had been gracious, it was only 'after the fact.' It was only the aftermath of the explosion that caused her to realize that he was right. And this highlighted to Jeff that he would always have this problem – if he ever warned anyone about anything, he would get the same reaction. Disbelief, incredulity, anger, and eyes that told him that they thought he was crazy.

Despite all the evidence that pointed to psychic ability being a real phenomenon, and despite people pretending that they were liberal enough to believe in it, when it became personal they refused to believe it. That was far too close to home for most people. So, he was kidding himself thinking that he could ever make a difference with his gift. And, he would have no choice but to live with the consequences, live with seeing something terrible in advance. Then watching it unfold – knowing in his gut that just a few words from him if someone had just believed him, could have prevented it.

It was an unsettling feeling. A feeling of absolute impotence.

*****

Dinner was great. Gaia was a wonderful cook. In fact she was wonderful at everything, in Jeff's mind. They had a great relationship, one that he never wanted to come to an end. He loved her, he knew, but hadn't told her yet. He didn't know why.

They moved to the living room after dinner, and sipped their wine. She had avoided talking about her new job so far, and Jeff had avoided putting her on the spot. But tonight he decided to find out how it was going.

"So, tell me sweetie, how do you like working for the 'big guy?'"

Gaia lowered her eyes. "I don't know, it's only been a couple of days. I guess time will tell."

"Do you know what your duties are?"

She raised her eyes and laughed. "Apparently, whatever he tells me he wants done. The joke is, Jeff, I've always worked for Brandon anyway. In my old job I worked for him along with all the rest of you senior folks. He never had a personal executive assistant before. Why he needs one now, I don't really understand."

"Is he perhaps busier than usual?"

Gaia laughed even harder this time. "Not that I can see. I have virtually nothing to do–the days just drag. Again, it's only been a couple of days…but I don't see the point."

Jeff drained his glass of wine. "But he's the Senior Vice President – surely he's busy?"

"No, I think Brandon is one of the world's great delegators. His desk is the cleanest in the company and when I worked for all of you guys, he only took up about 20% of my time. So, the need for this new role is a bit confusing to me."

"Did he give you a raise?"

"Yes – another thirty grand a year."

Jeff whistled. "Did he give you a choice?"

"No – he said he wanted my decision before he would even tell me how much more I would get. He said that I was the right person for the new job and that I was overqualified for what I was doing. He told me that he doubted I would have a future if I stayed in my old job."

Jeff put his arm around her shoulders and squeezed gently. "How did that make you feel?"

"Terrible – unappreciated. I did a fantastic job in my old role, and he didn't seem to care at all about that. He made it clear to me – work for him, or work for nobody."

A kiss on her beautiful soft cheek. " Did you feel like telling him to stuff it?"

"I sure did. I was really angry. But I hid it – I have a big mortgage on this house here and I need the job. So, I decided to just accept and then consider my options."

"Are you thinking of looking around?"

"You bet I am! I've had such little to do in this new job that I had plenty of time to update my resume. It's ready to go and I'm going to start searching. I don't know what Brandon's motivation is, but I know one thing – he doesn't need an executive assistant; he never has from what I've seen. This will be a boring, dead-end job for me and I'm too young and ambitious to languish away in some ceremonial position."

Jeff laughed. "You go, girl!"

Gaia giggled, reached over and tickled him. He tickled her back, then leaned over and kissed her hard on the mouth. She responded, tongue swirling against his, ducking out once in a while to ring his lips. He pushed her fringe back and kissed her silky forehead–she sighed.

In mere seconds Gaia had his jeans unbuttoned and she slid down his stomach until her mouth found its mark. Jeff gasped – her mouth felt so good, and it occurred to him that he couldn't imagine wanting any other mouth doing what hers was doing to him.

His hand found its way under her skirt and pulled down her panties while she was otherwise occupied.

The couch was a tight squeeze but the tightness and closeness felt wonderful. He put his hands on her bare buttocks and pulled her up on top of him, sliding her gently until his tongue found the right spot.

The breath escaped from Gaia's lips as she raised her head in ecstasy. Jeff lifted himself upward until his penis was back in her mouth again. The swirling of her tongue resumed as if on automatic pilot and he could feel himself getting close to reaching the point of no return. But not yet – he had to wait until he knew she was there too.

She whispered his name, over and over again. He whispered hers back. Jeff could feel the sweat on his back causing him to stick to the leather sofa. Gaia shifted her pelvis up away from his tongue, then back down again hard. Up, down, over and over. Hard, pounding his face. Her wetness was intoxicating to him – the wetter she got, the harder it was for Jeff to control himself.

He suddenly stopped, swept her up in his arms and staggered with her over to the wall, pushing her bare bottom up against the teal sheen. When he entered her she started crying. Crying and whispering at the same time. "Jeff, don't ever let me go. Ever."

Jeff finally just said it, said it with all his heart in between frantic rhythmic breaths. "I love you, Gaia."

It felt right.

CHAPTER 26

Dan Nicholson had a feeling this phone call was important. He could just tell. Was it the sound of the ring? Or maybe just his anticipation about the weirdest case he had ever had to tackle?

He picked up the phone on the first ring.

"Inspector Nicholson here. How can I help you?"

"Hello Inspector. This is Lieutenant Joe Granetelli of the Toronto Police – Homicide."

He felt his pulse begin to race. "Hi, Joe. I think we met at a charity ball last year. What's up?"

"Yeah, we did meet then. Good memory. 'What's up' is a possible murder. And it ties in to that 'tag alert' you put out on the firm, Price, Spencer and Williams. I'm supposed to shove this over to you, if I understand the terms of the alert correctly."

Dan could hardly contain his excitement. "Yes, that's right. It's all mine from this point on. Have you done any prelims that I need to know about?"

"Well, the body was found in the trunk of the man's car, in the company's underground parking garage. He's been identified as a Raymond Filberg, one of the vice presidents of the firm. We dusted his body and pants for prints. He was shirtless. Came up empty on the body prints. But we did find prints on the trunk handle; one set that was not the victim's. However, they weren't in the database so we couldn't identify them."

"Cause of death?"

"Coroner says heart attack. Darndest thing though, he discovered that there were two broken ribs, which in his guess was as a result of possible CPR being applied."

"Couldn't those have happened as a result of a struggle?"

"I asked the same question. Apparently not. There was one rib broken on each side of the chest. And a clean snap for each – not a shatter as you'd find with a violent blow. He says it was comparatively gentle pressure that caused these ribs to break. He's seen breaks just like these before, with people who've had CPR done on them."

Dan furiously jotted down notes as he was talking. "Any other signs of a struggle?"

"Yes, the man's groin area was bruised as was the underside of his chin. Looks like he was kicked or kneed in the balls, then got clipped with a pretty good punch. As well, there was slight redness on his neck area around the Adam's Apple, symptomatic of choking. Sputum in his throat, as well as some on the cement."

"So, he got a good going-over, did he?"

"Yes, he did. Then the killer tried to save him with CPR. When that proved hopeless, he gave up and threw him in the trunk of his own car."

"Family advised?"

"Yes, his wife. No kids. And the people at Price know he's dead as well. In fact, they reported him missing – he hadn't been into work for several days, yet employees saw his car in the parking lot."

"Time of death?"

"Coroner estimates that it was last Thursday or early Friday. Rigor has come and gone. So, it's been a week since he was stuffed in that trunk. But we didn't really need the coroner to tell us that anyway."

Dan pulled the mouthpiece up tight against his lips. "Why is that, Lieutenant?"

Joe chuckled in a way that told Dan that the detective had been just toying with him, and had saved the best for last.

"We've got the whole damn thing on film."

*****

Jeff's stomach was in his throat. Ray's body had been found. He knew it was inevitable, but he'd tried to just put it out of his mind.

With his jaunt down to Belleville and the near disaster there, it had been easy to force the tragedy out of his mind during the last few days. Except in his dreams. But now it was back in full force.

The office was a somber place right now. Ray hadn't been a particularly well-liked executive but he was still a familiar face, and since the slaughter of just a few months ago, his was just one more familiar face that had been stolen from the company culture. And once again, in violent fashion.

Jeff wandered down to Gaia's cubicle and sat down beside her. He needed to see her smiling face; it would be almost like redemption for him if she smiled at him today.

He rubbed her back. She looked up at him through teary eyes. He whispered, "How are you feeling?"

She shook her head and dabbed at her eyes. "I feel sick. I think I'm going to just go home. I've known Ray a long time – feel so bad for his wife. She's such a sweetheart."

Jeff twirled his fingers through her hair. She sighed.

"Maybe you're right – maybe you should go home. Would you like some company?"

She rubbed his knee.

"No, I think I need to be alone. This just brings back memories of last July so vividly – I'm reliving it."

"Yeah, I know what you mean."

She looked up at him with a question in her eyes. "Why?"

"It's only natural that this would remind you of July, Gaia."

She shook her head. "No, I mean why would someone do this to Ray? They say it was a botched robbery, but why kill him? He wasn't one of my favorite people, for sure, but he didn't deserve to die like that.

"I was angry when he'd hired that Walker character to spy on us; in fact I despised him after that. But, it was a mistaken identity thing – he was just trying to spy on his wife and he thought you were having an affair with her."

Jeff nodded. He didn't know what to say.

"Jeff, I really hated Ray after that incident – it scared me to death. Now I hate myself for hating him. Whenever he tried to talk to me afterwards, I ignored him. He tried to apologize, and I just cut him off. Wouldn't let him off the hook. And I could tell he was hurt by it, and felt really bad about it. But I wanted to make him suffer a bit. Now he's dead."

Jeff leaned in and kissed her neck softly. He wanted so much to tell her that Ray was the one who'd hired Walker to sabotage her fiancé's plane five years ago. That Ray was the man who his aunt had seen in her vision – the man who had a sick fixation on her, endangering her life and Jeff's.

He wanted so much to tell her all that – but he knew that he couldn't. Not now, not yet. Just the shock of hearing that her fiancé's death wasn't an accident could push Gaia over the edge. He had to wait for a better time.

Gaia suddenly shut off her computer, rose from her chair and brushed past him.

"I have to go, Jeff. I just have to. Please, call me later though, okay?"

Then, she turned around and stared at him. Blew him a kiss, and mouthed, "I love you."

That was nice – but he never did get the smile he'd been looking for. The smile of redemption that apparently just wasn't hers to give to him today.

*****

"Are you ready to step up?"

Jeff 's throat went dry. What was he talking about? What did he know?

"I don't understand, Brandon."

"Are you ready to be a man and step up?"

All Jeff could do was shrug – and brace himself. Just after Gaia had left to go home, he'd been summoned by the 'big guy.' He was sitting in the man's cavernous office feeling very uneasy, feeling as if this was going to be an inquisition.

"We have a vice president vacancy now, and we need to fill it. You're the only one with enough talent to fit the bill. So – I'll repeat, are you ready to step up?"

Jeff breathed a sigh of relief and hoped that Brandon hadn't noticed. "Yes, you can count on me."

Brandon smiled for the first time since their meeting had started. "Good, it's effective immediately then. Your salary will jump an extra 200 thousand a year, and your bonus scheme will change dramatically."

Jeff choked. "Okay, thank you. I'm honored."

"No need to thank me. You've earned it – you're a very talented young man. You can move your stuff into Ray's office today. He won't be needing it any more." Brandon laughed at his macabre little joke.

Jeff felt acid rising up from his stomach, lodging in his throat. He coughed. The idea of moving into the office of the man he'd killed had an instantly sickening effect on him. "Can't I just keep my own office?"

"No, absolutely not. There's a certain prestige that goes with being a vice president, and clients have to see that. His office is much grander than yours."

"Okay."

"I'll also want to have a meeting with you in the next couple of days. Get settled in and then we'll spend some time together. Your duties and responsibilities will change of course. You won't be just placing executives in jobs anymore – you'll be much more involved in coaching and hypnosis techniques with high-level clients. I'll want to demonstrate some of those things to you. And, as I said, your bonus scheme will change. It will be potentially in the millions each year, depending on how you perform towards certain objectives."

Jeff's mouth froze in the open position.

"I can see you're shocked. Yes, Jeff, you will get very rich being with me, providing you leave some of your morals at home. There's no room in business for morals; it's a 'dog eat dog' world out there. Are you ready for the big time?"

Jeff didn't really know what the hell the man was talking about, but he nodded his agreement anyway. He'd reserve judgment until their meeting.

In the meantime, the compensation package that came with his new position of vice president was causing his mind to think ahead – think of all the things he'd wanted, the kind of life he and Gaia could possibly have together.

And his final thought before he left the man's office was how unsettling it was that Brandon Horcroft had gotten over the death of one of his top executives so quickly. Was this an example of the kind of morality that Brandon had been referring to? An absence of humanity, of compassion?

Then Jeff reminded himself that he had been the one who had killed Ray Filberg. Had he already given up his own grasp on morality? Was he being a hypocrite in judging Brandon? Was he really no better than him, no better than a man he had actually despised right from day one?

When Jeff got back to his office, his new assistant, Carla Matthews, was just writing out a message for him. "Oh, Jeff, there you are. I was just leaving this for you. An inspector from the RCMP wants you to call him back. A…Dan Nicholson… seems like a very nice man. Very friendly. Anyway, here you go." She handed him the note with the phone number written on it.

Jeff mumbled, "Thanks Carla."

"Oh, and congratulations on your promotion. I'm so excited for you!"

"You know about that already?"

She smiled affectionately at him. "Yes. Brandon told me first thing this morning."

"Oh."

Carla drifted her fingers down his shoulder, onto his arm. "I think you'll make one very charismatic vice president." Then she turned with a flourish and flew out of his office.

Jeff thought: *Arrogant asshole. Told my secretary before he even asked me.*

Then he sat down and stared at the note in his hand. Feeling sick to his stomach. *The RCMP. What's this about? What do they know?*

CHAPTER 27

Dan shuffled his papers, then re-filled his coffee cup from the thermos that Chrissy had brought him. Lovely coffee, rocket fuel...he would need it today.

His guest would be here any minute – the 'guest of honor,' Doctor Jeff Kavanaugh: psychologist; hero; executive...killer.

He could tell over the phone that Jeff had been nervous – but Dan didn't show his hand. He wanted the man calm and off guard.

When Jeff asked him why he wanted to have a meeting with him, Dan replied simply that it was a follow-up to the office slaughter that had taken place in July. He wanted to fill in a few blanks.

But Jeff was sharp – he enquired as to why the RCMP was involved in that now, since the Toronto Police were the ones who'd investigated it. It wasn't a federal matter. But Dan was sharp too – and quick on his feet. He explained to Jeff that the Toronto Police called in the RCMP on numerous cases, just to get their expertise on mass killings since the Mounties had had much more experience with crimes of that nature considering their close ties to the FBI. Jeff seemed to calm down; he seemed to buy Dan's bullshit.

But Jeff had still been a bit on the suspicious side. He stated correctly that the case was closed, that Jim Prentice had been declared unfit for trial and was now safely locked away. Dan agreed, but pointed out that even after cases are closed, there are 'learnings' that go on sometimes for many years afterwards. They needed Jeff to help them with some of the 'learnings.' After that explanation, Dan was convinced Jeff was sold, and he seemed more than eager to come down to the detachment office on Dufferin Avenue.

Dan excitedly rubbed the palms of his hands together. The death of Ray Filberg, although tragic, opened up a valuable door into the secretive firm of Price, Spencer and Williams. And it led right to their newest vice president, Doctor Jeff Kavanaugh. Dan believed in taking advantage of opportunities when they presented themselves, and this time he had been presented with a pretty damn good one.

*****

Jeff parked his car in the underground parking garage of the RCMP office. He thought back to how odd it was being in his own office's underground garage this morning. Seeing the spot where Ray's car had been parked, now an empty lonely space that glared at him in anger.

Seeing that abandoned spot brought back the memory of having the knot of Ray's tie in his fist, shoving it tight against his throat, chokingly tight. His mind recalled the look on Ray's face, the bulge of his eyes, the desperate futile attempts to convince Jeff that he had had nothing to do with the death of Gaia's fiancé, that the spying on Jeff and Gaia was merely to check on whether or not his own wife was slutting around on him. What a ridiculous assertion, Jeff thought. Even if he thought that Jeff was the one fooling around with his wife, there would have been no need to take photos of he and Gaia together. That would have proved nothing to Ray, except that maybe Jeff had a thing for more than one woman.

No, the man was a menace and a killer. A killer with a dangerous obsession with Jeff's girlfriend. And he probably would have killed again just to have Gaia all to himself. He was probably the ultimate stalker – a man with the connections and the money to get what he wanted. And to kill for what he wanted.

Jeff knew he had to keep telling himself these things. Just to avoid the guilt he was feeling, and the nagging feeling that he'd made a mistake. He didn't know why he was feeling that but as the days had worn on, that thought had been creeping into his mind more and more often. And it made him feel very uneasy. Would he ever know for sure? Where were his psychic skills? Why didn't they come to him at times like this?

And he wondered, why had he never had an uneasy feeling about Ray? Why had he not seen halos and eyes like black lumps of coal? He had never really liked Ray, but he also never had those feelings about him either – those special feelings. The kind of feeling that he had when he was looking at Brandon and got that horrible vision about the Lakeside Psychiatric Hospital. He still hadn't reconciled that in his mind – he'd been puzzling about it for days. Why had Brandon triggered that? And he knew that his vision had clearly showed Jim Prentice as the target. His aunt had told him that there must be some connection between Brandon and the vision. Had Brandon hired those ex-military men to storm the hospital? To kill Prentice?

Jeff shook his head. He knew he was thinking too much, and was quite certain that it was causing him to become irrational. Too much thinking did that to a person— as a psychologist, he knew that only too well. He had to calm down and try to put some of these things out of his mind. Accept what had happened, what he had done – and just move on.

Yes, the right man was dead. Ray Filberg had been a killer, and a stalker. Jeff's original instincts had been right. He had to keep telling himself that—over and over.

He took the elevator up to the fourth floor, and walked up to a cute girl at the reception desk.

"Hi. I'm Jeff Kavanaugh – I have an appointment at 4:00 to see Inspector Nicholson."

The girl squinted at her computer screen. "Ah, yes, Doctor Kavanaugh. I'll let the Inspector know that you're here." She pushed a button on her console. "Can I get you a coffee?"

Jeff smiled. "No thanks." He took a seat in the waiting area, crossed his legs, and waited. And he thought some more. This time about how amazing it was that they were still studying the slaughter at Price several months later, even after the killer had been locked away. And it was the RCMP now, not just the Toronto Police. Jeff was still surprised about that. Well, he'd help in any way he could. He couldn't avoid it – whether he liked it or not, he was a big part of that horrible story.

A young lady was walking his way from down the corridor, one who was even prettier than the receptionist. She came up to him and held out her hand. "Hello, Doctor Kavanaugh. I'm Chrissy, Dan's secretary. Welcome to the RCMP."

Jeff stood and shook her hand. "Well, thank you. I can't say it's great to be here, but thanks anyway for the welcome."

Chrissy laughed. "I guess that's an honest reaction! Come with me, I'll walk you down to Dan's office."

Jeff walked beside her down the long corridor, past an area that opened up to what looked like a clerical zone with dozens of small cubicles. Then they turned a corner and passed by one private office after another until they reached the end of the hall. Chrissy put her hand on the door handle to a corner office while knocking with the other. Not waiting for an answer from inside, she opened the door and ushered Jeff through with a slight wave of her hand. "This is Doctor Kavanaugh, Dan."

A tall blonde man with piercing blue eyes stood up from behind a massive executive desk, and walked around to shake Jeff's hand. "Thanks Chrissy. Close the door behind you, please."

Jeff shook his hand and was instantly taken by the broad genuine smile on the handsome man's face. He felt instantly at ease. And the man's grip was strong – Jeff liked strong handshakes. It said a lot about a man, his confidence, his sincerity.

"Very nice to meet you, Doctor. Do you prefer I address you as 'Doctor' or is 'Jeff' okay?"

"I'd prefer you just call me 'Jeff.'"

"Alrighty, then – and you call me 'Dan.' Okay?"

Dan directed Jeff over to a comfortable living room area that had a couch, two leather chairs, and a coffee table, which already had a thermos and two mugs sitting on it. "Coffee, Jeff?"

"Yes, thanks." Jeff glanced around. He was impressed by the size and opulence of the Inspector's office. Quite a step up from other police headquarters he'd been in. The RCMP certainly was in a class of its own. He noticed also the nice framed portrait on the man's credenza – a beautiful dark-haired woman along with two young children, both of them blonde.

Jeff pointed towards the photo. "Is that your family?"

Dan smiled his big smile once again. "Yes, it is."

"Lovely."

"Thank you, I agree! Any family for you, Jeff?"

Jeff grinned. "I suspect you already know the answer to that question. But, no… no family yet. Hopefully not too far off."

Dan laughed. "Yes, I did know the answer already. But you neglected to mention your aunt. I'm sure that former Deputy Chief Louise Hanson of the Toronto Police Service would be very hurt indeed to hear you say that you have 'no family.'"

Jeff tapped his chin in a mock slap. "Can't believe I forgot that. Of course you would know my aunt. Even though you're RCMP, it's still quite a tight fraternal society, isn't it?"

Dan nodded. "It sure is, especially at us senior levels. We met on all sorts of issues that we had in common, and of course your aunt's specialty was homicide, so she was front and center."

"She was. Funny though, she's been retired so long now I tend not to think of her as a former police officer. She's just, well, my aunt!"

"Understandable. I didn't know her well, but the few times that we had the opportunity to chat, I was swept away by her. She's an impressive woman. And you know, I always got the feeling that she could look right through me, right into my soul. She just had that special something about her, all knowing. Not in a condescending way, but in a sincere interested way. She always seemed interested in what anyone else had to say…even if it was rubbish!"

Jeff laughed. "Yep. Sounds like my aunt!"

They exchanged a few more pleasantries together and Jeff felt more and more comfortable the longer he talked with Dan. It was comforting also to know that he knew his aunt. That gave them a connection.

Finally Dan got down to business. "Jeff, tell me your recollections from last July. Give it to me straight from the heart. What you felt, what you heard, what you saw, what you did. I know you've been through this probably a million times and I've read the entire case file, but I want to hear it for myself. It's not often we get to meet real life heroes, so I'd like to hear you talk about it."

Jeff told the story once again, even though it made him cringe. He didn't volunteer the psychic vision parts though – those parts he intended to still keep to himself.

Dan listened to him intently, nodding, taking occasional notes. But he let Jeff keep talking without interruption.

Once Jeff was finished, Dan spoke. "I understand you went down to Belleville to visit Jim Prentice at the request of the man's lawyer. What was that all about?"

"Yeah, I had a meeting with him. He just wanted some closure, I think. He seemed so normal when I saw him again though – it was a real disconnect from the madman I saw that day in July."

"Did you have a breakthrough with him?"

"No, not really. But there was one thing that was odd. He did tell me that he thought he'd been hypnotized. Now, we do an awful lot of hypnotherapy at my company, dealing with stress, panic attacks, etc. We use it to make good executives better. It's a recognized technique that has had excellent results – nothing unusual about hypnosis per se. But what was strange was that Jim thought that he himself had been hypnotized. I don't know if it was a cop-out, or what. But he did seem to believe that."

Dan jotted down some more notes, then looked up. "Did he say what he was thinking before or during his rampage?"

Jeff thought for a second. "Yes, he did say something kind of weird. He said that there had been a phrase running around in his head, and he couldn't remember the exact phrase. But he said it was something like 'go forth.'"

Dan sat forward in his chair. Jeff could tell he had caught his interest. Dan opened his mouth to ask a question, and then seemed to change his mind. He leafed through some papers in his binder and pulled out the one he'd been looking for.

"Jeff, I see that you were back at the Lakeside Psychiatric Hospital last weekend– twice as a matter of fact. On the Friday evening, and then again Saturday evening. In fact, you were there right at the exact moment that vehicle exploded near the hospital. The one that contained former military officers and heavy weapons. I see that they've just identified the second guy from his DNA. So, two mercenaries were in that car. Here's my puzzle – you were at a slaughter several months ago, and almost witnessed another one last weekend. What are the odds? And both of those incidents involved the presence of Jim Prentice. Very strange, don't you agree?"

Jeff gulped. "Well, I guess wrong place, wrong time. Happens sometimes."

Dan grimaced. "I don't believe in that happenstance stuff, Jeff. What were you doing there?"

"Just following up on the treatment of Jim Prentice."

"Why would you care about that?"

Jeff was speechless. He knew the answer he'd just given was about as dumb an answer as he could possibly have made up.

Dan continued. "The visitor records show that both visits you made there last weekend were with the administrator, Doctor Olivia Magnusson. Why would you see her about Jim Prentice? Does she have personal involvement with Jim's case?"

Jeff took a sip of his coffee. His throat was not working properly, and neither was his tongue. He didn't want to admit to Dan that he was psychic, and that that was the reason he'd been there. But he was reaching the point in this interview where he knew that, for his own defense, he might not be able to keep it secret much longer. This guy was good, very good.

Suddenly Dan stood up and walked over to his desk. Opened the top drawer, pulled out a pair of handcuffs, and threw them over to the couch. Jeff reached out and caught them in his right hand.

"Good catch, Jeff. Would you like to try them on?"

Jeff looked up at him, puzzled. "Excuse me?"

"Go ahead, try them on for size."

Jeff stood up. "Why on earth would I want to do that?"

Dan walked over to him, took the cuffs out of his hand, and spun him around – pinning Jeff's hands behind his back. Before Jeff could react he heard the snap of the cuffs around his wrists.

"Because you're under arrest for manslaughter."

CHAPTER 28

Gaia Templeton walked up the steps to the front porch of her cute little Leaside bungalow. She loved this neighborhood – one of the finest in all of Toronto. She grew up here, played here, loved here, and now lived here all by her lonesome.

She played around with the petunias in the flowerpot, dead-heading a few slumping petals, and straightening out some stems that had been flattened from the last rainstorm. While it was late Fall, the weather felt like Spring. Everything was still blooming.

Once inside, she strolled down to her little kitchen and poured herself a glass of juice. Her pet parrot, a little redheaded conure, perked his head up as she approached and started banging his beak against the bars. He wanted out. She opened the cage door and held her wrist up against the opening. He gently hopped on and chattered his approval. 'Bingo' was his name, and he knew it too. He loved to repeat it over and over again.

Conures weren't known necessarily for being the most prolific talkers in the parrot family, but this little gem was in a class of his own. He picked up words very easily, sometimes after he'd heard them just once. Gaia herself was surprised, because she had been warned by her veterinarian that these little guys were stubborn talkers, that she could repeat words until she was blue in the face and it still wouldn't make a difference.

Gaia just took that as a challenge – so she did indeed repeat words until she was blue in the face, until one magical day when he'd said his own name as clear as day. She was shocked, so shocked she'd almost dropped him. After that, he seemed to pick up everything. That first word was the toughest for him, and she figured that he must have been so proud of himself that he concentrated extra hard after that. Of course, Bingo always got her praise when he did learn new words, and he also got the occasional treat as well.

She loved her little pet. He was great company, and a very affectionate bird. And there was a certain thrill having him behave so affectionately and tame with her, when she knew that these birds possessed no less than 2,000 pounds of pressure per square inch in their powerful beaks. If he wanted to, he could bite right through her finger with ease. But he was always so gentle with her, and greeted her the same way every day when she came home. He would squawk loudly and bang his beak against the bars – then climb gently out of the cage onto her arm. He'd usually have a sip of whatever it was she was drinking, and even steal a morsel of whatever snack she was having. He always made her laugh.

She walked with him over to the buffet cabinet and gazed at the framed photos. Her mother and father who were now retired and lived up in Bobcaygeon, her two sisters and their large families…and of course, Matt.

Gaia marveled at how much she resembled her mother – dark hair, black eyes, and cute pixie face. While she loved her dad dearly, she was relieved that she hadn't taken after him – a large man – really, fat was more like it. He'd always been on the fat side, but was blessed with cheery chubby cheeks and sparkling eyes. Her two sisters had taken somewhat after their dad. Gaia was the exception, and she knew that her mother was thrilled that one of them had taken after her. And she also knew that her sisters were envious and a bit resentful.

She looked back at Matt's photo. This one had been taken just a few weeks before his death, and it was her favorite. He'd been a handsome man, charismatic as hell, and always hell bent on excitement. And a risk-taker. He'd filled her with so much joy over the years, and she'd been in love with him for what seemed like forever. They met when she was only sixteen, and Matt a cool eighteen – those romantic carefree high school years. They dated that year, and then Matt went off to the University of Western Ontario to study physical education. She joined him two years later and enrolled in a business degree program. They lived together near the campus and enjoyed university life together. The fun years.

Matt graduated first and landed a job at a local gym, putting in time until Gaia got her degree. Then when that happened, he suggested they just tour Europe for a couple of years, work here and there along the way. When they'd sowed their adventure oats they could come back and settle down for good, get married, raise a brood of kids and get the picket fence lifestyle.

So they did. They both landed great high-paying jobs, and then Matt managed to buy in to a gym, using his degree to design fitness programs and also tend to the business aspects of it all. Eventually he bought out his partners and he owned the lucrative place all by himself. He was thrilled – was talking about plans to expand, open some franchises, the whole nine yards.

Then he died. Gaia still had the picket fence…and now a parrot. And loads of debt.

She gazed lovingly at Matt's photo and mouthed the word, "Why?"

Yes, Matt had been a risk-taker all right – a reckless one. A quality she'd never seen in all the years she'd known him. But that reckless side of him came home to roost, in fact it was roosting on his broken wrist one day when he came from work. They were living together in this very house in Leaside, with only a tiny mortgage. Plans to get married, and have that brood of kids. But it wasn't to be.

She remembered back to that day. His wrist was in a cast; he sat her down at the kitchen table and told her what happened. What a pickle he was in.

As far as she knew, he'd arranged financing for the gym from a blue chip bank. But no, the money had come from a guy who's name sounded like the actor, 'Pacino.' Lots of money, no questions asked. An easy loan application. But the gym revenues couldn't keep up with the 30% interest. A 400,000 loan quickly turned into 500,000. So Matt's next reckless solution was gambling – he figured he could win a few hands and pay the loan off in no time. But typical of most dreamers who head to Vegas, that plan didn't turn out. All he did was empty their savings account.

So, finally he got a reminder that he was three months in arrears – that reminder was in the form of a broken wrist, from a guy who's name sounded like 'Martino,' an associate of Pacino. The wrist was just the beginning. More limbs would become useless if he missed another payment.

Enter Gaia.

She went with him to meet Pacino. He explained the facts of life to her, and it became apparent that the only way she could save Matt's life was to co-sign the note with him. His cash flow at the gym couldn't handle it alone, but with her salary thrown in as well, they could do it. That, and mortgaging their expensive little house to the hilt.

Gaia's life turned upside down that day – she lost her trust in Matt and met the scariest man she'd ever met in her life; a man whose name sounded like 'Pacino.' She knew that once she'd signed onto the note her wrist could be next...or worse. Matt knew that too, and it broke his heart. He was a good guy deep down inside, she knew that. But he just wanted too much too fast and had more confidence than was realistic. In fact, his confidence and view of the world was totally irrational.

On top of it all, they still owed a large loan on the airplane. The airplane. The thing that finally took Matt's life.

Gaia sighed and picked her mail up off the floor – Bingo reached down from his perch on her shoulder and tore the edge of the envelope to get it started. She laughed. How many people were lucky enough to have a bird open their mail for them? She never had to worry about paper-cuts with Bingo around.

There was only one piece of mail – a warning from her bank that she was two months in arrears on her mortgage payments. She started to cry. She still owed

Pacino the remainder of Matt's adventure – but it had gone down dramatically over the last five years since Matt's death. Gaia had made sure of that. Her salary was large and now she'd just received another big raise. The loan owing to Pacino was around 100,000 now, so she could see an end to this nightmare in just a few years. But her mortgage had risen to a whopping 400,000 and she was determined that she was not going to sell her little house. She wasn't going to give up what she and Matt had bought together. This was her home. So, once in a while, when cash became tight, she would skip a payment on the mortgage – the bank didn't like it, but Gaia knew that they at least wouldn't come and break her wrist. She never missed a payment to Pacino – she couldn't risk that.

She sighed again as she read the bank's warning. Then she said to herself, "I have to pay this up, no choice." Bingo, squawked and repeated, "No choice, no choice." Gaia wiped the tears away from her eyes, and affectionately stroked Bingo's back.

Gaia had never told Jeff any of this history. At this point, she didn't want him to know, didn't want to risk scaring him away. She had fallen for him big time, something she never thought she'd do again. He was the most special person in her life and she didn't want to lose him. She would tell him one day; one day when Pacino was out of her life for good.

Jeff was just as puzzled as she was about what her new role at Price was. Working only for Brandon was causing Gaia sleepless nights. For years he'd been trying to get her to go out for drinks or dinners with him – she had always rebuffed him. She hated the way he leered at her, the way he found reasons to lurk around her. And she really hated the look on his face whenever he saw Jeff and her talking together. It was like an anger, a seething anger.

But she needed the money. For now she'd suck it up, put up with the egotistical old pervert and do her job. But she was confident she could leverage her new role and new salary into an even better job.

The tough part was finding the time to hunt. Her days were full. She saw Jeff three nights a week…and…of course…she had her other job the other four nights.

Gaia walked solemnly over to her phone, and reluctantly punched the button to hear her messages. There were three from her second employer, and one from Jeff. She smiled when she listened to Jeff's message, but the smile quickly evaporated when she listened to the other three. She played them again, and jotted down the instructions onto a pad of paper.

Then she put Bingo back in his cage, and walked forlornly down to her bedroom. Gaia opened the drawer that held her special underwear, her work underwear. She stripped, hopped into the shower and slipped into a choice selection of that underwear. Then a sleeveless halter-top and a tight skirt.

Took a good look in the mirror – she knew she looked good. Not that she really cared about looking good for these guys. But she knew the better she looked the more she was paid, and she had to avoid having her wrists broken…or worse. Just for a while longer, then she'd be free. Free of Pacino and free of Moonlight Ladies.

When men visited the Moonlight Ladies website, the song playing as they browsed was that very song by Julio Iglesias: 'Moonlight Lady.' She wondered sardonically if he got royalties every time the site was visited.

She turned sideways in front of the mirror – yes, she was still a striking lady, and that was the only reason she commanded such a high price. She admired the beautiful tattoo that she had on the underside of her right forearm, a tattoo of Bingo himself. Beautiful shade of green with a red splotch on his head. If only Bingo knew how famous he was by now!

Gaia pulled on her high heels, and walked out to the living room to get her purse and keys…and of course the piece of paper with the three appointments notated in her perfect handwriting.

Her first date of the night was at the Airport Hilton. She couldn't be late. They tended to get real anxious…and kinda rough…if she was late.

CHAPTER 29

Jeff could feel his entire body shudder – like when you fall asleep in front of the TV and the nerves of your body just suddenly shake you awake for no apparent reason.

But this time, at this moment, there was an apparent reason.

He knew he mumbled something, some kind of pathetic protest, but Dan didn't pay any attention to it. The Inspector's demeanor had changed completely – he was no longer the friendly Mountie chatting with him about his aunt. Now he was all 'police.'

Within seconds Jeff was being marched out of Dan's office and down the hallway, into what looked just like one of the interrogation rooms on the TV show, CSI. Dan nudged him over to a wooden chair at the end of the table and Jeff noticed he was facing directly towards a large TV screen mounted on the wall. Dan sat adjacent to him at the bare wooden table. There was no friendly thermos of coffee at this table.

The next thing Dan did was read Jeff his Miranda rights. He did it off by heart – didn't need a little prompt card that the detectives on crime shows always seemed to need.

Then he spoke the official words. "You're charged with manslaughter, in the death of Ray Filberg."

Jeff nodded. He wasn't surprised – it was almost like he expected it would happen, and in a strange way it was a relief that it finally did. A weight was lifted from his chest, only to be replaced by a different kind of weight. He was no longer in fear of being caught; now he was in fear for his life. His life as he knew it. He knew that from this moment onward, nothing would be the same again.

"Anything to say, Jeff?"

Jeff swallowed. "Only one thing – on what evidence are you arresting me for this? I think I'm entitled to know, aren't I? If you don't want to tell me, I'll get my lawyer to ask you."

Dan smiled. "I have no problem telling you – no, showing you is more like it – and if you want your lawyer to see it after you, that's okay with me."

Dan reached across the table and picked up a small TV remote control. He switched the wall TV on. He hit another button and the lights in the room dimmed.

Then one final button, which brought a video image onto the screen. He sat back and crossed his legs.

Jeff watched intently as the video began to play. He saw himself leaning against his Corvette, the license plate of his car clearly visible. Then walking over to Ray when he came into the picture. The choking with the tie was next, followed by the loosening of the tie, some talking, then choking with the tie again. Next came the knee to the groin, the uppercut to the chin, then Jeff dropping on top of the prone Ray Filberg choking him one last time. It wasn't pretty.

It was like a bad dream – in fact Jeff had had dreams just like this ever since it happened, but the worst dream of all was the banging of fists against the inside of a car trunk.

He watched himself get up and start walking back to his car, then suddenly turning around and dashing back to Ray. Ripping off the man's tie and shirt, performing CPR.

He didn't know why he didn't just tell Dan to stop the film; he knew what was coming next. Perhaps his guilt was causing him to voluntarily suffer through this?

Jeff watched himself pocket Ray's wallet and begin rubbing his chest with the man's own shirt. On film it looked to Jeff like some kind of twisted religious burial procedure. Then he popped Ray's trunk, hoisted the body up over his shoulder and dumped him inside. Well, on film, it looked like he 'dumped' him – but Jeff knew he'd been gentler than that.

Dan pushed 'stop' on the remote, but left the lights in the room dimmed. He shrugged his shoulders, and glared at Jeff. "Not much more to say, is there?"

Jeff knew enough to say very little, or nothing at all. "No, not really."

"You probably didn't think there were any security cameras, did you? They were installed inside the ventilation ducts. Too many of these cameras are getting damaged these days, so they like to install them behind the vents now. Smart, eh?"

Jeff nodded. He could feel his stomach churning on him. His hands were starting to feel numb and his shoulders were stiff – having the handcuffs on behind his back was awkward while sitting in a chair. He just wanted to go home, go to Gaia. He could feel panic start to take over and he heard a little voice telling him that he probably would never see his house or Gaia again.

Without thinking, Jeff stood up from his chair just to give his shoulders and arms a break from the stiff position he was sitting in. Dan was up like a shot, shoving him right back down again. "You don't move unless I tell you to, understand?"

Jeff nodded. It was hard getting used to the idea of being a prisoner, not able to move or stretch if he wanted to, or go to the bathroom without asking permission.

This whole situation just seemed so surreal. " I forgot – just needed to stretch. Could you take these cuffs off? I'm hardly a danger to you."

"That's not what the film says, Jeff. On there, you don't look like someone I'd want living on my street."

Jeff had to agree. He could hear a million thoughts going through his head. Which lawyer should I call? Should I disclose to Dan about the psychic visions I had – that Ray probably killed Gaia's fiancé and had been spying on them? Would any of that make a difference?

He decided that he would just shut up. "I need to call a lawyer."

*****

Olivia Magnusson was sitting in her office. Thinking. And waiting. Waiting until it was lights out in the common areas and the guards had gone to their nighttime stations. The patients' rooms at that point went into lock-down and the corridors were empty.

She thought back over the incident last weekend and it frightened her to her core. They had come so close to a massacre, one that could have killed her and many of her loyal employees. As well as the patients on the second floor – but she didn't care about them as much. Almost all of them were sick beyond repair. And the sickest of all, the only mass murderer she had in her institution, Jim Prentice, was bait. Bait that could endanger everyone.

She thought back to her conversations with Jeff Kavanaugh, how she'd refused to believe him. How that stubbornness had almost cost her her own life. Those two commandos had been on a mission, and they were armed to the teeth. Someone had hired them to attack her facility. They had failed due to a fluke accident but more could come and most likely would. Someone wanted Jim Prentice dead. And next time she may not get a warning from one Jeff Kavanaugh. Olivia felt the most vulnerable she had ever felt in her life. And that was a feeling she wasn't accustomed to at all.

And one thing she remembered above all else – Jeff had said that in his vision Jim Prentice had seemed to be the target – that his image was larger than the others. And he was front and centre.

Someone had tried to kill Jim Prentice and had been willing to take the lives of many more just to cover up that murder – make it look like a slaughter by a couple of insane disgruntled former patients who just happened to be trained military killers.

Olivia shuddered and wrapped her arms across her chest, squeezing tightly, squeezing away the fear.

In all the private sessions she had had with Jim Prentice, one thing that stood out was that he was determined to kill himself. If he had the chance he would do it. He told that to everyone who would listen; every doctor, every nurse, every patient. But, the institution was very careful – nothing that could possibly be used as a weapon was ever in close proximity to a patient. Olivia felt some pity for the poor man. He was clearly remorseful and knew his life was worthless now. He didn't remember doing what he had done, but knew deep down inside that he had.

Olivia's job was to take care of these poor souls, try to rehabilitate them, even though most of them would never see the light of day again. Part of her brain was constantly saying to her, "Why bother? What's the point?"

The other part of her brain was saying, "They're God's creatures."

She stood. It was lights-out time. Lock-down time. She whispered, "Sorry, God." Then she made the sign of the cross.

She went over to her desk, opened the drawer and took out her surgical gloves. Then she took out a magnetic keycard – not the one she usually used, not the one that could be traced back to her. No, this was a special one that was scanned long ago as a 'master,' and couldn't be traced to anyone. No one even knew it existed. When the digital records were checked, the entries from this card would simply show as 'error.' After she was finished tonight, it would be destroyed. Olivia strode into her bathroom and took a thin package out of her medicine cabinet, and slipped it into her pocket.

Then she walked quickly down the dim corridor and used the master keycard to enter the secure section of the hallway – the hallway that led to the rooms. She used the stairs to reach the second floor, and swiped the card one more time to get out of the stairwell. She peeked around the doorway – all clear.

Room 207 was just a few feet from the stairwell. She withdrew the thin package from her pocket and slipped it under the door, giving it a good shove with her index finger almost as if the little package was a Crokinole disk. Then she rapped on the door with her knuckles three times.

As she disappeared down the stairwell, she made the sign of the cross again. "Forgive me."

But deep in her heart, Olivia knew that the remorseful monster, Jim Prentice, would simply see the razor blades as being a gift from God himself. That the Savior had come to him in the middle of the night and granted his wish – and had actually knocked on his door for God's sake.

And she consoled herself in knowing that very soon now Jim Prentice would finally be able to beg forgiveness. And thankfully it was for something far worse than what Olivia had just done.

*****

"Of course you can call a lawyer – that's your right." Dan pointed to a credenza. "The phone's right over there."

Jeff grimaced. "I can't exactly make a phone call while these cuffs are on."

"No, I guess you can't. I think I'll just make you wait a few more minutes, then."

Jeff looked up at him, noticing that he was pulling another remote gadget out of his pocket. "What did you say? And what's that thing?"

Dan pushed a button and a steel cover slid down over the one-way glass on the far wall. At the same time, Jeff could hear the door lock click and a strange humming sound starting from somewhere – background noise, slightly irritating.

"We're totally in private now, Jeff. No one can see in, no one can enter, and the scrambler ensures that nothing can be recorded."

Jeff didn't know what to say. He just stared at Dan, mouth open.

"Rest assured, I don't want you to say anything to incriminate yourself. I want you to just listen to me. I'll do all the talking. When I'm finished, if you want nothing to do with what I have to offer you, you can talk to your lawyer. But, and this is important, if you choose to do that, this conversation we're going to have didn't take place. I'll deny that I ever talked to you about this."

Dan then got up and walked behind Jeff's chair, slid out a key and removed the handcuffs. "Give yourself a stretch."

Jeff didn't need to be asked twice. He quickly got up and rolled his arms around, stretched his shoulders by lifting his arms up over his head, then rubbed his sore wrists.

He sat down again. "I don't have a clue where you're coming from, but go ahead, I'm listening."

Dan leaned forward with his elbows on the table. "Okay, here's the score. We have you dead to center. Indefensible. Manslaughter. Which carries a life sentence, but if you're a good boy you'll be out in ten or fifteen years. But here's the problem I have with that – you had some reason to threaten Ray Filberg, some grudge. I think it might have something to do with that little spying episode I learned about, where an ex-Ranger named Herbert Walker was killed by a car in front of your girlfriend's house. I know that Ray hired him. I'm sure you'll tell me more about that if you agree to talk with me.

"The problem I have is, people like you don't go around killing people. You're more likely to go around saving them like you did last July. So, something happened, and maybe this Ray guy is scum – I have a witness who has already come forward telling me something very disturbing about Ray Filberg and one other person at your company. So, you see, I'm already jaded somewhat in your favor."

"Okay, but what about..."

Dan cut him off, raising his hand in the stop sign. "No, don't say a thing yet. Hear me out. Okay?"

Jeff nodded reluctantly, finding it hard to control his brain, which was working on overdrive right now.

"Don't get me wrong – what you did was horrible. You used violence, which brought about the heart attack. But...you tried to save him. I felt kinda proud of you when I saw that part of the film – until I watched you hoist him up and dump him in the trunk of his car. He could have still been alive – you're not a medical doctor, you couldn't have known for sure. What if he came around and couldn't get out – died hours or days later. You abandoned him."

Jeff looked down at the table. What Dan had just said reminded him of the dreams he'd been having. Obviously that was a fear of his, that the man could have still been alive.

"But...I'm not into phony scare tactics. So, to put your mind at ease, we do have a report from the coroner that confirms that he had actually died around the time you were performing CPR on him. And he noticed two broken ribs, confirming that you tried real hard."

Jeff let out a long breath. "Thanks for telling me that."

"You're welcome...but I told you to shut up. Do that for me, will you?"

Jeff nodded once again. He was doing a lot of nodding in the last few minutes. This was a situation that he had no control over; a totally submissive situation and it unnerved him.

"You should know that the tape you saw has not been seen by anyone else – and I'm in the power position to keep it that way. Ray's death can just be confirmed as a robbery gone wrong. I will be in possession of the only copy of this tape – in essence I'll be blackmailing you."

Jeff frowned at him and was going to say something but thought better of it.

"I can make this charge go away and lower it to something far less damaging. At the right time further down the road you can come forward and confess, after which I will guarantee that you will be charged with the lesser offense of 'Criminal Negligence Causing Death.' I could also throw in 'Committing an Indignity to a Body,' and 'Obstruction of Justice.' I'll reserve judgment on those depending on how well we work together.

"The lesser charge of Criminal Negligence will carry a much lower sentence – you will do time, but most likely no more than two or three years due to the extenuating circumstances and that you did indeed try to save him. So, you're not getting off 'scot-free' here. But it sure beats a manslaughter conviction."

Jeff rubbed his hands together and almost opened his mouth – thought better of it and just pointed to the water jug on the credenza.

Dan chuckled. "Well, why didn't you just say so?"

He got up and poured both of them glasses of water.

"Now you can talk, Jeff."

Jeff guzzled his water, and then stared into the eyes of his captor.

"Obviously I'm intrigued…and relieved. But…what the hell do I have to do for this deal?"

Dan smiled in a confident knowing way, a way that said, 'I have you by the nuts.'

"I've got far bigger fish to fry than you. I have reason to believe that Price, Spencer and Williams is a front for something insidious—no, that's not even the right word for it. There probably is no word to describe how twisted it is. If I think of one, I'll let you know. But for now, and for the deal I've just offered you, I want you to be my 'inside man.'"

CHAPTER 30

Brandon wandered through the office – aimlessly in fact – but tried to make it look like he had a purpose about him. Glancing into offices, using his intimidating stare to remind people that he was in charge and watching them. He liked to do this once in a while. He believed in the old leadership tactic, 'Management by Wandering Around.' He didn't care about patting people on their backs, trying to make them feel good. These weren't kids, they were adults. They could pat their own backs, and he paid them good money to be fully motivated. That was another thing he believed in – motivation. But his tactic was 'motivation by humiliation.' It worked, as far as he was concerned.

As he got closer to Gaia's desk he pulled out his cell phone. He pretended he was reading the screen, but aimed it in her direction and took a photo. This was probably the fourth photo of her he'd taken today, and the twelfth in as many days. She looked particularly delicious today and he wanted to capture that. Dressed all in black, accented by a red scarf around her neck. She wore a ruby red necklace and her seductive mouth was adorned with a sexy nude shade of lipstick. He just wanted to kiss those luscious lips and keep kissing them for as long as she'd let him.

But she wouldn't let him – that was the problem. At least up until now. He knew she would need some convincing and he was now in the perfect position to do that. He had her now – she was his. She worked only for him, and he could invent plenty of excuses to get her out to dinner with him that would sound 'business-like.' She wouldn't refuse him now. Couldn't refuse him now. And then after dinner…well, anything was possible. Brandon was confident. Gaia was becoming more and more a 'mission' to him, and he felt powerless to stop himself. He knew it wasn't rational but he didn't care anymore. It hadn't been urgent before. He felt he had plenty of time. After Matt Fisher died in the airplane crash, he'd relaxed – he had showered her with sympathy, given her promotions, did all the little things that she should have appreciated. But she rebuffed his invites to dinner, drinks, little outings. That had bothered him, but he figured that in time she would come around. Because Brandon always succeeded at everything in life, everything he took on.

Except in the female department.

He never won over Juliet despite having smashed her boyfriend to death with a stolen car. He had reluctantly married his late wife and he knew she'd never loved him – but he didn't care about that because he hadn't loved her either. He'd just wanted her money, which came handily his way after she took her own life. And he'd tried so hard with Gaia, and been so patient – even hiring that Walker character to sabotage Matt's plane.

But that didn't push her closer to him as he'd hoped. And then, of all things, she started dating his young protégé, Jeff Kavanaugh. That was a slap in the face, considering how handsome Brandon was, how rich and powerful he was. Why would she choose Jeff over him? Well, sure, he was younger, but that was something that Brandon discounted as irrelevant. No, she was shunning him just like Juliet had done – and he was quickly running out of patience. He may just have to take what he wanted.

Brandon was actually feeling kind of good about things today, despite the anguish over Gaia. He'd received a call from the administrator at Lakeside Psychiatric Hospital informing him that Jim Prentice had committed suicide. With a razor blade. Doctor Magnusson mentioned that an investigation was underway, but at this point there was no clear answer to the puzzle over how he had gotten his hands on a razor blade – in fact a whole pack of the darn things.

So, the assault on the hospital had failed, but the end result was satisfying. Maybe the news of the attempted assault scared Prentice into just doing the deed himself, retain some control over his own death and spare the lives of the other patients. Brandon didn't care what motivated the man, he was just glad he was dead.

And Brandon was relieved that one other person was dead too – Herbert Walker, the man he'd hired to sabotage Matt's plane. Even though Walker'd been hypnotized to forget what he'd done, with the way some of their hypnotic techniques had been failing them lately Brandon felt better about the man being dead.

And Ray Filberg was dead now. The only other man, other than Walker, who could have tied him to Matt Fisher's plane sabotage. And Filberg had been a useless executive lately anyway, so good riddance.

Now he had a top-notch new vice president sitting in Ray's office. Jeff Kavanaugh. Despite his resentment of Jeff over the Gaia thing, Brandon knew that Jeff would be instrumental in the firm's success in the years to come. The man was brilliant, charismatic, and fearless. And on top of that, he was a living breathing genuine hero. How many real heroes were out there anymore? Most were dead and revered post mortem. But Brandon was lucky to have a real live one working directly for him. It would attract more clients, build confidence, and create almost a reverential feeling towards Price, Spencer and Williams – and in particular the tenth floor Artificial

Intelligence division.

And that was Brandon's baby – it mattered more to him than life itself. Well, lately there was one more thing that was coming awfully close, something that kept him awake at night, dreaming and scheming during the day. Gaia Templeton. His thoughts always came back to Gaia.

Was it because she was a stunning beauty? Or that she was the epitome of class and dignity? Because she was with someone else? Or was it simply because, irrespective of there being someone else, she'd made it clear to him that she wasn't interested?

Brandon figured it was 'all of the above.'

He looked at his phone messages. Brandon was old-fashioned. He insisted on all of his messages being written out on little green note pads – had to be green, the color of money. He didn't want to have to log on to the computer and check his inbox – he wasn't techno-savvy in the least, and had no intentions of being that way. He used the computer to the bare extent that he needed to and that was it.

Brandon also believed in paper – he didn't trust having everything online, even though he insisted on the systems they used being as secure as they could possibly be. But he still didn't completely trust automation, so he kept paper on virtually everything. And he never threw anything out. He thought of himself as being a lot like Richard Nixon that way – a little obsessive. Nixon had everything in the Oval Office recorded, and even when his world was crashing down upon him with the Watergate scandal, he still couldn't bring himself to destroy the tapes.

So, keeping paper on everything was probably a big risk, but Brandon also considered keeping everything online a big risk. Sure, it was backed up, but anything these days could be hacked. That had been proven true with the troubling news in the past year about the U.S. banks being accessed, as well as even the U.S. Treasury. No, Brandon would continue to keep everything on paper.

But he wasn't stupid. No one would see his paper piles. He had a vault for that, right there in the comfort of his own office. In the far corner, on the wall that divided his private boardroom from his office quarters was a walk-in vault. Built several years ago to exacting specifications, this little room protected all of Brandon's secrets – all of them. One day they'd simply be moved to the vault in his home, so he could look back over all of the triumphs of his career. His 'trophies.' His version of the 'Nixon tapes.'

And this vault in his office was hidden from view – behind wall paneling that needed to be tapped just a certain way in just a certain spot, to spring open. And once it opened there was the vault door of twelve-inch thick steel, embraced by ten-inch thick concrete walls, a six-inch concrete ceiling, and a six-inch raised concrete floor. The room was ten feet wide, twelve feet long, and eight feet high. It could even function as a panic room if needed, because there was an emergency ventilator and electric lighting on the inside.

Brandon spun the combination dial – he still preferred this traditional dial instead of the new digital versions – then turned the heavy handle. The door swung open to reveal neat shelves on two walls from the floor to the ceiling, all labeled and organized. On the third wall was a gun case, which contained several pistols and a sawed-off shotgun – because you just never knew.

Brandon stood on a stool and pulled down two large file folders from the top shelf. He closed and locked the safe behind him and shoved the wood paneling back into place to hide the vault door.

Then he walked over to his desk with the two folders, poured himself a glass of water and leaned back in his swivel chair to start his reading.

The first file he leafed through was his Russian file. He'd had a relationship with the Russian embassy for well over a decade. Little tasks performed here and there – but the big one he'd just tried to collect on hadn't worked out, so they still owed him. Sure, Jim Prentice was now dead, so the point was almost moot – but not quite. What the Russians had promised him didn't happen – the commandos they'd sent had failed. The stupid Russkies probably laced them with far too many microwaves, so much so that they couldn't keep their eyes on the road – hit a deer and killed themselves in the process.

So, the Russians still owed him a task.

In payment for the big one he'd given to them years ago.

They'd wanted to cause harm to Viktor Yushchenko, who was running for President of the Ukraine against the Kremlin's favored candidate. He was the leader of the Opposition at the time, and was gaining in popularity. The Russians didn't want to kill him; they just wanted him harmed in a way that his physical features would turn off the electorate. In their typical shallow way, they truly believed Yushchenko's popularity was based solely on his movie star looks – he was the Ukraine's equivalent to John F. Kennedy. And no one could deny that Yushchenko was one handsome devil, and he even had a gorgeous American wife. The Russians were furious – afraid that if this guy won, he would follow through on his electoral pledges to move the Ukraine away from Moscow's influence and move closer towards NATO and the European Union.

But they didn't want him killed – they knew that would be too obvious, that the finger would be clearly pointed towards the Kremlin. Yushchenko would become a martyr and whoever replaced him on the Opposition ticket would be almost guaranteed of victory. So, the Russians wanted him disfigured, hoping that the electorate would be disgusted. They wanted it to look like the man had a severe form of STD, perhaps Herpes, which if serious enough could cause terrible disfigurement. They wanted the people of the Ukraine to be disgusted, and what could be more disgusting than a venereal disease? Not just the disease itself but the implications of how he could have possibly contracted it. The man would be discredited very quickly by the image-conscious Ukrainians. And the Russians didn't want any of their people involved – they had to be as far removed from this as possible, due to a series of assassination attempts over the last few decades that had led directly back to the Kremlin. Embarrassing attempts. They couldn't risk any more of those.

Brandon had gone to work on that assignment himself. The idea excited him – the chance to wield his skill and power to impact a foreign election campaign. How special was that?

His team did the research and picked the day. The research indicated that the best poison to mimic a disgustingly bad venereal disease reaction would be Dioxin, but a particularly virulent form of it called TCDD. All that was needed was one milligram.

The date was September 5th, 2004. Smack in the middle of his election campaign, Yushchenko was having dinner that night with the government's two security chiefs. The meal was set in advance – sushi and soup. Simple. But what was also simple and predictable was Yushchenko's love for cognac – gallons of it.

And all it would take was one milligram.

The night before the dinner, Brandon paid the restaurant manager a visit. Brandon spoke fluent Russian and so did the manager. The man had respected Brandon's striking features, strong jaw, heavy brow – he looked Russian. He also respected Brandon's authentic-looking Kremlin credentials. And he listened. And he took. He took the tiny vial of TCDD. By the time Brandon was finished with him, the man's next day was established. He was to drop the TCDD into the cognac. Simple. Then the next night he would meet with Brandon again, at which time Brandon would do nothing more than repeat four words that he'd planted the night before: 'Thou shalt go forth.'

And he went forth.

The plan was successful in only one respect – it made Yushchenko very sick indeed, and grotesque to look at. His God-given handsome features were ruined, and for a while most people thought he would never get them back. The poisoning made headlines around the world, but what the Russians hadn't counted on was the reverse of what they wanted to happen. Yushchenko got the sympathy vote, and even though never proven, the electorate was convinced through local propaganda that the Kremlin had done this to their popular and handsome Kennedyesque candidate.

So, the now very ugly Viktor Yushchenko became the next President of the Ukraine. And Brandon Horcroft was still owed payment.

Brandon smiled to himself as he opened the second file. Yes, he would indeed collect from the Russians one of these days.

The second file was dedicated to the CIA. While the CIA used their own operatives around the world, they were prohibited by law against operating within the borders of the United States of America. So, while Brandon was a Canadian, he was the closest trusted contractor that they had for certain projects. It was almost as if he was operating within the United States because the border was relatively friendly. The CIA used contractors everywhere actually, but particularly for things they needed to do in the United States. They had no choice but to farm that out. And Brandon's firm had a lock on certain activities.

The CIA was infamous for their mind control project, termed MK-Ultra, which took place between 1953 and 1973. The project was terminated due to scandalous reports of people being experimented on without their permission or even knowledge. The project became an embarrassment. But it had indeed proved successful.

The general public had no idea that the project had actually produced results. And they enjoyed watching films like The Manchurian Candidate – pure fiction as far as they were concerned. Not exactly. There had been at least three Manchurian candidates within their midst, resulting in the assassinations of John F. Kennedy, Robert F. Kennedy, and Martin Luther King. One of them was an actual hypnotized and ELF-manipulated shooter – Sirhan Sirhan – but the other two, Lee Harvey Oswald and James Earl Ray, were simply hypnotized and ELF-manipulated patsies, scapegoats.

These three losers were perfect examples of just how powerful mind-control could be, either through hypnotic techniques or microwave technology.

And Brandon had been working with the CIA for years to continue the project that they had been ordered to quit. In fact, the CIA never quit anything – they just outsourced it if they weren't allowed to do it. And Price, Spencer and Williams was the outsource for mind-control.

Brandon chuckled to himself. He always thought that the United States Constitution was a joke. The Second Amendment to the Bill of Rights protected the right to 'keep and bear arms.' This stupid amendment was adopted in 1791 and was intended to allow citizens to carry weapons for service in the militia, or for basic purposes such as self-defense in the home. It clearly wasn't intended to allow people to walk around the streets with guns on their hips, or to brandish AK47 machine guns. Hell, the guns available for use back when the Second Amendment was drafted weren't much more advanced than muskets. Today, preaching the Second Amendment as a basic right to carry high capacity militarized weapons, was ludicrous.

But that's exactly the dilemma that the U.S. government had to deal with now. It had gotten out of hand. Witnessing uprisings in the Middle East – Syria, Egypt, Tunisia, Libya and more to come – scared the living shit out of American legislators. The Constitution had to be amended again, and quickly. They didn't want to see similar uprisings happen in America, with well-armed citizens at the ready. Sure, they could squash any uprising if they had to with their superior military firepower. But they never wanted to have to face that problem. It would be a lot easier and a lot less messy if Americans just weren't armed to begin with. If they could only get their guns away from them.

So, out of one corner of their mouths, legislators swore by the United States Constitution. But out of the other corner of their mouths, they wished the damn thing just didn't exist. Typical political hypocrites.

Enter the CIA. They had their own agenda on most things, and they knew how impotent the legislators were feeling about the entire issue. So, their solution was the one they usually used anywhere in the world where they wanted to create havoc – just manipulate the law of supply and demand.

The CIA knew that legislators just needed a helping hand – show that the gun laws were dangerous to the people, that the 'right to bear arms' was an archaic principle and the Constitution needed a Congressional amendment to keep with the times.

So, the CIA solution was to create slaughters. Create nut jobs, Frankensteins, armed with automatic weapons, shooting people to death in schools, theaters, shopping malls, and military bases. And all of these things they did, and did marvelously well.

With the expert assistance of Price, Spencer and Williams Inc. And specifically Brandon Horcroft. Master manipulator. Master at bending minds, creating crazy people who would do mindless unthinkable things.

The public outcry had started; the public horror was in full swing. Children lying in pools of their own blood did indeed create a 'supply and demand' problem. Soon, very soon, the U.S. government would be able to take the guns away from their people – and they'd be thanked profusely. And Congress would be able to finally pass legislation destroying that stupid amendment that went into effect way back in the days when Cowboys chased Indians.

After it was all over, Brandon would be able to look back and say, at least to himself, that he had done his part to change a Bill of Rights that no longer had a place in the American sphere of life. An historic moment to say the least.

Yes, Price, Spencer and Williams did a lot of things. His executives were primarily involved in the insider-trading activities. He left them to that – it was lucrative as hell and very illegal. But the projects he was personally involved in were much 'bigger picture.' They would change the world as we knew it. His projects would have lasting legacy, game-changers in the extreme. And Brandon had always fervently believed that he deserved – no, was entitled – to be a game-changer. It was his destiny.

CHAPTER 31

"Your 'inside man?'"

Dan smiled and nodded slowly. "That may sound kind of ominous, but I'm afraid to say that it's probably your only way out."

Jeff looked at him, stunned. "So, you're going to let me go?"

"In a sense, yes. But you'll be on a leash. And, as I said, you'll pay a price later – but definitely not as dear a price as you would pay if I sent you to trial now. You'll eventually be charged with a lesser offense, plead guilty, and you'll be out in two or three years. But that sure beats fifteen to twenty."

Jeff rubbed his sore wrists. It was amazing how those handcuffs had hurt so much after being snapped to his wrists for only a short time. He was glad to have them off, if only just for the subliminal feeling of freedom. All of a sudden he felt less like a despicable criminal. If just the simple symbolism of having his hands cuffed behind his back had made him feel that way, he could only imagine how bad it would feel sitting in a prison cell for the next couple of decades.

"Who are you after?"

Dan opened the file folder in front of him. "Jeff, I'm after anyone and everyone. To be specific, though, as with any crime, I want the man or woman at the top. And for Price, Spencer and Williams Inc., the man at the top seems to be Brandon Horcroft. You're going to help me get him and anyone else who's in on this."

Jeff frowned. "In on what, exactly?"

Dan leafed through some pages in his file, stopping at one. He began scanning quickly with his eyes, then his fingers flipped through several more pages in mere seconds. Jeff noticed that his eyeballs were flicking quickly from side to side as he did – the sure sign of a trained 'speed-reader.' He was impressed.

Dan looked up. "Before I tell you more, are you with me?"

Jeff was still rubbing his sore wrists. "How dangerous will this be?"

"Very."

"Are you shooting in the dark, or do you have real reason to suspect something bad is going on?"

"I never shoot in the dark."

"How much protection will I have?"

"Virtually none at all."

"What if something happens to me?"

"I'll pay for your funeral."

Jeff laughed. "You're kidding, right?"

Dan got up from his chair and walked over to the one-way glass that was now covered in a steel blind. He pulled the little remote out of his pocket and tapped on the metal blind.

"I don't kid very often, Jeff. Just say the word and I'll press this button. The blind will raise, the door will unlock, and the scrambler will be disengaged. Then I'll march you off to jail. You'll languish there for months awaiting trial. With the video evidence I have, you won't get bail. And it's a slam-dunk that you'll get life, with parole in fifteen. Do you still think I'm kidding? If you do, nod, and I'll press this button."

Jeff thrust his hands above his head in protest. "Okay, okay – put that stupid thing away. I'm with you. I have no choice. Tell me what I need to know, and what exactly it is you want me to do."

Dan nodded and walked back to his chair. "Smart boy. It will be a pleasure to work with you. Believe it or not, I'm one of your fans."

"Don't patronize me, Inspector. Just get on with it."

Dan leaned back in his chair and clasped his fingers behind his head. "Here's what I know about your firm. They're using hypnotic suggestions to obtain privileged information about the companies who hire them. Under the guise of coaching and personal development, they're turning the unwitting executives of their numerous clients into obedient little robots for Price's financial gain."

"Insider trading?"

"Yes."

"I find it hard to believe that Price, Spencer and Williams would blatantly participate in something like that. It could easily be traced by the Securities Commission. Unusual stock trading in companies who are clients of Price would be a pattern that would be picked up by the numerous system edits. It would be flagged."

Dan shook his head. "Not necessarily, Jeff. Not if they were sophisticated in how they were doing it. I doubt that trades are conducted in the Price name, and I doubt that they're even being done by entities incorporated in this country. Think offshore, and think also that just a handful of people are involved. Something like this has to be kept within a tight circle, very tight."

Jeff leaned back in his chair as well, tilting onto the back legs until he was almost perfectly balanced. "Why are you involved? Why isn't this a securities investigation by the OSC?"

Dan smiled. "Good question. Firstly, because Price is an international corporation with its fingers into pies all over the world. And secondly – because it appears to be much more insidious than just insider trading. At the very least, people are being murdered."

*****

Gaia got out of the cab and paid the driver. Then she just stood on the sidewalk on Front Street and gazed up at the impressive old structure for a few seconds. The Royal York Hotel was one of Toronto's most iconic buildings – she recalled the stories from her parents of its history. The Beatles, the Queen, Frank Sinatra, and every famous person imaginable who had stayed there. And the fact that at one time, this hotel had been the tallest building in Toronto. It was hard to imagine, with the gleaming skyscrapers that now dominated this world-class city. Hard to believe that at one time this hotel had been the tallest building.

As she walked through the lobby, she smiled. The lobby was so massive, and so opulent. And the hotel's famous Christmas tree was already in place, reaching to the sky – well, at least to the ceiling, which was about three stories high. The decorations filled her with warmth, filled her with a desire to visit here with Jeff. It was such a romantic old hotel and it looked just like a castle from the outside. On the inside it exuded class, style, privilege, and it was still, after all these years, one of the most prestigious hotels to stay at in the entire world.

She knew that Jeff would love coming here with her – she could picture them having a romantic dinner in one of the fine restaurants, then adjourning to one of the suites for a cozy night together.

All of a sudden her eyes started to tear up. Jeff – what would he think if he knew why she was really here tonight? All of the class and opulence of this place couldn't possibly compete with the sleazy reason she was here. She sullied the place, and she was suddenly ashamed of herself. All of a sudden she realized she was just a slut. A common slut.

She wiped away the tears and gave her head a shake. No, she wasn't a slut. That's not what she was. She was only doing what she had to do out of necessity – she didn't enjoy it. A real slut would enjoy it, and she didn't enjoy it in the least. In fact, it made her sick. After every encounter and when she was finally back home to the safety of her house and the comfort of Bingo, she always ran to the bathroom and vomited. And tried desperately to forget the dirty leering body she'd just spent an hour with.

She pushed the elevator button and waited. While she waited, she checked inside her purse – yes, her phone was there, as was her little can of Mace. A girl couldn't be too careful.

Gaia got off on the twentieth floor, and sauntered on down in the direction of room 2021. She glanced in the hall mirror as she passed it. She looked good – in a "hooker" kind of way. Certainly not the way Jeff was used to seeing her. Tight black leather trousers, a low cut silver blouse hanging low on the shoulders, high heels. She tried to remember back if Jeff had even seen her in high heels yet. Probably not.

At room 2021, she paused before she knocked. A brass plaque on the door said "Ambassador's Suite." She breathed easier. For a suite this expensive, he was probably a decent sort. Nothing to be afraid of.

She knocked. As was typical, he opened the door on the first knock. They never usually waited for the second. She always pictured them leaning up against the door… waiting in anticipation for the knock. Pathetic.

He smiled at her, apparently pleased at what he saw. Gaia wasn't too disappointed either. He was a good-looking guy, about fifty years old, distinguished, and well dressed. Didn't have the big potbelly that a lot of customers had. He seemed… well…decent. She chuckled to herself at her thought of the word 'decent.' The guy probably had a wife and eight kids, and maybe a grandchild or two. And here he was with a hooker. Yeah, real 'decent.'

He ushered her inside, and introduced himself as 'Jack.' Took her coat, threw it onto the chair and then guided her to the edge of the bed. He sat down beside her and immediately put his hand on her knee, rubbing the supple leather of her trousers, inching his fingers up towards her crotch.

"What's your name, gorgeous?"

"Amber. And I think we need to get something out of the way first, don't you think?"

"Oh, sure, yeah, right." He walked over to the desk and opened his wallet. "Three hundred, right?"

"Yes. That will do it." Gaia was suddenly feeling uncomfortable. The initial impression she had of the man had been totally wrong. He was acting like a disrespectful pig. She tempered that thought with reminding herself that she was a hooker, that she was here for one reason only, and that he was paying her for one reason only. But still, she couldn't help getting pangs of guilt and chest pains when she encountered men like this. She contrasted that in her mind with the tenderness and respect that Jeff always showed her. Gaia wondered how much tenderness Jeff would show her if he knew what she did in her spare time. A tremble went through her body – she suddenly had the urge to throw up now rather than later.

Jack threw three one hundred dollar bills onto the bed. "Here you go. Now, take your clothes off."

Gaia opened her purse and stuffed the bills inside. Then she walked over to the far side of the bed and put her purse on the night table. She withdrew a package of condoms, and tore open the edge. Then she began to strip – not seductively because this guy didn't seem to give a shit. She just took them off and lay down on the bed. He leered at her and took off his clothes as well.

Jack sighed in a hungry kind of way, and wrapped his left leg over Gaia's hips. Then he began sucking on her tits. Not in a gentle way. He began using his teeth and bit her right nipple. Gaia stopped him. "Please, don't. That hurts."

"Hey, for what I'm paying you, you can hurt a little."

"No, that's not the way this works. I'll leave if you don't stop."

"The hell you will, little lady."

He suddenly rolled on top of her and tried to penetrate. Gaia used all of her strength and pushed the brute off to the side. "No! We have to use a condom!" She reached over to the night table and grabbed the little package.

Jack grabbed her face in one big hand and turned it toward him. "Fuck the condom. I want bareback."

Gaia was horrified. "Absolutely not! I don't take risks like that! I have a boyfriend and you probably have a wife. We can't do something like that."

"Who gives a shit? You look clean, and I'm sure you'll agree that I look clean. I'll pay you extra to take the risk, how's that for a deal? An extra hundred?"

Gaia rolled off the side of the bed. "No, I won't do that for any amount of money. I'm leaving right now. This doesn't feel right at all."

Jack chuckled, just as the bathroom door opened and two shirtless men walked into the bedroom. "It may not feel right at this moment, sweetheart, but I guarantee it will feel real good in a couple of minutes." The two other men laughed as well and quickly slipped out of their jeans.

Gaia felt her stomach start to heave and she gasped. She heard them laughing again. She screamed...but it only lasted for a split second, because Jack was off the bed in a flash, his right arm around her neck and his left hand covering her mouth. He rasped into her ear, "Isn't this a funny situation? A hooker about to be raped?"

He threw her onto the bed. "I'm not gonna cover your mouth, because I want you to be able to breathe in ecstasy. But if you scream, I swear, I'll kill you."

Gaia nodded in agreement. Then she braced herself as Jack turned her onto her side. One of the newcomers crawled in behind her and she could feel him begin to penetrate her anus. The other one slipped in front and entered her without fanfare.

She called out. "Jack, please, get them to put on the condoms."

"Fuck you, slut."

Gaia found it hard to breathe as the man behind rammed her. She heard herself pleading, "Please, please, use some Vaseline or something. You're going to tear me apart."

She heard the brute behind her suddenly speak for the first time. "Hey, the effort is just part of the experience, slut."

The tears began. She hated hearing the word 'slut.' Even though deep down inside she knew that was really what she was, it had never hit home before until now. She just wanted to be home, be in Jeff's arms. But if he knew, would he want her anymore? She thought he would – thought he would understand. She pictured her hero in her mind, breaking down the door and killing these animals with his bare hands. The hero who had talked a madman out of shooting her in the head several months ago. He would save her, she knew he would. Or…would he just look at her in disgust and spit on her naked body.

Then she started feeling sick again. The guy from the rear had finally succeeded. He was ramming her forward, while the guy in front was ramming her backward. And Jack was still laughing. Stroking her hair. Then she heard him say, "I get more joy out of watching."

She heard the words coming in waves. "Slut." "Whore." "Bitch." Over and over again. Gaia felt no better than a piece of meat. Suddenly she felt an anger in her belly. Maybe more an anger at herself than at the animals who were tearing her apart.

The three of them were so preoccupied that they didn't notice her right hand slithering across to her purse on the night table. She reached inside and found the compact little spray can of Mace. She shoved her thumb upward and flipped the lid off the tip.

The next few moments were filled with screams of pain. Gaia swiveled the can around in an arc, hitting Jack first, then the other two clowns. She didn't waver – each of them got a good dose of the poison.

They clawed at their eyes at the same time as their penises became limp. Gaia felt the immediate relief of freedom as they quickly withdrew. They were cursing and swearing and sounded close to sobbing – she hit each of them again with another potent spray.

She didn't wait to get dressed. Running through the lobby naked was the least of her concerns now. She grabbed her purse, her shoes, and her clothes and ran for the door.

Gaia took one last glance back as she opened the door. The three animals were still scratching at their eyes. They were gasping for breath and she could hear them uttering what seemed to be their favorite word: 'Slut.'

She grabbed onto the toe of one of her high-heeled shoes and ran back to where Jack was squirming on the floor. She looked down at the sick evil man, raised her shoe above his head, and slammed the heel down onto his forehead with an intensity that shocked her.

It seemed otherworldly.

CHAPTER 32

Gaia drove her little Mini Cooper slowly along St. Clair Avenue West, hunting for a rare parking spot. She spotted a car just pulling out, so she put on her blinker and waited patiently despite the honking of the impatient driver behind her.

Once parked, she hopped out and popped a loonie into the parking meter. This would give her two hours – plenty of time. Her meeting was at a coffee shop about three blocks west. Luckily it was a nice sunny day, so the walk would be a pleasant one.

As she walked she reflected back on the past week – a week that had been hellish. Exactly a week ago today she'd been raped. And she knew full well that most people would say she had it coming – that she had a nerve calling it 'rape' when she'd gone there to have sex for money. And this was the dilemma that Gaia found swirling around in her brain: the shame of having been there to begin with; the utter degradation she'd suffered at the hands of those animals. And feeling like just an animal herself. A slab of meat, an object with no feelings or any right to self-respect.

Gaia was indeed ashamed of herself, disgusted at what she had allowed herself to become. She felt totally unworthy of Jeff. Every time he'd looked at her in the last few days, she couldn't help but lower her eyes. It felt as if he could look right through her, see past the classy façade right into the sleazy whore that she'd become. Part of her wanted to just blurt it out and tell him what she was, and what she had suffered. But the other part of her won out. What would that accomplish? She would just lose him, and that would truly break her heart as well as his. If Gaia lost Jeff on top of the loss of her self-respect, she didn't know if she could keep on living.

But she wanted his sympathy, wanted to hear his soothing words telling her everything would be okay. That he understood. That he forgave her. She wanted his strong arms around her, hugging her; protecting her from people like the three animals she'd spent an hour with a week ago. The hour from hell. An hour she would never forget for the rest of her life.

Ironic, she thought – a time like now when she needed Jeff's comfort the most during the biggest emotional crisis in her life, she couldn't even confide in him. Because if she did, she knew that her world would truly end.

Gaia walked along, gazing into the various coffee and ice cream shops, pasta outlets, and restaurants. This was an area of Toronto known as 'Corso Italia.' It was the sister neighborhood of 'Little Italy,' which was located a few blocks south. Both areas were populated mainly by Italian families and businessmen, and most of the businessmen were Mafia. No opulent offices in Corso Italia – just coffee shops and eateries that functioned as offices. Usually rooms in the very back, behind curtains or not so subtle locked doors. These were the rooms where the meetings took place, where the cheeks were kissed, rings were rubbed, favors granted, favors repaid.

There were always people hanging around on the streets outside the coffee shops. Looking like they had no purpose. But they did have a purpose – they were watching, guarding, greeting, and planning. And they were always friendly, particularly to women. Women were sacred in Italian families, as were the large broods of children they produced. Family was everything. And women were up on a pedestal. As far as Italians were concerned, women deserved respect and were also expected to earn that respect.

Gaia received a few nods from the loitering men as she walked along – no jeers or leers or whistles. No, just respectful nods and smiles. She liked that, especially after what had happened a week ago. If she got whistled at today or had to listen to some lewd comments, she was pretty sure she'd just break down, cry, and never stop.

She was sure that some of the men standing outside on the street recognized her. She had been making this trip every month for five years now, and with the thirty percent loan shark interest rate she was paying she'd probably be doing this for at least five more years. This was a cash business – no checks, no paper trails. The man whose name sounded like 'Pacino' was waiting for her.

She thought about the man as she walked. He was scary to her, because of what he did for a living. She knew he did a lot more than just loan-sharking. She could tell just by the reverence that others showed him. And she knew he was extremely wealthy, with a large house in a prime neighborhood in Woodbridge. He'd let that slip a couple of times. But the more she'd gotten to know the man, she realized that it wasn't him that was scary to her – it was just what he did that was scary. She knew he was powerful and probably capable of anything. She knew that he'd ordered Matt's wrist broken when he reneged on several months' payments. Pacino lived in a violent world and that was the way things were done. You paid your due, or you paid a price. Hard to argue with that logic.

But she was never really afraid of the man himself – a man who actually had a real name. It reminded her of the Godfather character, Pacino, but she knew that was only because she associated him with that character. His actual name was Frank Palladino, and his office was a room in the very back of a café called Frank's Espresso.

She knew that Frank had never had any respect for Matt. She could tell. Matt was reckless and undisciplined, and Frank had no sympathy or respect for people like that. In a way, he probably thought he was teaching Matt a life lesson by breaking his wrist. In a way, he did. From that point on right up until the tragic airplane crash that cost him his life, Matt never gambled again.

Matt used to make this little trip by himself before he was killed. Since his death, this monthly visit had become Gaia's duty.

Frank Palladino was indeed an enigma though, in Gaia's mind. He was always respectful to her, accepted the money-laden envelope with gratitude every single time. He always poured her a cup of his famous espresso and they chatted like friends. Gaia guessed that Frank was in his mid-fifties. A tough-looking guy as most Italian men tended to be – dark features, broad shoulders, hairy forearms, a bit of a paunch. But his eyes were gentle and knowing. His smile was easy. And on several occasions he'd acted almost fatherly towards Gaia. She knew he had two sons and three daughters, and he beamed every time he talked about them. Two of his daughters were close to Gaia in age.

Gaia was frightened of what Frank Palladino was, but not of who he was. She actually enjoyed seeing him irrespective of having to pay him exorbitant sums of money every month. And he had never ever threatened her. He had never had to wield the big stick warning her of what would happen if she didn't pay. He had even offered to give her a break the occasional month if money was tight – if she needed it. Gaia had needed it many times, but she never took him up on it. She hadn't wanted to miss a payment for any reason – didn't want to get in the habit of doing that. The interest mounted even moreso if she missed payments. And she was afraid deep down inside that if she also got into the habit of skipping payments, this enigma of a man might lose his fatherly touch.

She still owed 100,000 dollars. Right now, because of the higher mortgage on her house, she was only able to pay Frank the interest – which amounted to 30,000 dollars every year. And now she was going to start having problems with that. Something she had to talk to Frank about today, a conversation she wasn't looking forward to. For the first time ever, she may have to miss some payments – and she hoped that Frank would still be willing to extend her that privilege. Scary though, knowing how much the interest would compound. But Gaia didn't have a choice.

Gaia smiled at a nurse who was standing outside a medical clinic, smoking a cigarette. Seeing the clinic caused her to relive her visit to her own doctor a few days ago. Gaia had been overcome with anxiety after the rape, terrified that the three animals might have infected her with something. She'd seen Jeff a couple of times before she was able to get an appointment with her doctor. He'd wanted sex and she'd rebuffed him. Gave the excuse that she had a yeast infection. He seemed to buy it, but she could tell he was confused. Perhaps he could sense from her demeanor that something else was wrong. Gaia didn't think she'd done a very good job hiding it – she burst into tears several times, and Jeff just held her tight not knowing what else to do. She sure loved feeling his arms around her though, and wanted dearly to make love to him. But she couldn't take the risk of infecting him – that would be the worst possible outcome of her recklessness.

Her doctor, a woman thankfully, gave her some ointment to deal with the tearing she'd suffered. She asked Gaia if she'd been raped, and Gaia said no. Just rough unprotected sex. Then she started to cry, right there in her office. The doctor hugged her and seemed to sense that there was more going on than Gaia was admitting. After Gaia asked to be tested for STDs, including HIV, the doctor, Melany, seemed confused.

"Haven't you been in a serious relationship for a while now?"

Gaia lowered her eyes. "Yes."

"So, why do you need to be tested?"

She kept her eyes down. "It wasn't with him."

"Oh…are you going to tell him?"

Through a flood of tears, Gaia answered, "No, I can't."

"It might relieve some of this anxiety I'm seeing."

"It'll make it worse."

Then Melany rubbed her back. "It's okay, dear, we all make mistakes. Just don't make it worse. Hold off on sex with him until we have the test results."

Gaia nodded, rolled up the sleeve of her blouse and watched what she hoped wasn't tainted blood pumping into the vial.

Two days later she got the call. All clear for STDs. And the new 'rapid test' had been done for the HIV portion – there used to be a three-month wait for results. She was all clear on that too. A big cloud was lifted from Gaia's mind – and her breathing became easier. She was fine. She'd gotten lucky.

That night, she and Jeff had sex. And it was the tenderest sex she'd ever had – or at least that's the way it seemed. She knew deep down inside that her anguished brain was merely comparing it to the feeding frenzy she'd had to endure a few days before. Her encounter with wild animals. She thanked God there was Jeff in this world.

She opened the door to Frank's Espresso, and headed toward the room at the back – the 'office.' Frank's office. There were a few men sitting at tables in the coffee shop, each of them smiled and nodded pleasantly to her as she passed. Frank's wife, Maria, was behind the counter. She smiled too and called out, "Buongiorno Gaia!" Gaia smiled and returned the greeting.

The door to the office was closed. Gaia knocked respectfully and waited to hear the usual command, "Entrare! Entrare!" It came as expected, so she turned the perpetually sticky pasta sauce smeared door handle and walked in.

Frank was seated behind his massive desk, which was absolutely covered with papers, not a square inch of the desktop exposed. The floor was littered with file folders and there wasn't a computer in sight. Frank didn't need one or want one. He despised them. Gaia didn't blame him in the least.

He jumped up from his chair and came around to give her a hug – and a kiss on each cheek. "Sit, sit. Maria, bring coffee!"

Within minutes, Maria was back with two espressos, closing the door on her way out. She understood that this office was 'manland.' Frank's private refuge. Italian women knew enough to make sure they didn't know enough.

Gaia sat down in one of the two guest chairs. Frank went back behind his desk – very formal ritual. Business was business. He sat down and crossed his legs. He smiled. Gaia thought he looked quite spiffy today – red shirt, brown cardigan, gray slacks. And he'd shaved – something he didn't do very often.

"How are you, Gaia?"

She grimaced. "Not very good, Frank." She reached into her purse and pulled out the envelope. She passed it over to him. It contained exactly 2,500 in cash. He opened a drawer and threw it inside. He never counted.

"Why aren't you good, my dear?"

"Something's happened in my life – something really bad. And I don't know quite what to do about it."

Frank frowned. "Is your boyfriend not treating you right?"

Gaia started to cry. She couldn't help it. This tough man was so gentle and fatherly, she just wanted to pour her heart out to him. "No, he's wonderful. That's the problem. I feel like I just don't deserve him."

Frank came out from behind his desk and sat in the guest chair beside her. He rubbed her back. "Tell me what's wrong. I may be able to help. Yes, you pay me each month and we have a business relationship, but I really do look at you as if you were one of my daughters. I've come to love you just like them, Gaia. Tell me. Let me help you."

Gaia looked up into his gentle eyes, which were as wide as saucers. And she lost it again. The tears were flowing freely now. Frank's gentle probing personality was getting to her. She turned towards him and threw her arms around his neck, her tears dripping onto his red silk shirt.

Frank gently rubbed her back. "Gaia, we all screw up. Me more than most. I'll make a deal with you. I'll tell you something, then you tell me something. What do you think about that?"

Gaia pulled her head back and nodded.

"I never told you this. But I lost one of my daughters a year ago – Gina, my oldest. She was about your age. She collapsed in her home in front of her kids. Drug overdose. Crystal Meth. I'd had no idea she was doing drugs. I should have had an idea but I was just too busy."

Gaia just stared at Frank in shock – this 'man's man' now had tears in his eyes too. He turned away in embarrassment, but she pulled his head back to face her. "Frank, I'm so sorry. My heart is breaking for you."

"I was a lousy father, Gaia. She didn't come to me for help. I could have helped her. But I just didn't pay attention to the signs, although now when I look back I can see all the signs clearly. She was such a sweetheart, but she was depressed. I didn't know that either. Why didn't I pay attention, Gaia? Why didn't I? I can't go back and do it over again, but I sure wish I could."

"I'm sure that wherever she is, she knows that, Frank. And she probably didn't come to you only because she was afraid of showing a weakness to you – didn't want to disappoint you. So she just tried to deal with it on her own."

Frank lowered his head into his hands, and ran his fingers through his thick black hair. "I always put up a brave front, Gaia, but I'm not so tough. I've never gotten over this, and I don't think I ever will."

"You're still a tough guy to me, Frank." Gaia tousled his hair. He smiled.

Frank rubbed the tears away from his eyes. Then he turned his head toward her and looked straight into her soul. "We made a deal. Your turn, Gaia."

She nodded and pulled a tissue out of her purse. She knew she'd be needing it.

"I can't pay you for a while, Frank. I took on a second job when I inherited Matt's debt to you, but now I just can't do that job anymore."

"What was that job, Gaia?"

She told him. Then she told him what happened a week ago. Gaia didn't spare him the details – she told him everything. She didn't know why. In the back of her mind, she was thinking about how strange this was, telling a loan shark, a probable Mafioso, the most despicable aspects of her life. But…his fatherly nature, his strong protective spirit, somehow compelled her. And the compassion she felt for him after what he had told her about his daughter. They had bonded together…and it felt cleansing to her.

Frank got up and started pacing the office. She could see that he was crying. Then he stood in front of her and spoke. "I've done it again, haven't I? Forced someone else into a desperate situation. Just out of my obsession with money. Both you and my daughter. And probably a lot more good people too."

He then walked behind his desk and flopped his big frame down into his leather chair. He pulled the cash envelope out of his desk drawer and handed it back to her. "Here, take this back. As of now, your debt is forgiven. You owe me nothing. We're even."

Gaia was shocked. She didn't know what to say. And he didn't seem disgusted with her, even after all the disgusting things she had just told him. He seemed angrier with himself than anything else. She looked into those kind eyes and for just a brief moment wished that he were indeed her father.

"Thank you, Frank."

"Don't thank me, Gaia. I don't deserve it. Tell me this, though. If you saw this 'Jack' character again on the street, how would you feel?"

Gaia looked down at the floor. "I'm ashamed to say that I would want to kill him."

Frank frowned at her. "Don't be ashamed. Scum like that deserve to die." He picked up a pen and held it over a pad of paper. "This happened a week ago today?"

Gaia nodded.

"And it was at the Royal York?"

She nodded again.

"Room number? Do you remember it?"

"Yes – 2021."

Gaia didn't know why she was so eagerly providing this information. She knew in her gut why he was asking. She knew what was going to happen but was trying hard to deny it to herself. One part of her was starting to feel closure, but the other part just didn't want to know what it was that was going to bring that closure. She realized that for this brief moment, she had become an Italian woman.

"Frank, hotels don't provide the information you're looking for."

He smiled. "Yes, sometimes they do, Gaia. And yes, in this case they will."

CHAPTER 33

Jeff weaved his Corvette along Bayview Avenue North, heading towards Gaia's little bungalow in Leaside. He was amazed that it was only one month until Christmas and not a flake of snow was on the ground yet. Jeff was glad – he always hated the moment when he had to store his sports car away for the winter.

He was free! He still couldn't believe it, but for now he was free. And he considered himself very lucky. He knew of course that when this was all over, he'd have to do some time in prison. But he'd reconciled that in his mind already. He was getting off easy for taking someone's life. Even though Filberg had been a bad actor, he was still a living breathing human being who had a family and friends who loved him.

Jeff thought that Dan Nicholson was a good guy – smart as a whip, and while equally charming and disarming, he was as tough as nails. Jeff respected that. And he felt fairly certain that he could trust him.

They had an agreement between them now, a contract of sorts. But it wasn't the kind of contract that was in writing, and couldn't be enforced in a court of law. Dan could deny that he ever made such a deal with Jeff, but Jeff's instincts told him that he wouldn't do that. He was fairly certain that Inspector Dan Nicholson of the RCMP was as honorable as the symbolic message that the ceremonial Mountie red tunic famously sent out to the world every time it was worn. Jeff was determined to trust him.

He thought back over their conversation. Dan had filled him in on the interview he did of the executive from Advanced Technologies Ltd., a senior vice president by the name of Clark...something.

The guy had been headhunted by Price, Spencer and Williams for his job at Advanced, and then was sent back to Price for personal coaching on stress management. Clark's main contact at Price was Ray Filberg. Jeff gulped as he thought once again of the name of the man he'd killed.

The sessions involved hypnotherapy performed by Filberg – Jeff wasn't surprised about that, since hypnosis was a common tool used in coaching and stress management. And Price used that tool all the time.

But this Clark guy told Dan Nicholson that he actually faked being under, since hypnosis had never worked with him in the past and he didn't want his bosses at Advanced Tech to think that all this coaching was for naught.

Jeff could relate to the ineffectiveness of hypnotherapy on some people – he himself could not be hypnotized. Neither could his Aunt Louise, or his mother when she was alive. Jeff suspected that it had to have had something to do with the fact that all three of them were psychic. There was a block somewhere in their brains, a sensory resistance of some sort.

But then Dan told Jeff about the insider trading. Filberg, while thinking Clark was hypnotized, commanded him to phone with tips on insider information on Advanced Tech. He wanted any information at all that might have some impact, up or down, on the stock price.

That was bad enough but the kicker was what Dan told Jeff next. Apparently in walked Brandon Horcroft himself, right into this private hypnosis session that Filberg was overseeing with Clark. He said the phrase, 'Thou shalt go forth,' over and over again and instructed Clark that if he ever heard that phrase again, he was to take his own life.

Jeff felt like he'd been kicked in the gut. And he immediately remembered his interview with Jim Prentice at Lakeside Psychiatric, when he had told Jeff that he thought he was under hypnosis that day he committed the slaughter. And that he kept hearing a phrase in his head, something like 'go forth.'

Dan and Jeff concluded that Jim Prentice had indeed been given the command that Brandon had implanted in his brain. Long before Prentice had been fired, that phrase and the suicide instruction must have been planted in his head. It just had to be repeated at the right time.

Then, the day he was fired and ushered into Brandon's office, Brandon must have used that phrase again – wanting Prentice to do the deed when he got home and it would simply look to the world that he was depressed over being fired. But… something went wrong. Something misfired. Prentice instead killed his own family, and then came back to the office to massacre his coworkers. He never did kill himself or even try to. Jeff almost killed him though…

Dan and Jeff discussed this at length – Dan picked away at Jeff's brain, his knowledge of hypnotherapy. Wanted to know as much as possible. Jeff admitted that it was an inexact science; that it worked on some, didn't work on others. And sometimes latent commands worked and sometimes they got mixed up or didn't work at all.

While inexact, hypnosis was still a powerful tool if executed properly on a subject. And with the right subject, it could indeed be deadly. There was some truth in the movie, The Manchurian Candidate.

But, the fact remained; two men were fired at Price on the same day. Jim Prentice and Mike Slater. Prentice committed a slaughter three days later and Slater slit his wrists in the bathtub one day after that. It seemed as if the latent commands had failed – one guy killed nine people three days after being fired, and the other guy took four days before he finally got around to it.

Both men had been ushered into Brandon's office for a brief meeting the day they were fired – which was not protocol, because neither of them reported directly to Brandon. Neither were at the vice president level. They were obviously taken to him so that the latent command could be repeated.

Dan told Jeff that he was awaiting a detailed report on deaths, suspicious or otherwise, of Price employees and executives over the years, as well as a cross-reference against clients of Price. He would fill Jeff in on what he found.

Before Jeff left his meeting with Dan, he asked, with a considerable amount of sarcasm, if he could have a badge and a gun. Dan laughed and reminded him that he was lucky that he wasn't still in handcuffs. He added, "But I do like your style, son."

So, no badge or gun. But Jeff did have a new pen. It was gold and black, expensive-looking – a beautiful writing instrument. But it also took video and audio. It would clip nicely to his jacket or shirt pocket and look just like any other expensive executive pen.

The little bugger had 4 gigabytes of internal memory, fifteen hours of battery life before recharge, and eight hours of recording capacity. It separated in the middle, revealing its own built-in flash drive for USB download or upload to any computer. Operating it was simple – the camera and microphone were integrated into the top of the pen just above the clip. To turn it on, all he had to do was slip the clip upwards – to turn it off, he just had to slip it again. Very subtle, no one would notice. Jeff felt like James Bond.

Dan told him that they'd start off with the pen – get as many video recordings as he could of meetings with Brandon or any of the other executives who might be in on the insider trading schemes and murders. Now that Jeff was a vice president, and being incented with an exorbitant salary and bonuses, chances were very good that he would be privy to these things very soon.

And very likely that Brandon would attempt to hypnotize Jeff and plant the 'Thou shalt go forth' command. Dan was relieved to hear that Jeff couldn't be hypnotized, but he warned him that he'd have to fake it real well or he could be in serious danger.

Every Friday Jeff was to meet with Dan at the Dufferin Avenue RCMP headquarters. Jeff could upload the data from the pen to his computer each night, charge the pen back up, and go at it again the next day. Then before their Friday meeting, burn a CD with the entire week's capturings and give that to Dan.

They'd try the pen for a while, and then would advance to other techniques if needed. Dan didn't want to rush – they had to have some ironclad evidence before he was willing to authorize a raid and arrest warrants. There was a risk more people might die, but that was a risk that Dan was prepared to take, with the bigger picture in mind. A premature arrest would ruin everything.

Jeff pulled into Gaia's driveway. He sat for a few moments admiring her cute little red brick bungalow. It suited her – cute and sweet just like her. He was amazed that he had found someone like her. She had that special magic about her that made him think about her every hour of every day. He knew he was going to marry this girl someday. And he was determined not to wait too long to muster up the courage to ask her. But…there were obvious complications now. He wanted to confess to her what he'd done, that he'd killed Ray Filberg. Yes, he'd killed him, but it was inadvertent. He didn't intend it. But Jeff's actions had led to his death – he'd basically terrified the prick into having a heart attack. Then covered it up.

How would Gaia handle this if he told her? Would she understand? How would she feel if she knew he was now working with the RCMP to bring down her boss? And how would she feel if she knew he'd be spending a couple of years in prison after this was all over? Would she want to marry him? Would she wait for him?

Jeff decided that for now he would just keep his mouth shut. There were too many variables, too many possible outcomes. Best to shut up. And just love her the best way he could.

He climbed out of the low-slung Vette and walked up her front steps. Gaia must have heard the macho rumble of the muffler, because she opened the door before he could knock. She was as cute as ever – a big smile on her face, her body adorned in tight blue jeans and a pink t-shirt. He wanted to just rip her clothes off.

She threw her arms around his neck and kissed him gently. "We're going to celebrate tonight. I have some good news to tell you about, and I'm feeling on top of the world!"

"Alright. I'm in the mood for a celebration."

She led him into the dining room, the magnificent walnut table already adorned with her best china and two romantic lit candles. Jeff cooed, "Wow, this is special."

They enjoyed a nice pasta dinner, accompanied by a couple of liters of red wine. Jeff didn't care – he wasn't driving home tonight. The food was wonderful. He could tell that Gaia had gone the extra mile tonight. And the wine was making him feel tingly...and very horny. But that could wait. He wanted to hear her news.

"So, tell me."

"Okay, it's about something I've never told you about. I inherited a big debt when Matt died – from a loan shark. Thirty percent interest. I've been paying it off for the last five years, but still owed 100,000 dollars. Yesterday, the dear man let me off the hook. I'm free!"

"Geez, I had no idea. You never told me. I could have helped you."

"That's exactly why I didn't tell you. I knew you'd want to help, and I needed to handle it myself. It was my problem."

"But I love you. Your problems are my problems. That's the way it works."

"I know, I know – and that's sweet of you. But I had to do this on my own."

Jeff smiled. "I think I understand. You're an independent woman and all that crap. But it's not a sign of weakness to ask for help. I would have gladly helped you."

Gaia smiled back. "Well, it all worked out."

"Why did he decide to let you off?"

Gaia looked down at her plate. "His daughter died a year ago, and I think I reminded him of her. He had a touch of 'heart' I guess. He's a sweet man. We're going to stay in touch."

Jeff laughed. "He must be pretty special, for you to want to hang out with a loan shark!"

"That's not all – he's very wealthy and he works in the Mafia section of downtown. I'm pretty sure he's Mafia."

"God."

"Yes." Gaia laughed. "They do believe in God more than you and I ever could muster."

Jeff frowned. "You make good money, Gaia, but how on earth were you able to afford those payments on top of everything else. You have a big mortgage."

She looked down at her plate again, and Jeff thought he saw her lower lip quivering. It reminded him for just a second of the way she was a few days ago, when she didn't want to have sex because of the yeast infection. And the way she would burst into tears over just the slightest thing. This debt over her head must have been causing her a lot of stress the last few days. And...something was still lingering. He wondered what that was. He worried about what that was.

"I took out a higher mortgage – took out some of my equity. So I was paying him out of that. Now, at the very least, I should be able to start getting my mortgage down again now that I no longer have this hanging over me."

Jeff nodded. "What's his name?"

Gaia blinked rapidly. "Who?"

"The loan shark."

"Oh. Frank Palladino."

Jeff chuckled. "Yes, that does indeed sound very Mafioso."

"He's actually a very sweet man, Jeff. I think you'd like him."

Jeff got up from the table and started clearing the plates. "I probably would. Why don't we take him out to dinner some night to thank him? Where does he live?"

"He might feel uncomfortable with that – but then again, maybe not. The Italians are very big on respect and all that. Being thanked for favors is important to them. Anyway, he lives in Woodbridge. But he owns a coffee shop on St. Clair West called 'Frank's Espresso.'"

Jeff poured some more wine for both of them. "Okay, think about it. I think we owe Mr. Frank Palladino a nice dinner out."

Suddenly there was a loud squawking sound coming from the kitchen. And the incessant banging of an impatient beak against the bars of a cage. Gaia laughed. "I think my little buddy wants out!"

She walked into the kitchen and opened the cage door. The noise stopped as the little parrot climbed out onto Gaia's wrist. But then he started to talk. "Palladino! Palladino!"

Jeff was amazed. "Wow! He just heard that name for probably the first time, and now he's got it down pat!"

Gaia leaned in to her parrot and gave him a kiss on the beak. Bingo kissed right back and started chattering.

"This is the way he is. He'll ignore certain words, and then hear one that he likes and gets it right on the first try. Bingo is one very smart bird."

Jeff walked up to the two of them. Bingo leaned forward, gave him a gentle peck on the cheek, and repeated once again, "Palladino! Palladino!"

With her right arm raised in the air holding Bingo aloft, Jeff could clearly see the beautiful tattoo on the inside of Gaia's forearm. "That's such a perfect likeness of Bingo. The artist did a wonderful job on that. The green color is bang on, and the red just jumps out. It's beautiful, Gaia."

She winked at him. "I'm glad you like it, darling. Sets me apart, don't you think?"

"It definitely does – but then again, so does everything else about you." Jeff gently stroked her arm, tracing his fingers tenderly around the tattoo.

Gaia nudged Bingo back into his cage and latched the door. Then she took Jeff by the hand and pulled him towards the hall. "Let's go to bed. I need to feel you right now more than you'll ever know."

CHAPTER 34

Several days had flown by without even the tiniest bit of interaction with Brandon Horcroft. The days when he was in the office he kept to himself, and then he quietly slipped away on business for a couple of days. No management meetings were held, so everyone just did their own thing. Jeff noticed that on the few days that Brandon did show his face, he managed to squeeze in some time to hang around Gaia's desk. Gaia was bothered by it and because of what he now knew, so was Jeff.

She'd confessed to him that Brandon tended to be a bit too flirty with her, and it made her uncomfortable. He'd also asked her out to dinner a few times since she'd taken on her new job. She'd accepted once, because it purportedly had to do with an important presentation she was formatting for him – for a speech he had to deliver at the Chamber of Commerce. She'd brought her laptop with her to dinner so they could go over it together. But she was surprised to find that he hardly wanted to spend any time on it at all. Every time she tried to show him something on the screen, he would redirect the conversation to something personal about her.

Jeff asked her if Brandon had said or done anything improper with her. Gaia said that he hadn't, but she had the uncomfortable feeling that it wouldn't be long before he did.

In the meantime, she was stepping up her efforts to find another job. Her resume was already out there with about ten prospective employers and she was hoping to hear something soon. It couldn't come soon enough for her. She had a weird feeling about her boss, and no matter how hard she tried she couldn't make that feeling go away. There was just something about him – something that made her skin crawl.

Jeff couldn't disagree with her on that point. The man had had a similar effect on him too from time to time, but for different reasons. The most eerie feeling he'd gotten from Brandon came that day when he was standing in Jeff's office – the day when the man's eyes appeared to turn black and the vision suddenly appeared about Lakeside Psychiatric. And now he knew with almost complete certainty that Brandon himself had hired those two mercenaries to attack the hospital and kill Jim Prentice along with anyone else who happened to be in the immediate vicinity. Collateral damage.

After his discussions with Dan Nicholson about what was going on at Price, Jeff was convinced that Brandon was capable of anything. Despite that, he decided not to confide in Gaia about what he was investigating with the RCMP. And Dan had even warned him to keep it to himself. But he'd thought about telling her anyway, take her into his confidence. That thought only lasted a minute or two. He'd have no choice but to tell her everything, not just the parts that were safe to share. And he just wasn't prepared to be that honest yet. Bottom line, he was just too scared to do it. Hell, she didn't even know he was psychic yet.

Dan knew – Jeff had told him about his gift when they discussed how it was impossible for Jeff to be hypnotized. He also told Dan about the vision he had before the office massacre and the two other visions that he'd experienced before the Lakeside Psychiatric fiasco. Dan was intrigued, and he asked Jeff – begged him actually – to be particularly vigilante about any visions he might get during this investigation. They might be useful, and in fact might very well keep him alive. Jeff was impressed by how the man handled what he'd shared with him. No skepticism, no jokes – just a clinical approach to how the gift might be useful.

But it scared Jeff to think about Brandon trying to get close to Gaia. Knowing what he now knew about him, he wouldn't put anything past him. He was ruthless, and was accustomed to getting his own way. And...he was a killer.

He had no choice but to warn Gaia without giving anything away. He didn't want her to let her guard down. So, he told her simply that he'd heard some things about Brandon from the other executives – some abuse that other women in the office had suffered at the hands of the 'big guy.' She asked him to be specific, and Jeff said that he couldn't. That these were just rumors, scuttlebutt. Nothing verified, no complaints ever filed. She didn't seem surprised, and she promised him she'd keep her head up. Jeff felt better – what he'd told her was complete bullshit, but it was a lot tamer than the brutal truth.

But now, today, after days of being shunned by the great and powerful Oz, Jeff had been summoned. A meeting between the two of them in Brandon's office. Jeff looked at his watch. It was about that time. This was the first chance he would get to try out his new pen. He rose from his chair, took a deep breath and slid the clip on the pen upward. For just a fraction of a second a green light appeared on the tip – if you weren't looking for it, you'd miss it. The tiny little video camera was now activated.

He took another breath – one even deeper and more labored than the last one – and began his trek down the hall to Brandon's office. He passed by Gaia's desk and gave her a wink. She blew him a kiss. Jeff knocked on Brandon's door and heard the muffled command to enter.

"Hello, Jeff. It's been a while since we chatted, huh?"

Jeff walked toward his massive oak desk. "Yes, it has. You've been a busy man the last few weeks."

Brandon made a flourish with his hand, indicating that they would be sitting in the living room area. The less formal area. Jeff guessed this was going to be a comfortable chat, a pleasant one – at least as pleasant as a conversation with Brandon could be.

Brandon sat on the couch and stretched his arms out across the cushioned back. Jeff sat across from him in a leather recliner.

"Help yourself to coffee, Jeff." He pointed to a pot sitting on the credenza in the corner.

"No thanks. I've been guzzling far too much this morning."

Brandon crossed his legs. "So, tell me how you're adjusting to your new role."

"Fine. I've inherited a few of Ray's accounts, of course, so the load is a little heavy at the moment until I get up to speed. Some desperate executives amongst his stable of clients that will need a lot of coaching, a lot of hypnotherapy. I'm shocked at how stress is taking its toll on people these days. There are so many of these folks that I've chatted with who are approaching the edge of being totally burnt out. The demands being placed on their personal and professional lives is almost intolerable for them."

"Yes, for sure. That's where we come in. That's why we're in such big demand. Any tactics you're taking that I need to know about?"

"No, just the usual stuff. Role-playing, simulations, hypnosis to reduce stress and clear their heads. It seems to be gradually paying dividends for the ones I'm working with."

Brandon scratched his chin. "How many are you working with at the moment?"

Jeff counted on his fingers. "I have eight senior executives going through the process, three days a week for each of them."

"What kind of firms are they with?"

"Covers a wide spectrum: banking, insurance, energy, trucking, mining. All over the map."

"Publicly traded companies?"

Jeff nodded. "Yes, I'm pretty certain all eight companies are traded on the TSX. And maybe the NYSE as well. They're pretty large corporations."

Brandon rose from the couch and walked over to the credenza. He turned back to Jeff with the coffee pot in his hand. "Sure you don't want any?"

"Oh, okay. One more won't kill me."

"Good boy. That's the right attitude."

Brandon brought the coffees over and placed them on the table. "Cream? Sugar?"

"No, black is fine."

Brandon chuckled. "A real man. I like that."

Jeff watched him for a few seconds without saying anything. He could tell that there was something he wanted to get to, and was being very careful about how he said it. The man was no dummy. And, even though Jeff was now a vice president, Brandon didn't really know him all that well yet. Didn't completely trust him yet.

Brandon rubbed his forehead with his hands, took a sip of his coffee, and sunk back into the couch again.

"Well, Jeff. Now you're in the big time. Big bucks. Big clients. But we're a team here, you know that, right?"

"Of course, Brandon."

"Are you a pussy?"

Jeff's back immediately tensed up. "What?"

"I asked, 'are you a pussy?'"

"I don't know what you mean."

Brandon frowned at him, an impatient kind of frown. Out of nowhere, the man's demeanor had changed. "Do you have the stomach for real business, some ruthless business, 'take no prisoners' kind of business?"

"I can be as tough as anyone, Brandon. But I don't write blank cheques. You'll have to be more specific with me." Here it comes. Will he take the bait?

Brandon smiled. "Good answer. Here's my theory, Jeff. There are no rules in business. Winners take all. But they have to put themselves in a position to 'take.' For example, all these executives we coach and hypnotize, from a myriad of different companies, they all have stresses. We have to help them with those stresses. We have to teach them how to take, how to take advantage. That's what we get the big bucks for."

"Okay, I buy that. But, how specifically do we help them do that beyond what I'm already doing for them."

Brandon leaned over and took another sip of his coffee. He winced. "Boy, that's strong coffee. Okay, I'll tell you. We can't just deal with the surface – we have to deal with the specific pressures and events that cause these executives stress. In every executive's life, daily life, things happen that they aren't necessarily equipped to handle. It could be a budget deadline, an important speech, a public relations nightmare, a bad product line…or a good product line. It may be an acquisition of another company, or the pending sale of their own company. It could be a big contract that they are just about to sign with a third party. Do you get my drift?"

"I think so."

Brandon spread his fingers out over the table. "It's like this." He moved his hands around in tight circles. "Right now, you're dealing with them on a big picture basis – general stresses that they're feeling, without dealing with the specifics that they have to fight with."

Brandon suddenly tightened his hands into fists. He raised them. "This is what you need to deal with. Specifics. In tight balls. Help them deal with the incidents that are causing them stress."

"Okay."

"Which means you need to know what those specifics are in order to help them. You need to hypnotize them into feeling comfortable sharing those specifics with you. Only then can you custom-design the approaches that will be helpful to them in their career development."

Jeff knew this was a pivotal moment, and he was glad he was getting it on video. "But, these companies are publicly-owned, Brandon. Traded on the major exchanges. These executives will naturally be reluctant to share specifics with us that might affect share prices. Premature disclosure before the shareholders or general public hear such news would be illegal. These folks know that, they're not stupid."

"Yes, Jeff. You're right. And that's part of their problem. They're bottling up their stresses, and they have no one to talk to. But they can talk to us. We're their advisors, their coaches. Hell, it's no different than the relationship they might have with a lawyer or a doctor. And it is indeed very similar in a lot of ways – you're a psychologist and I'm a medical doctor, a psychiatrist. They have to trust us as they would any professional – and it's essential they do that if we're going to truly help them. If we don't help them, they will burn out completely and our clients – their employers – won't be helped in the least. Neither will their share prices."

"I see your point."

"Do you, Jeff? Do you really?"

"Yes, I do, Brandon."

"Good. So, let's start a program of special hypnosis with each of the executives you're counseling. And, by the way, this is what we do with every one of our charges. You're new to this, but it is our way of doing things. Anyway, you'll design and implement hypnosis techniques that will compel them to feel comfortable – and with total absence of guilt – phoning you with any specific events that are going on in their companies. Any particular stress points that we can help them deal with.

Any exciting opportunities that might be in the works but are being kept secret by their companies for strategic reasons. Those are the kinds of things that can cause an executive sleepless nights. We have to know what they are in order to be able to help them."

Jeff nodded. "And what do I do with this information when I get it?"

"You'll sit down with me and tell me – and as soon as you hear. Time is of the essence with stress therapy. Together we'll discuss specifics tactics that we can prescribe to help the executives deal with these particular stresses."

Jeff took a labored sip of his own coffee. "Okay, I'll start right away."

"Good. And Jeff, after the first session with each of these people taking this new approach, I'll want to add some of my own expertise with each of them. Some additional hypnotic suggestions that will relieve their stress even more. Just some things that are unique to my own style that I can guarantee will be helpful for them. Okay?"

"Okay."

"And I need to do the same with you, Jeff."

"Pardon me?"

"Being my newest vice president, I need a private session with you as well. Some calming techniques I use with all of my executives. Nothing unusual, and your colleagues have all gone through the same thing. It's protocol here."

Jeff crossed his arms across his chest. "Well, if it has to be, then okay. I don't think it's necessary, but I'll go along."

"Good man, Jeff. I'll ask Gaia to set up an appointment for us. Probably in a week or two."

Jeff suddenly felt himself being drawn into the man's eyes. His eyelids seemed to be blinking fast. Far too fast. Mesmerizing in their movement. Then they stopped blinking and his eyes just stared straight ahead, lifeless. It felt like they were trying to bore a hole into Jeff's skull. He felt a chill, almost like a breeze, rustling from down at his ankles up through his pant legs.

All of a sudden Brandon's eyes turned black, black as coal.

Jeff knew it was happening again.

He concentrated hard on what he was seeing. The image of Brandon was up now, walking towards a far wall. Then he spun around and stood there straight as an arrow – staring back at Jeff. Then the wall started to move, slowly at first, then fast. It looked like it was going to tip over right on top of Brandon. It stopped at the last second, but cracks started forming in the wood paneling. Deep cracks.

Brandon's eyelids started blinking again, very rapidly. Then they stopped, and

Jeff saw a number dancing in front of his face. The number fifteen. They started blinking again, then stopped as suddenly as before. Another number – twenty-eight. Rapid blinking again, then a blank stare. The number twenty-one made its appearance, dancing up and down.

Everything went dark. For a moment Jeff thought he'd gone blind. He felt a hand on his shoulder, shaking him gently.

"Jeff? Jeff? Are you okay?"

Jeff shook his head and his vision was clear again. Brandon was standing beside him, hand on his shoulder. Jeff cleared his throat. "Yes…I'm okay, Brandon. Just some light-headedness and stomach cramps. I've been suffering from food poisoning the last couple of days – bad pork."

"Geez. I thought I'd lost you there."

Jeff laughed. "No, I'm fine. You don't have to worry about me. How long did that go on for?"

"Just a few seconds. Glad to see you're okay. Hey, I like that pen you have there." Brandon pointed at his suit pocket.

Jeff stiffened and looked down. "Yeah, it is kinda nice, eh?"

Brandon held out his hand. "Yeah, I like it. Can I see?"

Jeff hadn't expected something like this. He felt cramps in his stomach for real this time. "It's just a pen, Brandon. No big deal."

"Gimme, gimme!" Brandon laughed. "I like it and I want to see it! I have a huge collection of pens, just random ones I've picked up here and there. But nothing like that one."

Jeff slowly slid the pen out of his pocket and handed it to him. Brandon spun it around in his hand and his face lit up. "I love the gold finish on the top and on the clip. Stands out nicely against the black. A nice smooth finish. The gold top is almost transparent too. Very unique. Where did you get this?"

Jeff felt as if his throat was constricting. It was getting hard to swallow. "My aunt bought it for me when she was in Italy."

Brandon turned it around in his fingers several times. "There's no brand name on it. No engraving – nothing. Very unusual." He bent over and stroked the tip against a piece of paper on the table. "Writes real nice – very slick."

Brandon smiled and handed it back to Jeff. As he did so, his finger accidentally slid the clip downward. Jeff saw the sudden flash of a tiny red light on the top of the pen. He had just turned the unit off with one slip of his finger!

Brandon's hand stopped in mid-air just as Jeff was reaching out to take the pen. "What was that? I saw a red light."

Jeff had to dance quickly. It felt as if his heart had stopped, and only talking fast would get it started again. "Oh, that's just the laser feature. You've seen those used before in presentations, I'm sure. This pen is one of those laser pointers as well as being just a nice pen. When you touched the clip, you turned the laser on. But the darn thing never works properly as a pointer – something's wrong with it. No beam comes out. All it does is flash its little red light, and then just shuts off."

Brandon stared at him for what seemed an eternity. Then he tossed him the pen. "Damn technology, eh? Why can't they just let pens be pens? I have no use for that kind of stuff. If I want to point, I just point." He added emphasis by jabbing his index finger into Jeff's chest. "See? Doesn't that work just fine? I don't need a laser pen to point with."

Jeff felt his stomach relax at the same instant he felt the jab of Brandon's finger. And his heart started beating normally again. A close call. A very scary close call.

"I agree, Brandon. Too many complications with everything these days."

Brandon stood up and ushered Jeff to the door. "Keep an eye on me, Jeff, and I'll show you how simple things can be. I can make anything look simple."

CHAPTER 35

"I told you a couple of weeks ago that I'm not doing this anymore. I've had it. I told you about that guy, Jack, and I hope you put him on your blacklist."

There was silence at the other end. Gaia could hear the woman breathing hard.

"Well, did you? You don't want any other girls to be hurt like I was, do you?"

"It sounds to me like you just overreacted. Some men just like the fantasy of a woman being gang-raped. It's just a fantasy – it's not real. I'm sure they wouldn't have really hurt you."

Gaia felt pressure in her chest, as she relived the experience in her mind. "I told you what they did to me. They were sick perverts. I told you Jack even threatened to kill me. Christ, they raped me, you stupid bitch!"

"No need to lose your temper. I called you today just to see if you might have changed your mind. Some of your regulars are asking for you…and a couple of new ones."

Gaia screamed into the phone. "I will never do anything like that again! I'm ashamed that I allowed myself to sink so low. Now, I want my photo off your damned website! I asked you to do that the last time we talked and if you're still getting requests for me, you obviously haven't done that yet. So, do it!" She slammed the phone down.

Gaia was trembling as she walked over to Bingo's cage. He was cocking his head, not used to hearing her raising her voice in anger. She whistled gently to him, and spoke his name softly as she opened his cage. He suddenly perked up and jumped out onto her wrist. Sensing that she was happy again, Bingo became happy. "So, do it! So, do it!"

Another new phrase for him to repeat over and over again. He bobbed his head up and down, "So, do it! So, do it!" Gaia laughed. The little guy always cheered her up, particularly when he picked up new words and phrases. It was amazing how selective he was – must be either the sound of the word itself or the enunciation of it when he first heard it. She thought it was amazing, especially knowing how long it took for human children to learn words and learn to say them properly. Parrots like Bingo, with a lifespan equivalent to humans, could learn to mimic words instantly. Of course, with humans it was a little different – we had to also learn the meaning of words, not just how to say them. But still, the 'saying' part took an awful long time with children – sometimes requiring the assistance of speech therapists.

She kissed his beak and he hopped onto her shoulder. "So, Bingo, what do you think of Frank Palladino?" He raised his head up upon hearing her bait him with one of his new favorite words, and there was no stopping him now. "Palladino! Palladino! Palladino!"

*****

Jeff was sitting in Dan's office while he watched the footage that Jeff had filmed. He hadn't bothered to burn a disc; there was only that one meeting on it, so he just plugged the pen's flash drive into Dan's laptop.

Dan watched intently, and jotted down some notes as it moved along. Jeff was impressed by how clear the footage was. Amazing technology built into the tiny head of a pen.

When it finished, Dan swiveled his chair around to face Jeff. "Good work, this is a real good start. He's being very careful, kind of feeling you out. But he's already eased into the topic of getting you to hypnotize these guys to give privileged information about their companies to you. That's a big thing to get on film. Of course, he's pretending that this information is needed to coach them properly, but you and I both know why he wants you to get it. It's quite an amazing command for him to give you – hypnotize them to obtain information. And I noticed that he wants you to tell him right away when you find things out, not to wait. Of course, the reason for that is so that he can buy shares quickly before the information becomes public and before the share prices go up."

Jeff got up and poured himself a second cup of coffee. "He's astute and careful – but he's not too careful. Those instructions he gave me put himself out on the limb quite a bit. And I admitted to him that I know it's illegal, but he managed to bullshit his way around that. He's cagey but I also think he's a bit reckless. Just an instinct I have about him. I think we can trap him."

Dan nodded. "Oh, I think you're right. I think that from what you've told me about him, he has a strong 'God Complex.' People who are that self-obsessed can get away with things for an awful long time, which only strengthens their complex even further. They honestly think they can do anything they want and that they'll always get away with it. That they'll never get caught, because no one is as clever as they are. They take more and more risks, and just take whatever they want out of a feeling of entitlement. And when they reach that point, that's when they usually screw up. Their recklessness becomes…well…even more reckless."

"Gee, Dan. That was good. You're starting to sound like a psychologist."

Dan laughed. "Yeah, listen to me, eh? Lecturing a psychologist about mental disorders!"

"You put it better than I could have, I have to admit."

Dan laughed again. Then he quickly changed the subject. "Boy, that was sure a close call on the pen! You must have really tensed up when he asked to see it…and then when he saw the red light. God, you must have been getting ready to run!"

"I was, I was. I couldn't believe the bad luck. I think he bought the story about the laser, though. One thing about Brandon – he's terrible with technology. Has no patience for it, or any interest in it. I think that worked in my favor."

Dan leaned his elbows on the desk. "Let's talk about that vision you had. About what it could mean."

"Yeah, a strange one. And it really knocked me back a bit. Very powerful sensations, and I think I was almost unconscious during this one. These visions seem to be getting stronger with the physical effects."

Dan frowned. "It would be a bad thing if you got one of these while you were driving."

Jeff got up and walked over to the window. He gazed out over busy Dufferin Avenue. "These visions aren't easy to decipher sometimes. They're never literal, always symbolic. It's frustrating sometimes – they never just get to the point. They always dance around it with symbolic images."

"But you usually do figure them out, don't you?"

"I'm getting better at it. For the office massacre, it was only after the fact that I put the pieces together. For the Lakeside Psychiatric, yes, I figured out that something was going to happen."

"So, think then. First, what does that moving wall signify?"

Jeff moved away from the window and started pacing. "I've been thinking a lot. I think we need to put two things together first. The fact that in my vision Brandon walked over to that wall, that means it's his wall – not some other wall. And since the wall started moving, that tells me it's not stable. The wall in my vision was a paneled one, and there's only one paneled wall there – the one between his office and his conference room."

"Okay, that makes sense."

"These visions are really just puzzles, Dan. Have you ever done a cryptic crossword?"

Dan shook his head.

"Well, it's kinda like those. Your brain has to come right out of the box. Gaia is really good at cryptic crosswords. I don't know how she does it. I just watch her in wonder. My brain could never think that far out of the box."

"So, it's trying to tell you something, but wants to make you work for it."

"Exactly. For the rest of the vision – the rapidly blinking eyes, the three separate numbers after each of the blinking sequences, the cracks in the paneled wall – I think I need Gaia to help me with this one!"

Dan jumped up from his chair. "I have someone for us. A code decryptor, or whatever the hell they call him. One of the best."

Dan flew out of the office. "Be back in a few minutes!"

After about five minutes Dan was back, with a tall bespectacled man in tow. He introduced him to Jeff as Lieutenant Jason Barrett of the Intelligence division. Jeff thought Jason looked a bit bewildered. But when Dan told him that Jeff had a puzzle for him to solve, his eyes lit up and he rubbed his hands together in anticipation. "Okay, let's get at it, then," he said eagerly.

Jeff told him about his abilities as a psychic, and described in detail the vision that he had. Jason listened carefully, taking notes as Jeff talked. He stopped Jeff a couple of times to clarify some of the images, and then let him carry on.

When Jeff was finished, Jason sat back and crossed his legs, notebook on his lap.

"Well, first off, you were right in thinking that wall isn't stable. It's not. It's the only wall in the office that's paneled, which is unusual. If Brandon were a woman, it would be easy to believe that it was done that way for aesthetic reasons. But I doubt that a man would panel one wall for appearances, especially a man such as this Brandon who you've described to me as someone who has a reason for everything he does."

Jeff was impressed. This man was decisive in his opinions and analysis.

"Okay, so what is that wall for?"

"It's a false front. There's something behind that wall. And the fact that you saw it moving and almost tipping is just an exaggeration of the vision. The vision is trying to get you to see that it's a false front, and that it's designed to move. It's designed to open."

Jeff opened his mouth to speak, but nothing came out. He could see that Dan was also looking perplexed right now.

Jason raised his hand to silence them. "Let me carry on. The paneled wall is hiding something, and it's designed to open up. Probably a spring release. What it's hiding is a safe or vault. The fact that you saw the wall cracking signifies 'cracking the safe,' so to speak. The rapid blinking of Brandon's eyelids and then suddenly stopping, stopping just long enough for a number to dance in front of your eyes, is symbolic of spinning the dial on a safe or vault. Then the dial stops at a number. So this blinking and number dancing happened three times – the typical set required for a combination lock. So – you now have the combination of the lock: fifteen, twenty-eight, and twenty-one."

Dan scratched his head. "Jason, I think you've done it again. You always amaze me. Everything you've said here makes sense."

Jason smiled, obviously very pleased with himself.

Jeff stood up and held out his hand. "You've been very helpful. I can't believe how quickly you got it."

Jason shook Jeff's hand. "You know, sometimes the best way to solve something is to have someone with a fresh brain take a look at it. We can be too close to things sometimes, and we try harder than we need to. We make things harder than they're meant to be. Anyway, the rest is up to you. Good luck."

With that, Jason was gone. Dan and Jeff looked at each other in silence. Then Dan spoke in a whisper.

"You have to gain access to Brandon's office."

CHAPTER 36

Jeff now had two more neat little tools. His super-spy utensil collection was growing.

The first was some kind of thing-a-majig. A ring with three little picks, all different sizes and each with different hooks at the end. Dan called them 'lock compromisers;' in other words – lock picks.

He showed Jeff how to use them, demonstrating them on the lock of his own office door. He explained that office locks were pretty simple things – they weren't deadlocks so they could easily be compromised. The ring of three picks would be sufficient – one of them would be the right one. All he had to do was insert, tap and twist.

The second tool was a tiny little camera that resembled a Pez candy container. Jeff had suggested instead that he could just use his own iPhone. Dan shot that idea down real fast.

"No, definitely not. Not secure – one hit of your finger on the wrong button or icon on those stupid things, and the photos could go anywhere. And once they're in the hard drive of your phone, sometimes they never leave even after you delete them. This little baby here is high resolution, easy to hide, easy to use, and looks just like a candy container. See, it even has candies showing through the sides – of course, they're not really candies and that's the only place they are, just lining the sides as a disguise. And after the camera has done its job snapping pics of documents and we've uploaded the photos, the entire thing self-destructs. We just apply gentle heat; like, even a match will set it off. The "candies" burst and emit an acid that incinerates the little bugger."

Jeff shook his head in dismay. "Dan, you're a cop. What are you doing with things like this?"

Dan smirked. "Well, you may not believe this, but sometimes we just can't be bothered waiting for a judge to finish jerking off before he ponders giving us a warrant. The system is frustrating, Jeff, I'm sure you know that. We have a job to do, and sometimes due process blocks us at every turn. We do what we have to do."

"Kinda like the deal you made with me, huh?"

"Yeah, kinda like that."

Jeff slipped his jacket on, and headed for the door. He turned back to face Dan, and pointed his finger at him. "I'll pick the right evening to get into Brandon's office. And if there is indeed a vault and I can get into it, I have a funny feeling that you're going to have to move real fast and find some judge who doesn't have his dick in his hands."

*****

Gaia pulled her Mini into the driveway. She noticed that parts of the pavement were starting to crack. She sighed – a project for next spring. At least now she'd have the money to fix it. A lot of projects around the house had been neglected the last few years due to the loan shark payments. She was so relieved that Frank Palladino had let her off the hook.

She opened her front screen door and a rolled up newspaper fell back onto the porch. She picked it up, opened her heavy oak front door, and walked into the living room. "Bingo, I'm home!"

She heard the familiar cackle, and then he started shouting. "So, do it! So, do it! Palladino! Palladino!"

She laughed as she opened his cage door. Bingo leaped eagerly onto Gaia's shoulder and gave her earlobe a gentle peck.

Sitting down at the kitchen table, she unrolled the newspaper. Strange, Gaia thought. Why was there a newspaper in her door? She got all her news off the Internet now – it'd been years since she'd had a paper delivered.

Then her stomach flipped. In the margin on the front page, there was a note written in red ink. 'Go to page ten.'

Gaia quickly flipped to page ten, and her eyes were drawn to an article at the top of the page, circled in red. There was another handwritten note in red ink in the margin beside the article: 'No surprise – his real name wasn't Jack'

Gaia's mouth felt like sandpaper as she read the article:

> *Welder Falls to his Death*
>
> *Local welder, Murray Feldhof, fell to his death from the fortieth floor of the new Prominence office tower on Thursday. Mr. Feldhof leaves a wife and two grown children behind. Pedestrians walking along Bloor Street West were shocked when the body of Mr. Feldhof slammed onto the pavement around lunchtime. At that busy hour, the street was packed with shoppers and diners. Some witnesses were treated at the scene for shock. The Workers Compensation Board has launched an investigation into the accident, but initial reports from other high-rise workers who witnessed the fall indicate that his safety harness may have snapped while he was dangling on the outside of the fortieth floor*

while inspecting the welds of supporting steel beams. A foreman at the project commented that he thought this was a most unusual accident, because as was typical when working at such heights, Mr. Feldhof wore two safety harnesses, so they both would have had to fail at the same time. The Prominence Tower is not scheduled for completion until July of next year, with five more floors still to be added to the forty already completed. Mr. Feldhof has been somewhat of a legend in the city of Toronto, having been the expert assigned to structural steel work on most of the office towers built in the city over the last two decades. He owned and operated the most respected structural steel company in the city – Feldhof Steel Works Inc. While being the President and CEO, he was also famous for being hands-on with most projects and insisted on always personally inspecting the welding work done by his crews. Funeral arrangements will be announced by the family within the next couple of days. It is expected that the ceremony will draw large numbers.

Gaia was surprised that she was crying. Bingo leaned over and rubbed his cheek against hers, sensing that she was disturbed about something. And she was disturbed. It didn't make sense to her. Why should she care? Shouldn't this bring closure? Why was she crying for that pig?

She walked into the kitchen on rubbery legs, pulled several tissues out of the dispenser and blew her nose hard. Then she leaned up against the kitchen counter – she needed the support. Her legs felt so weak at the moment. "Oh, Frank Palladino, what have you done?"

Bingo suddenly shrieked. "Palladino! Palladino!"

※※※※※

"I see on the itinerary that you have one of your clients coming in this afternoon."

Jeff looked up from his computer. Brandon had just wandered into his office, as he tended to do from time to time. "Yes, Brandon. A Mike Clootis, from Global Mining. He's an executive vice president of Finance. Major stress problems – he's been a challenge."

"Okay, let's go to work on him. You do your thing – as we discussed. Hypnotize him into providing us with information about his company, the privileged stuff. Then when you're finished, give me a holler and I'll spend some time with him. I'll be here all afternoon."

Jeff thumbed through the file he was keeping on Clootis. "Looks like they're aggressive right now in gold mining, despite the fact that the price of gold has tanked lately. But – seems they have a new lease in Indonesia. There could be some developments going on with that."

Brandon clasped his hands together. "The price of gold is going to rise again, and very soon. The U.S. Treasury situation is desperate. However, the fluctuations and the uncertainties may be causing this Clootis guy nightmares. Zoom in on it."

"I will. And I'll give you a shout when I'm finished and you can have your time with him."

"Good. I'm away on Tuesday, by the way, for four days. So, you can proceed with some of your other clients along the lines we discussed, and I'll see them when I get back."

"Vacation?"

"No – no time for that. I'm off to Quantico, Virginia, the FBI Training Academy. Then I'm spending a couple of days with the CIA in Langley."

Jeff grimaced. "That sounds pretty cloak and dagger. What's that all about?"

"No big deal. We've had contracts with the FBI and the CIA for years. I handle those myself. Special training in hypnosis, advanced interrogation techniques, mind focus. It's funny, though. They're still so jealous of each other–like little kids. The FBI and the CIA absolutely hate each other, and each resents that the other has a contract with me. It's silly – but I don't care. That's their problem. It's lucrative and that's all I care about."

"Will probably be a pretty boring trip for you."

"No, I enjoy it. They need me. And the facilities at Quantico are absolutely first class. The FBI Academy takes up about 550 acres on a Marine Corps base just south of Washington. Virginia just kind of runs into Washington, D.C. Anyway, the place has conference rooms and classrooms, dormitories, firing ranges, a gym and even a pool. There's also a library, a dining hall – and it even has a mock town. It's really quite amazing."

Jeff shook his head. "The U.S. always has lots of money for their military and intelligence establishments, don't they? But when it comes to health care, the wallets are empty."

Brandon chuckled. "It's a little bit twisted, I agree. Their priorities are clear – hey, just give a good listen to their national anthem. Listen to some of the words: 'twilight's last gleaming;' 'rocket's red glare;' 'bombs bursting in air.' Christ, they have little kids singing that shit in their schools! It's all about war, and death – and they're proud as shit when they sing it, you can see it on their faces. As they're also proud to say, they're the 'land of the free and the home of the brave.' And they say people in North Korea are brain-washed!"

Jeff smiled. "Yeah, while here in Canada we still sing 'God Save the Queen!'"

Brandon stood up. "That's almost just as twisted, in my view. Let's face it; it's all about manipulating what people think so they can be controlled. In the U.S., kids are brought up to think that war and killing for whatever stupid cause the government believes in, is a righteous and proud thing. In Canada, we're the peacemakers – that's our motto. That's something we're proud of. And each separate set of brainwashing creates the type of populace that the respective governments want."

Jeff jumped in. "And the mass media seems to be humming the same tune as the governments. What they report on and don't report on seems to support the agenda."

Brandon swung his fist in the air. "Bang on! The media is very helpful in mind control. Which is very helpful to us. As far as I'm concerned, all of these political clowns can do what they want – and I'll support them. It creates tremendous opportunities for our firm, and I can tell you, we've taken full advantage of them. We're internationally recognized now as the leader in 'performance enhancement,' not just at the business level but at the militarized level as well. You'll learn more about all these things we do, the longer you're here. Too much to absorb all at once. Next year, I'll take you down to Quantico and Langley with me, and get you familiar with what we do for the American spooks. It might scare you a bit, but I guarantee that it will also stimulate you."

Jeff nodded.

"Okay, gotta run. Bring that Mike Clootis in to see me when you finish with him today."

*****

"I'm always in the limelight, always on stage. At board meetings, at AGMs. I'm sick of it. And the over-regulation that we have to contend with is just mind-boggling. The amount of reporting we have to do to shareholders is reaching the point of anal."

Jeff poured Mike Clootis a glass of water. He could see beads of sweat starting to glisten on his forehead. The man was getting stressed out just talking about it with him.

"That's why you're seeing me, Mike. I promise you that we'll deal with your ability to handle all of this. I want you to just concentrate on me now. You've been talking for the last hour about how your job is tearing you apart. Now I'm going to put you back together again. Humpty Dumpty stuff."

Clootis laughed. "Just hearing you talk relaxes me. I'll do anything. Sometimes I just feel like I want to curl up and die."

Jeff punched a button on a remote control, and the lights in his office reduced to a calming blue glow. He hit another remote and the soothing sound of a babbling brook began resonating throughout the room. He could see that Mike almost instantly relaxed.

Jeff stared directly into Mike's eyes and gestured with two fingers. "I want you to just stare right back into my eyes and do nothing else. Just watch my pupils. Try not to blink, concentrate on not blinking."

Jeff then lowered the tone of his voice to the lowest softest octave. "You will need to give in to me, Mike. I'll be asking you to tell me things from time to time that your natural ethical resistance will try to prevent you from doing. You have no choice but to deny that resistance, for your own survival, for your very life. You will realize that what I am asking of you is for your own good and that all we are trying to do is help you. You have to trust me, Mike. You have to trust me…"

Jeff continued talking in a soothing monotone for about fifteen minutes. He could tell that Mike was now out. Gone. Totally relaxed, submissive and pliant. Completely hypnotized. He then planted the suggestions and he knew they were received. He had no doubt that this man would be phoning him on a regular basis now with insider knowledge about Global Mining Inc.

Jeff gently brought him back, handed another glass of water to him, then left him alone for a few minutes. He walked down to Brandon's office, smiling at Gaia as he passed her desk. She blew him a kiss as usual.

"Brandon, I'm finished. Mike Clootis is all yours."

"Good. Bring him to me."

Jeff gave him a mock salute. "Do you want me to bring coffees for us?"

"There's no 'us' Jeff. I'll be meeting with him alone."

"Oh, why's that? He's my client – shouldn't I be maintaining continuity with him?"

"No. Just bring him to me. Remember this – your clients are my clients. You have no proprietary rights and don't ever suggest such a thing to me again."

"I'd like to know what hypnosis treatment you'll be giving him, so that I'll know if it will conflict with what I've done."

Brandon let out a frustrated sigh and rose from his chair. He walked straight toward him and brought his face within inches of Jeff's. So close that Jeff could smell the garlic the man had obviously ingested over lunch. His voice seethed in anger as he spoke through clenched teeth. Jeff couldn't believe how quickly the man's demeanor could change – from 'buddy buddy' in the morning, to ogre in the afternoon. Jeff was watching a classic example of a volatile personality, in living breathing color.

"Watch yourself, Jeff Kavanaugh. You're on thin ice right now. Challenge me at your peril."

CHAPTER 37

"He inherited a fortune when she died."

Dan was on the phone, and Jeff was taking the last sip of his first coffee of the day.

"Well, good morning to you too, Dan."

Jeff could hear him chuckling into the phone.

"Sorry, Jeff, sometimes I just cut to the chase."

"I kinda figured that out about you already. So, who inherited a fortune?"

"Your boss, Brandon Horcroft. His wife, Hayley, committed suicide about ten years ago. And shortly before that, her parents died. After Hayley died, fifty million dollars fell into Brandon's lap as the sole heir."

Jeff whistled. "God."

"Yes, and that's not all. She was found dead in the bathtub in their Forest Hill mansion, her wrist slit. Sound familiar?"

"Just like Mike Slater."

Dan cleared his throat. "Are you thinking what I'm thinking?"

Jeff paused, the revelation starting to sink in. "He killed his own wife. Hypnotized his own wife. Gave her the command, 'Thou shalt go forth.'"

"Seems likely, doesn't it? But I'm not finished yet. I had my research people go into deep background as well as crosscheck with client lists. In addition to the deaths of Jim Prentice and Mike Slater, three more senior people from Price, Spencer, and Williams Inc. have killed themselves over the last fifteen years. All of them from slit wrists in bathtubs. And all after having been fired. One was a vice president, and the other two were senior account executives."

"Seems like more than a coincidence, doesn't it?"

"Sure does – but if no one knows to look, there wouldn't be a connection. Price is a big company, a lot of employees. And suicides, especially after job loss are quite common. But three from the same company plus the other two recent deaths is more than a coincidence. It's a stark pattern."

Jeff let out a heavy sigh. "The man's out of control."

"He is, but trying to prove murder when the official record states 'suicide' is very much next to impossible. He's getting away with murder, but he's keeping his hands completely clean. This hypnosis stuff is a different kind of weapon – leaves no residue, no fingerprints – it's an intangible, and only the victim and the killer know that a command was planted."

Jeff spun in his chair and gazed out the window. "Dan, the guy's brilliant, and his plan is brilliant. It's almost foolproof."

"That's why we desperately need to get one of his private hypnosis sessions on video. We need to record him commanding the subject to commit suicide, record him planting that phrase, 'Thou shalt go forth.'"

"I've been trying. He gets belligerent with me when I ask him to include me in the sessions. He just doesn't trust me enough yet. By the way, he's had private sessions now with three clients of mine – so I can pretty much guess that he's planted the suggestion in each of them.

"You should know that I've scheduled follow-up visits with all three so that I can hypnotize and de-program them, reverse what Brandon's done to them. They won't be aware, and won't remember a thing – but I'll feel better knowing that they're not walking around like ticking time-bombs."

"That's one of the reasons I like you, Jeff. Your humanity always takes precedence."

Jeff snorted. "Yeah, one of my faults – in addition to the fact that I occasionally kill people in underground parking garages."

Dan ignored Jeff's self-deprecation. "Brace yourself – we also did cross-checking with Price clients. Again we went back fifteen years, the entire time that Brandon has headed up the Artificial Intelligence division. Six senior executives from different companies have killed themselves over that period of time – but not from slit wrists. Three were from headshots, two from pills, and one from carbon monoxide.

"So, it seems as if the commands Brandon gives are not that specific – I doubt very much he suggests how they should kill themselves. In fact, we know from the interview I did with Clark Winston – you remember, the whistleblower on this whole thing, the one who couldn't be hypnotized – that he was told simply to take his own life if he ever again heard the command, 'Thou shalt go forth.' He wasn't told how he should do it."

"Jesus, Dan – six clients died? I can't believe this!"

"Yeah, pretty ominous. We have a serial killer in our midst – one in pinstripes. The man's a narcissistic psychopath, which is a pretty scary combination."

"So, why did the ones from Price use the slit wrists in the bathtub method?"

"I checked with one of our RCMP criminologists about that. She said that it's just luck of the draw. That in most cases, if the thought occurs to someone to commit suicide and it's going to be imminent as opposed to being pondered over for a few days, the choice will be slitting the wrists. And the bathtub is chosen because they don't want to leave a mess. Even at the very end, most people are still considerate. Ironic, eh?

"But if someone thinks about it over a long period of time, they might go out and buy a gun, or a hose to connect to their car's exhaust.

"The interesting thing these days is that the car exhaust method doesn't always work any more – if you have a late model car, the emissions systems are so advanced that the carbon monoxide is minimal. So, it seems it only works if you have an early model car. And the pill technique – still popular, but it's not guaranteed to work either."

"So the wrist method is more sure-fire."

"It is, and usually the least painful. The initial cut hurts, but after that it's kind of a dreamy way to die. Lying in a warm bath, lifeblood oozing out of the body. The victim just falls asleep and dies. Guaranteed death.

"Believe it or not, the biggest worry in a suicide victim's mind is that they'll fail. They fear the gunshot will go through the wrong spot and leave them doing crochet in a nursing home.

"Or the pills won't be enough – someone will find them still alive before the death knell, and they just spit drool for the rest of their lives in a hospital. But with the wrist slitting, it's guaranteed to work. You just bleed out until there's nothing left to bleed."

"Dan, this is such a lovely talk first thing in the morning. I think if you phone me this early again, I'm going to need some scotch instead of coffee. My entire day is ruined now."

Dan belly-laughed. "I'm sorry, Jeff." He laughed some more. "I guess I did get a little carried away."

"A little?"

"Okay, a lot. But I thought you'd want to hear what we found out. We're up against one scary guy, Jeff. And the scariest part of all is that he's probably a genius."

*****

She'd turned him down again. Simply glanced up at him from her cubicle and said that she had a date. No offer to change her plans. No smile, no apology, just a flat 'no.' Brandon didn't like receiving 'no' for an answer. In fact he hated it. Her inability to recognize his power and magnetism was driving him crazy.

Gaia looked intoxicating today too. That was the main reason he'd taken another stab at asking her out. It was an impulse, an urge.

He found his urges coming more frequently now – he couldn't really understand them sometimes. They visited him almost as soon as he awakened, and haunted him throughout the day. Even though he had better things to do, he found he was spending more and more time in his private washroom jerking off.

And lately it was always the same image in his mind – the same movie reel. Gaia. Naked. On his bed. Tied to the bedposts.

When he had first met her many years ago, his images were more romantic ones – Gaia leaning up on her tippy toes and kissing him softly on the lips. Unbuttoning his shirt and sliding her hand down his pants. Coaxing him, teasing him. He would always reluctantly give in and allow her to lead him to bed. She would do all the work – he would lie there and comply, enjoying every delicious moment.

She would whisper that she loved him, and he would whisper it back to her. She'd smile and say that she hoped they'd spend the rest of their lives together. Then she'd slide seductively on top of him and they'd gyrate – slowly at first then advancing to a fever pitch speed, bodies sweating and close to exhaustion until the screams and sighs came. She'd collapse and fall down next to him on the bed. Cradle his head in her hands and whisper once again that she loved him.

Yes, that was a movie highlight reel that he had always enjoyed jerking off to.

But now? Now it had all changed. It had been a gradual thing over the years. As the rejections continued and his frustration built, the movie reel evolved. He began taking the lead, being the aggressor. Then, eventually, total domination.

His vivid imagination now saw him dragging her into his bedroom, ripping her clothes off and throwing her onto the bed. Rope on the wrists and the ankles, tightly bound to the head and footboards. Her screaming, begging him to stop. Him climbing on top of her, or sliding under her – being any place he wanted to be. Ramming his dick into her mouth and demanding she suck it until he told her to stop. Cumming all over her pretty face. Domination. Degradation.

There were no whispered 'sweet nothings' anymore. There were no dreamy smiles or the affectionate stroking of bare skin. There was no 'give and take.' It was just 'take' now. And Brandon was doing all the taking.

He couldn't get her out of his head. Seeing her today in a black and green skirt, stylishly sliding up just past the knee. A green sleeveless blouse, swooping loosely across the chest. No bosom on display, but just enough of a strong hint that there was one waiting to be touched by the right hands. His hands.

And that tattoo of a parrot on her right inner forearm. He loved it. Brandon hated birds, but he loved that tattoo. He longed to touch it, lick it. It added incredible color to her naturally olive complexion. Her skin had such a lovely hue to it, and when she lifted her right arm up to hand him a file, that damn tattoo caught his eye every time. It was just such a beautiful contrast on such beautiful skin.

Brandon headed straight for his private bathroom and locked the door. He lifted the toilet seat and dropped his pants. It was happening again and he couldn't control it. The movie reel. The new movie reel.

As he began pulling hard with the thumb and forefinger of his right hand, he decided that he'd been saving himself long enough. He had to have the real thing again. Right now, Gaia just wasn't ready for him. He'd continue to be patient for her. He wanted the old movie reel back, the one where she wanted him as much as he wanted her.

So, in search of the real thing that would bridge the gap, one night very soon he would surrender and go online. He would look for someone who he could pretend was Gaia. It would cost him more than what a simple dinner with Gaia would cost, but Brandon didn't care. He'd even pay more if the girl would let him tie her to the bedposts.

And if she even just slightly resembled Gaia, he'd be satisfied for the moment. He'd look for someone like that. Yes, there had to be someone who could fulfill his fantasy until the real thing came along.

CHAPTER 38

Jeff gazed up at her from across the dinner table. They were in a nice quiet corner of the Paris Rendezvous, a popular eatery in downtown Toronto. It wasn't far from the office so they had walked there hand in hand after work. Nice. This is the way it should be.

Gaia could tell he was staring, so she stared right back and made a funny face.

"Hey, that's not very nice, girl. Here I am making goo-goo eyes at you and you mock me?"

"Well, I'm making goo-goo eyes back at you too. It's just that my version of 'goo-goo' has my eyes cross-eyed and my tongue hanging out! An attractive look, don't you think?"

Jeff winced. Then he quietly slid the loafer off his right foot. Gently, subtly, he slid his foot between Gaia's legs and edged upwards. Luckily the table was blessed with a long tablecloth. He watched Gaia's facial expressions – watched them gradually change until he knew he had met his mark. He could feel her wiggling her crotch against his toes. He pressed harder and she pressed back. She closed her eyes ever so slightly while slithering her tongue around the outside of her sensuous lips.

"So, can I interest you two in any dessert? The Crème Caramel is very special tonight."

The spell was broken. Jeff looked up at the tuxedoed waiter and shook his head, not quite able to muster the word 'no.' At this point the word 'no' was the last word he wanted to even think of. He slowly and quietly lowered his foot to the floor.

Gaia giggled. She'd recovered much faster than Jeff, which was surprising since she was the one getting 'it' done to. "No, thank you. Everything was wonderful." She winked at Jeff. "I think we'll just have some more coffee."

"Right away, ma'am." The waiter turned on his heel and disappeared into the kitchen.

Gaia smiled and caressed Jeff's hand with her fingers. "That was nice. Surprise me like that again sometime, but do make sure the tablecloth is at least as long as this one!"

Jeff laughed. "Yeah, I don't think we want to put on a show. We'll keep it a private affair. But I do want to hear fellow diners say, "I'll have what she's having!""

They talked about work for a while over coffee. Gaia told Jeff about the lack of success she'd had so far in finding another job, although her resume had been sent out to dozens of firms.

"But, the pressure is off me a bit with that debt being forgiven by the loan shark."

Jeff snapped his fingers. "I knew there was something I forgot. We were going to have dinner with him, to thank him. What's his name again?"

"Frank. Frank Palladino. I didn't forget – I've left a couple of phone messages for him but he hasn't phoned me back yet. I'll try again."

"Good. Let me know. Listen, there's something I wanted to ask you about. Way way back on our very first date, you were reluctant to talk about Brandon. You said when you knew me better, you'd tell me more. Well – you know me a lot better now."

She looked at him intently with her mesmerizing black eyes. "Why do you want to know?"

"Well, I work directly for him now too. And I'm a vice president, which puts me in the inner circle – although sometimes I feel like I'm not really there yet."

She nodded. "He's cagey. He's probably going to give you some time before totally trusting you."

Jeff cleared his throat. "Back on that first date, you mentioned something about 'cloak and dagger,' and 'scary clients.' What did you mean by that?"

Gaia picked up her spoon and began stirring her coffee. "There are some clients – the ones from the U.S. They're different. They're not like the executives who come from client companies here in Canada. These guys are just…different."

"In what way?"

"They're not friendly in the least. And, what's most strange is that Brandon seems to defer to them. They're the ones who seem to be in charge. They're not intimidated by Brandon at all."

"Who are they?"

"Seldom the same people. But they all look and act the same. Tall, confident, dark suits, dark ties – very conservative."

"But who are they?"

Gaia leaned forward and whispered. "Government. CIA. He does work for the CIA – a lot of work for the CIA. And it's very lucrative. A portion of the fees goes into the account of Price, Spencer and Williams, but a good half goes into Brandon's personal bank account."

"How do you know that?"

"I do the reconciling of the receivables before they go to Accounting. He gets two billings for any of this CIA work. One is for services rendered by Price; the other is for what's called a 'Personal Services' contract with Brandon himself. It seems that any training and coaching of agents at Langley by Brandon or other executives is payable to Price, but this 'Personal Services' stuff I have no idea about. I don't know what he does for that. But I can tell you that it's several million dollars a year."

Jeff whistled. "What could he be doing?"

Gaia shook her head. "I know that training and coaching is also done for the FBI at Quantico, but there doesn't seem to be a 'Personal Services' contract with the FBI, only the CIA."

Jeff already knew something about what Gaia was telling him. Brandon had admitted to him that he did training down in the States for the FBI and the CIA, and even suggested taking Jeff down there with him next year. But this 'Personal Services' aspect was a twist. He wondered what that was, and how it justified several million dollars a year going into Brandon's personal bank account. He didn't want to press Gaia too much on this, though.

"Again, back on that first date, you said something kind of shocking. You told me 'people seem to die.' What did you mean by that?"

She stared at him with a question in her eyes. "Jeff, if I didn't know better, I'd think you were a cop."

Jeff coughed. "It's just that what you said stuck with me. And now that I'm higher up in the organization, I'm curious – and maybe a bit concerned."

Gaia sat back in her chair and folded her arms over her chest. "I have no specifics at all, only office talk that I hear. Aside from the Slater suicide and the slaughter by Prentice and his eventual death, there have been several more over the years. Suicides apparently. And some client executives too. Seems odd."

"Do the staff that you talk to have any theories – conspiracy theories?"

Gaia laughed. "Oh, sure. All way out there. But most of us prefer to think that these are just coincidences – I mean, we are a big company and the firms we deal with are large also. So, it's probably just the 'law of large numbers.'"

Jeff held her gaze. "Do you really believe that?"

She gazed right back and was quiet for a moment. "No, I don't. There's something really odd going on at our company. I feel it. That's why I want out as soon as I can. In the meantime I don't want to rock the boat, and I prefer to believe in coincidences."

*****

One of Jeff's newest clients had just come out of hypnosis. Jeff had done his bit, planting the suggestions about insider information. The man had been totally under and Jeff was confident that he'd be receiving calls regularly now about happenings at the man's company that might affect their share price.

His name was Murray Maxwell, an executive vice president of operations at General Aerodynamics Inc. He was stressed beyond belief – Jeff felt sorry for him. Murray was a classic example of an executive who had surpassed the 'Peter Principle.' He was an over-achiever afraid of being found out. He had overachieved beyond his capability – now he had the big income, big mortgage, and expensive cars – so he had to keep up the charade, keep going because he didn't want to give anything up. But deep in his heart he just wanted to drop out. Jeff's job was to help him believe in himself again, get rid of the self-doubts, get his mojo back – and of course extract privileged information so that Price, Spencer, and Williams could buy General Aerodynamic stock and make a fortune.

In about ten minutes time, Jeff would be escorting Murray down to Brandon's office for the second phase of his 'programming.' Brandon would put the man under once again, very deeply this time – deeper than Jeff was probably capable of.

Brandon didn't know that Jeff knew what took place in those private sessions – Jeff only knew from what his new friend Dan Nicholson of the RCMP had told him from what he had found out from that one informant who couldn't be hypnotized. So Jeff was well aware, and made sure to go to great lengths after each and every session to arrange his own follow-up sessions to deprogram the hapless candidates. He didn't want them walking around with that ticking time bomb phrase in their heads: 'Thou shalt go forth.'

So far, Jeff had had no success at all in convincing Brandon to let him sit in on his private sessions with Jeff's clients. The man absolutely refused to include him – in fact had gotten quite angry with him for daring to challenge him. And, most surprising to Jeff, Brandon hadn't yet scheduled a private session with him – at which presumably he would attempt to plant that phrase in Jeff's head. And Jeff, being immune to hypnosis, would fake it and film it with his trusty little pen video camera.

But no luck on either front. He hadn't had the chance to film what Brandon did with Jeff's clients, because he wasn't allowed to sit in. And he hadn't been able to film his own session, because Brandon hadn't had one with him yet.

And Jeff's RCMP friend Dan was starting to get impatient. He wanted film and he also wanted Jeff to get into Brandon's vault.

First things first. Film first, then vault. And Jeff had a brilliant brainstorm that would get him that video footage. He would sneak the camera in under the cover of one unsuspecting Murray Maxwell.

Jeff looked at his watch, stood up, and motioned with his hand for Murray to do the same. "Okay, Murray, it's time for your private session with the 'big guy,' Brandon

Horcroft."

Murray laughed. "I'm kinda nervous. What's he going to do to me?"

Jeff squeezed Murray's shoulder. "Nothing to worry about. Just a 'meet and greet' session. And he'll try to add some aspects to the hypnosis session that I've just given you. He'll enhance it to help you deal with your stress even better. Brandon's a psychiatrist – he's capable of things way above my pay grade."

"Okay. I'll trust you on that."

Jeff smiled warmly at him. "You can trust me. And I'm going to give you something for good luck. It's my lucky pen."

Jeff pulled the video pen out of his pocket and deftly flicked the clip. He saw the green light quickly flash on and off. It was now activated. He slipped the pen into Murray's suit pocket, with the upper half of the pen sticking out.

"This pen has always been good luck for me. But don't use it or touch it – I've always been superstitious about this pen, and it seems to bring the best luck to me when it's left alone. Okay?"

"That's really something – a psychologist who's superstitious. Well, I am too, so I'll follow your instructions to the letter."

"Good. But I have to have that pen back. So, return to my office after your session with Brandon, okay?"

"I will."

Jeff led the way down the corridor to Brandon's office, made the introductions, and left them alone. It would be an hour. On his way past Gaia's desk, he grabbed her by the hand and said, "Let's go for coffee."

After a pleasant hour together at Starbucks, they agreed they'd see the new movie 'Gravity' tonight – the scary 'lost in space' story starring George Clooney and Sandra Bullock. They both loved anything to do with outer space. Jeff was excited. And excited also to see the footage from the video pen. This was turning out to be a good day.

He dropped Gaia off at her desk and made his way back to his office. There was a bounce in his step – he could feel it. His idea to plant the video pen on Murray was a stroke of brilliance.

Murray was waiting for him. He stood when Jeff came in and he had a big smile on his face. "I liked him. I think the session went really well. I've never felt so relaxed in my life!"

"Good. Glad to hear it." Jeff looked at Murray's pocket and his heart sank. The pen wasn't there!

"Murray, where's my pen?"

Murray looked down, and slid his fingers inside the pocket. Then checked all the other pockets. "Geez, I don't know. It was there when I went in."

"Did you give it to Brandon?"

"Not that I recall. But, I was kind of under the influence, if you know what I mean. I guess it's possible I could have given it to him and not be aware."

Jeff felt weak in the knees, and could hear a deep rumbling in his stomach. "Did Brandon ask you for it?"

"I don't remember, Jeff. Why don't you go check with Brandon yourself? I'm sorry; it sounded like you really loved that pen. If it makes you feel any better, I think you were right – it must be a lucky pen. I feel great after that session."

Jeff grimaced. "Yes, it is indeed a lucky pen."

Murray reached out his hand to shake. Jeff gripped it tightly, and wondered if Murray could detect the nervous sweat on his palm.

CHAPTER 39

"If he has the video pen and figures out what it is, you're in deep doo-doo."

Jeff had grown to like Dan Nicholson. He always came right to the point, no fucking around. He'd called him right after Murray left his office. Jeff didn't think Dan would be able to help with this problem but he just needed someone to talk to whom he could trust.

"Dan, do you think I should ask him if he has it, or would that be showing my hand?"

Dan was silent for a few moments. "I guess we can look at it this way. Let's assume he has the pen, and realistically, where else could it be? He has it, I'm sure of it. We know that he was interested in it when he saw you with it, so perhaps it's just an interest thing with him.

"Does he know that it's your pen, or does he think that this Murray guy coincidentally had the same type of pen? Either way, he might have just wanted it and decided to take it while Murray was under hypnosis. It sounds like Brandon's the kind of guy who just takes what he wants, and if he's brazen enough to steal insider information about these clients' companies so that he can stock-trade illegally, would stealing a pen be out of character?"

Jeff thought that Dan was putting things nicely into perspective. "No, it wouldn't be out of character at all. You're making me feel a bit better."

"Jeff, I'm just rationalizing – I'm not trying to make you feel better. I think it would be dangerous for you to feel too good right now."

"Okay, if I'm not supposed to feel better, how should I feel?"

"Scared. Regardless of whether or not he's figured out what that pen really is, he's in possession of it and it's only a matter of time before he figures it out or someone else figures it out for him. What if he's brandishing the thing around showing it off to one of his clients or colleagues, and someone tech-savvy recognizes it for what it is?"

"Yeah, you're right – only a matter of time."

"We can't afford to be complacent. As I said, we have to assume he has the pen, and we have to assume he's going to figure it out. That's the safest way for us to think."

Jeff switched the phone over to his other ear – he was so tense, even his ear was sweating. "So, where does that leave us? What the hell do we do now? If he figures it out, I'm a sitting duck."

Dan cleared his throat. "We have to move things up. We're not going to get video footage of him commanding people to commit suicide, so we'll have to rely on the testimony of that Clark Winston guy who came to me – you remember, that senior vice president from Advanced Technologies who couldn't be hypnotized? His testimony will probably not be enough, so if we did make some arrests we may have to scare the shit out of some of Brandon's other vice presidents. If they've ever sat in on one of his sessions, they might testify to save their own asses and thus corroborate what Clark Winston testifies to."

Jeff switched the phone back to his other ear. "I think you're still a ways off from making arrests though. You haven't got much yet."

"You're right – that's where you come in. We need you in that vault. Sooner rather than later now. This video pen creates a sense of urgency – if he figures out what it is, you'll be in danger."

Jeff could feel the sweat soaking the back of his white Pierre Cardin shirt. Despite the excessive sweating, he felt chilled. "Okay, I'll pick a safe evening this week or next. Have to get this over with."

"Good. Let me know. In the meantime, in light of what you've told me about the training Price, Spencer and Williams does for the FBI and CIA, and now the revelation from Gaia about this Personal Services contract that Brandon has with the CIA, I have to do some probing with my contact down at the FBI."

Jeff frowned. "Is that wise? Can you trust them? They have a relationship with this man."

"I have to trust them, Jeff. The RCMP and FBI always work together on cases that cross our respective borders – I have to bring them in on this. Just like they bring me in on cases that involve exposure in Canada. It's protocol – I have no choice."

Jeff started pacing his office. "Are you going to talk to the CIA as well? That's who he has the personal contract with that pays him millions a year."

"No, I have no regular contact at all with the CIA. The FBI is our equivalent down in the U.S. The CIA is confined to working outside of their own borders – they're not permitted by law to operate within America."

"But what's this contract Brandon has with them?"

"We might never know that. I'll inform the FBI and let them address it with the CIA if they wish. Not my concern. But I have to inform the FBI about the insider trading and securities fraud that Price, Spencer and Williams appears to be guilty of, and that we're trying to gather evidence about. And, of course, the mind manipulation leading to commanded suicides. They might have a few cases down there where this has happened too. Price has clients around the world. We only know about the Canadian deaths and the Canadian insider trading."

Jeff felt a headache coming on. "Okay, are you going to talk to them soon?"

"Today. I'll touch base with you later."

*****

Dan was waiting patiently. It had been three hours since he'd chatted with his contact at the FBI in Quantico: Vince Moon, the assistant deputy director. He and Vince had worked on cases together for years. They had a good relationship and had actually become good friends. Their respective families had vacationed together in Virginia, which Dan's wife and kids had just loved. A beautiful state. Vince even offered him a position in the FBI once upon a time, but Dan didn't relish the idea of living in the United States even though the state of Virginia itself was enticing.

He opened his file while he killed time—began reading once again the mounds of notes that he and Jeff had made together. Jeff – he'd come to like the young man very much. He was worried about him now. He had a funny feeling about how this was going. The sooner Jeff got into that vault the better. Hopefully, that's where the incriminating stuff was because, so far, Price's Wide Area Network had been impenetrable. If Jeff could get some good photos with his Pez camera, they'd be able to move on this.

But Jeff was exposed to danger now, and this made Dan uncomfortable. Before the video pen had disappeared he'd considered the assignment a fairly safe one. But now...

And Jeff was just a civilian. Dan used civilians all the time, but if things got dangerous he'd usually pull them in plenty of time. Was he being reckless this time because of the diabolical nature of the crimes being committed? Would Jeff even agree to be pulled, knowing that he needed to do this just to get a lower sentence for the killing of Ray Filberg? Dan and Jeff each had their own motives for bringing this to a conclusion.

But Dan had really come to like Jeff...

His thoughts were jarred by the ring tone of his phone.

"Nicholson here."

"Hi Dan. It's Vince."

"Hey, Vince. What were you able to find out for me?"

There were a few seconds of silence before Vince answered. "You'll have to leave this one alone, Dan."

"What?"

"Just bury it. Between friends, do this for me, will you? We've all done it from time to time. This is one you need to bury."

"Vince, I'm astounded. I've de-briefed you on all of this. We have massive insider trading and securities fraud here, and you probably have the same thing happening down there. But we also have a serial killer who kills by hypnosis! How can I ignore this, or...as you say...bury it?"

"I can't get into it, Dan. I've talked with a senior guy over at the CIA – okay, I'll give you a strong hint. Did you know that for all of the people who work for the CIA in every country around the world, only thirty percent of them are actual CIA employees? The remaining seventy percent are contract employees – contractors who work under the guise of other professions. I don't have to tell you what kind of deeds they probably do in those countries."

"Are you saying that Brandon Horcroft is a CIA contract agent?"

Vince sighed. "I said I'd give you a hint, I didn't say I'd confirm anything."

Dan ignored Vince's dodge. "So, the CIA sanctions insider trading and murder of innocent executives?"

Vince sighed again, a little louder this time. "Let's just suppose for a second that someone in a certain country does specialized contract work for the CIA – in that country, the U.S.A. or elsewhere. Remember, the CIA isn't allowed to operate in its own country, but sometimes they still do – but through contractors, so that they can't be connected to it.

"And let's just say that that contractor might get a bit power-mad, and thinks he can do anything. So, a little mischief here, and a little mischief there – nothing to do with the CIA but totally on his own. So, maybe that agent gets a little bored and decides to manipulate the stock market – and maybe some people get killed. That doesn't mean the CIA knows about those things or even cares. We're talking hypotheticals here now."

Dan raised his voice. "In all conscience, can you honestly ask me to ignore these crimes committed by a bored psychopathic narcissistic CIA agent? Is that something you can live with? You consider these crimes just 'mischief?'"

Vince raised his voice in reply. "Dan, I can't tell you what to do. Know this though – if there is publicity surrounding this, which there would be because the financial crimes are major and the killings are sensational, weird, and newsworthy – it will cause a firestorm. You don't know what his role is and what he does for the CIA. It would come out, and neither of our countries can afford that. Trust me. Best to just live with the insider trading and killings, and quietly make them stop."

"Quietly make them stop? Are you serious? No justice here – is that what you're saying? People have been ordered to kill themselves, for God's sake!"

"Dan, listen to me as your friend. And swallow the naïve crusader act. Save it for your priest."

"Fuck off, Vince!" Dan slammed down the phone.

He got up from his desk, walked down the hall to the elevator and took it down to the ground floor. Then he walked, and walked, and walked…

Two hours later, back in his office, Dan was feeling a bit better. The anxiety had been spent on the streets and he was calmly tired. But then his phone rang again.

"Nicholson here."

"I'm not going to give you my name, but I'm calling from Langley. That's all you need to know. I was hoping we could have a pleasant conversation together."

Dan caught his breath. He was now talking to a spook from the CIA. "I know what you're calling about."

"You were given some sage advice a while ago from Mr. Moon. I urge you to take it–it's in your best interests to take it."

"Is this some kind of threat?"

"Of course not. We don't threaten people. We just give direction."

Dan couldn't help but notice that the man's voice was monotone, expressionless, and emotionless – almost like it was computer-generated. It was all business, no attempt at a connection.

"You have your agenda – whoever you are – and I have mine. I suggest we agree to just leave it at that."

"That wouldn't be smart, Inspector."

Dan sneered into the phone. "Well, sometimes I'm just not that smart a guy."

He slammed down the phone for the second time in two hours.

*****

The Nicholsons lived in the Lawrence Park area of Toronto, a nice upper middle class neighborhood. It was the only house they'd ever had in the fifteen years since he and Caroline had gotten married. Dan couldn't imagine living anywhere else. He knew all his neighbors well, and they knew him – and they admitted to him on many an occasion that they felt a hell of a lot safer knowing that an RCMP inspector was living in their midst. One Halloween they even convinced him to wear his ceremonial red tunic and Stetson hat. They were thrilled – their very own Mountie.

This was one of the days that Dan would take the subway to work. He drove down on Tuesdays and Thursdays, but took the subway the other days. Like clockwork. In some ways he was a creature of habit. He enjoyed taking the subway – it was relaxing. He could read the paper and let someone else do the driving–all he had to do was tolerate the oppressive curry smell that always infiltrated the subway cars.

Dan playfully punched Wade on the shoulder, kissed Marilyn on the top of her curly blond head, and then embraced his gorgeous wife. Caroline held him tight, kissed him gently on the lips and slid her hands down to his ass giving it a good squeeze.

She smiled demurely at him. "Be home early tonight? Please?"

Dan smiled back, and lied as he usually did. "I promise – especially after that squeeze!" He never made it home early, and probably never would. But Caroline never stopped asking anyway, and he was glad she didn't. It showed she cared – and he knew she understood.

Off he went – a short walk to the Lawrence subway station. He'd take the subway south to Bloor, then change to the westbound line that would take him right to Dufferin Street where his office was.

Sitting in the subway, he thought back over his conversations with the FBI and the CIA. It had been three days since those encounters and he was still troubled by them. Jeff had phoned him asking for an update, but Dan didn't have the heart to tell him what they'd said. Instead he told him they hadn't gotten back to him yet. Which was kind of true, because he intended to ignore what they had asked of him anyway. His conscience and sense of what was right and wrong wouldn't allow him to do anything else.

It was true what some people said about him – he was the 'last of the good guys.' And he was realistic enough to know that sometimes 'good guys indeed finished last,' but he had to be faithful to himself first and foremost, be true to his integrity.

He got off at Bloor and walked down to the westbound platform to await the train that would take him the last few stops to his office. He detoured for a coffee first at the Starbucks kiosk. Dan loved his Starbucks in the morning.

He strolled onto the platform and waited. The train was coming. He could actually feel it before he saw it – the familiar rush of air from the tunnel into the station, blowing his hair out of place. Then the sound of the wheels on the tracks, the whistling of the brakes as the train emerged from the tunnel.

He took another long sip of his coffee, feeling the rush of the caffeine working wonders on his morning inertia.

Then he felt something else. Two strong hands against his shoulder blades, thrusting him violently forward.

Dan was airborne and helpless to stop his momentum. He was aware of his newspaper flying off in one direction and his coffee going in the other. Then he saw the faces of Caroline, Wade and Marilyn flash in front of his eyes. Happy and smiling. Looking peaceful and content, almost angelic.

CHAPTER 40

Brandon immediately minimized the website he was looking at—the knock on the door disturbed his pleasant voyeurism.

"Yes? What do you want Josh?"

Josh Carney took that as an invitation to enter the massive office. He made the long walk over to Brandon's throne, and made himself comfortable in one of the guest chairs.

"How have you been, Brandon? We haven't chatted in a while."

Brandon glared at him. Josh was his least favorite vice president—well at least he was now, now that Ray Filberg was dead and gone.

"I've been fine, Josh. Very busy—lots on the go."

Josh fidgeted in his chair. "Yeah, I've noticed on the itineraries that you've been down to Langley a lot lately. CIA keeping you hopping?"

"Yes, very much so—which is why I need you guys keeping things under control here. I haven't got the time to babysit."

Josh frowned. "Why do you feel the need to say things like that? I haven't talked with you in at least a week, and after just a few sentences you find a way to insult me."

Brandon rose to his full six foot, three-inch height and stared down at Josh. "This is coming from the guy who totally dropped the ball on Jim Prentice? Which led to a slaughter here at the office and at the man's home. And which led to unbelievable publicity and scrutiny that we just didn't need. Thank God one of our staff was a hero and managed to deflect all that attention away from the firm."

Josh stood up too. "Oh, you're referring to your golden boy who rose to vice president in just a matter of months, when the rest of us toiled for years to attain that rank. You have Jeff up on a pedestal right alongside Jesus Christ—it's nauseating to the rest of us, do you know that?"

Brandon sneered. "Well, poor you. If you had Jeff's talent and courage, maybe you'd be up there too. I've been remiss in not asking you this before—why was your office door closed that hot summer day when bullets were flying and people were screaming and dying? I was down in Vegas, but I received reports when I got back. People told me you were basically invisible. And you're one of our leaders?"

Josh didn't expect this attack. He stammered, "I...I...was on a...conference call."

Brandon laughed. "Yeah, right. The phone conversation was so loud you couldn't hear the terror outside your office door? I hear that you didn't show your face at all until after Jeff had subdued Prentice. You're a coward, Carney. And I'm ashamed of you."

Brandon turned and walked in the direction of the door, a strong hint that Josh should follow.

Josh called after him. "Why don't you just fire me?"

Brandon chuckled. "Why would I do that? I'd have to pay you severance. I'd kill you before I did that."

Josh walked up to Brandon and pulled an envelope out of the inside pocket of his jacket. His voice cracked with both anger and fear. "Here. Take this. There are some nice photos in here of your golden boy. You'll see the street number of the building he's walking into on Dufferin Street–and if you look really carefully you can read the name of the organization etched into the concrete edifice. I had him followed because, unlike you, I don't put people up on pedestals. Enjoy."

*****

Brandon had the four photos spread out in front of him. Indisputable. They were photos of Jeff Kavanaugh walking up the steps of RCMP headquarters. The date and time stamps showed that they were from two successive Fridays, around the same time on both days.

He turned his eyes back to his computer and maximized the website he'd been looking at before Josh had burst in. He needed a distraction for a few minutes–needed to see some different photos. He scrolled through the various ladies who were on display–this was an escort site called Midnight Callers. None of them excited him. None even slightly resembled Gaia. He clicked off in disgust. But there were still lots of sites to visit–he wouldn't get discouraged at this early stage.

He turned his attention back to Jeff's photos and tried to rationalize. There might be an explanation. Sure, there had to be. Jeff had been the hero in a high-profile mass murder. His face was splashed on the front pages of newspapers around the world. The world loved a hero. And surely the RCMP did too. Maybe they were holding regular briefings with him over that. Brandon nodded–Yes, it was possible.

He opened his desk drawer and pulled out the pen he'd stolen right out of the pocket of Murray Maxwell. Brandon chuckled to himself. Once he'd finished the special hypnosis session with Murray, and before he'd brought him out of his trance, he'd snatched the pen. Which wasn't actually unusual–Brandon's top drawer was full of pens he'd taken from his unsuspecting victims. Pens were Brandon's version of killers' souvenirs. Most killers took souvenirs from the scenes of their crimes. But the problem was, Brandon was a killer whose method didn't allow him to take souvenirs from the scene of the crime. He was never at the scene—well, except for Juliet's boyfriend and his own wife's death. But those were unique.

So he had to take souvenirs beforehand, while his victims were still alive. And because Brandon was at heart a corporate geek, pens were the perfect souvenirs. And, well, he just loved pens.

Of course, not all of his hypnosis victims would become murder victims. The planting of the phrase, 'Thou shalt go forth,' was just a necessary precaution in case they got out of control. In fact, only a small percentage of all those who had had the phrase planted had died so far. But Brandon never knew in advance which ones would have to die, so he had to take souvenirs from all of them.

But this particular pen that Murray had was a puzzle. It was identical to the one that Jeff had, the one that Brandon had admired so much. What were the odds?

He shoved the clip down and saw the green light flash on at the top. He aimed it toward the wall—no laser beam. Brandon flicked the clip again and the red light came on. He aimed it again. Still no beam. Strange—Jeff had said that the laser on his pen didn't work either. Both pens were lemons.

Brandon held the pen between the fingers of both hands as he gazed down at the photos again. He could feel himself tensing up as he thought about what the photos could mean. His fingers began twisting the pen. Suddenly it came apart in the middle.

He looked at it, stupefied. It was a flash drive.

Brandon plugged the flash drive half of the pen into a USB port on his computer and waited for the image to pop up. When it did, he clicked on it.

Then he sat back in his chair and watched a video of himself commanding Murray Maxwell to kill himself if he ever heard a certain phrase again.

*****

Jeff was busy doing prep work. A presentation for a speech he was scheduled to deliver at the Ontario Psychological Society's annual meeting. His notoriety had put him at the top of the list as the desired keynote speaker. They wanted to hear first-hand how he had talked down a mass murderer. But Jeff was going further than that—in fact he was sick and tired of talking about that day. Sick of being hailed a hero. So, he was preparing a Power Point presentation that would focus on the power of hypnotherapy in dealing with depression and anxiety. He had plenty of case examples from his own experience, and he was pretty sure that the audience would be captivated by the new techniques that he was advocating. Jeff enjoyed public speaking—he knew he was a good speaker and was usually able to hold the audience's rapt attention whenever he spoke.

Suddenly there he was. Right in front of him, smiling from ear to ear.

"Hello Brandon. You kinda snuck up on me."

Brandon sat down. "Sorry, Jeff. A bad habit of mine."

An awkward silence. Brandon just stared at him. Jeff cracked his knuckles.

"What can I do for you, Brandon?"

"No, it's what I can do for you." He reached into his pocket and threw a pen onto the desk. "This must be yours. I've been meaning to return it to you, even though I was tempted to keep it! As you know, I love this pen!"

Jeff started breathing easier. "I was wondering what had happened to this thing. Where did you find it?"

"Well, that Murray Maxwell guy must have picked it up off your desk when you were meeting with him. And then he left it on my desk when I was finished with him. I just noticed it yesterday."

"Thanks, Brandon. Nice to get it back."

"You're welcome. If you ever want to sell it, give me first dibs, okay?"

Jeff laughed. "I promise."

Brandon stood up and started walking to the door. Then he stopped and turned around. "I heard you'll be giving a speech at the Psych Society. Are you going to talk about last summer?"

"Yeah, for a bit. I can't avoid it, can I? But I'm going to talk about other things too—that's what I was working on when you came in."

"It's tough, isn't it? Talking about it?"

Jeff lowered his eyes. "It is, yes."

"It's okay. Normal for you to feel the effects months later. It'll pass. Have the police left you alone now? No more inquisitions?"

"No, that's long over with. They've moved on to other things."

"That's good. But I would have thought that they would have pestered you a bit longer. Even the Feds. The RCMP loves to profile everything and everybody these days. You're lucky if they've left you alone."

Jeff nodded his head up and down; trying to cover up the bulge he felt forming in his throat. "I am lucky. I want to just leave it in the past as a distant memory."

Brandon smiled. "Good. I want you in top form. I'm off to Langley today, so I'll see you in a few days."

Once he was out of sight, Jeff immediately plugged the pen's flash drive into his computer and waited for the image to pop up. It didn't pop. The drive was empty.

That all too familiar knot was back in his stomach. Did the video camera just not work when Murray was in there? Or had Brandon seen it and erased it?

Then he began pondering his answer to Brandon's questions about the police and the RCMP. Jeff was usually quick on his feet, but he started getting the sinking feeling that he should have answered differently. He should have said that the RCMP were talking to him about profiling of mass murderers.

The thing that was bothering Jeff at this very moment was that he knew for a fact that skilled executives seldom asked questions that they didn't already know the answers to. He had the sinking feeling that he'd just talked his way into a trap.

*****

Back in his office, Brandon immediately picked up the phone and hit the directory button. Then he clicked 'call.'

"Maxwell here."

"Hello, Murray. Thou shalt go forth."

Brandon hung up and then punched in another set of numbers that were etched into his brain. He'd used them so often. The call bypassed the reception desk at the Russian Embassy and went directly to his contact.

The man picked up on the first ring and Brandon recognized the thick harsh accent of the former KGB operative.

"It's me. I have another job for you."

"Okay."

"You can take a few days to plan it. I'll be away for three days starting today, but I'll want to be here, for appearances, when it happens. Just make sure to leave a message telling me the day that you're ready to go."

"Yes."

"It needs to look like a botched robbery, and he lives in a quiet neighborhood so you can't use things that go boom in the night."

"Okay."

"I'll leave a package with photos along with his name and address in our usual drop spot. I'll be dropping it there today at 3:00. Make sure your man is there to pick it up within two minutes. We've had some delays before and we can't risk that again. Agree?"

"Agree."

"Okay, then. And don't fuck this up like the last one."

CHAPTER 41

A cacophony of screams echoed around him. Perhaps his own screams were mixed in there somewhere too, he wasn't sure. And it seemed like he was suspended in air and that time had been frozen, just as if the 'stop' button had been pressed on a DVD player. Nothing was happening except the ghostly sounds of the screams and gasps.

Then it all sped up as if in 'fast forward.' His senses were on fire as he fell to the tracks and rolled dangerously toward the 'third rail.' His left leg actually came to rest on the wood planking that was encasing the top of the rail. Dan thanked God in that instant that no part of him had slipped underneath the wood protector.

The roar of the train was deafening and he dared to allow himself one quick look to see how close it was. Dan's terrified brain calculated that he had about sixty yards until he was pulverized. His heart was pounding in his chest as if struggling all by itself to burst free and make a run for it.

Dan jumped to his feet and dove for the edge of the platform, towards the countless pairs of hands reaching out to help him, and the choir of terrified voices yelling, "Hurry! Hurry!"

The rushing wind from the train got stronger as the train got closer. Dan managed to get one hand on the platform and another one into the hand of one particularly big man. The man pulled his one hand while Dan pushed up with the other. But his hands were wet with sweat–he couldn't hold on and slipped backwards. He took a glance to his right–he had to do something in about three seconds. He could try to run ahead of the train but that might buy him only two extra seconds until he was flattened.

Then he realized that his feet were actually standing underneath the platform edge–it had an overhang of about two feet. Dan dropped to his knees and rolled himself underneath the overhang and flattened himself up against the short wall that supported the overhang. He took a deep breath and held it–partly because he was scared shitless, but mainly because he had to make himself as skinny as possible as the train passed alongside of him. If it caught any part of his body or his clothes, he would be dragged along sideways to his death.

It arrived. It felt as if the shiny steel of the silver streak was scraping against him, but he realized with relief that it was merely the friction in the air as the space he was lying in became pressurized. He could feel his body bouncing with the air pressure. And just like on the highway when passing a big truck, he felt as if he was being sucked inward. He concentrated on flattening his back up against the wall—used every ounce of strength in his abdomen to push himself backwards to fight the horrifying beckoning of the train.

Then it was over. The train came to a stop, and he heard yelling from up on the platform. He couldn't look up to see anyone because the train was tight against the overhang with only about an inch of space. He knew that everyone up above would be wondering if he'd made it underneath the overhang in time, or had he instead been dragged underneath the beast.

Then he heard a subway official calling down. "If you're down there, crawl towards the front of the train! You can then climb back up! We won't be moving the train, don't worry!"

Dan called up. "Okay, I'm crawling."

And crawl he did—faster than when he'd been a toddler. When he finally got past the front of the train, he saw the same big hand reaching down to him again. This time he held on and the big man made Dan airborne once again.

Dan hugged the man hard and didn't want to let go. Others started crowding around him, patting him on the back, saying all the right things. He started feeling hot and took off his jacket. Suddenly everyone jumped back from him, including the gorilla of a man who'd yanked him to safety.

Then Dan realized why. He was wearing his shoulder holster and pistol. He called out, "No, it's okay, it's okay! I'm RCMP!" He pulled out his badge and flashed it around to sighs of relief.

Police officers arrived along with two TTC officials. He could see that other uniformed officers now blocked the exits from the station platform. No one was getting out of here for quite a while today. Especially not Dan.

*****

Jeff took a good look at his Pez camera. He chuckled—what a brilliantly disguised little instrument. Dan told him that the memory card in this camera was technologically brilliant—virtually unlimited memory. And a battery that was good for about fifteen hours once the 'on' button at the bottom of the container was switched into place. Long enough for what Jeff had to do.

Jeff had chosen tonight as his vault night. He couldn't wait any longer. Brandon was down in Langley so there was no chance he'd be popping into the office during the late evening. And Jeff knew in his gut that this had to be done fast.

He'd convinced himself that Brandon had discovered the flash drive in the video pen and had erased it. He was just toying with him when he gave the pen back to him. In some weird way, despite the seriousness of all this, Brandon seemed to consider this something of a game. He was relishing making Jeff sweat. Making him wonder what he knew.

And the question Brandon had asked him about the police and RCMP. Jeff was convinced now that somehow Brandon knew that he'd been meeting with the Mounties. He didn't know how he knew, but he was sure he knew. Had he been followed? Or was there a leak in the RCMP?

So he had to get this done, otherwise he might not get another chance. If Brandon fired him, he'd lose his access to the office. Then he'd have nothing whatsoever to offer Dan as evidence. Nothing that he could use to barter his conviction down from manslaughter for Filberg's death. For Jeff's own survival, he had to do this. And he prayed that there was indeed something incriminating in the vault. But there was a chance it could be completely empty. Jeff didn't want to think about that possibility. No, there was a reason Brandon had a vault. And considering how computer-averse Brandon was, Jeff was sure there was paper in there—lots of paper.

He glanced at his watch. Eight o'clock. Everyone should be gone by now. Jeff got up from his desk and began his reconnaissance. A nice leisurely stroll around the floor should give him peace of mind.

Ten minutes later he was back in his office. All clear. He had the floor to himself. Jeff unlocked his desk drawer and withdrew the little lock tool that Dan had given him. Then he took a deep breath. Butterflies were taking hold. He breathed through his nose, held his breath for ten seconds, and then exhaled slowly through his mouth. He repeated this six times until he felt better.

Then he stretched, clenched his fists, and cracked his knuckles. Ready.

Jeff walked down the hall until he reached the beautifully carved mahogany door marking the entrance to Brandon's private refuge. He looked left, right, and then inserted one of the little tools into the door lock. He twisted and poked—nothing happened.

Jeff switched to the next tool on the ring. This one worked. He took one last look around him, and then opened the door, re-locking it behind him by twisting the little button on the handle.

He walked into the cavernous office. It felt strange being in here all by himself. This was Brandon's private space, and even though he despised the man, Jeff felt like he was violating him just by being here. He shook his head in dismay. Get real. The man deserves to be violated.

Jeff sat down in the same chair where he'd experienced the vision of the wood panel wall moving and cracking. He looked towards that wall–it was the one separating the office from the boardroom area. He got up and walked slowly over to it, and then began sliding his hands across the surface of the wall. He was looking for any type of catch or button that might cause the wall to spring open. But there was nothing obvious.

He started pressing his fingers against the wood, starting at the right side of the paneling, along the bottom, then up the left side. When he pressed at a point about halfway up the left side, he heard a click. The wall sprung open.

Jeff's heart was beating fast. He took a deep breath, grabbed the edge of the wall and swung it out all the way.

And there was the vault. Shiny steel with a combination dial and handle. A hidden vault for God's sake, just like the RCMP decoder expert had predicted.

Jeff didn't waste any time. He spun the dial around to the numbers that his vision had disclosed to him. Fifteen–twenty eight–twenty one. He held his breath, turned the handle and pulled. It opened!

The door was at least a foot thick, and the floor was solid concrete. It was raised about six inches so Jeff had to step up when he entered. He saw a single light bulb in the ceiling, with a pull chord. The vault was lined with shelves, each laden with labeled files. And on the top shelf he saw several pistols and a shotgun. The vault was surprisingly large–about ten by twelve.

Jeff pulled out his Pez camera. He wanted to get this done and get out fast. He wouldn't read what he was snapping–he would just snap away. Jeff would leave the reading to Dan.

He was just reaching up for the light chord when something caused his hand to freeze in mid-air. A noise.

Jeff crept back to the vault door and stuck his head out into the office area. He heard voices, one particularly loud voice. "Joe, you do the big office tonight and I'll start on the hallway before tackling the other offices."

"Okee-dokee boss."

"And don't steal anything when you're in there!"

A laugh. "Would I do that?"

"Yes!"

Another laugh. Then the sound of keys jangling.

Jeff choked. *The cleaners! How could I have forgotten about the cleaners!*

He knew he only had seconds. The cleaners had their own master keys, so they'd be in Brandon's office at any moment.

Jeff slid his hand along the edge of the paneling, trying to find a ridge that he could pull on. Yes, there it was–a fault, sort of a semi-knot. He pulled on it gently, trying to get the panel closed as far as he could. But because the vault door opened outward and so did the paneling, he could only hope to get it partially closed. It would still be open a crack because of the open vault door. Jeff pulled on both the vault door and paneling, until both had about an inch of aperture. Then he stood back in the darkness and waited. And listened.

The door to the office opened and Jeff could hear the sound of shuffling feet and the dragging of some kind of equipment. Then the sound of a vacuum cleaner making its journey around the far section of the office. The sound got closer. So close now that Jeff saw through the crack the actual light beam from the vacuum head illuminating its path along the carpet.

The vacuum shut off.

Stark silence for a few seconds, then, "Hey, Ralph! Come in here for a second! I gotta show you something. You won't believe this!"

Jeff heard a second set of feet enter the office. "What the fuck do you want? We don't have time to snoop."

"Look at this, Ralph. It's a secret door!"

Jeff heard the wall panel creaking as it was pulled open again. Then he heard gasps from both men.

"Jesus Mother of God! There's a vault behind this thing!"

"The guy must have forgotten to close it."

"Ralph, let's check it out!"

"Fuck off, Joe. We're not taking that kind of chance."

"We could just take a peek."

"No! You've already got a record for breaking and entering, Joe. Haven't you learned anything?"

"I just wanna see. I wouldn't take anything."

"Joe, have you touched that vault door?"

"No. I only touched the edge of the wood panel."

"Okay, wipe it clean with your shirtsleeve. Remember, your prints are on record. Then use your foot–not your hand–to shut that vault door. After that, close the paneling. Don't touch anything with your fingers."

Hiding in the darkness of the vault, Jeff watched and listened helplessly as he saw and heard the vault door click shut.

He was locked in.

And he knew from experience that in just a few minutes he would begin to feel the sheer terror of claustrophobia.

CHAPTER 42

Breathing was becoming more difficult by the minute. Jeff sat on the floor of the vault and tried to focus. Claustrophobia only hit him once in a while, but whenever it did make its appearance it was a challenge for him to make his brain think rationally.

The last time this happened to him was last summer in the streetcar on his way to work–right after the massacre. People on the streetcar had been staring at him and grabbing for him. The feeling of containment and smothering was severe. He'd panicked so badly that he pulled the brake on the streetcar himself after the driver refused to do so.

But this was worse. He was in a windowless vault with limited air supply. Even though it was dark he could 'see' the walls of the vault closing in on him.

Jeff focused. He knew he had to practice what he always preached. He was a skilled psychologist and a licensed hypnotherapist. He knew all about self-hypnosis, he had taught it to countless others.

First things first. He knew he had to get the light on because claustrophobia was ten times worse in the dark. Fear of the unknown and the unseen.

He stood up and swung his arm up in the air, in the general area where he remembered seeing the light chord. There it was–he pulled it. The vault was now awash in a soothing blue light. Better now.

Jeff glanced around the vault and saw a switch on the wall about three-quarters of the way up. He reached up and flicked it. He heard the whir of a fan. An air ventilation system. Even better now.

Better for a second anyway. Knowing that he was locked in this tight space started eating at his brain. Jeff closed his eyes and focused again. His heart was pounding out of control and the irrational fear of having a heart attack started creeping into his mind. Jeff opened his eyes, pulled out his cell phone and hit speed dial for Dan's number. No signal. No surprise. The vault was solid steel and concrete. Impenetrable.

He closed his eyes again and began his deep breathing exercises. He did twenty repetitions and didn't stop until he started feeling light-headed. He didn't want to pass out in here…or, on second thought, maybe that would be preferable to being awake and aware.

No. He had to deal with this. Self-hypnosis. Jeff closed his eyes and concentrated on the images that he had long ago programmed into himself to allow self-hypnosis to take effect.

The dock at his cottage on Moon Lake. He was so well trained at this that it was easy to teleport himself to that spot. The trick was not to think about the predicament he was in. To actually believe he was there. To forget about where he was.

He could see himself now walking down the length of the dock, cold beer in hand, feeling the hot summer sun. He sat on the edge of the dock and dangled his feet in the water, swished them around a little bit, hearing the swishing noise as if he was right there. Because he was right there.

A boat came speeding by with a skier in tow—she waved at him and Jeff waved back. She was wearing a black bikini and her long blonde hair was flowing out behind her neck. She was stunning and she had the smile of an angel. The boat turned into a tight circle and made another pass—and another wave of her hand. A sweet wave—very feminine. Jeff nodded and smiled. She blew him a kiss.

Then she was gone. But the wake she left remained. It splashed against his feet and rocked the dock. Jeff enjoyed the swaying motion of the souvenir she had left behind for him.

A loon popped its head up out of the water and began making its own unique sound—kind of a high-pitched wail. He watched as it submerged and popped up again several seconds later, several hundred feet away. Oh, to swim with that kind of power.

Jeff looked up at the sky—it was early evening and the sun was just beginning to set. There were very few clouds but they were the puffy cumulous type that signaled possible thunderheads later. But for now they were turning revolving shades of pink and orange. The sun was a fireball now, and so low on the horizon that he could actually look at it without squinting.

Jeff took a sip of his beer and marveled at nature's wonders. With his feet still in the water he stretched out on the dock, enjoying the feel of the overheated cedar on his back. It burned slightly, but then eased up the longer he lay. He closed his eyes and breathed deeply with an exaggerated sigh. A sigh that let everything out—all the stress, all the fear.

When he opened his eyes again he was staring at the solid steel walls of the vault. He felt better but he knew he wasn't there yet. He still had more to do.

He closed his eyes again and did some more deep breathing repetitions. This time he imagined the vault itself, but he forced his imagination to put a steel penetrable saw in his hands. He cut through the walls and created four windows, each of them three feet wide by three feet high. Perfect squares. Perfect windows. Then he painted a blue sky through the windows and bright sunrays streaming onto the concrete floor of the vault.

Jeff knew he was done now. He snapped his fingers and came completely out of his trance. He smiled to himself, proud of himself. He'd conquered it this time. Jeff knew that he had, just by the frame of mind he was in now. Just by the smile he felt on his face and the relaxed pace of breathing he was experiencing.

The vault was no longer oppressive–it had windows and light now. He could even see Moon Lake through the windows. Peaceful, beckoning.

He decided to keep busy and begin doing what he came here to do. Jeff pulled out his Pez camera and opened the first file his eyes fell upon. It was labeled with the name of a U.S. Congresswoman whom most of the world was familiar with from an event that happened several years ago.

Jeff hadn't planned to read any of the files, but he couldn't resist. This name, and event, were so infamous. There were mounds of documents in the file and Jeff began snapping photos, stopping every few seconds to speed-read the occasional paragraph. He saw the name of the perpetrator on several documents with dates that pre-dated the incident with the congresswoman. It appeared as if Brandon had met with this man on several occasions prior to the tragic event. And he was paid 1,000,000 dollars to wield his magic. Jeff started feeling sick to his stomach.

Then there were several files labeled with the names of schools and shopping malls. And once again, meetings with the perpetrators prior to the events that had unfolded. And once again, million dollar and multi-million dollar payments. Jeff was feeling sicker the more he used his speed-reading skills.

He came across files that detailed certain strategic elections that had taken place in the U.S., but also several other countries unfriendly to the U.S. Documentation about meetings with electoral officials prior to the elections. Millions of dollars in payments.

Meetings with prominent radicals in the Middle East prior to well-publicized uprisings. Millions again. Brandon's minimum fee seemed to be 1,000,000 dollars.

Jeff opened the Russian file. He saw numerous references to experimentation with ELF waves, and the desired manipulative effects on the human brain.

Then he saw something that shouldn't have surprised him at all–but it still did. Notes by Brandon pertaining to Lakeside Psychiatric Hospital and discussions he'd had with the Russian Embassy. The name of Jim Prentice was scribbled in various sections of the notes, and the date of the attack was noted.

Jeff shook his head in disbelief. This guy was a one-man apocalyptic machine. His fingers had been virtually everywhere–he must clearly be the busiest CIA agent on the roster.

Before closing the Russian file, one more name caught Jeff's attention. Viktor Yushchenko, the former Ukraine President who had been poisoned and disfigured. A story that had hit all the major newspapers in the world. A story that had been laden with sad photos of the former movie-star handsome politician, looking grotesquely inhuman. But strangely, it didn't appear from the file that Brandon had even been paid for that one.

Jeff had lost count of how many photos he'd taken, but he was sure he had gotten everything. Every document, every file. And he was astounded. Before today, he and Dan had thought they were investigating Brandon for insider-trading and murder. What he'd seen tonight was way off the map, far above his pay grade and probably Dan's too.

The things that Brandon was involved in were absolutely diabolical. The events that he had had a hand in shaping, events that most citizens who read newspapers or news on the internet were fluent with, were beyond comprehension. Jeff could barely believe what he had just spent the last two hours looking at.

A part of him was suddenly ashamed of who he was. He was someone who specialized in understanding the workings of the brain, but he also knew how to manipulate the brain. Knowledge was power, no doubt. And his skills were dangerous if misused.

Brandon Horcroft was clearly a poster boy for misuse and abuse. But Jeff and Brandon had both been trained in a lot of the same skills. Jeff knew that he could manipulate anyone the wrong way if chose to do that. He hadn't chosen that…but Brandon had.

Finished now, he had to think about how to get out. At least he'd kept his mind occupied for the last two hours and the panic hadn't returned. He knew that in a few minutes it would return.

The self-hypnosis had a limited shelf life. He would have to do it again. Already, two of the 'windows' in the vault had disappeared from his mind, and the sun was no longer bright. He could no longer see Moon Lake through the remaining two windows.

Jeff checked all the file folders to make sure none were out of place on the shelves—everything would have to look untouched. It all looked fine.

He stood on his tiptoes and studied the guns. Some pistols and a shotgun. Jeff didn't know much about guns, but wondered if the shotgun would have enough power to blast through the vault locking mechanism. And if it didn't, would he get hit by the ricochet in such a small confined space? Well, it was an option at least.

He walked over to the vault door. Turned the handle. Nothing. He studied the door carefully—no visible hinges. Everything must be contained within the twelve inches of thickness. He pushed hard on the door while turning the handle—not the slightest movement. The thing was solid.

Jeff could feel his heart starting to pound again. Despite the ventilation system, his breathing was starting to become labored. He knew that within a few minutes he would have no choice but to hypnotize himself again.

He slid his fingers slowly around the handle.

Hello? What's this?

An indent in the round base of the handle. A compressed button of sorts. Jeff pushed it inwards and he heard a click. Jeff turned the handle and shoved—the door opened!

A safety release. It should have dawned on him that there would be one, especially since someone had gone to great trouble to install a ventilation system inside the vault.

Jeff was awash with an incredible feeling of relief. His heartbeat instantly returned to normal and he was now breathing like a healthy teenager.

He walked back into the vault and turned off the ventilation switch and the ceiling light. Then he left the vault without looking back. Closed the door and spun the dial. Pushed the false paneled wall back into place.

Then he practically ran down the hall towards the elevators. This was a night of terror that he would never want to repeat. Funny, he thought to himself, he'd been more terrified being alone in a locked vault than he had been trying to stop a mass murderer just a few months ago on this very floor.

The brain was a wondrous thing—but also a mystery beyond comprehension.

CHAPTER 43

He knew there was no way it would stay out of the news, and he was right. Dan picked up the morning edition of the Toronto Star and there was his face emblazoned on the front page. Well, at least it wasn't a bad photo. He was sure there were worse ones of him in the archives that they could have used.

He immediately sat Caroline and the kids down at the kitchen table and showed them. He knew Wade and Marilyn would hear all about it at school–it was inevitable that some parent would notice it, recognize him, and tell their child. So, they might as well hear it from him first so they wouldn't be shocked. And, they were pretty mature about things like this. They knew their dad was a police officer and that there were real dangers out there waiting for him every time he left the house.

Dan downplayed it though–told them the newspaper had exaggerated everything and that he was really in no great peril at any time. They seemed to accept that.

But after Wade and Marilyn left for school, Caroline cornered him in the bathroom. "So, tell me how close this really was?"

"It was a close call, hon. I was a second or two from being very very dead."

She hugged him hard. "Did they catch him?"

"No."

"Was he some drunken bum? Did anyone see him?"

"Not many drunken bums around first thing in the morning, Caroline. Yes, there were lots of witnesses. The Star didn't mention it but the guy was apparently well dressed–suit, tie, gray trench coat, black gloves. Not your typical subway platform pusher."

"Did anyone try to stop him?"

Dan nodded. "Two guys stepped up to the plate. They tried to grab him as he was running away towards the exit. But apparently he whirled around and flat-palmed them each in the nose. Broke them pretty good too."

"God."

"I know, I know–sounds like a pretty cool operator, doesn't he? And he got away clean after that, before they had a chance to close the exits."

"Dan, I don't like the sound of this. Doesn't sound like some crazy man doing a random crazy act, which is what these subway attacks usually turn out to be."

Dan put his arms around her waist and kissed her on the lips. "I don't think I was targeted, Caroline. Don't worry. But just in case, I've ordered a security detail to watch the house 24/7." He looked at his watch. "They'll be here soon."

Dan could see her lips quivering. He hugged her. "Don't worry, please?"

"Where will they be?"

"Parked on the street a few houses down. They'll move around a bit too—not wise to stay in the same spot for too long."

"But what about you?"

"I've taken care of that too. Until we figure this out I'll have a driver take me to and from the office and everywhere else I go in between. He's also an RCMP bodyguard—trained for things like this. And the security detail watching the house are Mounties too. So, we'll be in good hands."

Dan glanced out the window and saw a dark Lincoln sedan pull up in front. He pointed. "There's my ride now." He picked up his briefcase and headed for the front door.

Before leaving he scooted back and quickly kissed Caroline one more time, and added, "And in case you were wondering, that car out there is armor-plated and has bullet-proof glass."

*****

It was a different scene than Jeff was used to. Normally, Dan's floor was calm and peaceful—it always looked like it could be the suite of offices for a law or accounting firm.

But not today. Uniformed RCMP officers were stationed in the reception area, frisking every guest who came in regardless of whether they had an appointment or not.

Jeff took off his jacket, shoes, and raised his arms in compliance. He understood why they had to do this right now. Not only did he know first-hand what terrible things could happen in a usually calm office environment, but he had read the Toronto Star yesterday.

There was no one more shocked than him when he unfolded his paper and saw Dan's handsome smiling face staring back at him. And right on the front page too.

When the officers were finished searching him and his briefcase, one of them escorted Jeff down to Dan's office. Jeff had always kind of enjoyed the pretty Chrissy taking him down there, but for now he'd have to try his best to enjoy small talk with a serious and burly Mountie. Quite the demotion.

Dan bounced up from his chair as soon as Jeff entered. Big smile on his face, hand outstretched in welcome. Jeff thought it astonishing that this was the same man who almost got squished like a bug by a subway train a couple of days ago."

Jeff shook his hand heartily. "Wow, am I glad to see you alive!"

Dan laughed. "Now I know why most people hate riding the subway!"

"I can't believe you can joke about it. C'mon, admit it. You must have been scared!"

Dan smiled and whispered. "Don't tell this to anyone around here. I'm kind of a folk hero and I have a reputation to maintain. But I was fucking terrified."

"I'll bet. Any idea yet as to who did it?"

"No name yet, but we have a composite that will go in the papers tomorrow. So that may generate some leads. We got detailed descriptions of his face from witnesses, and all of the descriptions were basically the same. So we're pretty sure the composite will give an accurate image of the guy."

Jeff sat down in the guest chair while Dan moved around to the chair in front of his computer. "Well, good luck with it, Dan. I hope you get him. Glad to see you safe and sound."

"Thanks. So, you said on the phone that you had something for me."

"I sure do. But, you won't believe this." Jeff then told him about his adventure in the vault.

"Geez, we've both had some exciting times lately."

"Yeah, and like you, I was scared out of my mind too. Getting locked in a vault is not my idea of a good time, although I think I'd prefer that to lying on subway tracks!"

Dan rubbed his hands together in anticipation. "I want to see that camera."

Jeff held up his hand. "Wait until I tell you the rest first. Several days ago, Brandon came by and dropped that video pen on my desk. He said that Murray Maxwell had left it on his desk. I checked it after he left and it was blank."

Dan was writing notes. "So, he must have figured it out and erased it. Because you said you turned it on when you slipped it into Murray's pocket. At the very least there would have been footage of Murray walking down to Brandon's office."

"Yes, and there's more. Brandon then asked me if the police or RCMP had been talking to me in follow-up of the mass shooting. I told him no. But afterwards I could have kicked myself–it was an odd thing for him to slip into the conversation, so in hindsight I'm afraid that he might have been asking a question he already knew the answer to. I should have had my antenna up on that one–should have told him that the RCMP profilers had been talking to me, or something like that."

Dan was chewing on the end of his pen. Jeff could see that he was thinking hard.

"So, you suspect that he had you followed?"

"Maybe. Or maybe I'm just being paranoid."

Dan frowned. "No, I don't think you are. There's something I haven't told you yet."

He looked down at his notepad. "This…Murray Maxwell. I think I told you that I arranged for instant info on any crime or serious incident pertaining to employees of Price as well as any employees of their clients. That's how I found you–the Toronto police had to kick it over to me. It's called a 'tag alert.'"

"So, you found something on Murray?"

"He's dead, Jeff."

Jeff almost fell out of his chair. "What??!!"

"He was in a car accident. You might have heard about it, although no names were mentioned in the news. He drove onto the off ramp of the 404 and then headed north in the southbound lane. Cars were dodging him successfully for a while until he finally slammed head-on into a car driven by a young mother. She and her two toddlers were killed…and so was Murray."

It felt to Jeff as if his mouth was locked in the open position. He wiped away the sweat that had suddenly appeared on his brow. "Jesus, he killed himself. Why didn't he use the damn bathtub or a gun? Why a car?"

Dan nodded. "We talked about this before–suicide is a very personal choice kind of thing. When they get the idea to do it, sometimes it's the most convenient thing that they decide to use, or something they're most familiar with. In this case, his car was an Audi R8 Spyder. Maybe it was his favorite thing in the world."

Jeff rubbed his temples. "This is so sad–a mom and two kids."

"Yes, I hate hearing about things like this–and I unfortunately hear them a lot more than you do. It's hard not to take them home with you at night."

"Dan, I think we can assume that Brandon made a special phone call to Murray after he discovered that the pen was a flash drive. He must have thought that Murray was working with me to trap him."

"That's probably what happened."

Jeff stood. "Which means I sent Murray to his death."

"Don't beat yourself up. You couldn't have known this would happen. It was a good idea on your part–it just went wrong, which sometimes happens. Trust me, I've unwittingly sent people to their deaths too."

Jeff shook his head sadly, then reached into his pocket and pulled out the Pez camera. "Here's my trusty little friend. You can download the images and study them. You won't believe what's on there–I still can't believe it, and I only read a tiny fraction of the documents. Call me with directions on our next move, if there is one."

Dan walked Jeff to the door. Before opening it, he pulled a card out of his pocket and handed it to him. "I can't use RCMP resources to protect you, but call these people. They're a first-rate armed security service. We use them for any private security that's needed from time to time for witnesses and informants."

Jeff shoved the card into his pocket. "Okay, I'll call them."

"Do that. And give them my name and tell them I authorize them to bill the RCMP. They can phone me to verify."

"Much appreciated, Dan."

Dan squeezed his shoulder. "Stay safe, my friend. And…good work. I appreciate it very much."

CHAPTER 44

Dan had been up all night. Caroline had ventured downstairs a couple of times to entice him up to bed. But even seeing her in his favorite negligee couldn't change his mind. She knew he was troubled, and she knew enough not to press him.

He had spent twelve hours working on an executive summary of the documents Jeff had photographed. The more he read, the more troubled he became–and the more angry the verbage in his summary. He knew the angry verbage wouldn't make his case any stronger, but it made him feel better.

In his entire storied career, he had never seen anything like this. Never seen anything this diabolical. And masquerading the entire time as a respectable worldwide headhunting firm by the name of Price, Spencer and Williams Inc.

Dan rubbed his eyes, did one last quality check of the format of the report on his laptop, and then pressed 'send.' He looked at his watch–six o'clock in the morning. He hadn't slept a wink. He wandered into the kitchen and poured himself one more cup of coffee.

By now, his superior, Austin Chapman, Superintendent, would be reading the first words of Dan's report. Austin was always up at four in the morning and in the office by five-thirty. A dedicated career RCMP man, about sixty-five years of age now and most likely never destined to retire. Austin lived alone and not only loved his job but was splendid at it. Dan admired him a lot. He was a good boss and had been very protective of Dan's career–a true mentor if there ever was one.

He trudged upstairs to take a shower. After that, a small breakfast, a kiss for Caroline and the kids and then back to the office with his bodyguard. The man should be out front in about ninety minutes so Dan had to hurry. He knew it would be a busy and tiring day. He'd asked Austin to grant him a meeting at two o'clock in the afternoon. This thing couldn't wait. He wanted to push Austin to review his report quickly.

Caroline walked in on him just as he was getting into the shower. She looked at him in her knowing way and said, "This report you've been working on–it's related to the subway assault, isn't it?"

Dan nodded. "I'm not going to lie to you. I think it is. Now that I've seen what I've seen, I think they were motivated to take me out. I've gotten too close to something pretty horrible."

"Who's 'they?'"

"I have a good inkling, but I can't tell you that."

"Should I be worried?"

"Yes—but not much longer, I promise you. It's coming to a head today. I'm going to make it explode."

*****

When Dan walked into the eighth floor conference room at exactly two o'clock in the afternoon, he was surprised to see that it wasn't the intimate meeting he thought it was going to be. Austin was there of course, but in addition there were three more people: James Houghton, Chief Superintendent; Judith Merritt, Assistant Commissioner; and Perry Sutcliffe, Deputy Commissioner.

Austin stood up and walked around the long table. He shook Dan's hand and gestured to one of the chairs along towards the center of the table.

"I think you know everyone here, Dan."

Dan nodded and smiled around at the other three. They didn't smile back. Dan started feeling a bit uneasy. What was this entourage here for? The people in this room represented every ladder of the rung above him with the exception of just one more position, the Commissioner. He understood in his mind that the higher-ups would have to hear about this mess eventually, but he was hoping that he and Austin could have had a chance to chat strategy first.

He sat down and poured himself a glass of water. Austin returned to his seat at the head of the table.

"Dan, I read your report very carefully this morning, and looked at some of the supporting documentation that you provided. It was very well done. I was shocked as you can imagine. So, I provided copies of your report to the others around the table here, and we agreed amongst us that we should all meet with you today. It is that serious, I know you agree."

"I agree."

"Dan, who's your inside man who provided these materials?"

"Can't tell you that—not yet. I have to respect his privacy right now, it's too dangerous for him."

Judith jumped in. "I detect some feelings of mistrust in your voice, Inspector."

Dan turned to her. "I didn't intend any such thing, Judy. It's just that the man is really exposed right now and I promised him that for now his identity would be known only to me. I keep my promises."

Austin spoke again. "We all agree you've done tremendous work—very resourceful as you usually are. You've opened up a can of worms that you never anticipated when you started this. Do I read that right?"

"Yes, you read it exactly right. I was expecting evidence of insider trading and commanded suicides. That was bad enough–but while we did indeed get all that now, we got one hell of a lot more. I never could have imagined the stuff that was in those files–the stuff this guy has been into. The people he really works for."

Heads were down, everyone leafing through the report. The silence was deafening. Then James Houghton cleared his voice and spoke for the first time.

"Dan, I congratulate you. You've done impeccable investigative work here, and your report is very exhaustive. But we have a problem."

Dan looked up, surprised. "A problem? Yes, of course we have a problem. The report makes that very clear."

"No, not that kind of problem. We have a political problem. A sensitivity problem."

Dan scratched his head. "I'm sorry, James. I don't understand."

The most senior person in the room stood up and walked to the coffee machine. Perry Sutcliffe poured himself a cup, and then directed his gaze at Dan. "We can't arrest Brandon Horcroft. Nor can we expose any of this."

Dan was speechless. He opened his mouth to reply, but couldn't.

Perry was still standing, coffee cup in hand. "I can see you're shocked."

Dan found his voice. "Yes, but I don't think the word 'shocked' is strong enough. I don't understand. He and his executives have committed major crimes in this country, and now we know that unbelievably atrocious acts have been performed at the hypnotic persuasion of this man, not only in the United States but also around the world. And you don't want to see him arrested?"

Perry sat down at the table again and folded his arms over his chest. "You don't understand, Dan. There's nothing I'd like more than to see this man arrested–in fact I'd like to put a bullet in his brain to be perfectly frank. He's a psychopath, a monster–and he's exactly the kind of monster the CIA likes to hire."

Dan turned and looked at James Houghton. "You said before that this was a political problem. I think I can guess where you're coming from, but tell me exactly what your fear is here."

"It's not really a fear, Dan. It's a reality. Horcroft has been using the Canadian headquarters of a worldwide organization to launch his CIA activities. He's been using Canadian soil. In addition, if we arrest him on just the lesser charges the other activities will come out–guaranteed. The activities that we now know of are horrible–but they are the activities sanctioned by another nation who happens to be our best friend and closest ally. We can't blow the whistle on them."

Dan was dumbstruck. "Well, we can arrest him on insider trading, murder and conspiracy to commit murder. We stay silent on the other stuff we know about."

James shook his head. "Wouldn't work, Dan. He'd have nothing to lose at that point. His best defense is the threat to 'tell all.' We'd have to back off and drop the charges–and those kinds of charges once filed would have attracted a ton of publicity. If you were a newsman, wouldn't you jump all over a story about an executive hypnotizing other executives to kill themselves? Of course you would.

"So, backing out of those charges would be virtually impossible for us to explain. In essence, Horcroft would be able to blackmail us into setting him free by threatening to create an international incident. He'd threaten to disclose all of the horrible things he's been doing for the CIA, from right here in Canada. We're between a rock and a hard place here."

Dan rubbed his forehead. A fierce headache was coming on, he could feel it. "So, all this was for naught."

Perry spoke again. "No, Dan, not completely. I've already talked to the CIA. We had a good conversation. They know that we know everything, and they're scared. I've convinced them to take Brandon Horcroft off our hands. Basically, we'll quietly deport the man–revoke his Canadian citizenship–and the CIA, being who they are, will fast-track U.S. citizenship for him. He'll work for the CIA in Langley rather than Canada."

"So, we'll just move the problem and the murderous son-of-a-bitch south of the border."

Austin jumped in. "Cool down, Dan. And wake up. You're just aware of what one man's been doing–guess what, there are dozens of Horcrofts around the world doing despicable things for the CIA under the guise of service to country. Even if we could arrest this prick, it would only be the tip of the iceberg–and we're not about to take on the CIA and reform their habits. That's not our jurisdiction. And neither would we have a hope in hell of succeeding. Reforming the habits of the United States is not our purview. Exposing this will solve nothing and will only cause unspeakable unrest. It just can't be done."

Dan nodded and took a long sip of water. "What about the firm itself: Price, Spencer and Williams? And the executives who work for Horcroft?"

"We'll deal with that. It's a privately held company, so we don't have shareholders to worry about. We can use our influence with their President, Karen Woodcock, to close down the Artificial Intelligence division and have all of the executives thrown out in the street. We'll also arrange to pull their licenses so they'll never practice again as psychologists. That murderous insider-trading division will simply cease to exist and the company will have to carry on without it.

"But all of this is going to take some time—bureaucracy runs in slow circles. The CIA has promised to get back to us next month as to timelines. But at least it's all in the works and we'll get the bastard out of our country eventually."

Dan stood. "I understand. I do. I guess this is it, then."

Perry stood as well and shook his hand. "Glad to have your understanding. Yes, this is it. Leave it with us now. Destroy all of your documents and close the file. And call off your inside man."

*****

It had been a couple of days since Jeff's meeting with Dan, when he'd left him the Pez camera. He thought for sure he would have heard from him by now. He made a mental note to call him tomorrow to find out what the next steps would be.

Jeff got undressed and felt something in the pocket of his pants. He reached in and pulled out the card Dan had given him for the security company. He made yet one more mental note—to phone them tomorrow, first thing.

Jeff brushed his teeth and crawled into bed—under the warm soothing flannel sheets. He felt exhausted. The after effects of the vault adventure were still with him. The fear of claustrophobia and the stress in fighting it off always took a toll on him. He knew it would take a couple of days before he felt normal again.

He settled his head into the soft pillow and sighed. He sensed that this whole ordeal was close to an end. He'd have closure.

He would also have prison, but he'd just have to suck that up as the price for his huge mistake. A life had been lost and he had to pay for that. But at least he'd be nailing Brandon Horcroft before he had to pay his own price.

Jeff closed his eyes. But something made him open them again. He stared at the ceiling—and while he stared, two images began to form, floating above his head. They were wearing ski masks and he could clearly see the whites of their eyes. Each of them raised their right hands and the glint of steel appeared, flashing, stabbing. Then they disappeared as quickly as they had come.

But another image replaced them almost immediately. This time he saw himself hanging onto the branch of a tree, dangling above the ground, struggling, feet swinging towards the trunk. He could see his own face, sheer terror in his eyes. The image suddenly turned its face and stared at him.

Jeff was looking at Jeff. And the image of Jeff mouthed the word, 'run.'

Jeff lurched upward into a sitting position. Another vision!

He could feel his breathing getting more labored the longer he thought about what he'd just seen. He began to analyze it. He was starting to reach the conclusion that it was just his fear of the danger he might be in right now, particularly after what happened to Dan at the subway and the suicide of Murray Maxwell. And the fact that he'd found the card for the security company in his pocket and that he knew in his gut he should have phoned them already.

It was just fear. Irrational fear.

Jeff laid his head back down on the pillow again.

But then the neighbor's dog started barking. That dog never barked at night.

Jeff lurched up again and listened. At first he thought it was just his imagination. But then he realized the noise was familiar to him. It was the same metal on metal scratching noise that he remembered from when he was using Dan's lock pick tools on Brandon's office door.

CHAPTER 45

That sound was eerily familiar. It brought back the horror of being trapped in the vault. But now the sound had a new ring of horror to it. His own house might now become a trap.

Jeff tiptoed out into the hallway and looked down through the transom window above the front door. He could see dark shadows simulating figures on his front porch. Someone was definitely trying to get in. And they had chosen the front door because his back door had an integral bar structure that locked by slide bolts into the brick.

Jeff dashed into his bathroom and felt around for some kind of weapon. He picked up his electric razor, then a hand-held mirror, discarding each as being useless. Jeff knew he had to get down to the kitchen where the knives were. He grabbed his toothbrush just in case he didn't get that far. At least he could jab with it.

He crept back into the hallway and listened–yep, they were still attempting to get in. Jeff had a good lock on there so he was hoping it might take them a few more minutes. He picked up his phone and dialed 911.

"911 Dispatch."

"Someone's trying to break into my house."

"We're sending a car out right now, sir."

"How long?"

"About ten minutes."

"Don't you want my address?"

"We have it on the screen, sir. Hide yourself somewhere until we arrive."

Jeff hung up. Yeah, right. Where would he hide? It was a small house–and the idea of being trapped in a closet waiting for someone to yank it open made the feelings of claustrophobia start their haunting squeeze of his chest once again. No, he had to be in the open.

Jeff ran in his stocking feet to the top of the stairs. The shadows were still there and the metal scraping sound was getting more frantic. Whoever they were, they were getting frustrated now.

Deciding he had no time for the stairs, Jeff hoisted himself up onto the smooth mahogany banister railing. He put one foot on each side of the railing and then slid on his bum all the way down to the main floor. A smooth landing at the bottom—but then he heard a resounding click as the deadbolt slid inward. Jeff's chest began squeezing the breath out of him.

He leaped over to the side of the door opposite to where it would open. And waited. The door opened only partially and Jeff knew he would be exposed if they looked sharply to their right.

One dark figure entered cautiously. He had a penlight in his hand and began swooping the beam around in a gentle arc. Then he whispered something to the figure behind him—to Jeff it sounded like Russian. The first man moved forward and the second man began to enter. Once he was clear of the door, the second one quietly closed the door behind him. The first intruder moved slowly down the hall toward the kitchen and Jeff could see something in his hand that was reflecting the streetlights beaming in through the living room window. It was a knife, and a large one. They intended overkill.

Both men were wearing ski masks.

The second intruder had a knife out now too and he moved forward in a crouch, jungle ambush style.

Jeff decided not to wait. He decided not to ask why they were in his house. He already knew why.

He lunged from his spot against the wall and jammed the end of the toothbrush into the soft base of the second man's skull. The vulnerable area between the skull and the neck sometimes referred to as 'no man's land.' Instant paralysis if not death. The spine's Achilles' heel.

The man immediately stiffened and quivered, his upper body yanking itself upright at the thrust. An involuntary movement that lasted no more than a second. Then he began his collapse to the floor. Jeff's hand was still on the bristle end of the toothbrush, with most of the length of the instrument having disappeared through the base of the man's skull. The thug hadn't even had time for the brain signal to utter a scream. No sound had come from his mouth at all.

But there would be a sound now—the sound of him crashing to the floor. Jeff tried to catch him and ease him down but he was just too heavy. He was literally a 'dead weight.'

The other man was already in the kitchen, confident that his partner was right behind him. He was behind him all right, but about to make one hell of a noise. As he hit the floor Jeff yanked the knife out of his hand. He decided to leave his toothbrush right where it was.

Jeff dashed for the stairs, just as the other dark figure ran back out of the kitchen uttering some words that, once again, sounded Russian.

He ran up the stairs as fast as he could. He thought of using the front door, but he wasn't sure he would make it out the door without feeling a knife in his back. And he worried that someone else may be outside waiting for him in the unlikely event he escaped.

The dog was still barking, in fact louder than ever now. There was the sound of a woman's voice trying desperately to hush the dog up, but the animal clearly wasn't listening. Jeff thought it best to just buy some time until the police arrived, which would be any minute now. He had to just find a way to stay alive until then.

His outstretched legs took the stairs three at a time. The other man was on his way up now—he could hear his footfalls and his frantic angry breaths. He hadn't wasted any time mourning over his friend.

Jeff was almost at the top when he stumbled—then went into a terrifying slide down the stairs on his chest, getting perilously close to the pursuer behind him. He managed to stop himself after about six stairs but then felt a big hand on his ankle. Jeff whirled around with the knife and jammed it hard into the hand that was grasping his ankle. The knife went right through, the tip coming out through the man's palm right into Jeff's ankle.

Jeff gasped, the thug screamed.

Jeff pulled his leg upward, gasping again when the knife tore through his flesh as it came free. Then with his other foot he kicked the ski mask face as hard as he could, sending the man sliding back down the stairs.

He forced himself to his feet and ignored the temptation to limp. He gritted his teeth and used the best of his mind control skills to convince himself that he hadn't just stabbed himself in the ankle.

Jeff dashed into his bedroom, closed and locked the door behind him. He no longer had the knife and his trusty toothbrush was impaled in someone's head. He had absolutely nothing now, nothing to fight with.

In a matter of seconds he heard the guy at the door, twisting the handle, banging with his shoulder against the wood. It wouldn't be long—that door would give after a few more thrusts.

Jeff ran to the window and tried to slide it open. It was frozen in place. These old wooden windows had a lot of character but they weren't too dependable as escape hatches. He turned around and grabbed a side chair that was up against the wall. He stood back and heaved it with all his might through the glass.

To the incessant thumping of a heavy body against the door, Jeff brushed away the broken glass and wood strips and knelt on the windowsill. Then without much thought he just threw himself into the air, hands outstretched, towards the old oak tree that was about five feet away from his window. He had a particularly gnarly branch in mind and he aimed his open hands in that direction.

His left hand missed, but his right hand got a good hold. He swung himself around and managed to get his left hand up onto the branch. Then he began inching himself along to the trunk. When he was close enough, he swung himself so that his feet could wrap around it.

The thug was at the window, yelling something in Russian at him. Jeff ignored him and looked down.

No police yet. The dog was still barking. The woman was still shushing. And there were no branches he could see below the one he was holding that were big enough to bear his weight on the way down. He had to go up.

Jeff began to climb just as the stranger began squeezing through the opening. Branch after branch, holding onto each one as he shinnied himself up the trunk. In mere seconds he was at the top. And his new friend was already at the trunk and shinnying himself up the same way that Jeff did. He was matching his every move.

There was only one place to go now. Over to the roof. Jeff swung himself out onto a thick branch and inched his way across to the roof edge. With one hand on the shingles and the other on the branch he heaved himself up onto the steep incline, feet resting against the flimsy eaves trough.

Death was right behind him. Hands moving deftly across the thick branch to the edge of the roof. Jeff thought for a second that the guy must be inhuman. Just minutes ago a knife had gone right through his hand, yet here he was moving like a monkey as if nothing had happened.

Jeff scrambled upward, wincing in pain as his ankle began to throb with the effort. He heard the thump of a heavy body. The killer was on the roof now, beginning his scramble in Jeff's direction.

Jeff continued up–then slipped on a patch of ice and for the second time in just a few minutes he slid downward on his chest. And once again he felt a hand on his ankle–the man knew which ankle to grab. He squeezed it as hard as he could with his good hand causing Jeff to yell out in agony. Jeff wrested his foot free and frantically resumed his trek up toward the top of the roof. What he was going to do when he got there he had no idea whatsoever. As far as he was concerned he was just buying time–just trying to stay alive for a few more minutes.

He made it to the top and stood, grabbing onto the top of the chimney for support. One of the bricks broke off in his hand. He'd been meaning to get this chimney re-pointed, but had procrastinated. Jeff thanked himself for his laziness.

He had a weapon again.

Jeff put the hand with the brick behind his back. He stood at the top, one hand holding the chimney, the other holding the brick…and waited.

The beast was only five feet away now. A big brute—broad shoulders, well over six feet tall. Clad all in black, the whites of his eyes gleaming through the holes in the ski mask.

Even though the mask covered his face Jeff could tell he was smiling, sneering. His damaged hand was covered in blood but he didn't seem to care or notice. He kept coming, the shiny long knife in his good hand, no doubt excited as hell at the prospects of cutting Jeff's heart out.

Jeff didn't wait until he got any closer. He swung the brick out from behind his back and delivered a roundhouse to the would-be killer's head. Jeff heard the sickening sound of masonry against skull, and saw him teeter back on his heels for what seemed like an eternity. Then his white eyes looked skyward as he fell backwards and tumbled in reverse somersaults down the roof, over the eaves trough and out of sight.

The dog was still barking. The woman was still shushing. And into the mix now was the sound of sirens getting closer by the second.

CHAPTER 46

"How many times do you want me to go over this same story? It's late, I'm tired, and I'm glad to be alive."

"Well, Mr. Kavanaugh, two men died tonight. That's a serious matter."

Jeff was sitting in an interrogation room at the Toronto Police Service precinct on Church Street. It was 11:00 p.m. and he just wanted to go back home. Before they took him away at least they had the decency to let him change out of his pajamas. They even summoned a doctor to bandage up his ankle. Luckily, no stitches were needed.

"I could have been the dead man. They were in my house brandishing knives, for God's sake."

"Why do you think they were there?"

"Toronto isn't exactly crime-free. I guess they came to rob me."

"But you attacked them before they had the chance to even explore the house."

Jeff sighed with exasperation. "They broke into my house. They were prowling around with knives in their hands. Should I have waited? I took the only chance I had—caught them by surprise."

"You attacked one from behind."

"So what? He shouldn't have been in my house sneaking around with a knife in his hand. Would you prefer that I waited until he turned around and swung the knife at me? I was armed with a fucking toothbrush, for Christ's sake!"

"That turned out to be a pretty deadly toothbrush."

"Well, you gotta use what you have—and that's all I had."

"Is there someone you'd like to phone?"

"No, if you're done with me I just want to go home."

"You can't go home until tomorrow night. It's a crime scene right now."

Jeff crossed his arms over his chest and hunched his shoulders up and down. He was starting to feel stiff. "Okay, then, I'll go to a hotel."

The detective shook his head. "No, I think you'll stay here tonight. I'm obligated to tell you that we'll be talking to a prosecutor in the morning to recommend charges against you."

Jeff leaned forward. "What kinds of charges?"

"That's for the prosecutor to decide. But in my opinion, you used excessive force."

Jeff shook his head in frustration. "That's crap, detective. I'm allowed to defend myself and my property."

"Sure, but you can't go overboard."

Jeff pulled his cell phone out of his pocket. "Can I make that call now?"

The detective nodded.

Before dialing, Jeff looked across at the officer. "Privacy, please?"

Jeff speed-dialed Dan Nicholson. A groggy Dan answered the phone on the fourth ring. Jeff knew he'd ruined his sleep.

"Dan, sorry to wake you, but I have a problem."

He then told him what happened. Every detail, even the toothbrush.

Dan seemed genuinely concerned. "Don't worry, I'll fix it. And tomorrow you and I need to meet. I have to tell you something too. But right now, put that detective on the phone and I'll make this go away."

Jeff opened the interrogation room door, and hooked his finger at the officer standing impatiently in the hallway. "Here, take this. This is RCMP Inspector Dan Nicholson. He wants to have a chat with you."

The chubby detective took the phone. All Jeff heard from his end was, "Uh-huh. Oh. Uh-huh. Okay. Right away."

He handed Jeff the phone. "You're free to go. You'll hear nothing more about this, sir." *Now he's calling me 'sir.' Dan has some pull, that's for sure.*

"What about my house?"

"I'll have a couple of officers drive you back home, and they'll remove the tape when they drop you off. You'll have to clean up the blood and mess yourself, though. We don't do that."

*****

Jeff could see in Dan's eyes that he was troubled. Though, one of the reasons for the blood-shot eyes might have been Jeff waking him up with his late-night phone call about twelve hours ago.

He didn't waste time–typical Dan, he always cut to the chase. "We're wrapping up this case, Jeff. Closing down the investigation."

Jeff was shocked. His mouth hung open for about three seconds before he could find just one pathetic word. "What?"

"It's been kicked upstairs. The documents you photographed are nuclear. Political. Sensitive. It will embarrass and shame both America and Canada. The greater good demands we bury this."

"But what about the crimes? The people who've died?"

Dan shook his head. "Brandon will be forced to leave the country–the CIA will fast-track him to Virginia. He'll work for them there. He'll never be allowed back into Canada, not even for a weekend at Niagara. And the AI division will be forced to close, and all the executives who are psychologists will lose their licenses to practice."

Jeff couldn't believe what he was hearing. Both he and Dan had almost died during this investigation. And Brandon Horcroft was getting away with murder.

He got up and held his hands forward. "Well, I guess you might as well cuff me now and get it over with."

Dan stood too. "Put your hands down, Jeff. I'm not charging you with anything. How could I possibly justify doing that when my superiors have ordered me to ignore the crimes of a sociopathic serial killer? The very least I can do is ignore your one crime too, which was pretty minor in the scheme of things here."

Jeff breathed out heavily. "Thanks so much, Dan. I don't know what else to say."

Dan held out his hand and Jeff shook it vigorously.

"Jeff, you're one brave young man, and you've earned my admiration. I hope we can continue to be friends."

Jeff smiled into the blood-shot, but still sparkling, blue eyes of the man whom he'd become quite close to over the last few weeks. He was going to miss him.

"You can bet on it, Dan. But, tell me before I go–what are you going to do? I can tell by the tone of your voice that this isn't sitting well with you."

Dan allowed a grim smile. "Well, I'm not going to do anything more about this case, that's for certain. It's out of my hands. And in a few months, Horcroft will be out of this country once and for all.

"But it's left a bad taste in my mouth about law enforcement. Maybe I'm just too much of an idealist, but I can't stomach the fact that I'm letting a psychopath like Horcroft get away with this. I have no choice–but I also don't have to stay with the reminders of what I've been forced to do."

"What does that mean?"

"It means that I probably won't be here too much longer. Thinking of going out on my own and starting my own investigative service. I think I'll find that a lot more satisfying. And it will help me forget about this."

Jeff nodded. "Sounds like a good plan, Dan. Good luck with it."

He walked slowly to the door, and then turned around. "Dan, what about that video of me in the…parking garage…with…Ray Filberg?"

"It's already been destroyed–all the copies are ashes."

CHAPTER 47

Brandon was scouring the papers for the third day in a row–going through every section, every page. It had been three days now since the fiasco at Jeff's house, where once again the damn Russians had failed him.

But not one article, not even a tiny one. Nothing about the incident at all. Brandon knew about it only because Gaia had told him about Jeff's ordeal. He didn't hear it from Jeff, only Gaia. Which raised his suspicions even more.

So, it apparently wasn't news–even though far less sensational crimes made the pages of the Toronto Star everyday. And Jeff was being mum about it except to Gaia. That was strange too. Something was going on. And someone at a very high level had smothered this story.

And all his calls into his CIA controller in Virginia had been ignored. No one was calling him back.

Brandon got up and started pacing his office. He didn't like being ignored, hated being in the dark. He suddenly got an urge. Had to try one more time.

He opened his door and went out to Gaia's cubicle. He smiled at her and sat down in the guest chair. She smiled back. A nice smile, an inviting smile. He was convinced she wanted him. The countless rejections had probably been because he was her boss. That was probably it.

"Can I help you, Brandon?"

She looked nice today–red sheer blouse, gray skirt, and silver high-heeled shoes. The blouse was short-sleeved too, which gave him the chance to admire her parrot tattoo. And a beautiful shade of lipstick, kind of nude. Brandon liked nude, especially on Gaia. He could easily imagine her totally nude.

"That's a lovely tattoo, Gaia. I don't know if I've ever told you that before."

He could see that she was blushing. Cute, and it kind of confirmed to him that he did have some sort of flirty effect on her.

Gaia looked at her right forearm. "Thanks, Brandon. Everyone seems to love it."

"Why do you have a tattoo of a parrot?"

Gaia giggled. "Oh, this is my parrot. He's my pet–name is 'Bingo.'"

Brandon laughed. "I see. Well, he's one lucky parrot to have his owner endure a tattoo for him!"

"He sure is."

Brandon leaned forward in his chair. "Gaia, I know I'm your boss and it might make you uncomfortable agreeing to join me for dinner or drinks. But I want to put your mind at ease and tell you that it's okay. You're my executive assistant and sometimes it's good for us to talk outside of the office. More relaxing, know what I mean?"

Gaia nodded.

"So, that being said, I want you to join me for drinks tonight. And I'm not going to take no for an answer. Okay?"

Brandon could see that she was fidgeting with her fingers, and shuffling her high-heeled shoes back and forth against the carpet. "No, Brandon. I can't do that. You'll just have to take no for an answer, and I hope you understand."

Brandon wasn't one to beg. And no one would ever see him sweat either, even though he was feeling it dripping down the back of his shirt at this very moment. He stood up. "Okay, Gaia. Have it your way."

He closed the office door behind him and walked over to his full-length mirror. Took a good long look and gave himself a self-assured smile.

Then he went straight to his phone. He dialed a number that he used occasionally. Someone he contracted with when he wanted people fired and he didn't want to do it himself.

Sometimes he had to do the firings because of the commands he had to issue before they left the company…and the world…forever. But for these two, there had been no hypnosis done and no latent commands to activate. So these would be just normal firings–and Brandon didn't do normal firings.

The man was a consultant by the name of Paul Axworth. Brandon thought that he had the perfect name for a man who 'axed' people for a living.

"Paul, I have two people I want fired today. This afternoon. I'll give you the details. Got a pen and paper?"

*****

Brandon wandered around his Forest Hill mansion–a lonely place for one man, but it suited his prestige. He still needed this house. Even though his wife had died here, that didn't bother him. Because he had made that happen–that was his control, his power, and he'd never given a shit about her anyway.

Her death was a blessing–and it made him rich. It would have killed her just to know that Brandon had arranged for the hit and run on her parents. He regretted not telling her that just before he'd commanded her to kill herself. A missed opportunity. It would have given him pleasure just to see the look of horror and hurt on her face, and the reflection of sheer understanding of his power and determination.

He paced back and forth in his huge living room. Today the traitors were sent packing. Both Jeff and Gaia shown the door by the axeman, Paul Axworth. Unceremoniously sent to the street.

Well, at least Jeff was a traitor. Gaia was just tied to him at the hip; that was her main faux pas. And he'd had enough of her rejections. He deserved better, much better.

Brandon walked into the kitchen, and then suddenly yelled at the top of his lungs. He reared his fist back and slammed it into the wall leaving a bloody impression behind. He rinsed his hand under the cold water tap and pressed a hanky over his knuckles until they stopped bleeding.

He was feeling restless tonight. He needed something badly. He'd psyched himself up thinking that Gaia would be back here tonight with him. When he asked her out for drinks and told her he wouldn't take no for an answer…he really didn't expect to get no for an answer.

The audacity of that girl! How could she continue to ignore him, ignore his charms, his power? Christ, he was the one who signed her paychecks. That alone should have been worth something.

Well, now she was out of a job. That should show her his power, his control. That should make her regret causing him to feel like a foolish schoolboy.

Brandon went down to the den, turned on the light and sat behind his desk. Switched on his computer and waited for it to warm up. He knew what he needed–he needed to pretend. Pretend that Gaia was right here with him, making love to him the way he deserved. He would pay good money tonight for that fantasy.

He searched 'Toronto Escorts' and as usual a whole slew of them popped up. He scrolled down, passing by the ones that he remembered having checked out already. He clicked on one that he hadn't seen before: 'Moonlight Ladies.'

As he perused the front page showing the rates and 'menu' of services, he was forced to listen to Julio Iglesias singing the title song for the website. Then he clicked on 'Ladies.' They showed up in a sidebar, and all he had to do was scroll down until he saw something that struck his fancy. He scrolled. A couple of skinny redheads, far too many blondes, and a few sultry brunettes. All in a state of near-nakedness.

None of them were what he wanted. He wanted short-cropped jet-black hair and eyes as black as night. That's what he wanted, what he needed to make the fantasy as real as possible.

Then he saw her. She was a dead-ringer. Brandon clicked on the tiny picture to enlarge it. Up popped the big photo with all the vital statistics. Her name was Amber.

He read the stats first, and then allowed his eyes to float upwards to feast on the delight.

Brandon choked. His body stiffened and his hands formed fists; fingernails digging hard into the palms of his hands. He closed his eyes, and then opened them again to take another look. Was he imagining things? Was he going mad? The blood was rushing through his veins so fast now he was starting to feel faint.

No, it wasn't his imagination. She had the close-cropped jet-black hair and the eyes as black as night. Her beautifully round bare ass was facing him, body slightly turned away, left arm covering the hint of her breasts. Her right arm was raised above her head, and she was leaning seductively against a hot pink wall.

And the distinctive tattoo of a red headed green parrot was perfectly visible on her right forearm.

CHAPTER 48

There were things to do.

Brandon was still breathing hard as he searched his hard drive for the staff directory. There she was: Gaia Templeton, 1600 Manor Road. He wrote the address down on a piece of paper and stuffed it into his pocket.

Next he unlocked the top drawer of his desk and withdrew the only thing that was in it–a tiny remote control transmitter. He aimed it at the wall that was adorned with a magnificent bookcase. He heard the familiar click, then watched as the bookcase swung open wide, revealing a vault identical to the one he had in his office downtown. He spun the dial: fifteen–twenty eight–twenty one. Turned the handle and pulled hard on the foot thick steel door.

Brandon tested the ventilation switch, and then pulled the light switch. Everything was working fine. The vault was basically empty except for three Glock pistols and some ammunition. He removed those and stuffed them into the desk drawer along with the little remote.

Most of Brandon's snotty Forest Hill neighbors had invested in elaborate alarm systems. But not Brandon. He spent more money on his vault than any alarm system would have cost.

The trouble with alarm systems, you had to assign a trusted neighbor to be the contact for the alarm company if you weren't home when something happened. Brandon didn't trust any of his neighbors–hell, he didn't even know most of their names. And there was a tendency for false alarms with those sensitive systems, which was a nuisance. He wasn't a fan of technology.

No, his vault was the best security. Even if he had an alarm, it could easily be compromised by a pro. But it would be very tough to compromise his vault without explosives–and they had to find it first too, which wouldn't be an easy task. His bookcase hid it nicely away from snooping eyes.

Funny thing was, he never really kept anything of value in the vault for all that long a time anyway. Sometimes he'd be in possession of diamonds or drugs that were smuggled to him through CIA channels, and he'd have to hold onto them temporarily until he received instructions as to who and where they were to be delivered. But that didn't happen very often.

Tonight he would finally have something of lasting value in his vault.

Brandon went to his kitchen pantry and hauled out a large bottled water dispenser. Grabbed one of the big plastic bottles and fitted it onto the dispenser. And tested it. Brandon dragged it down to the vault and placed it carefully in the corner.

The next thing he did was march down to the basement to carry up a brand new chemical toilet. Tested that too, leaving a smelly little souvenir of his own. He chuckled and placed the toilet in the corner of the vault opposite to where the water dispenser was.

His last additions to the vault were an inflatable mattress, some sheets, a blanket and a pillow.

He stood back and admired his work. Very comfortable indeed. Brandon smiled at his genius. He decided to just leave the vault open; he'd only have to open it again in a very short time, so why bother.

He donned his Italian leather jacket and gloves and went through the Butler's Pantry into his four-car garage. He took a roll of duct tape off one of the shelves and stuffed that into the inside pocket of his jacket.

Then he realized he'd forgotten something. Old age creeping up on him. He walked into the house, back to his den, and unlocked the drawer of his desk again. Picked out one of the Glocks, checked the magazine, and reached into another drawer to retrieve a belt holster. Snapped it on, and shoved the pistol inside. Ready.

Back into the garage. A moment's indecision as to which vehicle to take. After a second or two of pondering, he chose the Land Rover–lots of space and heavily tinted windows. Perfect for what he had to do. For what he was entitled to do.

*****

Gaia had Bingo out on her arm. The cute little guy was eating Shreddies right from her mouth. She'd purse her lips and hold one piece of the cereal tightly–Bingo would gently pick away at it, morsel by morsel. She loved the little fellow. She chuckled as she thought that he'd probably outlive her–she might have to leave him an inheritance!

Gaia eased him back into his cage and locked the door. Then she went back to her computer to resume her search for another job. The termination from Price wasn't expected, but she wasn't all that concerned. With her education and resume, she should be able to find something. She'd been searching for a few weeks now anyway, but because she had a full time job at Price it had been hard to put a lot of time into it. Now she had lots of time.

At least she didn't have to worry about paying back a debt with thirty percent interest accumulating. She was so thankful to Frank Palladino for forgiving her debt. For a tough man who lived his life on the dark violent side, he had one hell of a gentle side to him.

Gaia and Jeff had both been 'walked' out of the office at the same time by a man aptly named Paul Axworth. Brandon hadn't even had the courage to do the deed himself. The man was a coward underneath his slick confident veneer–and he was someone who was clearly used to having someone else do his dirty work for him.

She was surprised–Jeff didn't even seem to care when he got the word. He just shrugged, and asked how much the severance package was going to be. Paul told them they'd receive a year's pay in a lump sum, to be sent by registered mail within a few days' time.

Jeff shook his head and said that wasn't acceptable. That they both were entitled to their pro-rated bonuses as well as the employer's share of pension contributions for that one year period. In addition, cash compensation for lost benefits.

Paul had balked a bit, but Jeff stared him down. Said that if Brandon wanted these terminations to be 'clean,' without a legal battle and the associated publicity–Jeff had emphasized the word 'publicity'–then he had better agree. Paul scurried off to Brandon's office and was back within five minutes agreeing to everything Jeff had demanded.

Gaia was proud of him. It was an unusual situation to have two people fired at the same time in the same meeting, but she was glad that it had been done that way. She'd benefited from Jeff's experience and negotiation skills. He'd looked out for her, as she always expected he would.

They parted outside the building–both of them financially secure for a little while at least. Jeff said he'd call her in a couple of days and they'd head out to dinner and a movie.

She missed him already. The one thing she enjoyed about working at Price was that she got to see Jeff everyday. Now she wouldn't have that. She smiled, thinking that maybe they'd be lucky enough to work at the same company again. She knew that was virtually impossible, but it was a nice thought.

Gaia was startled by the doorbell. She looked at her watch–11:00. Who could be at her door this time of night? She got up warily from her chair, tiptoed to the door and looked out the peephole.

Brandon! What could he possibly want? Something to do with her termination? Delivering her check in person? Or did he have a change of heart about firing her?

But alarm bells suddenly started going off in her head. He'd never come to her house before so why now after she'd been fired? And in the middle of the night?

Something just wasn't right about this.

She cautiously opened the door, but left the chain lock on so that the door was only open about an inch. "Brandon, what are you doing here?"

He smiled a friendly smile back at her. "Hi Gaia. I've been feeling badly about what went down the other day. I'd like to talk to you about it for a few minutes, if you don't mind."

"I do mind, Brandon. This is my house, it's late, and I didn't invite you here. If you want to talk, I can come by the office tomorrow."

His tone suddenly changed. "Are you telling me that you're not accustomed to men coming to your house at night?"

Gaia was startled by his question. "That's an inappropriate thing to say, Brandon. Good night." She started closing the door.

Then she saw his foot–swooping upwards and smashing into the door before she had the chance to latch it. The chain snapped and the door smacked her right in the forehead. She fell backward onto the hall floor, stunned and a bit dizzy.

The door slammed shut and he was standing over her, a half smile half sneer on his face. While he was a tall man, Gaia had never thought of him as so huge and imposing until this very moment.

He leaned down, grabbed her under the armpits and yanked her to her feet. Then his hand flashed to his waist–the next thing she knew there was a gun to her head. She started to scream, but his other hand clasped her mouth tightly before she could utter more than a pathetic squeak.

"We're going to sit down at your computer for a few minutes. If you make a sound, I'll kill you. Understand?"

Gaia could tell he was in serious distress. There was a rage in his eyes that terrified her. She nodded nervously and pushed her hand against her tummy. She felt like she was going to throw up.

Brandon marched her into the living room to where her desk was. He threw her down in the guest chair and he made himself comfortable in her leather executive swivel.

He clicked on 'Outlook' and got the sign-in prompt. "Give me the password to your email account."

Gaia swallowed hard. Her throat was so dry, and she was having a tough time generating saliva. In a crackly voice, she said, "Use lower case: 'jefflove1'"

Brandon snorted and said, "Isn't that sweet."

He punched in the password and her email page came up. He clicked on 'New,' then searched for Jeff's email address in her contact list. He clicked on it.

Then she watched him type: "Jeff, I need some time away from all this for a while. Losing my job is causing me more stress than I thought it would. I'm going to visit my parents for a few days. Don't worry about Bingo. I've asked my neighbor next door to pop in to feed and water him every day. Don't contact me please–I just need some space for a few days. Hope you understand. XXX Gaia."

Brandon pressed 'send,' logged out and shut off her computer. Then he swiveled around in her favorite chair and faced her. She could feel her hands and knees shaking as his eyes bore into her.

"You're a fucking whore."

Gaia just stared back at him. She decided it was best not to say anything at all. The man was clearly out of his mind. She couldn't believe her ex-boss was sitting here in her house with a gun in his lap.

Brandon suddenly swung the pistol up and pointed it at her head. "I saw you tonight, do you know that? I saw your naked ass on the 'Moonlight Ladies' website."

Gaia gagged. Her dry throat just got a lot dryer. She sputtered, "I quit that place. My photo shouldn't still be on there."

"Doesn't matter whether you quit or not! You were still there, which means you're a fucking whore!" Brandon was yelling now.

Bingo didn't like the raised voice. He started squawking, and then changed over to, "Palladino! Palladino!"

Brandon turned his head toward the birdcage. "Shut the fuck up, you stupid bird!"

Bingo went suddenly silent, as if he knew that danger was lurking.

Brandon turned his attention back to Gaia. "You wouldn't even go out with me to have dinner or drinks, but there you were fucking strangers the whole time. How do you think that makes me feel?"

Gaia started sobbing. "I had no choice. I owed a lot of money. I hated doing it."

"You could have come to me. I could have paid off your debts for you. I would have done anything for you."

Gaia's tears were flowing faster now. She could taste the saltiness as they washed down over her lips.

"Here I was showing you every courtesy, promoting you, giving you every opportunity–and you never showed me one ounce of gratitude or recognition. What was wrong with me? Eh?"

Gaia managed to spit out a reply. "Nothing. You were my boss."

Brandon lowered the gun. "Ignoring me, then turning around and fucking guys right off the street. What a slap in my face!"

He jumped up from his chair and slipped the gun back into his belt holster. "So, we're going for a little ride, you and I. You're going to have a new home."

Gaia panicked. She lurched from her chair and ran for the front door. But Brandon was fast—he lunged for her and had his arm around her neck before she could reach it. He yanked her backwards and threw her onto the floor. Her head bounced off the hardwood and she felt for a moment as if she was going to pass out. Part of her wanted to.

"Get up, bitch."

She struggled to her feet, and then in between tears, said, "Please fill Bingo's food and water dish before we go. He'll die in a couple of days otherwise."

Brandon sneered at her. "Why should I care about your stupid bird?"

"Because it would mean a lot to me if you did."

She could tell that she'd struck a chord. His face softened for just a second. He sighed. "Okay, where's his food?"

"Over there in that bucket." She pointed to a corner of the kitchen.

Brandon walked over to the bucket and carried it over to the cage. He opened the door, and reached his hand inside. Gaia knew exactly what would happen next. She braced herself.

Bingo immediately hopped onto Brandon's hand and plunged his powerful beak down into the soft flesh between the thumb and forefinger. It tore open a bloody gash with its 2,000 pounds per square inch of pressure.

Brandon screamed and cursed as he yanked his hand out of the cage. Gaia didn't waste a moment. She rushed him, head down, and caught him hard around the waist with her shoulders. He didn't see her coming, being preoccupied with the blood gushing out of his hand.

They crashed onto the floor together with Gaia on top. She jumped up quickly and brought a foot down hard on his nose. Another scream. Then she went for the gun.

And she would have had it if she'd checked the left side of his waist instead of the right. A costly miscalculation.

The next thing she knew the gun was against her forehead. "Find me some bandages, fast!"

Gaia opened one of the kitchen drawers as Brandon made his way to the sink. He turned on the water and rinsed it over his hand. Then he dried it and made Gaia wrap it tightly. She noticed that the blood was still pouring out pretty fast, so she applied an extra layer and taped it tight.

When she was finished, he encircled his arms around her waist. "Kiss me. Hard."

She did.

"That wasn't good enough. But you'll have plenty of time to practice."

Gaia cried out, "No, Brandon, please!"

His face twisted into a look of rage again. She barely recognized him. What had happened to this man? He'd always been a bastard, but this was way over the top.

"I have a very special place for you in my house. A place where I sometimes keep precious things. But you'll be the only precious thing there for now. Just you alone."

She stared straight ahead into space; numb, resigned.

"Don't you want to know what this special place is?"

Gaia shook her head.

Brandon grabbed her face between both his hands and squeezed hard until she could feel her cheeks puffing out. Then he yelled at her, his face inches from hers. "It's a vault, you whore! A vault!"

Gaia was shaking uncontrollably, her entire body this time. She'd never been so scared in her life.

Bingo objected once again to Brandon's raised voice. The squawking resumed, along with, "Palladino! Palladino!"

Brandon swore. "I should kill that stupid bird. But, just for you, I won't. Consider my restraint as partial payment for services you're going to render. You're used to that, aren't you? Being paid for services rendered?"

Gaia just sobbed. She couldn't stop.

He reached into his back pocket and pulled a fifty-dollar bill out of his wallet. Then he pried open her mouth and angrily stuffed the bill inside. "Here's a downpayment for you." He wrapped his arm around Gaia's neck as she gagged on the money. "Let's go to your bedroom and you can give me a little preview before I take you to your new home."

In an instant Gaia had a flashback. A guy named Jack and his two filthy friends, in the Ambassador's Suite at the Royal York Hotel. She'd been violated and terrified out of her mind that night.

But this time was worse.

Because she knew in her gut that she was about to lose the one thing that every human being valued the most.

Freedom.

Once they reached Brandon's house she would be his slave.

And no one–absolutely no one–would have any idea where she was.

CHAPTER 49

Jeff stared at his computer screen, puzzled. He scratched his head and re-read the email. Maybe he just didn't understand women all that well, but why would Gaia just up and leave for a few days without talking to him? He deserved more than a cold email; at least he thought so anyway.

The last time they'd talked had been the day they'd both been fired, and they tentatively set up a dinner and movie date for a couple of days later.

It had been a couple of days already.

First he'd phoned and got her voice mail–then checked his emails, which had been neglected for a while. And there it was. A strange email to say the least–not because it said anything strange, but because it was out of character for Gaia to take such an impersonal approach. She would always phone before choosing to use email. And what was with the X symbols at the end of the message? Gaia always used smiley faces.

Oh well, if that's the way she wanted it to be, there was nothing he could do about it. She was away at her parents and didn't want to be disturbed. Jeff figured she must be more stressed out at being fired than she'd expressed to him. He wished she'd taken the time to call him though. He could have helped her deal with it–he was, after all, a psychologist and a stress management expert.

And...he was her lover.

He looked at his calendar. Christmas was only a few days away, and he'd been so wrapped up in all this intrigue that he'd totally neglected the holiday shopping and card sending. He hoped Gaia would be back for Christmas–she didn't say in her email how long she'd be gone for. Strange. He couldn't imagine spending Christmas without her.

Then he thought of his Aunt Louise. He hadn't talked to her in the longest time, and here it was almost Christmas. She was probably wondering where her card was, not to mention the poinsettia he always sent her. A tradition that was broken this year because of everything else. Jeff had to phone her, apologize, and wish her the best of the season.

He usually spent Christmas Eve with her up in Port Perry. He wanted to ask her if Gaia could join in this year for the big feast...assuming she was back from her parents by that time. And after that, Gaia would probably want him to go with her to Bobcaygeon for Christmas Day with her parents. He'd never met her parents so he looked forward to that. He'd talked to them on the phone before and they seemed very nice–just like their lovely daughter.

Jeff picked up the phone and dialed.

She answered on the first ring. "Well, it's about time you thought about me!"

"Always the psychic, eh? You knew who it was right away."

She laughed. "No, Jeff. Just call display!"

He chuckled at that admission. "Hey, I wanted to call and apologize for not being in touch. And for not sending my usual card and poinsettia. It's been hell down here in Toronto. I'll have to tell you all about it when I see you."

"That's okay, Jeffy. I'm a tough old broad–I can handle rejection."

"No you can't. You're just saying that to let me off the hook."

"Yes, you're right, nephew."

"So, do you still want me there on Christmas Eve, even after I've slighted you?"

"Of course I do, silly boy! I can't imagine Christmas without you!"

"And can I bring Gaia? I'd love for you two to meet each other. You'll adore her and she you, I guarantee it."

Jeff heard a sudden gasp at the other end of the line. Then silence.

"Louise? Are you okay?"

A long drawn-out sigh haunted through the earpiece.

Jeff was getting frantic now.

"Louise, Louise–answer me! Should I call 911?"

Then she whispered. "She's gone, Jeff."

"What?"

"She's gone away."

Jeff breathed easier. "You're having another vision. I was scared for a second there. Yes, Gaia went to see her parents for a few days–they live up north in Bobcaygeon."

He heard another long sigh, then, "No, Jeff. She's been taken."

Jeff's stomach was in his throat. "Louise, what do you mean?"

"Someone's taken her–that's all I can see right now. Go–check on her. She's in danger. I hope I'm wrong."

*****

He pulled into Gaia's driveway and went right to her front door. Rang the doorbell. Then peeked in through the front window. No signs of activity or disturbance. He then walked over to the neighbor's house and knocked. A young lady opened the door.

"Hello, can I help you?"

"Hi, I'm Jeff Kavanaugh—Gaia's boyfriend."

She smiled. "Oh, yes. Gaia's told me all about you. Nice to meet you."

He forced himself to smile back. "I just have a question for you. Did Gaia ask you to look after her parrot for her while she was away?"

She looked puzzled. "No, I haven't seen Gaia in quite some time. I guess winter has a way of keeping most of us inside."

"Okay, thanks very much." Jeff was in a hurry and didn't want to get dragged into a discussion.

She frowned. "Is something wrong?"

"I don't know yet. I hope not."

Jeff then walked over to the other neighbor's house. Gaia did say in her message that it was a 'next door neighbor' that she'd asked to look after Bingo, so if that was true it had to be this one.

An elderly man answered the door. Jeff introduced himself and asked the same question—and got the same answer. No, he hadn't seen her in quite some time.

Jeff was panicking now. He wanted to phone her parents but he knew their number was unlisted. Gaia had the number written down in a directory book in her kitchen. He needed to see inside the house anyway now.

Jeff didn't have his own key. They'd never exchanged keys with each other; in some small way he guessed that had been their way of still asserting their individual independence.

He checked underneath the flowerpot on the front porch. No key. Walked around to the backyard and slid his hand underneath the obvious sources—flowerpots, benches. Still no key. Gaia didn't take chances.

Then he noticed the old mailbox. It was adjacent to the side door. These old boxes weren't used anymore but were typical of wartime-built homes. A small child could easily squeeze through, but a man's long arm could also easily reach through and around to the inside latch on the side door.

He opened the tiny door to the mailbox and pushed his hand in to the back of it. The inside door to the box didn't budge—it must be hooked shut from the inside. He looked around for something to bash it with. Walked to the back of the yard behind the garage where Gaia had some old items stored under a shanty.

A softball bat.

Jeff grabbed it and headed back up the driveway. He reared it back and then rammed it forward as hard as he could. The inside door on the box popped open easily. Jeff leaned in as far as he could and bent his arm at the elbow so it could wrap around the wall on the inside. His fingers found the door latch and he flipped it up.

Then he opened the door and walked cautiously into the kitchen, still holding the softball bat. He didn't think it would be as effective as a toothbrush, but it was better than nothing.

The first thing he noticed was Bingo sitting on the top of the cage, looking as forlorn as a parrot could possibly look. His feathers were fluffed up and his head was hanging down. He cocked his little head towards Jeff as he came in and perked up a bit–but not as much as he usually did. Jeff wondered why the cage door was open– Gaia never left it open when she wasn't there.

He ignored the bird for the moment and continued his inspection of the house. Everything seemed intact–no signs of a disturbance. He walked into her bedroom and was surprised to see the sheets in disarray. Gaia always made up her bed.

He walked back into the living room. Her car keys were on the ledge; Jeff assumed that her Mini Cooper was parked safely in the garage. Gaia's purse was on the desk along with her laptop.

Jeff's mouth felt like sandpaper. These items indicated that Louise was right. All the indications were that Gaia had left the house not of her own accord. Which meant that the email he'd received had not been typed by her…or she'd typed it under duress.

His knees felt rubbery as he made his way back to the kitchen. He glanced at Bingo–the poor little guy was looking so sad. He looked like Jeff felt.

Jeff's eyes were drawn to the kitchen linoleum. The stains stood out dramatically against the light colored tile. Dried blood stains–he had no doubt. And quite a bit too. Then he noticed the sink and counter had the same stains. Someone had been bleeding and had done their best to try to stem the flow.

Jeff held out his arm to Bingo. He reacted immediately–squawking appreciatively and climbing onto Jeff's forearm, then working his way down to his hand. Jeff put his lips up against Bingo's head and blew softly. Bingo chattered appreciatively. Then Jeff noticed darkness around Bingo's normally yellowish beak. He looked down at the tile, then back at Bingo's beak. The same shade. Bingo had bloodstains on his beak!

Jeff eased Bingo back into his cage and then took out his water and food dishes. Both were empty. He filled them up and put them back onto the floor of the cage. Bingo pounced on them right away. The poor bird had been wasting away.

Jeff locked the door of the cage. He opened one of the drawers in the kitchen and took out the phone directory book. Looked up the number for her parents and dialed it.

"Hello?"

"Hi Mrs. Templeton. It's Jeff Kavanaugh calling."

"Well, isn't this a nice surprise! Hello Jeff! Is Gaia there with you?"

Jeff paused. He had his answer.

"No, she went out for a while. But she wanted me to call you to see if you wanted us both up there for Christmas Day dinner."

"Well, of course we do! We were waiting to hear what your plans were. Nice to know you want to come. It will be lovely to finally meet you rather than just talking over the phone."

"I look forward to it too. Okay, I'll let her know and we'll see you and Mr. Templeton then."

"Jeff, you can call me 'Grace' and Gaia's father will insist you call him 'Harry.' Okay?"

"Okay, Grace. It's an honor."

Jeff hung up and sat in a kitchen chair. He rested his head in his hands and tried hard to think. His first thought was to phone the police, but would they really take this seriously at this point? She had sent him an email and the police would suggest that she just wanted him out of her life for a while and lied about where she'd be. The bloodstains indicated some kind of wound, but there wasn't enough blood to indicate serious violence. Gaia was a grown woman, not a child. She had the right to give him the brush off and go away with someone else. There were no signs of forced entry, nor signs of violence in the house, bloodstains notwithstanding.

Jeff decided that he didn't have time to involve them and their bureaucracy. Maybe tomorrow, but right now he had to move on his own. He was worried sick.

Bingo seemed happier now. He jumped up on his perch and started chattering. He'd had a good meal and a good long drink of water. Life was slowly returning to the normally lively little guy.

Then the chattering got louder and Bingo started bobbing his head up and down. He jumped onto the side bars of the cage and stared out at Jeff. The word came next, his favorite word: "Palladino! Palladino!"

Jeff lurched from the chair, knocking it backwards. He ran to the telephone table and pulled out the phone book. Looked up 'Frank's Espresso." There it was: St. Clair Avenue West.

Frank Palladino was the obvious suspect here. Why hadn't that occurred to Jeff before now? Thanks Bingo!

The loan shark had apparently forgiven the loan, but he must have changed his mind. He came back. Jeff asked himself one question: What did Gaia have in her life that could possibly bring danger to her? A 'loan shark' was the logical answer. That was the only dark side to Gaia's life and she thought she'd extricated herself from it. But maybe she'd just deluded herself into thinking she was free. Maybe she wasn't so free after all.

Jeff ran from the house, closing the door behind him. He didn't lock it–he'd be back shortly.

His mind was racing and he was finding it hard to think clearly. All he could think about and see within his powerful brain was the image of Gaia being taken. Being held against her will. By a Mafioso loan shark who had changed his mind, or who just wanted something else from her now in payment.

Jeff jumped into his Corvette and raced in the direction of St. Clair Avenue West, towards Frank's Espresso.

*****

His heart was pumping hard when he burst through the front door of the coffee shop. Jeff's face felt heavily flushed and very hot, and his hands were clenched like fists of iron. He dashed past the tables and headed right for the back room that Gaia had told him about–the room with the perpetually closed door.

A woman at the counter yelled at him as he ran through the shop–two men jumped up from their seats just as Jeff reached the door to Frank's office. He didn't check to see if it was locked or not–he just raised his foot and kicked it open.

The heavy-set man sitting at the desk looked up, startled. Jeff dove over the desk and toppled him to the floor, chair and all. He put his hands to Frank's throat and squeezed. "Tell me where Gaia is! Tell me now or I swear I'll kill you!"

Then Jeff was flying backwards. Four hands were on him, dragging him across the desk he had just flown over, and then ramming him up against the wall. A fist went to his solar plexus and another one to the side of his face. Then a gun was out, the cold steel against his temple.

Then he heard a deep gruff voice. "No. Let him go."

The four hands backed off and Jeff was left slumped against the wall, groaning in pain. His stomach was in turmoil. He bent over and rubbed it gently with his hands. Blood was dripping down from his right eyebrow, some of it finding its way into the corner of his eye.

Then Frank was in front of him, his face just inches away.

"You must be Jeff."

Jeff looked up into his eyes and was surprised at how gentle they looked. For such a big man, and a man who did what he did for a living, it was unexpected.

"Yes."

"Tell me—what's happened?"

The two goons who had attacked him were standing by the door, obviously still wary of him and worried about their boss. But Frank didn't look scared at all, nor did he even seem angry over what Jeff had just done. Jeff knew in his gut that he'd made a big mistake.

"She's missing—been taken by someone."

"And you thought I was that someone."

"Yes."

"I want to help you if I can. But first you need to know something. I love Gaia like a daughter. I would never harm her. I forgave her debt, I'm sure she told you that."

Jeff nodded.

"I forgave her debt because she told me what she'd been doing to help pay it off."

Jeff frowned, puzzled.

"I didn't want her doing that anymore. She's a lovely lady, a classy lady—and she loves you dearly, you should know that."

Jeff managed to stand up straighter. The pain was starting to ease, but a new pain was starting—this time in his heart. He asked tentatively, "What was she doing?"

Frank ignored the direct question. "She promised me she was going to stop."

Jeff asked again. "What was she doing?"

Frank put his hand on Jeff's shoulder. "She was an escort, Jeff. A hooker."

Jeff screamed. "No! She wouldn't do that!"

Frank continued, his hand still on Jeff's shoulder. "Sometimes the truth is hard to face. It was for Gaia, too, believe me. She was gang-raped one night. That's what finally convinced her that what she was doing was far too dangerous, and I think she hit rock-bottom. And I was scared for her—knowing she had been doing that to pay me off. I felt terrible, so I erased the debt. And I also erased the main guy who led the attack on her."

Jeff felt like he'd been punched in the gut a second time. Gang-raped? His Gaia? A hooker? His Gaia?

"No, I don't believe any of this. You're lying to me." Jeff started sobbing.

Frank turned his head toward his two goons. "Tony, get me a laptop, will you?"

Tony was back in seconds with an HP notebook. Frank took it over to his desk and sat down. Jeff could hear him tapping away on the keyboard.

"Okay, come over here, Jeff."

Jeff moved slowly around the corner of Frank's desk and reluctantly looked down at the screen. He knew he was going to see something that he'd regret seeing for the rest of his life. He knew his life would never be the same again after he looked at this computer screen. But he had to look. He had no choice.

Frank was talking as he scrolled. "This is the agency she worked for: 'Moonlight Ladies.' I figured that even if she had quit, her photo would still be up here. These scumbag companies hardly ever delete photos."

Jeff could see small thumbnail photos of women, mostly naked women. Frank scrolled down, then stopped and clicked.

Jeff put his hand up to his mouth and gagged. He had to concentrate hard to avoid throwing up in Frank's lap.

There she was—in all her naked glory. Black close-cropped hair, hypnotic black eyes, and a tattoo of Bingo on her right forearm.

This was his lover. His Gaia. The girl he loved and trusted. The reason he'd risked his life today barging into a Mafia coffee house.

CHAPTER 50

Jeff drove around in circles for at least an hour. He didn't know where to go or what to do. Right now he just needed to drive.

Sometimes when the coast was clear, he'd rev his Corvette up to the red line, just to hear the roar, just to feel the power. It was a release of some kind to him—but it wasn't enough. He needed something else.

His emotions were racing all over the map. All he could see in his mind was Gaia, naked on a bed with a man's hands all over her. He could hear her moaning, could see her mouth wandering down to the man's penis. Then the thrusts would start—a faceless man with his hands on her buttocks, raising her up as he thrust himself inside of her. More moaning.

He shook his head, trying to chase the images away. He'd never felt this much hurt in his life, never felt so much pain in his heart. And he was a pro—capable of making such feelings go away. Hell, he taught people how to make those feelings go away.

But it wasn't working on himself. He'd tried to soothe his mind with self-hypnosis, tried to picture the dock at his cottage. But the image wouldn't stay. It would be replaced immediately by Gaia and a faceless stranger.

He pulled the car over to an empty curb, jumped out and threw up. An old man walking by asked him if he was okay. Jeff just nodded and hopped back into his car. Then resumed his aimless wandering.

He couldn't relax—there was a knot in his stomach that wouldn't go away. He needed a drink. Maybe that would work.

He passed by an infamous bar called Mingles, on Mount Pleasant Avenue. Jeff pulled a u-turn and headed into the almost full parking lot. He was amazed that it would be so full so early in the evening.

He knew this bar by reputation. If you were a man, or a woman for that matter, and wanted to get laid, this was the place to go. Jeff never went to places like this—he had never been a 'pick-up' kind of guy, and had no urge to be with women who were 'pick-up' kind of women. But tonight, a part of his soul was saying, "Who gives a shit."

He locked his car and walked toward the front door. Along the way he passed a car where there was obvious activity going on in the back seat. He could hear it, and could almost smell the sweat of the desperate bodies. The car was shaking slightly and the kind of moaning he'd been haunted by during his aimless driving was seeping through the closed windows. He shuddered and kept on walking. *What am I doing here?*

No matter. Something was drawing him here. The dark side that he'd never had an urge to experience before? Maybe?

He opened the door and headed straight for an empty bar stool. He ordered a scotch neat and sucked it back. Then ordered another. Jeff allowed his eyes to wander around the bar. Lots of single women and just as many single men. All posturing, flirting, drinking. All seemingly there for one reason and one reason alone.

Girls wiggling and gyrating on men's laps, tongues swirling—oblivious to the fact that at least a hundred people were watching. Women seductively dancing all alone on the floor, crooking their fingers at guys drooling on the sidelines. Most of the men being too lazy or inept to dance, preferring instead to wait until the women were drunk enough to head out with them to their cars, their apartments or hotel rooms; it didn't much matter where. This was just that kind of place.

Jeff started feeling disgusted with himself for even being in this place. He wasn't one of these people. He was too good for this. But a big part of him seemed to want to stay; maybe being too good was a fool's paradise. Maybe Gaia had just taught him that tonight.

He ordered another drink. Then looked around again. He was suddenly struck by an amazing observation. Most of the women getting hit on were really fairly normal and plain looking. But they were dressed to kill. Men were being drawn to them because of how they displayed their wares, not by how attractive they were. Strip away the slutty outfits, and most men probably wouldn't give them a second glance.

But there was another group of women in the bar also—they weren't like their drunken counterparts near the dance floor or off in cozy corners. There were about twelve of them occupying two tables, sitting just back from the action. All well dressed and all very classy looking. And these women were beautiful; in fact most were downright striking.

Jeff guessed that they might be a business group or perhaps even participants in a stagette. But he observed something that sociologists would appreciate. None of these women were getting hit on. Sure, some men were staring at them but for the last hour that he'd been observing, not one of them had been approached. They were laughing and sipping their drinks and certainly looked friendly enough. But they weren't sending signals—only the trashy ones were sending the signals, and they were the only ones getting hit on. Jeff thought this was interesting.

The party girls were advertising—and men felt comfortable hitting on them because they dressed and acted as if they wanted it.

Jeff knew full well that what the average man feared most was rejection—he had to have a reasonably good idea in his mind that what he was proposing would be accepted. Otherwise he wouldn't dare take the chance of being humiliated. Classy women scared these guys, because they weren't interested in one-night stands. And for most of the men in clubs like this, that was all they wanted. So they were out of their league with these classy ladies.

The other types were sending signals that they'd be open to suggestions. Dressed and acting in such a manner so as to answer the question before it was even asked.

Just like Gaia advertising her wares on the internet. Men knew what she was selling and she displayed herself to entice them to buy. There was no seduction needed, no real work to do—all she had to show them was that she was easy and up for sale. Jeff shook his head from side to side, once again trying to dispel the images that kept creeping back into his brain. He took another long sip of scotch to help kill the horrible daydream.

Jeff never usually thought about these things—and he never usually came into places like this. But being clinical, he realized that places like this were an interesting study of human nature and behavior. And he was in the mood to analyze tonight.

The shock of his life had happened to him today, and he was struggling to understand it. He couldn't help but look at every woman right now with a jaundiced eye. Most of the women here were looking for a recreational night in the sack. To them it was just fun, throwing their bodies at any eager male. But in Gaia's case she had done it for money. Jeff was certain she hadn't done it because she enjoyed it—he knew her heart and soul better than that. She was one of the classy ladies who in better circumstances would be sitting at that table with those other dozen classy ladies. She would fit in well with them. However, Jeff knew that she wouldn't fit in well with the girls who were gyrating on the laps of strangers over in the corner.

But he was conflicted. Part of his brain told him to get past this and forgive her, and the other part was telling him to just run for the hills. That part of his brain was yelling at him that she'd deceived him, been unfaithful to him—and she'd been paid very handsomely for doing both of those things. And just like those party girls, she had been having sex with complete strangers, a thought that was like a kick in the gut to Jeff. That thought, and the images it produced, really hurt.

To complicate things further, Gaia was missing. Should he care? Did he have a choice? Could he just shut it off because of what he'd discovered?

Jeff was already feeling a bit light-headed so he decided he was heading in the right direction. The knot in his stomach was disappearing the more he drank. So, he ordered another.

He'd just tipped the fresh glass up to his lips when he felt her hand on his shoulder. Then she slid onto the stool beside him.

"Hi there, handsome."

Jeff turned his head to look at her. Not bad. Not great either, but not bad.

"Back at ya."

"What? You're calling me handsome?"

"No. I'm just saying 'hi there.'"

"Do you think I'm pretty at least?"

"Does it really matter what I think?"

"Boy, aren't you the grumpy humpty tonight!"

"Sorry, just a bit preoccupied."

She rubbed his arm. Even though it didn't feel good, Jeff let her.

"I've been watching you ever since you came in. You haven't talked to anyone, haven't gone up to any of the girls. Why?"

Jeff just shrugged.

She persisted, and rubbed his arm with a bit more pressure. "You don't look like the kind of guy who frequents a place like this. A bit too well dressed, a bit too good looking."

Jeff didn't need the flattery. It meant nothing to him coming from a stranger who had an ulterior motive. It had only meant something coming from one special person whose only motive had been to love him.

"Needed a drink. Then I needed two. And after that, one more."

She laughed. "If you drink that much, then you're my kind of guy!"

That comment made Jeff's stomach jump. *No, honey, I'm not your kind of guy. And you're not my kind of girl.*

She slid her hand off his arm and onto his chest. Jeff let her do that too; the booze was the only thing keeping him from pushing her hand away in disgust. Tonight he just didn't care. He wondered if he really cared about anything anymore.

"You're not a very talkative man, are you?"

"I'm just drunk."

"I live right around the corner. Why don't you come back to my place and I'll make you some coffee?"

Without a second thought, Jeff nodded and stood up. *Why the fuck not?*

They headed out together arm in arm. Jeff was staggering a bit and she supported him quite nicely.

In five minutes, maybe less, they were sitting on the couch in her spartan apartment. There was no attempt on her part to make coffee. Unless the coffee maker was down around his crotch somewhere.

She was rubbing him gently, but nothing was happening. "Don't you like me?"

Jeff shrugged. How could he answer a question like that? He didn't even know her, not even her name. *What am I doing here?*

She stood up and wiggled out of her alluring little dress. Then she paraded herself back and forth across the tiny living room. "Does this help?"

He studied her. Figured she was in her late 30s or early 40s, and judging by the heavy makeup and the dress she'd just shimmied out of, she was someone who was trying desperately to look younger. The only word that came to his mind was 'pathetic.'

In the bright lights of the apartment she wasn't that pretty even with the layers of makeup. She might have been when she was younger, but that had long since passed her by. But her body–that was a different story. She was gorgeous from the neck down. Voluptuous.

Jeff instantly compared her and Gaia in his mind. Gaia had a petite little body, sexy as hell, but not what one would call voluptuous. But this girl, wow, she was a fuck machine. If he was that kind of guy, he would get off on a girl like this, then just get the hell home as fast as possible.

But…he wasn't that kind of guy. He needed more than a body. He needed Gaia. This girl had a killer body, but it wasn't the body he loved.

She sashayed over to him and slithered onto his lap. Started undoing the buttons of his shirt. Jeff grabbed her hand and stopped her.

She cocked her head. "What's wrong, honey?"

Jeff licked his lips. "This isn't for me. It's not you, it's me. You're very seductive but you're not what I need."

He gently eased her off his lap, and rebuttoned his shirt.

"What do you need? I can do anything."

He smiled at her and suddenly felt very sober. "All I know is that I don't need this."

Then he left.

*****

Somehow Jeff managed to drive back to Gaia's house. He was drunk, but typical of most drunks, he felt he was sober enough to drive. He knew, somewhere deep down inside that it was wrong, but he drove anyway. Took the side streets. Luckily Gaia's house was only about ten minutes from the girl's apartment.

Strangely enough, Jeff felt guilty. Despite what he'd learned today about the woman he loved, he felt guilty. Guilty for even entertaining the thought of being with someone else. He was glad he'd gotten himself out of there before he actually did do something to feel guilty about. He just wasn't that type of guy—sometimes he wished that he was, but most of the time he was glad about who he was. He couldn't be anyone else and still feel proud.

He decided to sleep at Gaia's tonight, then face the morning with a fresh face.

Jeff went into her bedroom and started straightening out the sheets on the bed. Then he saw it—a stain as large as a baseball. He knew what it was and he gagged. Dashed for the bathroom as fast as he could and emptied the contents of his evening's adventure. He knelt on the floor with his head over the toilet and just started crying. So hard that his entire body went into a spasm-like shaking.

About fifteen minutes had passed before he'd calmed down enough to venture back into the bedroom. He turned his head away, rolled the sheets up into a tight ball, and threw them into the bathtub. Took the pillowcase off and tossed it in there too.

Jeff stretched his tired body out onto the bed, sunk his head back into the soft foam pillow and pulled the duvet up around his neck.

He forced himself to crawl back out again to turn off the ceiling light, and then saw something that he absolutely needed in bed with him. He went over to the easy chair and cradled it. Gaia's teddy bear. She always had it with her when she slept, even when they were in bed together. Jeff wasn't going to let it sleep alone tonight.

He flicked off the light switch and eased himself back under the warm duvet, teddy bear squeezed tightly in his right arm; the same strong arm that was usually wrapped underneath Gaia's shoulders.

The images started coming back again as he was staring at the ceiling. The images of other men, other arms, other hands—grabbing, squeezing, caressing. But this time he was successful in chasing those images away. He used the full octane of his powerful brain to block them out. They weren't going to hurt him—he wouldn't let them.

He was not going to let those images torment him into ignoring the obvious.

And the 'obvious' was…Jeff loved Gaia deeply. He knew that now more than ever. He'd sorted it all out in his mind, and perhaps his experience tonight at that club and with that girl had helped him do that.

He was going to find Gaia and bring her home.

And God help whoever had her.

CHAPTER 51

It was a bright morning—the sun streaming through the window woke Jeff up earlier than his hangover would have liked. He reluctantly rolled out of Gaia's bed and for a moment he couldn't remember where he was. But the teddy bear crooked tightly in his arm reminded him.

He headed straight for the bathroom to have a quick shower, then saw the rolled up sheets in the bathtub. He felt that familiar knot in his stomach once again but managed to fight it off with some deep breathing. He wouldn't let this thing possess him. There were more important things to think about.

Things like—where was she? And—who had taken her?

There had to be a clue somewhere in the house…or, maybe, somewhere else. After his shower he phoned Frank Palladino. No time to spare.

"Hello?"

"Hi Frank. It's Jeff Kavanaugh."

"Oh, hi Jeff. How are you feeling today?"

"Better, Frank. But first I wanted to apologize to you for jumping to conclusions yesterday. After meeting you, I know you wouldn't have hurt Gaia. I know that."

"Thanks for the apology, Jeff. And I'm sorry for shocking you with that information about her. I know that must have been hard to take."

"It was—and I'm still grappling with it. But right now, the most important thing is to find her. I can deal with the blow to my self-esteem later after she's safe."

"Glad to hear that you've rationalized it. How can I help?"

"Well, I was wondering if you knew who the other two guys were who were involved in the gang-rape. I know you've dealt with the leader, but could one or both of the others have possibly taken her? It's kind of the only lead I have."

"I don't know who they are, and it would be difficult if not impossible to track them down. The room was registered to the leader…who's now gone. His friends could have been any two guys, hell they could have been guys he just met in the bar."

"Yeah, okay. I was hoping that might be a lead. But…here's another question. Since Gaia's photo was still up on the website for that escort agency, she might not have quit like you thought. I saw evidence here at her house…that…she…might have had…sex with someone recently."

"Oh, I'm sorry, Jeff."

"I'm okay, thanks. But, my question is—do you have any pull or influence with that Moonlight Ladies escort agency? Is it possible to find out the names of whoever came here to her house for…sex…within the last few nights? In other words, the names of her most recent clients, particularly the last client?"

A pause at the other end.

"Frank? Are you there?"

"I'm here—and yes, I can find that out for you. Leave it with me. And once we have those names, you'll have to let me help you. We have some means at our disposal."

"Great, Frank. Give me a call back as soon as you can. You have my number."

Jeff hung up and made himself a pot of coffee. He felt better. At least he was doing something. He'd be on pins and needles now waiting for Frank to call him back.

He opened Bingo's cage and gave him some fresh food and water—then let him crawl onto his shoulder for some tender loving care. He could tell that he was missing Gaia. His behavior was different and he was a lot quieter—he hadn't said a word all morning. Jeff was starting to miss his rendition of 'Palladino.'

*****

Two hours later the phone rang. Jeff could see on the call display that it was Palladino. He picked up on the first ring. His heart was pounding.

"Talk to me, Frank."

"Good news and bad news."

"Give me the good news first."

"She quit when she said she did. She hasn't taken on any clients at all, not a one."

Jeff let out a long breath. "That is good news. What's the bad news?"

"She quit when she said she did."

"Huh?"

"In other words, no leads. And this information is valid. We tracked down the headquarters, if you could call them that. Simply one woman operating from a phone and a computer in her own home. I sent a couple of men over there and they looked at her records. Scared her a bit too—while they were there, they convinced her to delete Gaia's photo from the site. I don't think that photo will ever pop up again."

"Thanks for that, Frank. So, another dead end."

"Looks like it. If I think of anything else I'll get back to you, Jeff. Good luck to you and keep me posted. I'll pray for her safety…and yours."

Jeff hung up the phone and started pacing the house. No leads now whatsoever.

He had high hopes that Frank would find something. Now, he wondered, who did she have sex with before she disappeared? That stain on the sheet was unmistakable.

The knot was returning to his stomach again.

Maybe one of her ex-clients that she invited over on her own and bypassed the agency? More money in her own pocket that way.

He rubbed his temples. A headache was coming on. And he once again felt the familiar frustration of knowing that he had this wonderful psychic ability but could never summon it when he needed it. Where was it? Why didn't it appear for something as serious as this? Why did it appear when mere acquaintances or virtual strangers were about to be killed, but it was nowhere in sight when the person he was the closest to was in danger? It didn't make sense. What was the point of having this stupid gift…or more appropriately, this stupid curse?

Jeff snapped his fingers. Louise! He'd call her! Her visions were much more frequent and more powerful than his, and she was the one who told him that Gaia had gone missing in the first place!

He dialed.

"Hello, Jeff. I've been anxiously waiting. Is she okay?"

Jeff told her the basic details–how the email seemed to have been sent by someone else on her account. That no one had been asked to look after Bingo. That her car, purse, laptop and phone were in their rightful places. How all the evidence pointed to her being taken as Louise had warned him.

He didn't tell her the other things he found out though–that was too sordid to share with his aunt. At this stage, that was information he didn't think she needed. Unless she was able to 'see' it herself, he wasn't going to tell her.

"Oh, Jeff. I'm so worried for you. Have you 'seen' anything? Any visions?"

"No–none at all. I was hoping that you might have had one. You're my last hope. She's disappeared into thin air."

There was silence for a few seconds. Then, "Jeff, I want you to email me a photo of Gaia, or even better, one of you and Gaia together. Do you have a nice one you can send?"

"Hardly the time for family photos, Louise."

"Jeffy, you're not thinking straight. I understand–you're stressed and anxious. A photo, silly boy, might trigger something in me."

"Right. Of course. Let me check my iPhone. I should be able to send you one in a few minutes."

*****

About half an hour after he'd emailed her a beautiful photo of him and Gaia at

Niagara-on-the-Lake, Louise phoned back.

She was short of breath. Jeff knew something was happening to her. He sat down at the kitchen table and waited patiently. Holding his breath–and praying silently.

She started crying.

"Jeff, she's in a small space. Very small. She's sobbing and whispering your name."

Jeff felt tears forming in his eyes. His lips were quivering as he asked, "Is she hurt? Can you see that?"

"There's a bruise on her forehead. Other than that, she seems fine. But she's been hurt in other ways, Jeff. I think you know what I mean by that–I'm sorry."

Jeff choked up. "Yes."

"I see a mattress, a portable toilet and a water dispenser. That's all."

"Can you pinpoint where she is?"

"No. Nothing's coming to me on that."

Jeff was getting frantic. "Look at the photo again, Louise! Look hard!"

Silence for about ten seconds. Then, "Oh my God! It's that man!"

"What man?"

"I never saw his image when I last told you about him. But I sense that it's the same one I told you about–the one who'd been obsessed with her for many years. The one who arranged for her fiancé to die in that plane crash."

Jeff's hopes sank. Ray Filberg. This was another dead end.

"No, it can't be him. That man's dead now, Louise."

"He's not. I can see him."

Jeff sighed with exasperation. "Describe him to me."

"Tall, well over six feet. Thick white hair pushed back–stylish. Blue eyes–piercing blue eyes."

Jeff's heart was in his throat, could feel the pulse there and everywhere. He jumped up from the table. "Are you certain?"

"Yes. I see him standing over her, smiling. But not really a smile, more like a sneer."

Jeff's pulse continued its pounding pace. Could it be true? If it was, he'd caused the wrong man to die. But right now, that was the last thing he was going to worry about.

He shouted into the phone, excited. "Louise, that sounds like our ex-boss, Brandon Horcroft!"

Suddenly the birdcage rattled and the squawking started. Bingo was clearly agitated. Jumped from his perch down to the floor of the cage, and back up again. Then he leaped onto the side bars and screeched, "No, Brandon! No, Brandon!"

Jeff felt the color drain from his face. "Louise, it must be Brandon! The parrot is going crazy! Sounds like he's repeating something he heard Gaia say! Almost like she was pleading with him!"

"Be fast, Jeff. Time is running out. I feel it."

Jeff swiped his car keys off the table. "I'm on my way out the door, Louise. I'll phone you again en route. Maybe when I get closer to his house, you'll pick up more visions, maybe some specifics that can help me."

"Just move quickly, Jeff...very quickly."

CHAPTER 52

The constant whirring of the ventilation fan was driving Gaia bonkers. But she knew that it was the only thing keeping her alive, so she was glad for it. By her calculation, she was into her fourth day of captivity—which constituted four days of a torturous and continuous humming noise.

But that was the least of her problems. The isolation was the worst torture imaginable. And the absence of windows. It was wearing her mind down, almost to the point where she welcomed the end of the day when Brandon returned home from work. She knew then that the vault would open and she'd see something outside her confines. She'd see him too, which was a perverse diversion from the long lonely day in the vault. At least he was something different from the mind-numbing routine. Stockholm Syndrome?

Gaia tried not to think ahead to what life would be like a month or two from now—she knew for sure that a deep depression would set in if she allowed that thought to linger.

She was allowed two meals a day. The morning meal was cereal, toast, honey, and coffee. And the evening meal…well that was when she got to dress up. Got to venture out of the vault and be allowed to enjoy the fantasy of being a human being again.

That was her privilege time if she'd been a good girl. Gaia made sure she was as good a girl as she could possibly be, while keeping an eye out for the opportunity to slit her captor's throat.

She would try to keep him calm in the meantime—but she'd get a chance eventually. He'd have to let his guard down sometime.

Her job right now was to live to fight another day.

On the very first day when Gaia was thrown into this vault, Brandon had gone right back out again and bought her several expensive outfits to wear. He tossed them into the vault and told her she would have to wear a different dress every night for dinner. Then he gently slid two rings over the fourth finger of her left hand. A wedding ring and an engagement ring. He said they were his beloved wife's. He proceeded to play the 'widower card,' extolling the virtues of his dead wife and telling her that he'd never been the same since she took her own life. Gaia didn't believe any of it. This man wasn't capable of feelings or compassion. He loved himself far too much to care for anyone else.

Gaia knew she had to keep him calm. She had to be polite. He was deranged now, out of his mind. There was no rationality to a man like this. She wasn't a psychologist but she had a boyfriend who was and she'd worked around dozens of them for years. She knew she was looking at a man who was drunk with his own power and entitlement. And Brandon was also someone who had been overtaken by obsession. He was clearly obsessed with her and finally decided to just take her. Since he couldn't win her, he had to take her.

Gaia knew she was partially to blame–not deliberately, but still to blame. He had wanted her and had tried to entice her to go out with him. Many men in the office had flattered Gaia over the years; chatted her up, paid attention to her. But she'd never reciprocated, never fallen for their lines. Never did with Brandon either.

After Matt's death in the plane crash she'd become despondent. And then she allowed herself to sink to the lowest depth of self-loathing...she became a prostitute. How could she possibly have a relationship with anyone?

And then there he was. Jeff came along. Suddenly she wanted a relationship.

Something about him just hit her like a ton of bricks. Perhaps it was the intense experience they'd had together when Jeff had been her knight in shining armor, saving her from certain death at the hands of Jim Prentice. He'd been her hero.

And they'd been scared to death together–probably in some weird way a good formula for love to happen between two people.

But no, not quite–it was even earlier than that. Jim Prentice's office slaughter had just been the catalyst. She'd felt the chemistry with Jeff long before that–knew that he'd dated others, but she didn't know how to break the ice with him. Occasionally they'd chatted at coffee breaks, had lunch in the cafeteria together, but nothing ever escalated. He never pursued her. And he was the only one in the office whom she'd wanted to pursue her.

But then it all changed. It changed that horrible summer day when he'd saved her life from a man who'd put a gun barrel to her head. It was karma, fate.

Knowing she was with Jeff probably infuriated Brandon–fueled the fire of his obsession even more.

But then the absolute kicker was when he discovered she'd worked for an escort service. That pushed Brandon and his obsession over the edge. Her rejection of him, her acceptance of Jeff...and then Brandon finding out that she was having sex with paying customers. All of this contributed to a psychotic breakdown and his only solution was to just take what he wanted and possess it. Angry that she'd had sex with strangers while shunning him. His ego had taken a terrible hit, and to Brandon his ego was everything. His entire existence depended upon it being secure and unassailable.

And now Gaia had to use that knowledge to survive. She knew in her gut that he was dangerously fragile. Brandon could easily erupt right now on the wrong cue.

So she dutifully dressed up every night for him. He cooked nice dinners, and set the table. He'd open the vault door, offer her his arm and walk her into the dining room. Lights were always dimmed, candles lit, expensive china laid, and wine glasses filled. The sick man actually considered these to be dinner dates. It was like he was courting her.

But he didn't act deranged. He seemed to have control of everything–there was no confusion or bizarre behavior. Well…aside from taking a woman captive which was pretty bizarre–but it seemed to have a purpose with Brandon. It wasn't something that he seemed spaced out about–he didn't talk in riddles, didn't ramble on about nonsense. He just still seemed to have it together. He still seemed to be…Brandon.

Gaia was a bit puzzled about this. Maybe she'd seen too many movies, but for some reason she was expecting him to be 'talking in tongues' by now. He wasn't. He was just Brandon. In control, quick-witted, dominant, brainy as hell–and scary as hell. He'd always been scary. But he was even more so now; now that Gaia knew what he was truly capable of.

And anyone who was capable of 'collecting' a human being for his own amusement was capable of virtually anything.

After dinner they always went upstairs. There was a collection of lingerie that she was expected to choose from, which she did. He'd hide in the bathroom until she'd changed–he wanted to be surprised. He didn't seem concerned that she would run at those moments. Seemed confident that she wouldn't get very far.

Then, after she'd changed into the sexy outfit and he eagerly emerged from the bathroom…

One benefit of Gaia's second career as an escort was that she'd become skilled at turning herself cold and detached with the men who'd paid her for sex. Those encounters meant nothing to her–she'd gone through them like a zombie; no feelings, no enjoyment, and no memories. Thank God, no memories. Except for the gang rape–unfortunately she'd never forget that one.

After all of her encounters she could hardly wait until her and Jeff were together–it was intense because she loved the man. She felt guilty and ashamed, but was afraid to tell him what she did. She thought for sure she'd lose him. Gaia always used protection with the strangers, was always careful–terrified of the thought of infecting Jeff. That would have been the ultimate betrayal–doing what she did on the sly, and then infecting the one she loved, the one who trusted her. He would have been the innocent victim of her behavior and the thought of that ever happening made her feel sick.

With Brandon, she just put her mind in a similar place as to when she'd been hooking—he was nothing to her and she numbed herself out. This allowed her to get through it without the effects of it lingering on her mind. Unfortunately, Brandon refused to use protection. She worried about this. If she was able to somehow get out of this alive, she'd have to get herself tested again, just like after the gang rape.

The very first day when she was thrown in the vault, he'd taken a hammer to the safety release catch. He wanted her to see him destroying it. She watched as he bashed away at it, pleased with himself that there was no possible way now that she could let herself out of this metal box.

The days were long. No books to read, no music to listen to, no TV to watch. It wore Gaia down. She wondered if her parents were worrying about her. She wondered if Jeff had been puzzled when he received that email that Brandon had sent from her computer. Was he missing her? Concerned about her?

She missed Jeff's smiley face, his laugh, his teasing, and his body. She missed him terribly and tried not to think that she may never see him again. Gaia thought about the future they would have had together—the fun things they'd been planning to do. Those might never be now. She could possibly be in this vault forever. There were all sorts of stories in the news where women had been kept for decades. Hard to believe that was possible until it actually happened to you.

Gaia rubbed the bruise on her forehead where the door to her house had smacked her hard when Brandon kicked it in. Then she started whispering Jeff's name, willing him to come to her rescue as he had before. She wanted her Sir Galahad, wanted him now. Wanted him forever.

Suddenly the room went pitch black. And something disturbed the silence. Ironically, it was the absence of a sound that actually disturbed the silence.

The whirring noise had stopped. The air ventilation fan that had been annoying Gaia so much for four straight days had just come to a silent ominous halt.

Almost immediately, she began imagining that she was suffocating.

CHAPTER 53

Jeff had the address. The entire roster of executive addresses and phone numbers was in his iPhone. It was 6:00 p.m. and already quite dark. Brandon usually didn't leave the office until at least 8:00. Jeff prayed that tonight was no different.

Forest Hill was one of the most upscale neighborhoods in Toronto–a mixture of different styles. Buying into that area usually required a minimum of five million. It was quiet and snotty–people kept to themselves. There was very little neighborly socializing that you would find in the average area. Jeff thought that this might work to his advantage.

He was winding his way down toward the Bathurst area. Brandon lived on Briar Hill Avenue; Jeff was fifteen minutes away. He gunned the Corvette through a caution light and glanced quickly around to make sure there were no cops lurking. His heart was pounding and his palms were soaked with sweat. All he could think of was Gaia and what she must be going through. If she was still alive.

Louise had told him to hurry, and that time was running out. Those words lingered in Jeff's mind–daunting words that filled his heart with fear. He couldn't lose her, he just couldn't.

Five minutes away. He was on Bathurst Street now. Jeff pulled over to an empty spot near a phone booth–one of the few remaining booths in the city. He needed to phone the office to make sure Brandon was still there, but he didn't want call display giving him away.

He dialed Brandon's direct line. He answered on the first ring. Jeff hung up quickly, and hopped back in his car again. The coast was clear. Brandon's house was his for the taking.

As he was driving he pulled out his cell and called Dan's office landline. No answer–he left a message giving him brief details about Gaia's kidnapping and Louise's vision. He told him what he was doing and gave him Brandon's address. He then tried Dan's cell–no answer there either. He left the same message.

He was all alone. He thought of phoning Palladino and then just as quickly discarded the idea. He didn't know him well enough and wasn't sure he wanted the Mafia's help on something like this. Jeff wanted Dan–shouldn't take long for him to phone Jeff back. He always returned calls within minutes.

The sleek Vet was making good time. Jeff wound his way through the picturesque streets of Forest Hill until he came to Briar Hill Avenue–drove east and counted down the street numbers.

There it was–an imposing French Colonial on a corner lot. The land area was huge and there was at least a hundred feet of detachment from his closest neighbors. And lots of trees and shrubs. Jeff was glad for that–for what he had to do. He drove past the house and parked on the street a few houses down.

Time to phone Louise again.

"I've been waiting."

"Hi Louise. I'm near his house. Do you feel anything?"

"Yes, I can see it. Tell me if I'm right. It's a large house, cream-colored wood frame with brown accents. And brown concrete roof tiles too. Lots of sharp angles and points to the house–looks like a country manor."

Jeff was excited. She described it to a 'T'.

"Bang on, Louise. Tell me more–anything at all that you're feeling, seeing."

He could hear her sigh, and then sob. "Oh, Jeff. She's choking, gasping. Hurry up, hon. Get into that house. Keep the phone on and I'll try to help you."

Jeff leaped from the car, ran down the street and up Brandon's front walkway. He could barely see where he was going; his eyes were so blurry from tears. Choking, gasping! The bastard! What has he done to her!

He reached into his jacket pocket and pulled out the lock pick ring that Dan had given him. He tried each of the three picks but none would work–the locks were just too secure. He looked around and didn't see any signs warning of an alarm system. Jeff was surprised but maybe good fortune that Brandon's arrogance had perhaps kept the house unprotected.

He was going to get into this house, nothing would stop him. He ran around to the side of the house and yelled into his phone. "Louise, I'm going to break a window! Do you see anything else?"

"Nothing yet. But I hear her crying, Jeffy. She's in despair."

Jeff resisted the urge to throw up. He stuffed his phone in his pocket, grabbed a shovel leaning up against the side of the house and tossed it like a javelin through a stained glass window.

He pulled the sleeve of his jacket down over his right hand and chopped away at the shards of glass. Then he climbed through the opening.

It was a music room. A baby grand piano sat majestically in the middle surrounded by high-back chairs and occasional tables. He walked down a long hall past several rooms and into the living room–a huge space filled with expensive couches and cabinets.

Jeff pulled his phone out of his pocket.

"Okay, I'm in! Talk to me, Louise!"

"I'm getting a rush of images, Jeff. Look for bookshelves."

Jeff ran, through the kitchen, the dining room, another living room—then he saw a door leading to a separate little wing.

It was an office. Large executive desk, bookshelves built into the walls.

He was finding it hard to breathe. Every second he wasted was one more second that Gaia was choking and gasping. He wished Louise hadn't told him what she'd seen.

"I've found the bookshelves! It's an office! What else do you see?"

He could hear Louise breathing hard at the other end. And sobbing. She was seeing things again, and Jeff didn't want to know. "Just tell me how to find her, Louise! Please!"

Her voice cracked. "Jeff, she's behind one of the walls."

Another vault! At least the fucking guy was predictable!

"Which wall?"

"I don't know. Start banging on them."

Jesus!

He remembered how the wall back in the office opened. It sprung outward once it was pressed at the right spot. He circled the room, pulling books from the shelves, pounding on the wood finish. Then from the third wall he banged he heard a sound that was different. More solid than the others—a solid 'thud' noise. He was sure this was it. He pressed on all the corners, down the sides, along the bottom. No give at all.

"Louise—I think I've found the right wall! But it won't open!" He was panicking. More seconds being wasted.

"Jeff! I see a man's hand, his thumb on a button!"

A remote control! Jeff dashed over to the desk and rifled through all the drawers. Until he got to a special one—it was locked. He pulled the lock pick ring out of his pocket and inserted one of the picks. It worked! He pulled the drawer open.

Sure enough, there was the remote. There were three guns too. Jeff pulled one of them out and checked to make sure there was a fresh magazine. Satisfied, he shoved it into his waistband.

"Okay, Louise! I've found it! Testing it now!"

"Oh, God. Hurry, Jeff!"

Jeff spun around, aimed the tiny remote at the wall and pressed the button. He prayed.

There was a loud creaking noise as the bookcase began to open—slowly but surely. Exposing a vault that looked identical to the one back at the office.

"I've got it, Louise!"

Jeff hoped that Brandon was a creature of habit. He ran to the vault door and spun the dial. Fifteen–twenty eight–twenty one. Turned the handle. His heart sang as the heavy door surrendered.

Then he saw her. His sweetheart. Lying on a mattress in the fetal position, hands covering her mouth.

He ran to her and turned her onto her back. He could hear Louise screaming into the phone.

"Louise, I've found her! I'm going to hang up now and get her out of this place!"

"Thank God! Call me when you're free, Jeff. Good luck. Praying for you both."

Jeff tried to shake her awake. No response. He checked for a pulse. It was weak, but at least she had one. He began CPR. Breathing, pressing, breathing, pressing. Frantically trying to bring her back to life.

More repetitions. Then he took a break for a second. Was he doing it right? He thought so, but it had been so long since he'd taken the course. More repetitions.

Then she coughed! A small one, but still a cough! A sign of life!

He gently slapped her face. Then her eyes opened and she screamed, "No!"

Jeff wrapped the underside of her shoulders with one arm, and cradled her head with the other. Pulled her up into a sitting position and kissed her forehead.

He could feel her arms slowly encircle his waist. Then she pulled her weary head back and whispered in a groggy voice, "I knew you'd save me again."

Jeff felt a soothing warmth surge through his body. He'd never felt so much love for someone as he did at this very moment. He thought he'd lost her, and he almost had.

"We have to go, Gaia. Can you move?"

She nodded. Jeff helped her to her feet. She was shaky, but he thought she could make it. But then she just went limp and collapsed back onto the mattress. Gaia looked up at him helplessly, tears in her eyes.

Jeff didn't waste any time. He reached down and lifted her off the mattress. Hoisted her over his right shoulder and ran. Out through the vault and into the office area. Desperately tried to remember which way the music room was, where the broken window was. He ran into the living room—then a chill ran up his spine.

The unmistakable sound of a key being inserted in the front door!

Gaia was moaning as he raced down the hall with her slumped over his shoulder. He ducked into the first doorway he came to. It was some kind of butler's pantry.

Jeff laid her down gently and positioned himself in front, shielding her from the doorway.

Then he pulled the Glock from his waistband.

CHAPTER 54

Jeff heard him curse, "Fuck!" Brandon had obviously seen the open vault.

His footsteps sounded like thunder. Echoing through the house as the maniac went from room to room. Hard-soled Italian leather shoes pounding on the hardwood floors. A man on a mission.

Jeff brandished the gun in front of his face and aimed it halfway up the doorway, right where the man's heart would be. He braced himself.

Then his phone rang! *I forgot to put it on silent!* He frantically reached into his pocket and shut it off. Hoping against hope that Brandon hadn't heard it.

But he had. He was suddenly in the doorway looming larger than life. Kind of the way Brandon looked on any given day.

He was smiling. Amazing. He had a briefcase in one hand, and a gun in the other pointed right at Jeff's head. The pinstriped killer.

"Playing the hero again, eh, Jeff?" He chuckled. "She's mine now and you can't have her back."

Jeff gritted his teeth. "Fuck you!" Then he pulled the trigger.

A resounding click.

Brandon laughed, then took a step forward and kicked the gun out of Jeff's hand.

"You forgot about the safety. Not so smart after all, are you?"

The next kick came at Jeff's head. He fell backwards onto Gaia. Then he felt himself being pulled off of her and flung unceremoniously to the floor.

Through his blurry eyes he saw Brandon drop his precious briefcase, lift the limp Gaia up onto his shoulder and then point the gun back at Jeff's head again.

"Move! You're going into the vault until I decide what to do with you. As for Gaia and I, we're going upstairs." The man laughed again, a haunting laugh that Jeff knew would echo in his brain while he languished away in a vault. He mentally braced himself for the return of claustrophobic horror.

He struggled to his feet. Brandon motioned with the gun, directing him out into the hallway. They walked; Jeff in front, Brandon pulling up the rear with an unresponsive Gaia draped over his shoulder.

Then there was the sound of shattering glass somewhere near the front of the house. Brandon whirled around, swinging his pistol in the opposite direction.

Jeff reacted on instinct. He rushed him like a linebacker, with no regard whatsoever for the fact that Gaia was hanging over his shoulder. She would thank him later.

He hit him hard–harder than he ever remembered tackling someone in college football. His rage was overwhelming. He wanted to break the man's back, hips, and virtually every other vital part.

Brandon grunted and went down. The gun went skittering down the hallway in one direction and Gaia went skittering down the other. Jeff slithered himself up the length of Brandon's body, flipped him over onto his back and clasped his hands around his throat. Something primal was in control now and Jeff knew that no one was going to stop him from choking the life out of this monster.

But someone did stop him. He was standing in front of them, gun in hand.

"Let him go, Jeff."

Jeff immediately released the pressure. Dan's words always had a powerful effect on him.

Jeff crawled off Brandon and rushed over to where Gaia was lying. She was okay. A bit stunned, but otherwise fine. She shifted herself up into a sitting position.

In a shaky voice, she asked, "Are we safe now?"

Jeff kissed her lips. "Yes, we're safe, hon. I want you to meet my friend, Dan Nicholson."

She smiled wearily and looked up at Dan. "I don't have a clue who you are, but it sure is nice to meet you."

Dan smiled back. Then he nodded down at Brandon. "What should we do with this piece of scum?"

Jeff stood up. "Shouldn't you arrest him?"

Dan didn't answer. He averted his eyes.

Jeff got the silent message. And an idea came to him in an instant. He leaned down and grabbed Brandon by the collar of his shirt.

"What's the password for your email account?"

Brandon just stared back, eyes as cold as ice. "Fuck off."

Dan leaned down and put his gun to Brandon's forehead. "I don't know why Jeff wants that, but I trust him enough to know that he has a good reason. Tell him, or I'll put a bullet in your brain."

Brandon just shook his head.

Gaia came alive. She crawled over to Brandon's prone body, reached up and took the gun out of Dan's hand. "He probably doesn't believe that you'd kill him in cold blood. But I think he knows that I would." She rammed the barrel hard against his temple and glared into Brandon's eyes.

"Tell us the password or I swear I'll kill you without a moment's hesitation, you bastard!"

Brandon blinked twice. Then he muttered, "It's 'weaklings.'"

Jeff ran back to the butler's pantry, opened Brandon's briefcase and pulled out his laptop. He sat on the floor and entered the password. Opened his email account and clicked on every address in the man's contact list. Then he sent the following message: *I'm leaving for an extended trip. Dropping out for a while. Will probably be gone for at least a year. Time to enjoy life a bit. Brandon.*

He showed the message to both Brandon and Gaia. They nodded and he clicked on 'send.'

Dan grabbed Brandon under the armpits and lifted him not so gently to his feet. He put the gun to the man's head, and turned towards Jeff. "Okay, I'm with you, whatever you want to do."

Jeff turned his gaze to Gaia, a silent question. She just nodded.

"Put him in the fucking vault."

Dan grabbed Brandon around the neck. "You heard the man. Walk."

Brandon tried to resist, tried to fight, but it was to no avail. His fighting skills were no match for the RCMP. Before he'd even had the chance to swing his second attempt at a punch, Dan had hit him with lightning speed in the face, stomach, and groin. Then he roughly shoved him in the direction of the office.

Once they were in front of the vault, Gaia spoke. "The air ventilation system failed when I was in there."

Jeff laughed. "Good. All the better."

Dan squeezed Jeff's shoulder. "No, not good. Check the circuit box. I'm betting it just blew a breaker with both the light and the fan on at the same time. Overheated."

Jeff ran down to the basement. Sure enough, the breaker had tripped. He flipped it back up into the 'on' position.

When he returned, he said to Dan with a question in his eyes, "Okay, it's fixed. But why do you care?"

Dan smiled sadly. "Because the fear of being held captive with no hope whatsoever is a far worse punishment than being actually held captive. I don't think either you or Gaia want to think of him dying in a mere hour or two. And knowing what I know about this psychopath, I don't either. Let's give him a long time to think before he dies. To think about all the people he's killed."

Jeff nodded. He looked at Gaia. She nodded too. Dan spoke again, slowly and softly. "He could be in here forever or at least until this house gets demolished one day after years of being unoccupied. No one will know where he is. How long he lasts is anyone's guess. But the three of us will have a secret between us that will bind us together. Are you two okay with that? Can you live with that?"

No hesitation—unanimous nods. They shook on it.

Brandon had been watching and listening, his eyes as big as saucers. "You can't do this! What's wrong with you people? It's barbaric!"

Jeff lunged at him and squeezed his hands around his throat one last time. He pressed hard until the man choked. "Brandon, I would suggest you keep the light off so that you don't blow the breaker again. Now that would be barbaric."

Then he shoved him backward into the vault. To the sound of Brandon screaming at the top of his lungs, Jeff closed the foot thick steel door and spun the dial. Finally, silence.

He took the tiny remote out of his pocket and pressed the button. The bookshelf wall creaked back into place with a decisive thud. He put the remote back in his pocket; a little device that would never be used again.

The three of them just looked at each other. There was nothing more to be said—the thud of the bookshelf wall said it all.

CHAPTER 55

Jeff raised his glass high and toasted.

Toasted to 'freedom.'

Gaia smiled knowingly and clinked her wine glass against his.

They both knew that the word 'freedom' meant something different to everyone. And for the two of them there was stark realism to the concept. They had each come close to losing that precious right, but there was also the knowing that they had conspired in robbing one of God's creatures of ever being able to enjoy it again.

But was he truly one of God's creatures…or had he perhaps been working for the other guy?

They were having dinner tonight at Jeff's house–which was now also Gaia's house. And Bingo's house.

Gaia hadn't been able to go back to her little house in Leaside. It brought back too many memories of Brandon's brutal invasion of her sanctity. It had been her safe place, her happy place–but that had all vanished in the blink of an eye.

Jeff had his own horrifying experience in his house too of course. He could still picture in his mind, in brilliant 3D Technicolor, the Russians slinking through his house with knives in hand. They had come to kill him in his own home.

But that memory hadn't chased him away. Perhaps because he'd succeeded in taking the offensive against them. So he didn't feel so vulnerable or weak. For Gaia it was different–she'd tried the offensive but it was feebly inadequate against an opponent who'd had the upper hand from the beginning. And then, before Brandon stole her from the sanctity of her home, he'd raped her–right there in her own bedroom. Jeff knew that memory would never leave her and staying in that house would only recycle it over and over again. Particularly whenever he and Gaia went to sleep together in the very room where it happened.

No, she had to get out of there. And Jeff had been more than happy to have her move in. Bingo too, of course.

It had been six months since the ordeal had ended. Ended with Brandon being entombed in his own palatial home. They never talked about it–it wasn't something to be proud of, rejoice over, or even toast to. It was always just there, in the background. A promise of secrecy made between three people…and a promise to be kept forever.

It was a secret that would always bind Jeff, Gaia and Dan together. Which actually made their friendship stronger and more meaningful. They had made a pact against the devil, and they'd been triumphant.

And they even worked together now too.

True to his conscience and determination, Dan left the RCMP. He couldn't stomach how he'd been asked to look the other way, allow a brutal psychopath like Brandon Horcroft continue to enjoy his freedom despite the heinous things he'd done.

So Dan formed a new company, 'Nicholson Investigations Inc.,' and since both Jeff and Gaia were out of work at the time, they were the obvious choices for his first two employees. And as of now, still his only two employees.

Gaia was the office administrator. Jeff and Dan were the investigators. And once in a while a psychic vision helped Jeff solve a case faster than anyone could have dreamed possible. He still wasn't able to control them or summon them on command, but they would pop up once in a while at moments that always took him by surprise.

They really enjoyed the work and loved working with Dan. Jeff thought that it sure was strange fate that brought him and Dan together. Way back those many months ago Dan had been ready to charge Jeff with the manslaughter of Ray Filberg. Who could have thought that less than a year later they would be working in a business together?

With Dan's RCMP credentials and experience, plenty of work came their way. Most of the cases involved embezzlement or missing persons…and of course there were the predictable number of infidelity investigations.

The missing person cases usually involved teens taken off the streets and forced into prostitution. They had to be tracked down, rescued, deprogrammed, and detoxified. Those were sad cases–Jeff didn't enjoy those too much. They were personal to him. They reminded him of Gaia, and of how her situation had been totally different–she'd done it out of choice. That was the part that Jeff still agonized over at times. He was handling it pretty well, but once in a while it would creep back up behind him and bite him in the ass. But he knew time would be a good healer–for all three of them.

*****

The house on Briar Hill. Jeff had driven by it just the other day. Cruised by slowly and then parked his car a few houses away. Got out, leaned against his car and just stared at the imposing French Colonial. It was a pretty house, but it now held an ugly secret. A man had been entombed alive in there.

Jeff watched as the gardeners went about cutting the lawn, trimming the bushes. Brandon must have had an account where the landscapers were paid on a monthly basis straight from his bank account. It had been six months now and the gardeners were still working hard to satisfy their client. A client they would never see again. And a client who would never enjoy the fruits of their labors.

The house still looked occupied and full of life. But there were three people in the world who knew that it was instead full of death.

Brandon had to be dead by now. There was no way he could have survived longer than two or three weeks. He had water, but that was it. And if he left the light off, the circulation fan would have continued working without blowing a breaker. So that would have bought him some time. But not much.

Jeff had at least one nightmare vision a week. Showing a man still very much alive, pacing the tiny room, clawing at the walls. And trying frantically to undo the damage he had inflicted on the safety release button. Pushing at it with his fingers, banging on it with bloody fists. Ironic that smashing it beyond functionality just to keep Gaia imprisoned was now his own undoing.

But of course, Jeff knew all about that safety release, having been trapped in the office vault. So, if Brandon hadn't already destroyed it Jeff would have had great pleasure in doing so.

He didn't tell Dan or Gaia that he'd driven by the Briar Hill house. He didn't think they'd be too happy to hear that he'd done that.

But the main reason he hadn't told them was because he saw something else that day. More than just gardeners toiling away. Something that puzzled and troubled him in more ways than one.

A 'Sold' sign was proudly mounted on the freshly manicured lawn.

*****

"Jeff, you haven't told me everything, have you?"

"Do you need to know everything? Is that going to help in any way?"

Gaia topped up her wine glass. "Well, for one thing, have you been honest with me about how you feel? About what I was doing, I mean. That's a tough thing to forgive."

Jeff smiled wryly. "I've rationalized it, Gaia. I love you, that's all that matters. And I guess my love for you is strong enough to get me through this. I'm just glad you're alive and still in my life. You have no idea how panicked I was when I was trying to find you. And at that time I already knew about the…escort…thing."

Gaia nodded. She reached over the table and gently caressed his hand.

Then Jeff just blurted it out. "I killed Ray Filberg."

Gaia choked on her wine. "What?"

"Not intentionally. I roughed him up after finding out that he'd hired that guy to spy on us and take photos. And, I've already told you about my psychic abilities. Well, my aunt's are even stronger than mine. She told me that there was someone who had been obsessed with you for a very long time. I assumed incorrectly that it was Ray. Had no idea she meant Brandon.

"Anyway, Ray had a heart attack. I tried CPR on him, but it was too late. I then tried to cover it up. That's when Dan stepped in—threatened to arrest me for manslaughter if I didn't help him investigate Price, Spencer and Williams for insider trading and commanded suicides. I agreed—and that's what brought us all to this point today."

Gaia just stared at him for a few seconds, then, "That's one hell of a secret. Is that all? Anything else you need to share?"

"No." He lied. Jeff didn't have the heart to tell her that Louise had also visualized that Brandon arranged for her fiancé, Matt, to die in that plane crash almost six years ago. He didn't think that was information she really needed right now.

And I sure don't want to tell her about the 'Sold' sign on Brandon's property.

Gaia allowed for a small smile. "I guess we both had some secrets."

"Yes. But we kept them for good reasons. We didn't want to hurt each other."

Gaia poured some more wine. "I think I'm ready to hear about these commanded suicides that Brandon was doing."

Jeff frowned. "Are you sure?"

"Tell me. I want to know."

Jeff took a long sip of his Chianti. "Okay, in a nutshell, with the illegal insider trading that was going on, Brandon protected himself by putting executives under very deep hypnosis. He used his own radical techniques—very dangerous. In his mind he needed to plant some kind of protection for himself in the subconscious of these innocent victims. If things got dicey and risky, he could command them to carry out an act that he'd already pre-determined and commanded in their minds."

Gaia leaned her elbows on the table and rested her chin on her tiny fists. Jeff could see she was intrigued. "My God. How did he do this?"

"Well, he used a phrase—he picked one that was obscure and would never normally be heard in normal day-to-day life. So as to prevent accidental premature suicide. He'd tell them that if they ever heard that phrase again, they would have to kill themselves."

"What was that phrase?"

"It was, 'Thou shalt go forth.'"

Gaia let out a long breath. "Wow. That is pretty obscure."

"Yes, and it had to be."

She shivered and folded her arms tightly across her chest. "It's chilling, Jeff. Absolutely chilling."

"Yes, it is."

"I think I've heard enough. And I'm feeling kind of cold right now. Do you mind terribly if I leave you with the dishes? I feel like I need a nice hot bath. I'll take my wine with me, and maybe you could join me in a few minutes?" She smiled coyly at him.

Jeff smiled. "I like the sound of that. You go ahead—and yes, I'll wait an appropriately respectful amount of time and then I'll come up and slide in with you."

Gaia came around the table and planted a big kiss on his lips. "I do love you, you know. And I'm so grateful that you've kind of forgiven me for what I did. I don't think I could have gone on if you didn't."

Jeff hugged her. "I had no choice but to forgive you. I love you too."

Gaia smiled and headed up the stairs. Jeff could see that she was taking the steps slowly; holding tight to the railing with one hand, glass of Chianti in the other. Jeff chuckled to himself—*a bit too much wine tonight.*

He cleared the table and started loading the dishwasher. He was getting excited thinking about the bath they'd be taking together. As he listened to the water filling in the tub upstairs, he thought about how well she'd taken that stuff he shared with her tonight. It was pretty shocking stuff, but she'd handled it like a trooper. But after what she'd been through, it was probably minor in her mind.

As he poured himself one more glass of wine, he gave thanks for having Gaia in his life. He'd never loved anyone as much as her. Clearly, they could deal with anything in their lives now. They both now knew things about each other that would make anything else pale in comparison. If they handled these things they could handle every hurdle thrown their way.

Suddenly Jeff lurched back against the kitchen counter, almost as if he'd been shoved. He held on tight to the edge, afraid he was going to topple over. His eyes became blurry and he saw the number '1' dancing in front of his field of vision. Then he saw Gaia's smiling face mouthing the word, 'goodbye.'

She had a halo of yellow surrounding her head, rays of light pulsating upward. And held a razor blade in her right hand.

Jeff staggered forward into the living room and almost fell over the coffee table. He felt drunk but he knew that he wasn't. Lurched toward the stairs and fought with all his might against the strange gravity that seemed to be trying to pull his body down to the floor. He had to get upstairs!

Jeff screamed, "Gaia! No!"

As he grabbed onto the railing, the same one that he'd surfed down on his ass just seven months before, he agonized over one of the last things he'd said to Gaia tonight just before she suddenly decided to take a bath.

'Thou shalt go forth.'

About the Authors

Peter Parkin was born in Toronto, Ontario and after studying Business Administration at Ryerson University, he embarked on a thirty-four year career in the business world. He retired in 2007 and has written seven novels, the last five with co-author, Alison Darby.

Alison Darby is a life-long resident of the West Midlands region of England. She studied psychology in college and when she's not juggling a busy work life and writing novels, she enjoys researching astronomy. Alison has two grown daughters, who live and work in the vibrant city of London.